DOMENICO'S TABLE

Domenico's Table and Casala

DOMENICO'S TABLE

TERESA NEUMANN

ALL'S WELL HOUSE
LEBANON, OREGON

All's Well House
PO Box 2489
Lebanon, Oregon 97355
www.teresaneumann.com
www.domenicostable.com

Printed in the United States of America

ISBN (print): 978-0-9831210-2-2
ISBN (ePub ebook): 978-0-9831210-3-9
Library of Congress Control Number: 2012924096

Cover Design by Luke and Marika Neumann, Neumann Films
Text Design by Jennifer Omner, ALL Publications

In loving memory of
Violenza "Babe" Bertozzi Neumann

✝

March 22, 1918 – May 13, 2011

*All my grandfather's descendants deserved nothing
but death from my lord the king, but you gave your
servant a place among those who eat at your table.*

2 Samuel 19:28

Pronunciation Table
Note: Pronunciations are not exact.

Characters

Domenico Sacchelli: [*Doh-MAY-nee-koh Sahk-YELL-ee*] Owner of a little piece of paradise in Tuscany, and the best chef around

Mariella: [*Mahr-ee-AYL-lah*] Bianca's niece (daughter of Rina), Domenico's wife

Orazio: [*Oh-RAH-zee-oh*] Domenico's father

Elvira: [*Ell-VEE-rah*] Domenico's mother

Marco Bertozzi: [*MARK-oh Bare-TOTZ-zi*] Bertozzi cousin

Rina: [*REE-nah*] Bianca's sister & Mariella's mother, Domenico's mother-in-law

Bianca Corrotti: [*Bee-AHN-ka Cohr-ROTE-tee*] Rina's sister, Mariella's aunt

Lucia Corrotti: [*Loo-CHEE-ah*] Bianca's daughter

Carlo Stellati: [*Stay-LAH-tee*] Bianca's son-in-law, husband of Lucia

Dolphus Geller: [*DOLE-fuss*] former WWII German soldier

Oden Geller: [*OH-dun*] Dolphus's father

Primus Geller: [*PREE-mus*] Oden's brother, Dolphus's uncle

Ralf Geller: [*Rahlf*] Dolphus's cousin, son of Primus

Aarika Geller: [*AIR-ee-kah*] Dolphus's granddaughter

Poppy Doyle: Aarika's half-sister from America

Signor Cavalleri: [*See-nyoor-ay Cah-vah-layree*] Franciacorta vintner

Elisabetta Cavalleri: [*Ay-lees-ah-BAY-tah*] the vintner's
   daughter
Mariesole: [*Mah-ree-so-LAY*] Signor Cavalleri's
   housekeeper

Places

Capri: [*KAH-pree*] an island off the northern tip of the
   Sorrentine Peninsula in the Bay of Naples
Lago d'Iseo: [*LAH-go Dee-SAY-oh*] lake in Lombardy where
   Armida died
Monte Montignoso: [*MOHN-tay Mohn-tay-nYO-soh*] a
   small mountain between the towns of Massa/Carrarra
   and Ripa. Casali di Montignoso is the community
   where Domenico's inherited property is located. It
   consists of two buildings: a fattoria and a casala, and
   also a small vineyard.
Praiano: [*Pray-AH-noh*] a delightful village on the Amalfi
   Coast just south of Positano

Italian and German words

Casala: [*Kah-SAH-lah*] a small dwelling separate from
   Italian main house
Chiusura: [*Kee-ew-SUHR-ah*] closure
Comparaggio: [*Cohm-pay-RAZH-zhee-oh*] kinship by choice
Fattoria: [*Faht-TOR-ee-ah*] Italian farmhouse
Pietra del tavolo: [*Pee-AY-trah dell Tah-VOL-oh*] a stone table
Oma: [*Oh-mah*] "Grandmother" in German
Opa: [*Oh-pah*] "Grandfather" in German
Vati: [*VAH-tee*] "Daddy" in German
Vater: [*VAH-ter*] "Father" in German

PART ONE

Passato

❖ The Past ❖

Prelude

Domenico Sacchelli, whom I love like a son, is a man after my own heart. Unfailingly warm, friendly, and cordial, he is also a master cook, shrewd businessman, and a generous hospitalier. Indeed, I've always said he was quite the catch for my niece Mariella when she married him thirty years ago. There's only one thing about Domenico that troubles me, however: for him, World War II has not yet ended.

Oh, I realize wars don't start one day and end on another simply because signatures on a document decree it to be so. Wars simmer for years before they erupt and fester long after the final truce. It's the pretense of peace I find disturbing.

You see, Domenico is so naturally buoyant, so delightfully down-to-earth and confident in his identity, that if you met him you would never dream he is living a life of stoic resignation; that he is in denial of the unresolved memories fermenting in his soul. Indeed, it threatens to upend his existence in the here-and-now.

Domenico once broached the subject with me.

"Bianca," he said, "after all you suffered in the war, how is it you are not bitter and angry? I rarely hear you talk about the Germans who did such unspeakable things to our families and friends."

"I no longer speak about the Germans," I replied, "because I have forgiven them. You, too, can forgive them while there is yet time. You'll be surprised how much lighter you'll feel if you do."

He dismissed my advice then, telling me there was no rush. He was convinced he had many years left in him to deal with his past. But I warned him that time is deceptive. "It runs through our fingers like sand," I said. "At my age, I know these things, Domenico. When your time is up, there is no going back."

Domenico has never confided in me about what exactly happened during the war that still haunts him, but I want to see him at peace before I die. Is that asking too much?

That said, it was with great curiosity I learned Dolphus Geller—a former German soldier who rents Domenico's mountain home every summer—was bringing his granddaughter Aarika with him to Tuscany again. It was highly unusual, as she had accompanied Dolphus here only one other time, many years ago when she was a little girl. Was Aarika needed to keep her widowed grandfather company? Had Dolphus reached that stage in life where he required medical supervision? I contemplated the various reasons why Aarika was coming with him this summer and it struck me that a portent was brewing. Her coming was a sign, a harbinger of change, although for good or bad I could only guess.

Even the weather foreshadowed change.

By the end of June, it was already so hot and muggy few of us could sleep through the night. July was even worse. And, oh, the storms! Nearly ever afternoon or evening in August we endured at least an hour of lightning, thunder, wind, and rain. Who could forget the night terrors they brought with them? Of course, my bad leg gave me fits as it always does when the temperatures are extreme. It was so sticky, my compression stockings and undergarments clung to my body like cellophane and the clothes I hung on the line to dry never really did. Everyone was on edge, distracted and discomfited by the unusually oppressive atmosphere bearing down on us.

Yet, despite the weather—or perhaps, because of it—this was to be the summer Domenico Sacchelli finally faced his demons. In fact, he found himself so immersed in the Geller family's lives, he had no choice but to confront them. As a result, well, that's what this story is about.

· 1 ·

The Feast

Casali di Montignoso
Toscana, Italia
August, 2001

Why is it *that I can seem to do nothing but feast on my memories these days?*

Domenico rested his elbows on the marble countertop stained by decades of food preparation and tried to refocus; tried to convince himself that not every unbidden thought popping into his head was a threat to his peace.

Like spores of yeast, tested and coddled in the bakery of my mind and then kneaded into my soul, my memories could nourish me if I'd just let them. At least the good ones could. The bad ones, well, I wish I could scald them out of existence. The problem is, without both, life could be rendered flat and tasteless.

Lifting his elbows from the counter, Domenico frowned as he reasoned a life of mediocrity was out of the question. Even if he could cherry-pick which memories to retain, selective amnesia would be the result, making him less than the sum of himself.

If only I could blend my good and bad memories together with a perfect balance of firmness and delicacy—just like the dough beneath my fingertips—then, perhaps, like a flaky-layered cornetto, it might be worth all the worry and waiting.

Domenico Sacchelli, alone in his family's *casala*, continued preparing a batch of sweet dough that would later be made into *cornetti*, or croissants, and then served to his guests the following morning. He felt harried and rushed for good reason. After spending most of his morning ferrying his newly arrived boarders from the Pisa airport to his *fattoria*, and with dinner expected to be served in just four more hours, Domenico knew that in order to pull off the evening he had so meticulously planned, he must keep focused on the task at hand. So, tossing a pinch of salt over his shoulder, as though trying to blind the hovering spirit causing his mind to wander, he resumed kneading.

When the *pasta dolce* reached the correct elasticity, he placed it in a greased bowl to proof. Then, reaching up to a thick wooden shelf above the counter, he peered beneath a muslin tea towel to inspect a dozen pillowy mounds of pizza dough. Deeming them perfect, he moved on to check the progress of his rustic bread, which had been rising in a cubbyhole beneath the blackened terra-cotta oven. It was ready to shape into loaves. He slathered some garlic-infused Colonnata lard on his hands and divided the dough, massaging it into two elongated ovals.

As he worked, he looked out the open windows of the kitchen at his wife Mariella as she prepared the long oak table on the patio for dinner. The scrape of chair legs dragging across fieldstone, the swish of tablecloths being shaken, and the clatter of silverware and clinking of plates and wineglasses, all produced an aura of tranquility contrary to Domenico's niggling thoughts.

All is well with the world, he thought. *Why, then, do I let my memories interfere so often with the present? Why do I feel tense every time Dolphus arrives for the summer holidays?*

Pausing to reach for the salt, he again threw some grains over his shoulder before placing the loaves on a baking sheet and covering them for their final rise. That done, he shifted his gaze toward the fattoria next door—the ancestral farmhouse he rented out—and wondered what his guests were doing. *Probably unpacking and washing up. And resting.*

Domenico reasoned that his third guest—the surprise one—must surely be jet-lagged, having flown overseas to meet the Gellers at the Pisa airport. As he pondered the day's unexpected turn of events, Mariella poked her head in the door to let him know she was finished setting the table and ask if he needed any help in the kitchen.

"No," said Domenico, untying his apron. "I am finished. Shall we go back down the mountain and rest at home for a while before returning to prepare dinner?"

"Do we have time to do that?"

"We'll make the time," replied Domenico, knowing his wife could use a short nap. Then he asked Mariella what time her cousin Marco—whom they had hired to be their guests' translator, guide, and companion during their stay—was expected to arrive.

Pointing out the messy counters and flour-covered floor, Mariella quipped, "He'll hopefully be here soon to clean up after you and water my plants."

Domenico grinned. It was a luxury to have help this year, and he was thankful Dolphus was willing to cover the cost for it. The German had told Domenico that hiring Marco was "worth it to have my granddaughter get the most out of her summer here. I want Aarika to experience Italy at its best and suffer nothing in the way of misunderstanding or ignorance due to language barriers or cultural unfamiliarity."

Domenico's smile faded. "I wish we had cell service up here so we could call Marco and warn him there's an extra person in the Geller party," he said. "I hate to surprise him like this at the last minute."

Mariella's hand flew to her mouth. Stepping closer to her husband, she lowered her hand and whispered, "I wish I could have gone with you to the airport this morning to see her for myself! Why, I knew Dolphus was bringing Aarika with him this summer, but I had no idea he had two granddaughters. And an American at that!"

"The American is not Dolphus's granddaughter," said Domenico, his voice lowered as well. "She is Aarika's half-sister." Mariella inquired further, but Domenico told her it was far too complicated to explain. "I don't understand it all myself," he said. "All I know is that Dolphus has been coming here nearly every summer for the last twenty years, requiring almost nothing from us except his meals, and now we have triple the guests to look after every day for six weeks. It's a good thing we have Marco to help us."

"Marco will be perfect," agreed Mariella. Lifting the fingers of one hand, she counted off the reasons. "After all, he is fluent in English—which is how the Gellers will communicate most often—and he speaks German well enough to get by. He's a master of Italian history and knows Tuscany like the back of his hand. He's young and *molto fusto* . . . so handsome!" Pausing to reflect a moment, she added, "And if I recall, Marco has already met Aarika. Remember the summer Dolphus brought her and his wife with him for two weeks? I wondered why they didn't stay longer, and why his wife and granddaughter never returned after that."

Domenico shrugged. "Dolphus has always seemed a bit of a recluse. For whatever reason, it is not for us to know. I'm just thankful we own the only rental house on the mountain and that Dolphus pays to come back here every year." Hanging his apron on a hook near the door, he added, "And as for Marco and Aarika, that was years ago, Mariella. Marco is older than her, but in reality they were both children. I doubt they remember each other very well, if at all."

Mariella waved her hand. "But who could forget Aarika? She was *bellissima*; so sweet and so well mannered. And such blue eyes she had! The color of my potted anemones in the front yard."

Domenico placed his hand beneath his wife's elbow and steered her out of the kitchen. "Come," he said, "we can continue our conversation in the car. Before we know it, it will be time to come back up and serve dinner."

As Domenico drove slowly down the driveway, trying not to kick up dust as they pulled out, he caught his wife gazing back at the fattoria. "Aarika's eyes are still incredibly blue, Mariella," he teased. "You will see for yourself tonight. And so will Marco."

LESS THAN TEN minutes later, Marco Bertozzi pulled into his cousins' driveway. The first thing he did upon getting out of the car was to go into the kitchen and clean up after Domenico. He placed dirty dishes in the sink to soak, wiped off the counters, swept the floor, and spent considerable time tidying up the casala in general before heading outside to water Mariella's flowers and shrubs.

Uncoiling the garden hose, he began spraying the beds along the side of the casala. He assumed the guests were in the fattoria, so when he rounded the corner he was shocked by what he saw. There, basking in the sun, was a fair-skinned blond lying facedown on a beach towel; the top of her lime-green, two-piece swimming suit untied, its loose strings splayed out from her like two neon-colored shoelaces. Marco took a step back, hoping she hadn't noticed him. But the girl lifted her head at the same moment, and as she did, Marco was blindsided by two things: her dimples and a tiny silver ring in her nose.

"I don't appreciate being snuck up on," said the girl, speaking English with a thick German accent. She snatched her towel to her chest and rotated her torso toward him before adding, "Or stared at, for that matter. But then, I suppose leering at women is normal for Italian men."

"Sorry?" Stunned by her impertinence, Marco said, "You must be Aarika."

"And you must be Marco." Aarika lowered herself back down, closing her eyes as she pressed her face sideways against the ground. "The last time I saw you," she sighed, "you were just a silly boy who couldn't take his eyes off me. It appears you haven't changed much."

"And if I remember correctly," countered Marco, "you were a spoiled little girl who thought the world revolved around her." He pointed the hose at Aarika and pressed the nozzle. It was a quick spray, lasting no more than a second or two, but Aarika gasped as though she'd been soaked. Wrapping the towel securely around her, she leaped to her feet.

"*Dumm junge Italienisch!*" she shrieked. "What do you think you're doing?"

"This 'dumb Italian boy' is teaching a *tipico* German girl a lesson," growled Marco.

"Exactly what do you mean by 'typical'? Because if you're insinuating Germans are . . ."

"Bigoted? Pushy? Arrogant?" Marco paused at the sound of Domenico's car pulling into the driveway and said, "You may want to get decent, *fraulein.*"

Aarika returned his suggestion with an icy, uncomprehending glare.

Marco pointed to her still-loosed bikini strings. "Unlike you, my cousins are modest." Then, turning his back on her, he walked away.

"How dare you insult me! It was you who invaded *my* privacy," Aarika called out after him. "We're renting this property and I can sunbathe as I please!"

When Domenico and Mariella, making their way from the car, saw Marco coming toward them, his eyes blazing, they asked him if something was wrong. Before he could answer, Aarika came storming around the corner of the casala. Trembling, she shook her finger in Marco's direction and addressed Domenico.

"Signor Sacchelli," she blustered, "my grandfather made a mistake when he agreed to hire this, this *Schlot!* We don't need anyone to . . ."

"Excuse me." Dolphus had snuck up on them and judging by the pained look on his face, he had overheard Aarika. Offering Marco his hand, he said, "It is a pleasure to meet you again, Marco. It has been, what, ten years since I last saw you? You have turned into quite a gentleman, I see. I understand your parents are joining us for dinner tonight. I look forward to meeting them."

Aarika grunted in disgust. As she turned and crossed the lawn to go back to the fattoria, Dolphus apologized to Marco. "You must excuse Aarika," he said in broken English. "It has been a difficult year for my granddaughter. I am hoping our stay in Italy will prove refreshing for her as well as therapeutic. And I trust your guidance and communication skills will help her to that end."

"Marco will be at your service every day," said Domenico, motioning to Marco that he would handle the conversation from this point. "As noted in the rental contract, Herr Geller, your payment includes round-the-clock translation; lessons in Italian if you wish; and tours and chauffeured transportation to beaches, museums, art galleries—anywhere you choose. Marco will be driving our extra car, so it is no problem. You need only pay for gas and your own accommodations on overnight trips. Of course, I was only notified this morning of Aarika's American sister joining you this summer. But it is of no importance where we are concerned. Within reason, if there is anything else you need help with, Marco is at your disposal."

Listening to his cousin recite the litany of services he had agreed to, Marco shuddered. *If it weren't for the fact that I need the money for school, I'd walk away right now and let someone else deal with the Gellers.* Swallowing his pride, however, he simply smiled at Dolphus and said, "I am at your service, Signor Geller." Then, excusing himself, he followed Mariella into the kitchen to help prep the dinner.

"What was that all about?" asked Mariella, once inside the casala.

"I take it you're referring to Aarika's hysterics?"

"That, and your change in attitude," she said. "I thought you were excited about helping us this summer."

"I was," said Marco. "Until I met Aarika the Hun."

Thrusting her hands into the sink, Mariella began scrubbing dishes and handing them to Marco to dry. "You need to give her another chance, Marco. Everyone has a bad day."

"I have a feeling every day will be a bad day with her. She's German."

"Marco! You know better than to say things like that."

His cousin's rebuke stung him, but Marco was only voicing what everyone else said about German tourists. Domenico and Mariella may have developed a friendship with Dolphus over the years, helping them not to be as unforgiving and intolerant as other Italians. But not knowing any Germans himself, his encounter with Aarika fit all too well with the stereotype. "And what's this about Aarika's sister being here?" he asked.

"Apparently it was a last minute decision. She's American." Handing one last bowl to Marco to dry, Mariella gave him a motherly wink. "Maybe things will go better with her."

Now an American, if she's not like Aarika, I can handle, thought Marco. *I guess I'll see tonight whether this summer can be redeemed or not.*

DINNER WAS A smashing success. Everyone raved about Domenico's cooking. The pizza was *perfetto*, the wine superb, and the conversation—which grew louder and more weightless as the evening wore on—was as steady and unimpeded as the waves pounding the beach on the coastline below them.

Marco, Domenico, and Mariella spent most of their time attending to the needs of their guests, but took part in the lively discussions whenever they were able. As matriarchs of the Bertozzi family, Bianca and her sister Rina sat at the head of the table. Marco's parents sat next to them; his mother keeping a sharp eye on his father to make sure he didn't overindulge, as was sometimes the case. Dolphus was more talkative, especially with Marco's father, and less retiring than anyone had expected him to be, while Aarika was predictably more subdued.

But it was Poppy Doyle who carried the evening, making sure there was no shortage of topics to discuss. She embodied everything Italians and Germans assumed Americans were. Chatty, energetic, bursting with self-confidence, earnest, inquisitive, edgy, opinionated, and impatient, her personality teetered on the extreme but never quite tumbled into excess. In short, as long as she was capable of keeping her enthusiasm in check, she was quite entertaining. After answering a few questions about where she lived in St. Paul, Minnesota, Poppy inquired about the history of Domenico's property.

"Bianca loves to tell that story," said Mariella, apparently too modest to talk about their rental. "She and her husband witnessed Domenico do much of the work here over the years. But, Marco, you'll need to interpret for her."

Motioning for Marco to take a chair next to her, Bianca rose to the occasion. "It is true I love to tell the story of Domenico's casala and fattoria," she began. "I am very proud of what he and Mariella have done here."

"As you can see," she said, "we are sitting high up Monte Montignoso, overlooking the Ligurian Sea. The mountain is so quiet, if you listen carefully you can hear the distant surf at the mouth of the Cinquale Canal. And on a clear day, you can see the islands of Elba, Capraia, and Gorgona—even Corsica, if you know where to look and are lucky. Today, Domenico and Mariella reside in the village below us. But when Domenico was a boy, his parents and his grandfather lived up here in the fattoria. It is nearly two centuries old, built on the order of Tuscan architecture of the time; two stories, with a kitchen and living quarters on the lower level and two tiny bedrooms upstairs."

"It's so awesome!" said Poppy. "I love it!"

When Marco interpreted Poppy's comment, Bianca smiled at her in agreement. Then, sweeping her hand across the moonlit landscape, she continued, as Marco translated. "With the exception of a narrow, terraced backyard, this property is framed by a forest of *pini, tigli,* and fir trees rising up the mountain behind it. The building we are sitting in front of now, next to the fattoria, is what we call a *casala*—a small structure separate from the main dwelling. Domenico built it with his bare hands after the war, when he was still a schoolboy. It is made entirely of limestone, and is also two stories high. Inside, there is a winding stone staircase leading up to a tiny lone bedroom on the top floor. From all the windows facing west, you can look out across the lawn and see the earth's horizon above the sea. The views are the best on the mountain."

"Over there," she added, "on the edge of the courtyard, near the retaining wall dividing the driveway and the vineyard, is a *pietra del tavolo*—a stone table wide enough to seat four people. Perhaps you've noticed it already? It was also built by Domenico and consists of a thick slab of granite placed atop a petrified tree trunk. The massive chestnut tree it is built beneath shades the entire yard. Close to the *tavolo* is an ancient stone winepress, or *torchio,* which to this day Domenico uses to make his wine."

There was a collective sigh heard around the table as Bianca finished.

"I feel like I'm living in a fantasy," enthused Poppy.

Inclining her head toward the casala, she added, "This is all like, you know, Snow White and the Seven Dwarfs or something."

"Of course you would compare this to a movie," said Aarika, shadows from the candlelight making it impossible to read the expression on her face. "Americans always see the world through an artificial lens. Life isn't make-believe, Poppy."

The quiet that followed Aarika's statement was a sharp contrast to the lighthearted discourse that had preceded it. Dolphus stood to his feet. "I didn't realize how late it was, Domenico," he said. "It's been a long day for all of us. Would you mind if we excused ourselves and retired to our rooms for the night?"

"Of course not," said Domenico, waving his hand toward the fattoria. "Go, go, and sleep well!"

Mariella bustled around the table to escort her guests across the lawn, lest they trip over something in the dark. Before setting out, she turned to Marco and said, "Would you mind taking Bianca and Rina home for us while Domenico and I begin cleaning up?"

"Not at all," replied Marco. He said good night to his parents and then gingerly, as though handling fine china, helped the elderly sisters to their feet and led them to the car. After making sure they were safely seat-belted in, he slid into the driver's seat and turned on the ignition. Bianca, sitting in the passenger seat next to him, asked how he thought the evening had gone.

"Fine," he replied. "I think nearly everyone enjoyed themselves."

"I hope my description of Domenico's property was

detailed enough for Poppy. She's seems very inquisitive. An interesting girl, isn't she?"

"I guess," he shrugged, wary that Bianca was baiting him.

"Poppy was right. The casala Domenico built *is* like something out of a fairytale, but it is really Mariella and Domenico who are the secret to its charm. Their warmth and amiability, their generosity and devotion to help others, built it as much as any hammer or saw. I told them long ago, when they married, that they would touch many people's lives."

"Did you?"

"Oh, yes. And I have seen it come to pass time and again over the years they've been married."

"Hmm."

"But I pray this year Domenico will begin to reap what he has sown."

"What do you mean?"

Bianca placed her hand on Marco's forearm. "You know I can't explain these things. I simply sense a breakthrough for Domenico."

"And what kind of breakthrough would that be? Because I can't see how anything connected with the Gellers, other than their money, will benefit Domenico."

Bianca tapped her head. "In here, where memories torment him. And in here," she lowered her hand to her heart, "where the empty places will be filled back up again."

But Marco's mind was elsewhere. He was no longer listening to Bianca. He was contemplating his run-in with Aarika Geller earlier in the day and thinking he had never seen eyes so blue as hers. That, and he found himself wondering how he was going to manage to survive the next six weeks serving her and her grandfather.

· 2 ·

Gnashing of Teeth

THE FOLLOWING DAY Marco took great pains in grooming himself before leaving his parents' house. His purpose was not to impress anyone, but to stifle any preconceived notions based on his appearance. Didn't Germans deem Italian men to be attention-seeking, overdressed lady-killers? So, he opted for a more casual shirt, switched out his designer sunglasses for a common brand, and refrained from using gel, as was his custom, on his thick black hair. He even shaved twice in a futile attempt to prevent a five o'clock shadow. In addition, because he wanted Dolphus to be pleased with his services, he vowed to be more stoic and less spirited.

Steeling himself for his first full day with the Gellers, he checked out his reflection in the mirror one last time and then took off for Domenico's. Because he didn't live far from Monte Montignoso, his routine involved riding his bike to his cousin's house. Once there, he would then park it and take Domenico's extra car, an older model BMW, up to the casala.

The road from the base of the mountain to its crest, via Metati Rossi Alti, was steep and riddled with hairpin curves. Even longtime residents dreaded navigating it at certain times of the year. But Marco tackled the drive as he intended on tackling his day, with concentrated resolve. He would not allow anything, not even Aarika, to get under his skin today. When he arrived at the mountaintop retreat, he found Dolphus was already up, sitting at the stone table beneath the chestnut tree, taking in the stunning views.

Marco parked the car. "*Buongiorno*, Signor Geller," he said, approaching him.

"*Guten Morgen*," said Dolphus. "You are here early."

Marco checked his watch. "I was told to be here at eight o'clock. I am a bit early."

"I suppose you have our day planned out for us already?"

"Domenico said I should ask you what you would like to do."

"Well," replied Dolphus, glancing at the fattoria, "it is the girls we are bound to please, no? Aarika is in the house showering, but I'm afraid jetlag has overtaken Poppy. If she sleeps most of the morning, are you averse to simply staying here and helping us with translating?"

"Of course not," lied Marco. Actually, he had hoped to take them all someplace where a multitude of distractions would limit personal interaction. "However," he added, "I think your English is better than you let on, signore. And Aarika's also. There should be no problem speaking to, or understanding, Poppy. Are you sure you need me here today to translate?"

"I fear without the use of an interpreter there could be misunderstandings that arise between myself and Aarika and Poppy. This summer is too significant for us to allow that to happen. You realize, Marco, this is the first time Aarika and Poppy have met each other."

"I did not know," said Marco, trying to conceal his surprise.

Dolphus stumbled over his words. "It is, how would you say in Italian . . . ?

"*Complicato?*"

"Yes, quite *complicato.*"

While the men had been talking, Aarika had finished her shower and was now walking briskly toward them. "Good morning, Opa," she said. Reaching her grandfather, she hugged him and kissed him on the cheek. Then, she turned to Marco.

"*Buongiorno,*" she said, not unkindly.

Taken off guard by Aarika's civility, Marco nodded. "Signorina."

"Where is breakfast?" she asked.

"Domenico made croissants yesterday. They are in the casala. I can bring them over to the fattoria and make a cappuccino for everyone if you wish."

"Is there no bread, or eggs, or meat of any kind?" Aarika seemed genuinely surprised. "My grandfather needs more than croissants for breakfast."

"I will check," said Marco, his guard back up. "But you realize that three times a week Domenico will be coming up here to prepare a different breakfast for you if it is required. Because of the big dinner last night, he felt lighter fare this morning would be more welcome than something heavy."

"We Germans don't consider a daily breakfast of eggs, meat, and bread as being 'heavy,'" retorted Aarika.

"Fine." Marco made a move toward the casala. "I will look in the kitchen to see if—"

Dolphus stopped him. "No, Marco, please do not bother. I love croissants, especially the ones Domenico makes. He knows they are my favorite." Turning to his granddaughter he said, "And Aarika, you mustn't worry so much about me. While we are on holiday I will eat as I always have."

"But, Opa . . ."

"Wait until you taste Domenico's croissants, Aarika," said Dolphus. "You will love them too." Addressing Marco again, he added, "I need to go back to the house. Go ahead and bring the *cornetti* over, and while you're doing that, I'll boil some water for the coffee."

Aarika, instead of going with Dolphus into the fattoria, followed Marco into the casala. "My grandfather is sick," she explained, when they entered the kitchen. "Before coming here, he was put on special medication. His doctor insisted it was imperative he change his diet as soon as possible."

Marco began transferring the croissants prepared by Domenico to a ceramic serving tray. "What is wrong with him?"

"He has hyperlipidemia. It is an excess of cholesterol in his blood."

Marco stopped what he was doing to study Aarika's face. "Is it fatal?"

"No, but . . ."

"It is treatable, then."

"Well, yes, but . . ."

"I understand your concern, signorina," said Marco. "But your grandfather's condition is common for his age, is it not? There is no worry."

Aarika seemed to hesitate, as though she might be weighing whether she should be angry at Marco's presumption or comforted by it. "What would you know anyway?" she sputtered finally. "Are you a doctor? And who are you to tell me I shouldn't worry?"

Marco picked up the tray of croissants and, with Aarika at his heels, headed out the kitchen door. As they traversed the lawn toward the fattoria, she kept up her diatribe about the necessity of Dolphus following doctor's orders. "I don't want you influencing my grandfather otherwise," she warned. "I need your support on this."

"Don't you think you're overreacting?" said Marco. "If your grandfather wants to enjoy his holiday by eating what he pleases, why should he be prevented from doing so? Besides, Dolphus is the one paying me to be here this summer, so it is his decision. Six weeks is nothing in the grand scheme of things."

"Of course. The Italian mindset. Eat, drink, and be merry, and who cares if you die tomorrow? I should have guessed I couldn't depend on you to help me. I'll have to speak with Domenico then." With that, Aarika sped away from Marco as fast as she could, leaving a trail of disgust in her wake.

Just as Marco reached the back door of the fattoria, Poppy leaned out her upper bedroom window and waved good morning to Marco. "I can't wait to see what you've brought us for breakfast," she chirped.

Marco held up the tray to show her. "Domenico's home-made croissants. Coffee will be ready soon."

"You look different from yesterday," noted Poppy. "Are you dressing to impress someone?"

"You don't like it?"

"It's okay," she replied, tilting her head to one side. "But you look a little too American. I like the yesterday you. The sizzling, Italian Marco."

"Really?" asked Marco, caught between embarrassment and curiosity.

"Well, of course!" Poppy laughed. "I didn't come halfway around the world to drool over the same thing I could see back home."

"What did you do to yourself?" I asked Marco as he stopped by my villa later that afternoon on his way home. He had been instructed to deliver a bag of fresh green beans from Mariella's vegetable garden to me.

"What do you mean?" he replied, dismounting from his bike.

"That shirt you're wearing looks like one my Danilo, God rest his soul, would have worn." Then, I pointed to his head. "You've combed your hair differently. And those sunglasses on top of your head are not Italian. They look so plain."

Getting only a shrug from him in response, I changed the subject. "How did it go with the Gellers today?" I asked.

"They wanted to rest, so I spent the day translating for them as needed and answered any questions they had. Domenico is going up there now to prepare dinner for them."

"Did they talk much?"

Marco set the sack of beans on the counter. "Dolphus was anxious for Aarika to get acquainted with Poppy, but it was he and Poppy who did most of the talking. I suppose it was a good thing I was there. There were quite a few times Dolphus called on me to interpret or explain something to Poppy and vice-versa."

"Why didn't Aarika take part in the conversation?"

Frown lines creased Marco's forehead. "It's clear she is not going to warm to her sister quickly."

"But, of course not. A lifetime of separation isn't broached overnight."

"Aarika was also angry with me because she thought I made light of her grandfather's medical condition."

"Dolphus is sick?" This was news to me.

After Marco explained Dolphus's diagnosis, I told him I agreed that if Dolphus wanted to wait until after his holiday to begin a strict diet, it was probably of no consequence.

"It is natural Aarika would be worried for him," I said. "Domenico says the Geller family has suffered great tragedies, but Dolphus has never revealed what they were. He keeps it a mystery. It's all very . . ."

"I know," said Marco, rolling his eyes. "*Complicato.* Domenico tells me the same thing. Something about Aarika's troubled parents and childhood. Why don't they just sort out their problems and get on with their lives?"

"To do that," I replied, "the Gellers must trace their history back to where the complications and the unraveling began. I am convinced that it is there, at that point in time, probably in childhood, that the map for their healing is buried."

·3·

Blood Ties

Passau, Germany
March, 1938

On his eleventh birthday, a plucky Dolphus Geller finished his morning chores, kissed his mother good-bye, grabbed his fishing gear, and headed down to the docks south of Passau. His father Oden, a farmer by trade, was there doing business with the town's fishermen. Herr Geller often traded small amounts of grain for barrels of fish refuse, which he used to fertilize his fields. The fishermen often teased Oden whenever Dolphus was with him, ribbing him about having fathered a son so late in life, but having a sixty-five-year-old father didn't bother Dolphus. His twin sisters, who were born when his parents were yet in their teens, were married with children and grandchildren of their own. It seemed perfectly normal for him to have siblings as old as his friends' parents, and grandnieces and nephews not much younger than himself. Uncle Primus, Oden's younger brother by a decade, had fathered a son, Ralf, late in life as well.

Oden Geller was known to dread taunting, so on this unseasonably warm spring day when his son Dolphus approached him on the docks, he said, "This is not a place for you, Dolphus. Go home."

"Mother said I could go fishing, but she said I must ask you first."

"*Ja, ja,*" replied Oden, engrossed in inspecting a pile of severed fish heads buzzing with flies.

"I'm going to meet Ralf, Father. Remember? He called last week to see if we could fish the River Inn on my birthday."

"Ah yes, yes. It's your birthday today."

A few fishermen, watching the father and son interchange, began smirking.

Oden blushed. "Can't you see I'm busy now, Dolphus? Run along and stay out of trouble. And be home in time for supper."

Dolphus hesitated. His mother had said he could go fishing with Ralf only if his father agreed to it. *He didn't exactly give me permission to go fishing,* he reasoned, *but he didn't say I couldn't either.* He glanced south at the railroad trestle crossing the River Inn, separating Germany from Austria. His cousin Ralf lived less than a mile across the river in a small Austrian village called Ingling. He had told Dolphus to meet him at noon next to the pilings beneath the trestle on the east side of the Inn.

To Dolphus, Ralf Geller was larger than life. He had a way with people that made them treat him with respect. And he was clever too, with a quick answer to everything. As a matter of fact, he was so convincing, Dolphus once watched a stranger give up his seat in a crowded theater for him. Nothing scared Ralf. That's what really impressed Dolphus.

I hope I can be just like him someday, thought Dolphus, taking leave of his father and setting out toward the river. *If I could be half as smart as Ralf, I could be anything I want to be.*

Trekking in a southerly direction for about a quarter of a mile, Dolphus scaled the wooden supports anchoring the trestle to the west bank of the River Inn. It took him awhile to find his balance as he walked, to pace his steps so that his feet landed firmly on each plank. He forced himself not to look down. One errant peek between the railroad ties and he might freeze, or worse yet, totter, tip, and plunge over the side into the deep, cold, swirling current below.

When he was halfway across the bridge, he heard someone shout his name. He paused, scanning the riverbank for Ralf. Adjacent to the pilings, he spotted him; a scarecrow of a boy with hair that looked like unraked straw. People often told Dolphus that he and Ralf looked more like brothers than cousins, but looking at him standing barefoot in the sandy muck separating the river from the sloping forest behind it, a self-fashioned fishing pole outstretched in one hand, Dolphus couldn't imagine ever looking so tall and strong and fearless as Ralf. Excited to begin fishing, Dolphus hurriedly resumed his advance. Less than ten feet from the last abutment, however, he stumbled. He tried catching himself, but before he knew it one of his legs was propped up at an angle in front of him while the other dangled below the deck.

Ralf's hoarse laugh reverberated against the embankment. "Clumsy oaf!" he hooted, throwing his golden head back.

Dolphus pushed with all his might until he was able to free his leg. Then, steadying himself, he squatted on his heels and adjusted his backpack. It was an old-fashioned, harness-like thing containing all his fishing gear, and unique in that a leather strap stretched across his chest, connected to the two shoulder straps beneath his arms. Slowly, he rose to his feet, his fishing pole clenched in his hand, but his embarrassment at having Ralf see him fall had cost him his self-confidence. He took two steps and lost his balance again, falling backward.

Angrily, Dolphus reached back with his free hand and yanked on the right strap of his backpack, which had slipped down his shoulder on impact. To his horror, he realized that in doing so, the strap had wedged around an iron rod, pinning him to the rail. This time, when Ralf's laugh filled the air, it was met with a high-pitched whistle blasting through the mouth of the west bank's hilly corridor leading to the bridge.

Dolphus panicked. What should have been a simple maneuver—pulling the rucksack over his head so he could free himself—turned into a series of mad flailings. The great, smoking iron beast heaved its engine onto the trestle deck. Every inch of Dolphus's body vibrated in sync with the pulsating frame and pile bents that supported the trembling structure.

Sure that he was facing certain death, Dolphus closed his eyes. *Gott, hilf mir,* he prayed. *Save me!*

As the words rolled off his tongue, he felt a pair of hands seize his shoulders. Ralf had scaled the pilings as soon as he'd heard the train whistle, raced the distance to where Dolphus lay trapped, and was now slicing through the tangled strap of his cousin's knapsack with a fillet knife, shouting, "Drop the fishing pole, *dummkopf!*"

Dolphus threw his pole over the side of the trestle just as his shoulder was freed, and in one fluid movement he and Ralf rolled over, no more than a split second before the first wheels of the train sparked by. They dangled side-by-side off the edge of the bridge, their fingers clinging white-knuckled to the tracks and their arms shaking from the effort to not let go. As the cars hurtled past them, the wind they generated blew Dolphus's cap off his head, sending it floating down into the river after his discarded fishing pole, like a hawk swooping down on its prey.

When the last car rumbled off the bridge the boys hoisted their bodies back onto the trestle. For several moments they lay motionless, gasping for breath, not daring to speak. Then, still not saying a word, they got to their feet and scuttled down to the end of the tracks where they leapt the short, final distance to the ground. Though Dolphus noticed that Ralf's hand trembled as he picked up his pole to resume fishing, his cousin immediately began acting as though nothing had happened.

"*Danke*, Ralf," stuttered Dolphus.

"Forget it." The tone of Ralf's voice implied there was to be no talking about his heroics or their near-death experience. "I've been here an hour already and haven't caught a thing."

Dolphus couldn't stop his legs from shaking, so he collapsed next to Ralf's tackle box and wrapped his arms around his knees. Still in shock, his eyes followed the river downstream for a trace of his fishing pole.

Ralf read his mind. "Your pole's gone Dolphus. So is your pack. Open my tackle box there and get me a cigarette and a match."

While Dolphus leaned over and did as he was told, Ralf continued, "Did you notice who was on that train?"

"*Nein.*"

"Soldiers. The Wehrmacht. Hundreds of them, I'd say."

Dolphus held up the cigarette to Ralf, who traded him for the fishing pole. "Here, maybe you'll have better luck than me."

Though a bit wobbly, Dolphus stood up. He threw his arm back and tossed the fishing line into the same dark eddy Ralf had been trawling.

Ralf lit the cigarette and inhaled deeply. "There weren't any guards at the border crossing outside Ingling this morning."

Dolphus, still fighting to stay composed, could only shrug.

"Something's happening," murmured Ralf. "Perhaps Germany is finally invading Austria, like father said they would."

Dolphus didn't like being reminded of his Uncle Primus. Ralf's father was a man to be reckoned with. Expecting perfection from everyone but himself, he was a notorious Jew-hater who was also obsessed with being right about everything. He could be vicious too. Rumor had it that any man who crossed Primus Geller could count on suffering his revenge, regardless of how long it took. Even Oden kept his distance from his brother. Primus had flown into a rage when the family farm was bequeathed to Oden after their parents' death and he was left nothing but his father's WWI uniform and an heirloom Bible. He burned them both, and never got over the slight.

Then, there was the mysterious death of Primus's first wife. Local authorities in Passau couldn't prove she had been killed, but many believed Primus had pushed her down their home's steep staircase and left her there to die. According to the neighbors, Primus had kept her confined for years, not letting her go anywhere without him. Several women even claimed she had suffered multiple miscarriages because of his brutality and when she finally threatened to leave him, she suffered the consequences. After her death, Primus quit his job in Germany and crossed the border into Austria where he got a young Ingling girl pregnant. She fared no better than his first wife, other than she was able to bring Ralf into the world nearly full term. Her subsequent "illnesses," however, frequently rendered her incapable of caring for the child.

With Primus either drunk, absent, or unwilling to assume

responsibility for his son when his wife was incapacitated, Ralf's mother—who had no relatives of her own—would send her son back over the border into Germany to stay on the farm with Oden. It was during those visits that Dolphus and Ralf spent a good amount of time with each other. But now that Ralf's mother had passed on, and Ralf was old enough to work a steady job, it had been several years since he had last stayed on the farm.

Dolphus studied Ralf. Oden always said he feared Ralf would turn into his brother Primus someday, but Dolphus couldn't imagine that ever happening. Although Ralf certainly seemed to crave his father's approval, he was far too charismatic and fun-loving to be compared to Primus, who was dark, morose, and exceedingly dangerous.

Ralf blew a smoke ring in the air and turned to Dolphus, breaking his cousin's reverie. "What are you staring at?"

"Nothing."

"Nothing? You look like you're a million miles away. Guess what, Dolphus? My father has become a member of the Austrian Nazi Party. He's sure they're going to elect him as an officer. He's going to be a big shot soon."

Dolphus felt a nibble on his line. Lifting his pole slightly, he replied, "I don't know anything about it, Ralf."

"Of course you wouldn't. You're too young."

"I'm not much younger than you."

"Yes, you are," countered Ralf. "I'm almost fifteen. You're only ten."

"I'm eleven today and you won't be fifteen for three more months."

Scowling, Ralf continued, "Father says he hopes Germany wins Austria to our side since so many Austrians are really Germans anyway."

"They are?" asked Dolphus.

"That's what Father says. As for me, I hope the Führer goes to war and takes over the whole world."

"Why?"

"I want to fight, that's why." Ralf rolled his eyes as if it went without saying. "So does my father. Your father must want to fight too, Dolphus. It's the best profession for a man. Everyone loves soldiers. Especially girls."

"*Verflucht!*" Dolphus reeled in his line to remove a tangle of debris from the hook. "How old do you have to be to be a soldier, Ralf?"

"I could be one now, if I wanted. The problem is, there's no one to fight yet."

Dolphus sat back down. "*Vater* says Herr Hitler has become dangerous."

"Your father better watch what he says," Ralf warned. "Someone might think he's a traitor."

"He is not a traitor!" Dolphus thrust Ralf's fishing pole at him.

"I'm not saying he is," replied Ralf. "But others might think so unless he proves himself by fighting for the Führer." Grabbing the pole from Dolphus, he stood up to stretch. "Germany will be the leader of a great empire. Mark my word, Dolphus, someday I'll be a war hero and all the girls in Vienna will love me."

"Vienna?"

"It's a great city, don't you know? The capital of Austria. Soon, it will be in German hands."

Dolphus felt a rush of confusion come over him. Awkwardly, he brushed a layer of sandy dirt off the seat of his pants and made a move to leave.

"Where are you going?" demanded Ralf. "We just started fishing."

Staring eastward, Dolphus said, "If there were soldiers on that train, and it's true there's going to be a war, I need to get home."

"Oh, well," sighed Ralf. "The fish aren't biting anyway." Gathering up his gear, he added, "I don't know when we'll see each other again, Dolphus."

"Why? If my father has to fight in a war, maybe I will too, Ralf."

"Maybe." Ralf slung his knapsack on his back and nodded good-bye to Dolphus. "See you around then, Cousin."

Dolphus wanted to thank Ralf again for saving his life, but feared it would only embarrass him, so he just stood mutely as Ralf ambled his way along the train tracks back toward Ingling. When his cousin had disappeared from sight, Dolphus turned and sped home, confused and deeply troubled by his conversation with Ralf. Voices in his head shouted at him to run faster, lest he arrive back at the farm to find his father already snatched away to fight a war for the Führer, leaving him behind to care for his mother. Worse yet, were the visions flashing in his mind of Ralf's father Primus becoming a powerful leader in Austria. The prospect lit a fire under Dolphus's feet, and it was only when he reached his house and found his family safe and secure that he was able to breathe a sigh of relief.

"Don't worry, Dolphus," his mother told him, when Dolphus explained what Ralf had said about a coming war and Primus's ambitions within the Austrian Nazi Party. "People always talk of war, but your father and I pray that's all it is. Just talk. And your Uncle Primus? He will never be a leader of anything. He doesn't have the common sense or fortitude to excel in any occupation. I can't even imagine the army wanting him."

Oden, however, disagreed with his wife's assessment. "Since when does common sense and fortitude count for anything in the Third Reich?" he grunted. "If things don't change soon, there will not only be war, there'll be thousands of little Primus Gellers throwing their weight around with the government's blessing. Primus is exactly the kind of man the army will want."

Dolphus's mother shushed her husband. "It's Dolphus's birthday today, Father, and there'll be no more talk of war or your brother. Come to the table both of you and let's eat."

Sitting down opposite his mother and father, Dolphus bowed his head to pray. Silently, he asked God to bless their meal. But before saying "Amen" he also prayed for peace and his family's protection, realizing that Ralf seemed set on a path completely different from his.

· 4 ·

Bread of Defiance

Dolphus, dozing in the front seat of Domenico's silver BMW, woke up with a jolt when Marco slammed on the brakes.

"You could have made it," complained Aarika from the backseat, as the arms of a rail crossing guard lowered in front of the car. Fanning herself with a magazine she added, "We'll probably be sitting here forever now."

Seconds later, a southbound Trenitalia express train zoomed by them, causing the car and its occupants to rock wildly. Dolphus turned white. Tensing his neck and shoulders, he reached up and squeezed the grab handle on the ceiling.

"Are you all right, Signor Geller?" asked Marco, looking sideways at the German.

"I . . . just don't like trains." Beads of sweat glistened on Dolphus's forehead.

"I didn't know that, Opa," said Aarika. "Why not?"

"I was nearly hit by one when I was a young boy." Looking over his shoulder, Dolphus waved away his granddaughter's concern. "It's nothing, Aarika."

The train took nearly five minutes to pass. When the guardrails rose again, Marco drove over the tracks and continued west a few blocks before turning left onto the frenetic Viale Italico, running parallel with the sea the entire length of Versilia. Even though it was only ten o'clock in the morning, the palm-lined promenade was already teeming with tourists, shoppers, and beachgoers. Performing a series of deft moves, Marco found a temporary parking spot close to the Monte Cristo beach club where the Bertozzi family owned a cabana. He turned off the ignition, helped everyone retrieve their belongings, and then escorted his party to the admission desk where he would sign them in as Domenico's guests.

"Will you be joining us for a swim, Marco?" asked Dolphus, as Marco began filling out the required forms.

"Thank you, Herr Geller, but I have some errands to run. What time would you like me to return?"

Dolphus deferred to Aarika, asking her when she thought Marco should come back.

"*Nie,*" she said.

Marco paused to look up at Aarika. *Never? Really? What kind of immature answer is that?*

Before Marco could summon a reply, Poppy jumped into the conversation. "Aarika may not care if you never come back, Marco," she said, "But I care. You're the expert. How long do you think we'll want to stay here?"

Marco signed his name on the last form and handed it back to the clerk. "Most people find the afternoon sun and sand too hot on the beach this time of year. By one o'clock, they have gone home to eat. If you wish, I can make lunch for all of you at the casala afterward."

"Perfect," said Dolphus. "We'll see you at one then, Marco."

Marco, lingering near the club entrance, watched as Dolphus began following the girls down the boardwalk. A middle-aged Italian man stepped around Poppy and the Gellers and approached Marco. As he did, he paused and turned to stare at Dolphus. "Go home, *Deutsch*," he called out loudly. "You don't belong here."

Other than a momentary stiffening of his spine, Dolphus showed no sign of having heard the comment. But Aarika, on the other hand, glared at the man and protectively looped her arm through her grandfather's, slowing her pace to match his. Marco felt an unexpected flash of sympathy for the Gellers, the only Germans he had come to know personally. Making his way back to the car, he wondered—for the first time in his life—if the war had ever really ended.

Not long after the Gellers had left for the beach that morning, Domenico had driven up the mountain to his casala. When he entered the kitchen, he found it stuffy, so he opened the windows as wide as they would go to let in a breeze. If there was one thing that impeded his baking enjoyment and creativity, it was stale, stagnant air.

With *bucatini all'amatriciana* as his choice for dinner later, he decided some fresh bread and a lemon-fig *crostata* would go perfectly with it. Gathering together all the necessary ingredients, he tied his apron on and set to work. In the midst of slicing some purple-green figs, a voice startled him.

"Domenico! Made you jump, did I?"

Domenico looked up to see his neighbor, Sergio Petrosello, leaning through the open window. The old man's crossed arms rested on the marble sill, and when he laughed his rotten teeth looked like irregular rows of pegged corn.

"I noticed you had quite a group up here the other night," said Sergio, his smile fading.

Domenico turned back to slicing his figs. "You being my closest neighbor, Sergio, I can always count on you knowing what goes on here. It was a family get-together."

"From my place, it sounded like someone in your family is American."

"Yes, an American guest joined us. Is there something you need, Sergio?"

"I take it the German is here again too. I could hear his guttural voice last night as well." Sergio paused to stare at Domenico's hands. "What are you doing, Domenico—preparing dinner for the barbarian?"

"He's not any more of a barbarian than you, Sergio."

"How would you know? What is his name, anyway? I always forget."

"Do you? Dolphus Geller has been coming here nearly every summer for the last twenty years."

"Exactly," hissed Sergio. "And *why* does he come here?"

"Because as you know, he spent time in our area during the war. Behind the Gothic Line."

"And why is it that it's your house he rents year after year? Eh?"

Domenico silently counted to ten before replying. "Because I am the only one on the mountain who has rental property. You could make an income from your property, Sergio, if you would move out and rent it. But I realize it might be too much work and sacrifice for you to pursue."

Sergio stopped grinning. He leaned his bony torso further into the kitchen, his puny, prying eyes probing Domenico's face. "Why Dolphus?" he countered. "Why rent to a German? Tuscany is full of American and British and French tourists these days."

"Dolphus Geller has always paid a premium price to

stay here. He provides me with a reliable source of income over the holidays. And . . ." Domenico almost said that an unusual friendship had sprouted up between Dolphus and himself through the years, but decided against it. "And that's all you need to know, Sergio."

"But why do you go to such lengths to treat a German so well? He doesn't deserve it. If it were me, I would soak those figs you're slicing in rat poison and feed him a great big piece of *crostata* for dessert."

"I'm sure you would." Domenico set his knife aside and reached up to close the windows. "Excuse me, but this breeze will prevent my bread from rising."

Gently, Domenico pushed the windows against Sergio's elbows until he unwillingly relinquished his post, and then watched as his nosy neighbor hobbled down the hill toward his home. When he was sure it was safe, he reopened the kitchen windows. He finished scooping the sliced figs into a prepared crust, and shaping some bread dough into a loaf, he finally placed both the bread and the *crostata* into the oven.

He checked his watch. Marco had called Domenico at home earlier to tell him he'd have the Gellers back up the mountain to the fattoria by one thirty. Figuring he had plenty of time before they returned, Domenico grabbed a plastic tub of fresh green beans and an empty wooden bowl. He went outside, walked across the lawn to the stone table beneath the spreading chestnut tree, and sat down. As he began snapping beans, the dappled sunlight dancing across the pitted surface of the table distracted him, and soon he was lost in thought. His eyes grew heavy. His chin dropped to his chest, and before he knew it, he was dreaming.

Deep in his subconscious, he heard is mother Elvira call to him, "Domenico! Come quickly!" There she was, standing in the doorway of the fattoria, a broom in her hand, calling to him as he swung like a performing monkey from the bottom limb of the chestnut tree. "Your father wants to talk to you," she said.

Domenico dropped to the ground and dutifully obeyed his mother, his five-year-old mind fretting that he must be in trouble if his father wanted to "talk" to him. Try as he might though, on the walk from the tree to the house, Domenico could not think of a single thing he might have done that would cause his father to be angry with him. Nearing his mother, he noticed she was crying.

"Hurry," his mother whispered, pulling him into the house. Before closing the door, she scanned the horizon intently, from the Cinquale Canal at the base of Monte Montignoso, to the beaches south of Forte dei Marmi.

Orazio Sacchelli, lean and overly tanned from years of hard work in the sun, sat hunched over the kitchen table, a note and several maps spread out in front of him. He looked up as his son sat down opposite him, his face expectant.

"You deserve to know what is happening, Domenico, even though you may not fully understand." Orazio held up a sheet of paper covered with cryptic writing. "I received this from someone warning us of what will happen now that the Americans are defeating the Germans in Florence. It says the Nazis plan to retreat and set up a new line of defense called the Gothic Line near our mountain. Do you understand, Domenico?"

"You're talking about the war, Papa."

"Yes, son, the big war that has been going on ever since you can remember. Until now the fighting has been far away, but soon it will be here. Perhaps, at our house. We must decide what to do."

Domenico's eyes widened. Although war was a concept he knew little about, other than what he had overheard his parents talking about behind his back, the word "we" implicated him in the decision. He glanced at his father's hunting rifle hanging from a rack above the door. "We will have to fight?"

Elvira's hands flew to her mouth. Domenico noticed her eyes were glazed over as though she was watching something she didn't want to see.

"It will be impossible to stop the soldiers from coming here," replied Orazio. "Whether they make their stand to the north of us, or to the south, it doesn't matter. Either way, we will be at the center of the battle. We can't stay here."

The thought of fleeing his home was incomprehensible. "But, where will we go, Papa?"

"That's what we must decide."

"I still say we should try to go to my sister's in Milan," said Domenico's mother.

"The Germans are entrenched in Milan, Elvira. The city is overrun with them. If we are in Milan when the Allies invade there, which I believe they will, we would only be facing this moment yet again."

"What are you saying, Orazio?" asked Elvira, panic in her voice. "There is no hope? No way to escape what's coming?"

Orazio placed his hand over his wife's hand and glanced at Domenico. "There is always hope. The question is, where do I send you both?"

"Send us?" said Elvira. "What about you?"

"I must stay here as long as I can. Who will care for our animals?"

Clenching her fists, Elvira stood up. "You are separating us?"

"How will we eat when all hell breaks out around us? You

have heard the stories from the south, families dying of starvation . . ." Orazio nodded toward Domenico, intimating he didn't want to frighten their son. "And worse."

Elvira's eyes fluttered, as though trying to block out horrific scenes her imagination was conjuring up in her mind.

"Once you and Domenico are established in a safe place," continued Orazio, "and I can no longer stay here, I will bring all of our goats and rabbits and chickens with me to meet you. I cannot expect someone to take in our family *and* care for our animals so we can eat."

For the first and only time in his life, Domenico saw his mother explode with rage. He noticed, with boyish fascination, how her nostrils flared out and her lips curled back, baring her teeth.

"If you do not leave, I do not leave," she threatened, her voice resolute.

Orazio stared at his wife who now leaned across the table toward him, no longer a meek and frightened woman, but a fury not to be crossed. With the slightest movement of his eyes he stole a look at Domenico as if to say to her, "What about our son?"

Unflinching, Elvira stood her ground. "We stay together."

Domenico was roused from his nap by distant thunderclaps rolling along the front range of the Carrara Mountains. He rubbed his eyes and blinked at the blinding rays of sunlight searing through a thin gap in a band of quicksilver clouds gathering off the coast. His dream had left him feeling dirtied with memories. Still half-asleep, he stood to his feet and shook his shoulders, as if by doing so he could fling the gritty residue of his dream off of him. Then, he glanced at his watch and realized with a start that the Gellers would be returning from the beach any moment. Leaving his bowl of unsnapped peas on the table, he raced to the casala to check on the bread and *crostata.* They were done to perfection.

As he pulled the bread from the oven, his mother's long-ago words, "*We stay together,*" reverberated through his mind like the thunder that continued to boom along the foothills. His mother, he recalled ironically, had baked bread the very day they were forced to flee their home. Though she knew the threat was imminent, she couldn't possibly have known how close at hand it was when she got up that morning to prepare the dough.

That long-ago morning at the fattoria just wouldn't let go of Domenico. Setting his bread on a rack to cool, he fell into a trance-like state, his mind reeling back to the year 1945. He could hear his father telling his mother, "Elvira, you might as well hang a sign on our door that says, *Come, German Dogs— Dinner is Ready.* What is this? Your Bread of Defiance?"

By then, nearly everyone on the mountain had already escaped. The only "defiant" ones seemed to be his family and the few stubborn neighbors who remained. While those neighbors may have stayed behind because they were in denial about the danger, or physically incapable of fleeing, Domenico knew his father had every intention of leaving, because he had spent the last week fashioning cages for their animals and loading their wooden cart with feed and what few possessions they needed. All he would have to do when the time came, Orazio had assured his wife and son, was grab his rifle, harness the mule, and they could go.

Try as he might, Domenico couldn't shake the memories of that brilliant summer day—the day his mother had baked her Bread of Defiance. Absently, he used his index finger to trace the etching splayed across the top of his own *pane rustica*. His mother had always marked her baked goods with the signature three strokes, like a fleur-de-lis, though it more closely resembled a small sheath of wheat than a flower. It represented, she used to tell him, their family: Orazio, Domenico, and herself.

We stay together.

The aroma of fresh-baked bread also reminded him of their old neighbor, Signora Gabrelli. Smelling his mother's Bread of Defiance wafting out of their fattoria that day, the signora had appeared at their door to barter half-a-dozen small eggs for one slice of Elvira's bread.

"Our flour is gone," the old woman had explained, her hungry eyes fixated on the great round loaf cooling on the counter. Noting that the Sacchellis were busy packing their belongings, she added, "I see you'll be leaving the mountain soon. Our children wanted Mario and I to come live with them in Livorno. We would have left last week—it would be much safer there, of course—but Mario's gout has returned . . ."

Domenico roused himself and looked at his watch again. Where was Marco with the Gellers? What was taking them so long? He stepped back outside and began pacing in front of the casala, praying for a distraction, anything, to stop the uninvited memories bombarding him. No matter how hard he tried, however, he couldn't get the picture of old Signora Gabrelli's worried, wrinkled face out of his mind. Nor could he forget the gunfire that had erupted below them just as his mother began to slice the bread that day, and the sound of the serrated knife clattering across the granite floor when she dropped it. He heard the panic in his father's voice as he told Signora Gabrelli she had better return home at once. But the old woman had hesitated. Even when Elvira tried to shoo her home, the signora had remained frozen in their driveway.

Domenico raised his hands to his ears in a vain attempt to stop the sounds haunting him from the past.

"Hurry!" he heard his mother shouting at Signora Gabrelli. "Go home to Mario. Tell him you must leave the mountain *now!*"

They never got so far as being able to hitch the mule to the cart. Signora Gabrelli never made it home. German troops had already scaled the mountain, their jackboots, motor-cycles, and trucks kicking up clouds of dirt as they rounded the bend in the road below the fattoria.

A hint of rain blew into the kitchen, dissipating Dome-nico's reflections. Somberly, he closed the windows, covered the warm bread with a towel, and then reached up to pull his right ear lobe. It was a habit he had developed over the years, doing it whenever voices from the past invaded the present. The words haunting him now were the voices of soldiers shouting, in broken Italian, as they stormed the mountain-top houses, "*Arrendetevi e vivrete. Lottate e morirete!*" Surren-der and you will live. Fight and you will die.

His family did neither. They barely escaped with their lives. *But then,* he thought to himself, *escape comes with dan-gers all its own. It did then and it does now. If I don't confront my past sooner or later, I'm bound to die an incomplete, unre-solved man.*

And that, he realized with a jolt, was the dilemma he had always faced. His options were mutually exclusive. Either he continued living an easy, but shallow life marked by a façade of happiness, or he must take the plunge and pursue truth and real peace. But at what cost?

·5·

The Truth About Secrets

Marco waved at Domenico as he passed him driving up via Casone to the fattoria. *He must have been baking at the casala,* he thought, his tongue toying with the roof of his mouth. *Domenico is such a great cook; if it weren't for Aarika, I'd find an excuse to stay and eat dinner with the Gellers tonight.*

Yes, Aarika. On the ride back from the beach club, she had been acting especially aloof and superior, as though Marco were nothing but a speck of lint on her cotton sundress. Marco was so put off by her attitude that, when they arrived a few moments later at the fattoria, he intentionally opened the car door for Poppy first and helped her unload her beach gear, leaving Aarika to fend for herself. As he was doing so, Aarika dropped her towel and bags to the ground and screamed.

"Opa!" she cried. "What is it? Did you forget to take your pill?"

Dolphus, barely able to stand upright, steadied himself by placing his hands on the hood of the car. Aarika, trying to support him as best she could, turned to look at Marco. Her eyes were wild with fear.

"Not to worry," Dolphus mumbled weakly. "I'm sure it's just angina. The doctor warned me this could happen as a result of my condition. I thought it wouldn't matter if I waited and took my pill with lunch. Perhaps I should have taken it this morning."

All the color drained out of Aarika's face. "You told me you took your pill this morning when I asked you, Opa. You lied to me?"

"No, Aarika. When you asked me this morning if I'd taken my pill, I didn't say anything. I simply nodded," argued Dolphus between labored breaths. "Besides, we were in a hurry to leave and I didn't want to worry you."

Meanwhile, Marco had come around the car and was now stationed next to them. "Here, let me," he said, tenderly removing Aarika's arm from her grandfather. Then, in a firm voice he added, "Run to the fattoria, Aarika, and get your grandfather's medicine and a glass of water. I'll stay here. And Poppy, go with her and bring me back a cool, wet towel."

Both girls raced to the house while Marco tended to the old man. "Tell me what's going on, Dolphus," he said.

Dolphus inhaled sharply.

"Are you feeling short of breath?"

Dolphus nodded.

Marco put two fingers over the German's wrist and felt his pulse. Next, he placed his palm over Dolphus's forehead. "You feel cool," Marco noted. "Does your chest ache, as though a ton of bricks is resting on it? Does your arm hurt?"

"I feel no weight on my chest and my arm is fine. My heart is just racing, that's all. Once I take my pill, I know I'll be fine."

Marco looked up to see Aarika sprinting toward him, still alabaster pale, carrying a glass of water in one hand and a bottle of pills in the other. Poppy followed close behind, holding a large wet towel out in front of her. Moments after swallowing his pill, Dolphus began breathing easier. His pulse returned to normal. When Marco was sure Dolphus was sufficiently able to walk, he helped him into the house while Poppy and Aarika brought their beach towels and bags in and set them on the kitchen table.

"I can't thank you enough, Marco," said Aarika, her voice trembling. "I'm not sure what I would have done if you hadn't been here."

"I'm sure you would have risen to the occasion."

"Perhaps."

Taking her grandfather's hand in hers, Aarika insisted Dolphus take a nap while Marco prepared lunch. "I'll help you to your room, Opa. I don't want you trying to climb the steps yourself quite yet."

Grudgingly, Dolphus went along with her. "Just a fifteen-minute nap," he muttered. "Do you hear me, Aarika? Only fifteen minutes and then I want to be woken up."

When Aarika returned to the living room, she caught Poppy and Marco huddled together. Eyeing them suspiciously, she asked, "Is there something I should know?"

"I was just telling Marco how glad I was that he was here to help with Dolphus," said Poppy. "He said you told him the same thing."

Without replying, Aarika pointed to a mountainous pile of laundry stacked in a basket next to the fireplace. "You left those wet clothes in here last night, Poppy. Would you mind hanging them up outside before they get mildewed? That's something we would never do in Germany, you know."

Poppy shot Marco a glance that seemed to say, "What did I tell you?" Then she picked up the basket and trudged outside where she began hanging clothes on a thin frayed rope stretched between the kitchen door and a nearby *pino* tree.

"What was that all about?" asked Aarika after Poppy was out of earshot.

Marco, reasoning he had nothing to lose by being honest, said, "Your sister was just surprised that you thanked me for helping your grandfather."

Aarika looked down at her feet, her cheeks suddenly flushed. "Did she say anything else?"

"She said it's hard to believe that you and she have the same blood running through your veins. Your sister is trying her best to get along with you, Aarika. She can't understand why you don't make an effort to reciprocate."

"Poppy's my *half*-sister."

"Half-sister, whole sister, she's still your family."

"What Poppy and I are to each other, and how we get along, is none of your business."

"Unfortunately," replied Marco, "in a way it *is* my business. Your grandfather has requested that I help make your holiday here a memorable one, as enjoyable as possible. I could be the best tour guide and translator in the world, but if you spend the entire time resenting your sister's presence here then . . ."

"You will have failed."

"Exactly."

Aarika bristled. "Let me understand this correctly. The only reason you care if Poppy and I get along is because it will reflect poorly on you if we don't."

"You're twisting my words," said Marco. "I was simply responding to your accusation that your relationship with your sister was none of my business."

"And you would have me pretend to like a girl I've only just met, who I have little in common with and who may have ulterior motives for coming here, as a favor to you?"

Marco knew he should drop it. He knew he shouldn't let Aarika goad him into an argument. Her life *wasn't* any of his business. Yet some unexplainable urge to see the two sisters get along better compelled him to press her on the subject. "Would it really be so difficult for you to be nice to Poppy, Aarika?"

Aarika crossed her arms in defiance, but her voice was almost childlike. "Put yourself in my shoes, Marco. My mother abandoned me when I was three and moved to America where she gave birth to Poppy. I haven't seen my mother since she left and, honestly, I hope I never do. Poppy's coming here was her idea. My mother called Dolphus and talked him into agreeing to let her come here this summer. She probably thinks this is a way of winning me back."

"What's wrong with that?" asked Marco. "Making amends with your family is a good thing."

"You don't get it," frowned Aarika. "How could you? You probably have a family who sticks together when times are tough and would do anything for each other."

"My family is wonderful, it is true. But I have often imagined what it would be like to have a sibling. A brother. Someone who understands my history, who can help share the burden of caring for my parents when they are older. You have been given an opportunity to have that kind of relationship, Aarika. You should take advantage of it and be thankful. Not bitter."

Aarika had not removed her purse from her shoulder since coming into the house. Now she pulled the strap around and clutched it close to her abdomen, shielding herself from Marco's words. "Forget it, Marco. You'll never understand. I don't know why I even bothered telling you about my mother." Then, loosening her grip on her purse just enough to open it, she pulled out a book. The worn cover featured a German title Marco understood to be an anthology of English poems.

"Opa doesn't want to sleep very long," she said, icily. "Can you wake him when it's time for lunch? I won't be eating this afternoon. If anyone needs me, I'll be outside reading."

An hour later, when lunch was over and the kitchen cleaned, Marco pulled the lace window curtain back just enough to peek outside and see what Aarika was doing. Curled up in a lawn chair beneath the chestnut tree, her book and purse tossed to the side, she was cradling the resident cat, patiently plucking clods of dirt from its long orange tail. In the stillness of the afternoon, above the muted hum of a few lone crickets, Marco heard her singing a lullaby to it in German, in a voice so tender it could have been a mother singing to her child.

On his way home later that afternoon, Marco stopped by my house to deliver a bag of lemons from Domenico's lemon tree. It took a fair amount of prompting on my part, but eventually he told me about the conversation he'd had with Aarika—how her mother had abandoned her when she was a child and gone back to America. It was so reminiscent of my Uncle Egisto's wife Armida, who had left her children in America to come back to Ripa during the war, that my heart went out to Aarika.

Marco told me he was puzzled that Aarika seemed to regret opening up to him about her past. "She probably thinks I'm heartless," he told me. "A shallow Italian who can't be trusted with a confidence."

Marco, heartless? Why, he was the kind of boy who rescued stray kittens when he was little, set the broken wings of birds and ducks and geese, and talked to dogs as though they were human. He has, what we call in Italian, a *grande cuore*: a big heart. "Oh, it's not about you, Marco," I said. "It's about Aarika not trusting her feelings."

"Her feelings about what?"

"Her ability to love and be loved."

"Her grandfather being the exception. If that's the case, then I can tell you she is going about it all the wrong way," said Marco. "If Aarika wants to love and be loved she shouldn't be acting the exact opposite. She acts as if she doesn't want anyone to love her. And she's impossible to read most of the time. It's as though her life is a pad-locked box of secrets, and she's swallowed the key so that no one will ever be able to really know her."

Secrets? I explained to Marco that humans are complex creatures remarkably clever at concealing their fears and extremely selective with which memories they want to retain and which they want to suppress. "We can all be notorious secret-keepers," I said. "Not just Aarika Geller."

Marco didn't look convinced. "Regardless, I don't think it's healthy."

"But of course it's not healthy to harbor secrets. They are often lethal."

"Deadly? I wouldn't go so far as to say that."

"It is true that during the war, for example, it was some-times necessary to keep secrets to save the lives of others. One slip of the tongue and a partisan could lose his life, and with him an entire village. But that is the exception, Marco, not the rule."

"What is the rule?"

"The very nature of secrets," I said, "is to keep some-thing hidden; to conceal the truth from others. Usually, the motive behind a secret is to protect someone's reputation. It could be a crime, big or small, or a moral failure of some kind. Any deed that might invoke judgment or shame if it's exposed is apt to be buried, Marco."

"What secrets could Aarika be hiding?"

"I don't know, but whatever they are, she is paralyzed by them. They are preventing her from being herself."

Marco shrugged, as if all this talk about feelings and secrets and love was too much for him. "Aarika just needs to bury her secrets deeper or get them off her chest and get on with life," he said. "I'm willing to be a good listener for a day or two if that would help her, and I can offer a shoulder to cry on as well as anyone. But her thanking me today for helping with Dolphus was an anomaly, Bianca. A second later, she was storming out of the house, angry at me for who knows what? Spending six weeks trying to please someone like Aarika Geller isn't exactly what I signed up for this summer."

"I know, Marco," I said, reaching out to stroke his cheek. "Just try to look for something you may have in common with her. Maybe then, she will be comfortable enough to let go of her secrets."

Marco glanced at his watch and stood up. "Sorry, but I have to go, Bianca. I'll think about what you've said." Then he kissed me good-bye, stepped outside, picked up his bike, and rode away.

Watching Marco disappear down via Strettoia, I reflected on our discussion about secrets. I recalled that long ago Domenico had shared a secret with me that only he and his wife knew about. To be honest, I don't understand why he is so intent on keeping the incident under wraps. But Domenico is a man of good character, so I trusted him and listened as he unburdened his soul.

All I will say is this: It had to do with two German soldiers stationed at his fattoria during the war.

IN ALL THE years Domenico had rented his fattoria to Dolphus Geller, he had never broached the subject of the war with him. At least, he hadn't asked specifics. It would have been rude and unprofessional to do so. But now he knew that if he was going to pursue the truth, Dolphus would be the perfect person to talk to. He glanced over at the German, who had fully recuperated from his angina attack and was now intent on eating his dinner.

What is the truth? mused Domenico. Perhaps the truth was that he didn't really want to know the truth. *After all, what if Dolphus took offense and I ended up losing the income he brings me every summer? But then, the old German is almost seventy-five-years-old. He isn't going to live forever. When Dolphus is dead and gone, I'm going to have to find another renter anyway. Hopefully, it will be someone as well-to-do, trustworthy, and reliable as him.*

Certainly, reasoned Domenico, he could rent out his fattoria to any number of tourists, as Sergio had mentioned the other morning. But Domenico guessed the Americans would find his farmhouse too rustic for their tastes, the French would think it was located too far from the beach, and the British would balk at his asking price.

"Delicious, as always," said Dolphus, setting his fork down and pushing his plate away. "You are surely the finest chef in Versilia, Domenico."

Domenico snapped back to attention. "Not in Versilia, I'm not. No. Perhaps on Monte Montignoso?"

Dolphus raised his glass of wine to Domenico. "Ah then, to Domenico Sacchelli, the culinary King of the Mountain!"

Poppy scooted her chair away from the table and stood up. She looked tired. "I must still be jet-lagged," she said. "Think I'll call it a night. Thanks for dinner, Domenico. It was delicious."

"Are you sure you wouldn't like dessert?" Domenico asked. "I made a lemon-fig *crostata*."

"It sounds wonderful, but not right now. Could you save some for me?"

"Of course."

Aarika excused herself also. "I need to walk off dinner," she said, getting up from the table. "Thank you, Domenico. The *bucatini* really was . . . perfect." She paused behind Dolphus and leaned down to embrace him, her arms crossing over his chest. "I'll be back in awhile, Opa."

"Be careful, Aarika," he replied, patting her hand. "It's starting to get dark."

"I will."

As the two men watched Aarika saunter along the twilight-shadowed footpath, Domenico said, "Your granddaughter enjoys walking?"

"She does. Taking a stroll outdoors does for her soul what listening to music does for mine. Oddly enough, this is the first time she has gone for a walk here. The heat is typically too much for her. She likes walking when it's a bit cooler."

"At least she came with you to Italy this year, despite our hot summer. That is a good thing, no?"

"I would say so, although I'm not sure she would agree. Normally she would have stayed back in Passau with her grandmother." Dolphus's face fell as he mentioned his deceased spouse. "Except for that one summer long ago when she and Aarika came with me, my wife insisted I spend my holidays alone. She knew how difficult it was for me to relax at home."

"Farming is hard work," agreed Domenico.

"Yes it is, and my wife—as always—was right. My holidays here were very therapeutic. At least, in some ways they were. I remember the first time I saw Tuscany during the war, I thought I had never seen anything so beautiful."

Domenico raised his hand to his mouth and coughed. It was a nervous gesture, one that indicated he might want to say something but couldn't quite formulate the right words quickly enough.

"As for Aarika," continued Dolphus, "I really think the only reason she accompanied me this summer is because she's overly concerned about my health."

"I'm sure she came with you because she loves you." Domenico struggled to sound reassuring. "You raised her, after all."

"My wife did most of the raising. I wasn't the husband or father, or even the grandfather, I should have been." Dolphus seemed to be stricken again as he mentioned his wife. He rose to his feet, his voice faltering. "You know, Domenico, suddenly I'm tired also."

Domenico rushed to Dolphus's side. "Aarika talked to me yesterday about your heart condition. Do you not feel well?"

"I refuse to have my entire summer in Italy ruined by questions about my health!" Dolphus growled.

"Forgive me." Domenico took a step back. "I didn't mean to . . ."

But Dolphus was already apologizing profusely, his hands raised in peace. "Please, Domenico, I am so sorry. It is me you must forgive. It is just that ever since my diagnosis, Aarika has hovered over me trying to control everything I do. She does this despite my doctor assuring me that with medication, more exercise, and some slight changes in my diet, my heart is strong enough to carry me along for a while longer. I wish my granddaughter would listen to reason."

Without Marco there to translate, the two men had been communicating in broken English. Not knowing if he understood Dolphus completely, Domenico made a stab at humor. "I would hate to think what my wife's reaction would be if I had your condition, Herr Geller. I wouldn't be allowed to eat my own food!"

With a thin smile, Dolphus said, "Let's hope you never have to find out." Then, stepping away from the table, he added, "Dinner was wonderful, Domenico. Nothing will stop me from enjoying your food while I am here. It's one of the reasons why I keep coming back every year. I've warned Aarika not to mention my name and the word 'diet' in the same sentence again until we return home. Oh, and speaking of Aarika, would you mind keeping an eye out for her? If she's not back from her walk in twenty minutes, let me know."

"*Certemente,*" said Domenico. "I see it's not only the granddaughter who worries about the grandfather."

Dolphus raised a finger. "Aha! Clever, Domenico."

"Oh, and before I forget it," said Domenico, "you said you were going to talk to Marco about arranging an impromptu trip to the Amalfi Coast next week. Have you done that yet?"

"*Ja, ja.* He is looking for suitable accommodations in Praiano. We hope to leave as early as Monday and return on Friday. You have a remarkable young man working for you, Domenico. Your cousin has been an excellent guide and interpreter for us so far."

"You are happy with his services?"

"Very much so." Turning to leave, Dolphus said, "*Gute Nacht,* Domenico."

"*Buonanotte,*" replied Domenico. "Sleep well."

After Dolphus disappeared into the fattoria, Mariella emerged from the casala to help Domenico clear the table. "Is everything okay?" she asked, noting her husband's drooping shoulders.

"Si."

"Don't lie to me, Domenico."

"I just hope Dolphus lives to come back again next year."

"You are worried about him dying? Marco said if Dolphus takes his medication and makes some lifestyle changes, he should be fine."

Domenico shrugged.

Placing her hands on her hips, Mariella asked, "Is it because you really care about Dolphus that you are worried, or would you simply miss the income he brings us?"

Stunned that his wife even asked the question, Domenico said, "We have become friends over the years. You know that."

Mariella pressed him further. "Then you must be worried you'll lose the opportunity to talk to him about the war if he dies. That's it, isn't it? I tell you, this worry of yours is going to give you the same sickness as Signor Geller."

Domenico wagged his head at his wife and stepped around her without responding. She had succeeded in piercing the very heart of his indecision. Dolphus was the only person he knew who might be able to give him the information he needed to fill in the missing pieces of the puzzle of his past. Maybe Dolphus knew the soldiers who had been involved in Signora Gabrelli's death. Perhaps he had heard about the attack on his mother from his fellow soldiers. If Dolphus died before Domenico could ask him, his opportunity to find out would be lost forever. But then again, he thought, if he questioned Dolphus and he became angry, he would get nowhere either. The German may not have any information to share, and even if he did, nothing could make him confide in Domenico if he didn't want to.

Ironically, while Domenico was in the casala's kitchen agonizing over his predicament, Dolphus Geller, now stripped down to his boxers, was lying on his bed upstairs in the fattoria examining his own situation in excruciating detail. He stared up at the moon-shadowed ceiling above him, his hands folded over his chest, asking himself questions he hadn't dared to ask himself since arriving last week at Domenico's.

Was letting Poppy come here to meet Aarika and spend the summer with us the right thing to do? What if the whole plan to reunite the girls gets out of control and backfires on me? What does Domenico know about what happened here on the mountain during the war?

Ten minutes passed, with Dolphus fretting the entire time. He heard Aarika enter the house and climb the stairs to her bedroom, her steps heavy. Not much later, Domenico's car pulled tiredly out of the driveway, its headlights flashing an arc of light into Dolphus's room as it turned onto the road. In the dense stillness of the night, Dolphus felt utterly alone and exposed, as though he was frozen on the ledge of a jump plane's open exit door. He could see himself as though it were real: his hands gripping the edge of the metal doorframe, his feet glued to the floor, a parachute strapped to his back.

Looking down, he watched the surface of the earth roll beneath him. It was like seeing his life from a bird's-eye view spread out in neatly groomed sections; broad fields of manicured habits and routines, resplendent meadows of longing and passion; dense, dark forests choked with fear and doubt. In the distance, he caught the outline of a golden city splayed against the horizon. Mesmerized, he allowed his torso to lean forward, his fingers still clinging to the edge of the door, his feet immovable. As the city zoomed closer to him, he could make out hundreds of fine architectural details. A massive medieval wall surrounded magnificent domes, soaring spires, towering operas and libraries and museums, and enormous palaces fit for emperors. His heart skipped a beat. There was no mistaking it. He was hovering over Vienna. And in that revelatory moment, he knew if he wanted to be set free, he had to jump.

Suspended in time somewhere between youth and old age, Dolphus let out an anguished cry. *I can't do it! Dear God, I want to, but I can't!*

Faster than a shooting star, a giant hand—as invisible as it was real—slapped him on the back and shoved him through the door of his indecision. Dolphus felt his heart stop as he spun helplessly into a dizzying free fall. Desperately, he fumbled to find, and then pull, his ripcord. When he finally succeeded in deploying his parachute, his body yanked back a second before floating down into the heart of Vienna where it crashed through the roof of Café Central and into the body of his formerly younger self.

Back to 1944 where it all began.

· 6 ·

Vienna

Vienna, Austria
July, 1944

WHILE SITTING IN the sumptuous Café Central, staring into his lukewarm *helles* Stiegl beer, a disturbing memory burst unbidden into Dolphus's mind. *Ralf enjoys killing. It excites him.* Just as quickly, Dolphus shoved the thought back into his subconscious. Having only just arrived in Vienna two hours earlier, Dolphus chalked up his mental turmoil to the culture shock his father had warned him about. After all, fresh off the farm, a country boy like him was sure to be overwhelmed by a city like Vienna. Indeed, the café's avant-garde clientele, high-brow ambiance, five-star food and service, and live string quartet performing Beethoven's "Septet" in the background all made Dolphus feel as though he was quite literally in another world.

But seconds later, when he looked up from his beer and saw Ralf across the table from him pulling the rhinestone straps of Fraulein X's ivory silk evening dress down over her shoulders, Dolphus knew this was no dream. He watched the woman demur, or at least pretend to be embarrassed, which seemed to excite Ralf even more, because soon his cousin was attacking her slender white neck and daring décolletage as though it were the evening's entrée.

Reluctantly, Fraulein X pushed Ralf away. "*Bitte,* Herr Geller," she squealed loudly. She then made a show of pulling her straps back up.

The fraulein's false modesty, heavy makeup, whiny voice, and cheap mannerisms annoyed Dolphus, which was unusual because few people had that effect on him. But in fact, he was so nauseated by her behavior, he wondered if he should warn Ralf. Perhaps his cousin was too inebriated to discern the woman's poor moral character. But as Dolphus was debating what to do, Ralf looked sideways at him and smiled, his eyes glazed over with a savage, insatiable hunger. The eyes of an animal. The same memory and the same conclusion exploded again in the forefront of Dolphus's brain, but this time he couldn't push it away: *Ralf enjoys killing. It excites him.*

Dolphus had seen the look on Ralf's face before, when as boys they had gone hunting on the farm and in the forests along the River Inn. They had both relished the chase. Each had rejoiced when they bagged their prey. Yet Ralf, though he was a good marksman and could shoot to kill, rarely did. He would hover over the animal he'd shot, spellbound by its suffering. The first time Dolphus witnessed his cousin doing this, he wrote it off as Ralf simply being curious. But as time went on, Ralf's emotional detachment turned to unnatural fascination, and then to calculated cruelty. Even then, Dolphus excused the troubling signs because Ralf was *sehr charmant,* or so charming, in so many other ways.

Now, faced with what he knew was the undeniable truth, Dolphus could no longer ignore it. The fraulein had become his cousin's prey. No longer concerned about her motives for being with Ralf, Dolphus began to worry about what Ralf's intentions were with the fraulein. Thinking he might at least be able to talk Ralf out of pursuing the woman, he waited until she excused herself to visit the powder room. When she had melted into the long queue outside the women's lounge, Dolphus said, "Let's go someplace where just you and I can talk, Ralf."

"About what?"

"Well," said Dolphus, trying to ease into his plan of action, "I wanted to thank you for pulling strings to get me into the army so quickly and . . . and for giving me the opportunity to serve with you in the war."

The corners of Ralf's mouth stretched into a self-congratulating smile. "When you are me," he waved nonchalantly, "it takes nothing to get what you want."

"No doubt that's true. It's just that I think . . ."

Ralf lifted his martini glass in the air. "Stop right there. That's your problem, Dolphus. It always has been. You don't need to think, you need to *live*. You are in Vienna, after all, the pearl of the Führer's crown. Now, tell me cousin, are you Dolphus the dull, serious farmer, or are you Dolphus the soldier?"

"I'm a soldier now, of course," said Dolphus, aware that several officers at the table next to them, and the women keeping their laps warm, were glancing his way and chuckling. He wished Ralf would lower his voice.

Ralf took a sip of his drink. "So then, I'm telling you, Soldier Dolphus, live it up! Soon enough the party will be over and we will have to leave here to defend the Fatherland. But for now, we are in a city that allows us to live life to the fullest in the midst of war."

Leaning back in his chair, Ralf tilted his face from side to side, taking in the opulence of their surroundings. "I mean, look around you, Dolphus. What war, right?" When Dolphus surveyed the room with a vacant look, Ralf laughed so uncontrollably that he spilled his drink. "Oh, Dolphus, I had forgotten how truly entertaining you can be."

"I . . . wasn't trying to be entertaining, Ralf."

Another round of gut-wrenching laughter followed Dolphus's admission, and when Ralf finally came up for air, he said, "We are dining in one of Vienna's finest districts, in one of its most popular cafés, surrounded by beautiful women hungry for real men, and you ask me to go somewhere else so we can 'talk'?" Without skipping a beat, Ralf narrowed his eyes suspiciously and growled, "So, what is it you're trying to tell me, Dolphus?"

"I want to know what you see in her." Dolphus lowered his head and leaned over the table, closer to Ralf, so he could speak in confidence. "I mean, the fraulein; she doesn't seem . . . your type."

"Ah, so that's it." Smirking, Ralf twisted around in his seat so he could cross his legs. His polished black boots gleamed in the candlelight. Draping one arm over the back of his chair, he dangled his Overstolz cigarette between his index and middle finger for a moment before asking, "How old are you, Dolphus?"

"Eighteen."

Ralf arched one eyebrow.

"Almost eighteen."

"And tell me again how a seventeen-year-old *bauernjunge* like you ended up in a place like this?"

"You arranged it."

"That's right. Me. And how old am I?

"You're twenty-one, Ralf."

"It follows then, since I'm older than you, that I am also wiser than you when it comes to women, no?" Ralf paused to take one last drag from his Overstolz before smashing the butt in a silver ashtray next to his plate. "Or perhaps I should say I know women very well, whereas you don't know them at all."

Dolphus felt a blush creep up his neck. He'd never been with a woman, and his cousin—in that typically uncanny way of his—somehow knew it.

Appearing to change the subject, Ralf pointed to the insignia on the collar of his field-gray military uniform indicating that he was an *Obersturmfuhrer,* or first lieutenant, in the 16th SS Panzergrenadier Division, Reichsführer-SS. "See this?" he asked. "I earned this rank, Ralf. You know how, don't you?"

Dolphus nodded, taking note of the angry, puckering scar crisscrossing his cousin's left temple. It ended in an almost perfect check mark along his upper cheekbone. Ralf's head, Dolphus knew, had nearly been blown off after he'd taken over command of an anti-tank unit at Kursk during the Battle of Prokhorovka. He was lucky another soldier took the main hit from the explosion that blasted both of them twenty feet from their position, leaving Ralf in a coma with a piece of shrapnel buried in his skull.

"They didn't think I'd make it, but look at me," said Ralf, stroking the gleaming Iron Cross 2nd Class medal dangling from his chest pocket. "I never gave up."

Dolphus stared at the medal. He couldn't help but be impressed. *The Iron Cross!*

"The war is not for cowards," continued Ralf. "You have to be ruthless, Dolphus, or you won't survive. The same goes for how you must treat women. Watch your back and always keep the upper hand with them, because if you don't, *boom!*" Ralf rocked back in his chair to emphasize his point. "They could blow up in your face, *ja?*"

"I . . . wouldn't know," blustered Dolphus. He hadn't realized before the depth of Ralf's distrust and hatred of women. Only now was it beginning to dawn on him just how much he had misread his cousin all these years.

"Of course you wouldn't, Dolphus. So like I said, take it from me; let a woman know you mean business from the very beginning and never give her the opportunity to turn on you. If she won't submit the first time you put your heel to her neck, throw her out. It's the best thing my father ever taught me."

Shock raced down Dolphus's spine. "Your father—Uncle Primus—taught you to treat women like that? But, Ralf, what about your mother? Didn't she . . . "

Before Dolphus could finish his question, Fraulein X returned to their table, sporting a fresh coat of bright coral lipstick. She lowered herself into a chair with exaggerated wriggling so as not to rip apart the seam of her body-hugging dress. Then she scooted close to Ralf and pressed her body against his. "I'm ready to go," she purred. "You promised me an evening I'd never forget, remember?"

Ralf turned from her and snapped his fingers at the waiter to bring him the bill. After signing his tab, he tossed several *Reichsmarks* on the table. "Go wait for me at the front door," he told the fraulein. "I want to talk to my cousin awhile longer. Alone."

Fraulein X began to pout, but seeing the effect it had on Ralf, she stopped, and picking up her purse, made her way toward the café's entrance. When she was gone, Ralf rose and nodded for Dolphus to follow him out of the dining room. He led him down an empty corridor and stopped in front of a great iron door separating the café's cavernous wine cellar from the restaurant.

Pulling another cigarette from his pocket, Ralf lit it and said, "I'm sure you've heard of Major Alfons von Stillfried."

"Of course," said Dolphus. The major's signature had appeared on the official notice he had received calling him to duty.

"Major von Stillfried has approved my requisition for you to be commissioned immediately to my division," said Ralf. "We're in the process of coordinating bomb squads to accompany some anti-tank units to northern Italy. I gave the major the impression you were an expert on assembling explosives."

"What?"

"You've used them on your farm to clear land before," reasoned Ralf. "So, you know more than most, I'd wager."

"But," stuttered Dolphus, "an *expert?*"

Ralf shoved Dolphus against the cellar door. "Don't question how I got you here, Dolphus. Just be thankful I did. Like I said, this is no time for cowards. The future of the Reich rests on the outcome of the war in Italy. Indications are we might lose Florence, and if the Allies reach Milan, it will be over. As we speak, a defensive line is being drawn near La Spezia. They are calling it The Gothic Line. We will both be stationed there and you will be under my command. That means you will do whatever I tell you without question. *Verstehen sie?*"

Dolphus pushed back against Ralf, forcing him to let go. "Yes," he growled. "I understand." In his entire life, Dolphus had never butted heads with Ralf like this. A clarity of mind descended on him as they stood face-to-face in the hallway, and the realization that their relationship had forever changed steeled his resolve.

"*Gut,*" said Ralf. "I'm glad we're in agreement and you know who's boss." Catching his reflection in a hall mirror hanging opposite where they stood, he straightened his uniform and smoothed his hair. "I'm catching a taxi to the Hotel Bristol. Room 256. You'll be sharing it with me until we leave for Italy. Tomorrow perhaps, maybe the next day."

Dolphus had no doubt Ralf would be sharing the room with the fraulein as well. "I'll find my own way to the hotel," he said.

Ralf winked. "You learn quickly, Dolphus. Take your time coming back."

Dolphus stepped outside the Café Central and dawdled. He realized he had no idea in which direction the Hotel Bristol lay, but it didn't matter as he intended on sightseeing for a while anyway. So, he shifted his satchel, which contained the few possessions he had brought with him from home, and set out, figuring he'd give Ralf a few hours with the fraulein before showing up at the hotel.

Though it was early, only eight o'clock, the Strauchgasse was littered with drunken soldiers and couples seeking temporary respite from the war at whatever concert hall or theater or tavern was open. Having never been outside of Passau before, save on his hunting and fishing excursions over the border of Germany with Ralf, the only thing Dolphus knew for certain about Vienna was that he was in the Innere Stadt, the city's ancient inner ring. He might walk around in circles, he reasoned, but he couldn't get lost. By the time he arrived at the Michaelerplatz, an enormous square lined with historic fountains and monuments and grand public and imperial buildings, the crowds had thinned and the sun was setting, bathing the entire plaza in shades of saffron and raspberry. Carried away by the beauty around him, Dolphus found a bench on the edge of the square and sat down. He pulled his knapsack onto his lap and retrieved a pen, some colored pencils, and a notebook, and began sketching the scene unfolding before him.

He didn't notice that a woman had come to sit down near him until she said, "You're really good."

The pen in Dolphus's hand slipped. "Oh," he muttered, closing his notebook hastily, "*danke.*"

"Sabine," said the woman, introducing herself with a pat on her chest.

"Dolphus," he replied, bowing his head. Her perfume reminded him of the lavender his mother grew in her flower beds back home.

"This is your first time to Vienna, isn't it?"

Dolphus nodded without meeting Sabine's gaze.

"You're not in uniform, but I'd guess you're a soldier. A new one. German?"

Dolphus nodded again, wondering how she could possibly know so much about him.

"Don't worry," said Sabine, as though reading his mind. "Vienna is filled these days with hundreds of boys just like you. A five-year-old could look at you and figure you out. How old are you?"

Dolphus turned to look full-on at Sabine. She was slender as a disc on his father's plow, with blond shoulder-length hair, full lips and a fine narrow nose. Her large, unblinking eyes were the color of distant mountains, lending her an air of innocence. "Eighteen," he lied.

She tossed her head. "I'm nineteen."

A silent pause passed between them. "Do all the girls in

Vienna walk around by themselves at night?" asked Dolphus. He regretted the question immediately. It was just that in Passau the only people his age who were out in the streets at night were troublemakers and Hitler Youth—usually one and the same.

Sabine lifted her hands to the twilight sky. "It's not night yet." Frowning, she added, "And I don't have anyone to answer to, so it really doesn't matter. Besides, there's no curfew."

"You're alone? No family?"

"*Ja.* That's me."

"Where are your parents?"

"They're in Mauthausen-Gusen."

"The work camp?"

Sabine nodded. "My father tried to help the family of a fellow professor at the university who was . . . in trouble. I was in a boarding school at the time and wasn't aware of what was going on. It was only when the SS came to interrogate me that I discovered my father and my mother had both been arrested." She paused to rub her shoulder. "The Nazis know how to rough you up to get what they want out of you. I was lucky; I walked away with only a torn rotator cuff."

Dolphus stood up. Stuffing his pencils and sketchbook back into his knapsack, he said, "Are you with the Resistance?"

"Do you know about the Resistance?"

"I know that people who resist the Third Reich are executed on the spot. Anyone who is against the Führer is a traitor."

"Well then, I'd be crazy to be involved in the Resistance, wouldn't I?" countered Sabine.

"You're not answering my question."

"I truly am just lonely," she admitted, looking up at him. "Today was one of those beautiful summer days that had me thinking about my parents and how carefree life used to be and . . ." Her voice trailed off. "Everyone else in my family has either died, or been killed in the war, or fled to the country because of the bombings. Even though I know I should be more cautious, I saw you sitting there soaking up the sunset and sensed a kindred spirit in you."

"Kindred spirit?"

"You seem like a sensitive soul caught in the crosshairs of a brutal war. Like me. You see, Dolphus, I have an unusual knack for recognizing like-minded people when I meet them."

Dolphus looked nervously over his shoulder. "I don't even know you."

"What's to know?" replied Sabine. "I'm simply having an innocent conversation with a soldier who's in Vienna for the very first time."

Dolphus stepped into the street. "I have to get to my hotel."

"Which one are you staying at?"

When Dolphus hesitated to tell Sabine, she reached out and tugged on his arm. "I can direct you to your hotel and show you some highlights of the city along the way, if you like. Come on, Dolphus. I don't bite."

Dolphus, having never had a girl challenge him the way Sabine was challenging him tonight, muttered his appeasement. "I'm booked at the Hotel Bristol."

Sabine pointed to her left. "Hotel Bristol is south of here. You're lucky I don't have anything else to do tonight. Let's go."

They walked together silently past several blocks of shops and cafés before Sabine asked, "Do you know where the army will be sending you, Dolphus?"

Dolphus abruptly stopped. "Just how lonely are you, any-way?" he asked. "Because if you keep talking about the war, you'll have to find someone else to annoy this evening."

"Agreed," smiled Sabine, waving aside his irritation. "I'm lonely enough to shut up."

The city's streetlamps had come on, but only dimly. Sabine told Dolphus that several days ago Allied warplanes had bombed some warehouses and supply bases around Vienna. As she was explaining that everyone feared the city itself would be the next target, a vivid flash of lightning, fol-lowed by a deafening crack of thunder, startled the two. Sabine pulled Dolphus into the doorwell of a nearby store and searched the sky intently before announcing, "It's just a storm."

Dolphus took note of the goose bumps that had crept up Sabine's bare arms and wondered if it was from the sudden drop in air temperature or from fear. Seconds later, a cloud-burst ruptured directly above them.

"We're not far from Café Mozart," cried Sabine. "Follow me!"

They raced several city blocks in a blinding downpour, and when they finally arrived at the café entrance, they found it had standing room only. Sabine looped her arm through Dolphus's and steered him through the crowd to the only spot available near the bar. She spoke briefly to the bar-tender, a broken-nosed bear of a man about forty or so, and ordered two beers. Dolphus offered to pay for their drinks, but she refused.

"My parents were able to transfer enough money to me at school before they were arrested to get me through the war," she said. "I've got it."

"I didn't know being a professor was such a lucrative career."

"It's not," replied Sabine bluntly, slapping some coins on the counter after their drinks were handed to them. "My parents inherited their wealth."

They both nursed their beers for a while without speaking, letting the bohemian atmosphere distract them from the quirkiness of their newfound relationship. Café Mozart was a popular after-show venue for actors and actresses, opera singers, and dancers from the nearby Burgtheater, so the air reverberated with lively banter and laughter, but it also buzzed with undercurrents of rebellion and repressed rage. They were just getting ready to vacate their seats when a ruckus broke out in a far corner of the dining room. Through the thick haze of tobacco smoke, a swarm of Nazi officers could be seen bullying and harassing some local men. Quickly, it escalated into a shoving match with curses and threats being leveled at everyone in the vicinity.

"Time to leave," said Dolphus, escorting Sabine toward the door. "Before it gets any uglier."

"What did I tell you about the SS, Dolphus?" snapped Sabine. "They're animals."

"From what I've seen, I might have to agree," Dolphus hissed. "But this isn't the best place to be airing your views of the war. Besides, you agreed not to talk about it, remember?"

Inching their way through the crowd, they peeked outside the door to see if it was still raining. Catching sight of a nearly full moon emerging from the clouds, they set out again, with Sabine playing the amateur tour guide. After admiring the landscaping and architectural details of the University of Vienna campus, Sabine pointed down an alley to their left.

"Let's take this shortcut," she said.

Although dank and narrow, the alley was surprisingly

clean. "I don't live too far from here," said Sabine, nodding toward the end of the alley. "I share an apartment, at least for the next few weeks, with a friend's family in the 6th district. It's called the Mariahilf."

"Look," she continued in a whisper, double-checking their surroundings to make sure they were alone. "I have a confession to make, Dolphus. It's true I'm lonely, and I was definitely waxing nostalgic today, but there's another reason I approached you tonight in the plaza where you were painting. I saw you first in Café Central. You were with an officer named Geller."

Stunned, Dolphus said, "He's my cousin. My name is Geller also."

Sabine's mouth dropped open. "He's your . . ." She took a step back, a look of stark fear passing over her face.

Dolphus drew close to her. "What has this got to do with you, Sabine? And how do you know my cousin?"

"Even though your cousin has only been in Vienna but a month or more, he already has a chilling reputation," Sabine's resolve seemed to surge as she spoke. "I had to deliver something tonight to a friend of mine who works in the kitchen at Café Central. She was on break and we were talking in an alcove around the corner from the entrance to the wine cellar. We heard everything you and your cousin said, Dolphus. I heard him threaten you."

"Why would you care one way or the other about a conversation you overheard at Café Central?" asked Dolphus, suspiciously.

"I've been on the receiving end of Nazi threats before, Dolphus. Let's just say I have a soft spot in my heart for their victims."

Dolphus narrowed his eyes. "You *are* with the Resistance."

"No," Sabine insisted, "I am not. Just look at me as an angel who was sent to give you some good memories to take with you to the front lines."

Motioning for Dolphus to follow her, she added, "And by the way, you earned points with me for the way you stood up to your cousin. Come on, let's go. Your hotel isn't far from here."

Dolphus didn't budge. "I don't believe you. Nothing you're telling me adds up."

"Fine," retorted Sabine, throwing her hands in the air. "I guess that's what I get for being honest." She turned her back on Dolphus and began walking away, calling over her shoulder, "You can follow me or find your own way to your hotel. I told you I don't bite."

Grumbling under his breath, Dolphus warily made his way down the alley, following in Sabine's footsteps. Once they exited the alley, they turned right and walked several more blocks, Dolphus wondering to himself if Sabine's presence was as circumstantial as she made it out to be.

At one point, they stopped in front of the Anker Bakery. Sabine directed Dolphus's attention to the mouthwatering breads and pastries showcased in the window. Then she turned and pointed at an elegant nineteenth-century structure across from the Vienna Opera House. "There it is," she said. "Hotel Bristol."

Dolphus was speechless. He had never stayed in a hotel before, let alone one fit for a king.

Together they crossed the Opernring, approaching the hotel from the west. "I don't know why they still call it a hotel," groused Sabine. "It might as well be a bunker for as many Nazis stay in it. And since our walk is over, and we'll probably never see each other again, I'll just go ahead and say it: A Jew by the name of Samuel Schallinger was forced to give up his share of the hotel two years ago. He was sent to Theresienstadt and is, as they say, no more."

Dolphus, however, hadn't heard a word Sabine had said. He had caught a glimpse of something gleaming white in the shrubbery on the side of the hotel. As he drew closer he could tell the form was human. Then he saw it was a woman. He crouched down, Sabine close behind him, and turned the body over. He lifted her gently off the ground and as he did, her head flopped back and rolled over toward the lighted street as though it was disconnected from her body. Her neck was broken. Her flesh was still slightly warm, but her eyes were cold and lifeless. He felt her neck for a pulse and detected none.

It was Ralf's fraulein from Café Central.

"Is that you, Dolphus?" The voice, familiar and playful, came from a third-story balcony directly above them.

Dolphus eased the woman back onto the ground and looked up to see Ralf leaning over the railing, hailing him with a drink in one hand and a cigarette in the other.

"Don't worry about her," shouted Ralf, referring to the fraulein's corpse. "Someone will find her in the morning. So you brought a girl with you, eh? I'm impressed. Bring her up!"

Dolphus looked at Sabine to gauge her reaction. He expected her to be in shock, overcome with fear, or at the very least, livid with rage. Instead, she calmly drew near and made a pretense of nuzzling with him.

"Of course I'm not going up there," she hissed. "And be careful. Let your cousin take care of the body and don't let him get you involved in it. He could easily blame it on you."

"Sabine, I'm sorry you had to see this. My cousin is . . ."

"He's sick. I know. He has a reputation around here, remember?" Cautiously, as though weighing the wisdom of what she was about to suggest, Sabine whispered, "I'm taking a big risk here, but—can I trust you, Dolphus?"

As Dolphus studied the dead woman lying next to them, he heard Ralf snickering above them on the balcony. Whatever it was Sabine was about to say, he had an eerie feeling that it could be something he might benefit from someday. Taking a leap of faith, he replied, "You can trust me, Sabine. I swear."

Sabine placed her lips next to Dolphus's ear. "If you're ever in trouble, go to Café Mozart and tell the bartender, Kurt—and him only—that you need to see me. Just tell him, 'Jael has Sisera's head.'"

Without another word, Sabine fled like a wisp into the night, leaving Dolphus standing over a dead woman who just moments before had been alive in the room he was about to share with his once-idolized cousin Ralf.

·7·

Praiano Unmasked

DOLPHUS WOKE UP the next morning feeling emotionally wasted. So much so that it took him at least a half hour to muster the strength required to get out of bed. His dream of Vienna had seemed so real—so *now*—that he could still feel Sabine's breath in his ear and hear Ralf's maniacal laughter. *Why did I have this dream now, while I'm in Italy?* he asked himself. *Is it a warning of some sort, or was it simply the result of mentioning the past to Domenico last night?*

Continuing to feel out of sorts, Dolphus didn't bother shaving before going downstairs for breakfast, as was his custom, but instead grabbed a cup of coffee and headed out the kitchen door in search of a private refuge. Catching sight of Domenico and Aarika conversing with each other underneath the chestnut tree, he skirted them in a wide arc and set a course away from the fattoria. Eventually, he found a haven of solitude in Domenico's olive orchard; a half-acre of gnarly-trunked, velvet-leaved trees sloping downward in tight formation on the other side of the driveway. Dolphus strolled slowly, pensively, among them until he emerged into a small clearing next to a cement-and-limestone wall separating the orchard from the vineyard. With a heavy heart, he sat down on its ledge and sighed. He simply couldn't shake the mental images of last night's dream: the fraulein's dead body, his cousin's leering face, and Sabine's expression of not being at all surprised by Ralf's calculated cruelty.

A goldfinch, which had been worming its way along the aisles of grapes opposite Dolphus, paused and tilted its pale, downy head toward him, as if asking permission to come nearer. Dolphus waited motionlessly as the bird hopped closer, until, in one feathery leap, it was on top of the wall not four feet away from him. They stared at each other, the finch taking in the brooding German and Dolphus studying the winged creature's delicate beak, curious black eyes, and the way its tiny head rotated effortlessly on its neck.

"You are lucky, Little One, to have wings," said Dolphus out loud. "To be so free, to not be burdened with memories. I'll wager you weren't up all night like I was, remembering terrible things that happened a lifetime ago."

In response, the finch let out a high, single-syllabled chirp.

"Perhaps what I need is a change of scenery. Fly away to somewhere different. Just like you, eh?" Dolphus shrugged. "Soon, we will go to the Amalfi Coast. It is only for five days, but I'm thinking it could be just what the doctor ordered. Ach!" Dolphus angrily dug in his shirt pocket and pulled out a small brown plastic vial. "I almost forgot."

He downed his pill with the last of his coffee and when he looked up the bird was gone. His eyes roamed along the row of tilled earth tilting up toward the fattoria, trying to find it. The finch was nowhere in sight, but in the distance—as though he were at the bottom of a Roman arena looking up at an amphitheater lined with trees—Dolphus could make out Aarika and Domenico still talking.

Aarika is all I have left, Dolphus said to himself. *Please*

God, let me see her healed before I die. And restore her relation-ship with her mother and sister this summer. That's all I ask.

But if Dolphus had been a bird, sitting on a branch of the chestnut tree above his granddaughter, where, in fact, his goldfinch confidant was now singing, he might have changed his prayer to include more than Aarika's immediate family.

He might have asked for wisdom in how to deal with maddeningly inquisitive Italians.

"Do you remember my grandmother?" Aarika had asked Domenico this question shortly after watching her grand-father disappear into the olive orchard with a cup of coffee in his hand.

"I do." Domenico had been puttering around the casala, fixing leaky outdoor hoses, leveling out the bocce ball court, and pruning and tying up vines. Now he was cleaning off his tools scattered about on the stone table. "Why do you ask?"

"I was thinking of her this morning when I woke up; recalling some of the advice she gave me when I was younger. I could always count on her to be honest with me."

"From what I remember of her, your grandmother was an impressive woman," said Domenico. "You resemble her in many ways."

"She was remarkable," agreed Aarika. "I miss her."

"How long has it been now?"

"She's been dead ten months."

"I am sorry for your loss, signorina. Your grandfather loved her very much, you know."

A spark flickered in Aarika's eyes. "Did he tell you that?"

Domenico wiped some oil from a wrench before dropping

it into his toolbox. "He spoke of her as though he could not live without her."

Aarika ran her fingers along the rough, pitted rim of the stone table, her lips moving wordlessly. Waiting politely for her next question, Domenico put the last of his tools away and snapped the box shut. When it appeared she was finished talking and was going to say no more, he made a move to leave.

"Is Marco in a relationship with anyone?" she blurted out.

Domenico turned. "Why do you ask?"

Aarika tilted her head slightly so her profile was partially obscured. "He never stays around in the evenings, and when he brings us back from the beach or from shopping or sightseeing, he just drops us off and leaves. He doesn't talk much with us when he is here. He's very businesslike. I was hoping it wasn't because he's upset with me." She rushed to add, "I mean upset with *us*. Poppy's the one that noticed Marco's behavior and brought it up. I think maybe she . . . likes him."

"Perhaps you should ask Marco yourself," said Domenico. "Marco doesn't discuss his love life with me."

"Yes, of course. It's just that Marco and I don't really get along, you see, so I'd rather not ask him."

"I am sorry you feel that way, signorina, but if Marco is not aware of the problem then it appears it will have to take care of itself. Now, if you will excuse me . . . "

"Wait," said Aarika, slipping around the table to confront Domenico. "It's just that I would feel much less responsible for Marco's . . . detachment if I thought it was due to the fact he has a girlfriend, rather than something I've said or done to offend him. *Capisce?*"

"My English isn't the best, but I think I understand." Domenico's eyebrows puckered as he carefully chose his next words. "Marco, by nature, has always been a playful, easygoing boy. It is not like him to be distant or withdrawn. I can tell you this: he takes his work very seriously. If you feel Marco is avoiding you, it could be because he is simply trying to be as professional as possible toward you."

Aarika lifted her chin. "I never said I thought Marco was avoiding *me*," she said. "I told you it was Poppy who mentioned his behavior. She's the one who noticed it."

"Oh, yes," smiled Domenico. "Then perhaps your sister should ask Marco these questions herself? He will be by this evening to finalize the details of your trip, since you leave tomorrow morning. She can talk to him then."

Tipping his cap, Domenico turned and strode away. When he was nearly to the shed, Aarika called out after him. "Domenico, please don't tell Marco I asked you about him."

Domenico turned around, and placing two fingers together, slid them across his sealed lips. Then, swinging the same fingers out toward her, he yelled back, "On my honor! Your secret is safe with me!"

THAT EVENING MARCO arrived at the casala as expected, loaded with notes and maps and travel brochures and detailed checklists. Herding everyone into the living room, he instructed Dolphus and the girls to sit down while he went over last-minute instructions with them.

Aarika balked. "We have so much to do to get ready. Must we do this right now, Marco? Just leave all your information here and we'll look at it when we have time."

Something about Aarika's attitude, the way she minimized his expertise on arranging travel in Italy, made Marco's blood boil. To him, she was insinuating that all the work he had gone to preparing for this holiday was inconsequential. Steeling himself for a possible showdown, he waited patiently until Aarika finally sat down before speaking again.

"We'll be gone a total of five days," he began. "But of course, two of them will be spent mostly in the car, which leaves us with only three full days to tour the Amalfi. It's summertime and peak tourist season, so be forewarned that it will be crowded and everything will be a challenge."

"What time do we need to be ready to leave tomorrow?" asked Poppy.

"I will be here at six o'clock to pick you up," he replied. When the girls started to complain, Marco held his hands up. "If we leave any later, we won't get to Praiano at a decent time. As it is, I was lucky to book the last two rooms available at Tramonto d'Oro. I don't want to risk losing them."

"Two rooms?" Aarika looked dumbfounded. "You mean . . ."

Marco nodded. "You and Poppy will have to share a room. Dolphus and I will share the other."

Aarika protested, but Marco cut her short. "I'm sorry, but there are no other options." Then he broached the subject of the weather. He told them it would be hotter on the Amalfi Coast than what they'd been experiencing in Versilia. "Temperatures are supposed to be at least a hundred degrees each day we're there," he said. "So, bring sunscreen and pack accordingly."

"If it's going to be that hot, what's the point in packing anything?" said Aarika, sarcastically.

Marco grimaced.

"I'm just kidding. You're such a *spielverderber*, Marco."

"A spoilsport?" replied Marco. "No, I learn quickly, Aarika, and what you have taught me so far is that you either have no sense of what appropriate behavior is here, or you don't care. Giving good advice is part of my job description, and if I recall, you didn't take kindly to it when we first met."

Poppy's eyes opened wide. She glanced back and forth between Aarika and Marco. "Dish, Marco. What am I missing here?"

"Nothing," said Aarika, her face livid.

"Aarika seems to think Italians are stuck in the past—in the sixties—when it comes to beachwear." Giving in to his temptation to goad Aarika, Marco spoke dismissively, but a smirk toyed with the corners of his mouth. "If you care about being acceptably fashionable while you're here, look around and see what Italian women are wearing. At the very least, take note that they're wearing *something*."

"Ooh, I've got it!" beamed Poppy. "Aarika was sunbathing in the nude when you first met, right? Let's see. It must have been the day we arrived, when Dolphus and I were napping. Behind the fattoria?"

Dolphus sat bolt upright. "Aarika, is this true? This is how Marco first saw you when we arrived?"

"No, Opa!" Aarika glared at Marco. "Tell my grandfather the truth."

Marco, realizing he had taken the jibing too far, backtracked. "It was really nothing," he assured Dolphus. "When I first saw Aarika she was . . . " He paused, using his hands to make various motions around his chest and shoulders to indicate that Aarika's swim top had only been partially removed. Then, noting that Dolphus looked confused, Marco said soberly, "Herr Geller, I assure you, your granddaughter was not trying to seduce me. I simply stumbled across her while she was sunbathing. She didn't even know I was there."

"Seduce?" Aarika gasped. "You?"

"All I am trying to say," said Marco, desperately trying to climb out of the hole he had dug himself into, "is Italian women are very style conscious. Rarely will you see a topless woman on a beach these days. It's not *d'avanguardia*. And if you do see it, you can be sure it's probably a German or French tourist. Also," he said, placing his finger against his nose as he looked at Aarika, "few Italians have their noses pierced. I say all this only because I feel it is my responsibility to ensure your holiday is free from disappointment and ridicule."

Aarika sputtered, "So you're saying German women are backward exhibitionists?"

Poppy, equally incredulous, rose to her sister's defense. "I happen to love Aarika's nose ring, Marco. As a matter of fact, I want to get one myself. You talk about protecting us from ridicule? What about all the Italian men I've seen wearing Speedos at the beach? I mean, really. If anyone's deserving of being made fun of it's . . ."

Dolphus clapped his hands, calling their meeting back to order. "Enough!" he growled. "Come, come, Marco. Let's finish up so we can all go to bed."

Marco, flushed from having to vigorously defend himself, passed out photocopies of the itinerary to the Gellers and Poppy. "You each have your own copy," he said. "Keep it in a safe place in case we get separated. It has emergency numbers, a few important Italian phrases, the name of our hotel, and other important information. I've researched the region and have come up with some ideas for what we can do while we're there. I've noted some of them on your itinerary, but I suggest we play it by ear once we get to Praiano. Any questions?"

Poppy folded her paper without looking at it. "You're the

expert, Marco. As long as we have you as our fashion coordinator we'll be fine. Oh yeah, and to deflect any ridicule that might come our way."

As Aarika began to chime in with some cutting remarks of her own, Dolphus rose from his chair. Shaking his head at the girls, he turned and addressed Marco. "Thank you," he said. "You have done an admirable job organizing this trip for us. I appreciate all of your hard work, Marco. Is there anything else you require from us?"

Marco looked over Dolphus's shoulder at Aarika and Poppy. Apologetically, he said, "Look, I realize we are all from different cultures and may not agree on everything, but we're going to be together exclusively the next five days, so . . ."

Poppy finished the sentence for him. "Let's get along?"

"Exactly. And don't take things so personally."

"No problem," said Poppy, giving Aarika a nudge, as though their mutual disagreement with Marco on the subject of women had instantly made them comrades-in-arms.

Aarika, however, didn't seem quite ready to acknowledge an alliance with her newly discovered sister. Ignoring Poppy, she addressed Marco, "I'm just fine with my own culture, thank you," she sniffed. "You can have yours to yourself, Marco."

"Aarika!" barked Dolphus. "He is simply making a legitimate request." Turning around, he extended his hand to Marco. It was an abrupt motion, signaling his desire to wrap up the evening. "We'll see you tomorrow morning then, Signor Marco. *Gute Nacht.*"

After Marco left, Dolphus lowered himself back into his chair and picked up a book he had been reading earlier. As he opened it, he muttered, "Is finding common ground with others really that difficult, girls?"

Poppy's face lit up. "I have an idea." Pulling Aarika to her feet, she dragged her reluctant sister into the kitchen. "I think tonight we may have found some common ground between us," she said. "It's a start anyway."

"What are you talking about?" asked Aarika.

"Men! Tonight, we both called Marco out on his double standard." Seeing that Aarika wasn't fully understanding what she was getting at, Poppy asked, "Look, we both like men, right?"

Cautiously, Aarika nodded.

"We're in Italy, which is filled with good-looking men, right?"

Again, Aarika nodded.

"Marco's being a bit overprotective, don't you think?"

"He's egotistical, is what he is."

"Regardless," said Poppy, "we could have fun at his expense on this trip and teach him a lesson or two."

For the first time since Aarika and Poppy had met, they giggled. Dolphus looked up from his book, startled by their laughter, and watched as the two girls talked in hushed tones at the kitchen table, their heads bent close together in conversation. He had always thought Aarika favored his son, with her blond hair and intense blue eyes. But tonight, studying the girls' profiles in such close proximity to each other, he realized Aarika and Poppy shared the same small ears and sharp chins. The same sculpted tip to their noses. And in that moment, he saw their mother as he remembered her from long ago. The image rattled him. He wondered if Poppy and Aarika could see the resemblance in each other.

"Don't stay up too late," Dolphus called out to them. "Marco will be here early, remember?"

Barely skipping a beat in their conversation, the girls replied in unison, "We remember."

"Humph," grunted Dolphus to himself. "I wonder what they have up their sleeves?"

At six fifteen the following morning, just as the sun's first rays broke through the dark crevices and valleys of the Carrara Mountains, Marco and his passengers pulled out of Domenico's driveway. They descended Monte Montignoso, Aarika and Poppy grumbling about the early hour, and by they time they reached Querceta they both were asleep. Dolphus rode shotgun. With a roadmap of Italy spread out on his lap and a magnifying glass at the ready, he looked like an advert for *Senior Travel* magazine. He said little, gazing spellbound out his window at the unfurling glory of the Tuscan countryside.

Marco followed the Variante Aurelia south, guiding the car onto the A-11 to Florence. Once there, he caught the Autostrada del Sole toward Rome, where he was finally able to relax behind the wheel. For the next hour, they cruised effortlessly through Tuscany's villa-studded hills and golden valleys lined with *pini* trees and terraced vineyards. It wasn't until they were near the town of Levane that the girls finally woke up. Marco and Dolphus informed them they had missed some spectacular sights while they were sleeping. "But now," noted Marco, "look there to our left. That is the town of Arezzo. And there," he added, pointing in the opposite direction, "is the countryside we call Chianti Classico, between Florence and Siena. The drive is one of the finest in Toscana."

"Dreamy," said Poppy. She dug her camera out of her

backpack and took aim through the window. "Italy is *so* amazing."

"You've never seen Germany," said Aarika.

"Hoping you'll invite me." Without any warning, Poppy turned and snapped a picture of Aarika. "For posterity. Thanks, Aarika."

As the conversation in the car continued, light and friendly with no complaining or drama, Marco thought, *Perhaps this trip will actually be more enjoyable than I expected it would be.*

Four long, uneventful hours later, they exited the autostrada south of Pompeii and merged onto the SS145 out of Castellammare di Stabia onto the Sorrento Peninsula. At first, the radical shift in scenery awed them into complete silence. Marco tensed as he began maneuvering the Nastro Azzurro, The Blue Ribbon highway. It consisted of two standard car lanes, but due to seasonal congestion, he soon discovered it might as well have been a one-lane road. Now strung tighter than a new violin string, Marco spent the next two hours avoiding haphazardly parked cars and hordes of pedestrians spilling off the sidewalks into his path. He cursed other motorists' complete lack of driving etiquette and shook his fists at foreign tour bus drivers who continually hogged the lane. Worse yet was the narrow highway itself, which zigzagged along the treacherous coastline like a serpent coiled against the rugged towering mountains.

Dolphus hung on to his door handle for dear life. The girls gasped every time Marco screeched around a hairpin turn. At one point, Poppy begged to be let out of the car, claiming she was going to be sick. They stopped briefly at a roadside fruit-and-vegetable cart squeezed into a tiny roadside pull-off barely wide enough to accommodate their vehicle. When they climbed back into the car, Poppy switched places with Aarika, but it didn't help. She continued to moan, clutching her stomach as Marco resumed zooming past dizzying drop-offs and death-defying cliffs.

By the time Marco finally pulled into Praiano, their nerves were so frayed they all leapt out of the car as though they'd been chained together underwater for hours with no air supply. Aarika let loose a volley of pent-up criticism, accusing Marco of making them all nauseous with his aggressive driving. "Typical Italians," she groused. "Driving as though they own the world."

Marco gritted his teeth. "Now's not the time, Aarika."

Poppy, her complexion sickly pistachio, groaned, "Can we please not talk about the drive?"

Even Dolphus griped, "If I didn't know better, I might have thought you were trying to give me a heart attack, Marco." Lifting his hand to his heart as if to emphasize his point, he added, "I need to go to the lobby and sit down."

Aarika reacted with alarm and hurried to accompany her grandfather into the hotel. Poppy lingered near Marco, asking if he needed help even though she looked incapable of doing so.

"No," he replied. "Go with the Gellers, Poppy. I'll take care of the car and checking us in to the hotel."

As Poppy stumbled away, Marco unloaded all of their suitcases onto a rolling luggage cart and handed it off to the valet. Then he parked the car and returned to the hotel to register at the front desk. Taking the room keys from the clerk, he rounded everyone up and escorted them to their rooms. He had a sinking feeling that the day, which had begun with such promise, had turned into an omen of what

the next four days were going to be like. The thought made
his stomach churn more than all the terrifying curves on the
Blue Ribbon Highway.

DINNER THAT EVENING at Hotel Tramonto d'Oro, perched
majestically over the Tyrrhenian Sea, was a muted affair.
Marco, still on edge from the drive, acted especially out of
character. He stabbed at the tomatoes on the *caprese* tray as
though he was spearing predatory fish, and flipped the meats
and cheeses and olives on the antipasti platter over dis-
tractedly until he finally selected some for his plate. When
an acceptable amount of time had passed, an immaculately
suited waiter brought them each their *primo piatti* and
poured more wine into their glasses.

"So," said Poppy, her coloring back to normal. "What's on
the agenda for tonight?"

Dolphus tucked his napkin into the neck of his shirt. "I'll
be going to go to bed," he muttered. "It's been a long day."

"Aarika?" asked Poppy.

"Why don't you ask *him*." Aarika pointed her fork at
Marco. "He's the tour guide."

"Well, I say we take a walk around town," said Poppy, her
eyes trained on the floor to ceiling windows directly behind
Marco. "Praiano looks like it was made for exploring. After
the drive today, I need some exercise."

Marco paused from eating to turn and follow Poppy's gaze
out to the Chiesa di San Gennaro. The resplendent church
was one of the most famous in Campania. He studied it a
moment, registered its magnificence, and resumed eating.

When no one responded to Poppy's suggestion of an
after-dinner stroll, she pushed her plate away, drank the rest

of her wine in one long gulp, and stood up. "Well, guess I'm going solo," she said. "See you all later."

Aarika, watching her sister exit the dining room, clicked her tongue. "Impulsive Americans. I wouldn't be surprised if she forgot to take her room key with her. It would serve her right if the hotel locked their doors at midnight and she didn't get back in time."

Dolphus shot his granddaughter a disapproving look, wiped his mouth brusquely, and rose from the table. "I'll put our meal on my tab. I'm calling it a day. I'll see you both in the morning. *Gute Nacht.*"

Marco frowned at Aarika and excused himself also, leaving Aarika with her mouth agape at being abandoned by everyone to finish her dinner alone. Catching up with Dolphus in the lobby in front of the elevator, Marco asked, "Are you not feeling well, Signor Geller?"

"Oh, I'm fine, Marco. I'm just an old man who gets frustrated easily. Please forgive Aarika and I for our comments this afternoon about Italian roads and drivers. You did much better today than I ever would have." Dolphus smiled. "Even though at one time in my life I might have bested you on a German autobahn."

"As you can imagine, the drive was not an enjoyable one for me either," replied Marco. "Even for Italians, the Amalfi roads are treacherous. But your granddaughter should take responsibility for her own words and not expect you to apologize for her."

"Give Aarika time and she will ask for your forgiveness. She is a good girl. Actually," sighed Dolphus, "I am surprised how much you two are alike."

"Sorry?"

The elevator signal pinged and the doors slid open.

Merging into the midst of hotel guests stepping off the lift, Dolphus turned and said, "You are both easily misunderstood. Oh, and remember our agreement. Would you make sure the girls get safely to their rooms tonight?"

The elevator doors closed before Marco could assure Dolphus that he would do as asked. Not wanting to return to the dining room just jet, he dawdled in the lobby, musing over what Dolphus had said about he and Aarika being alike. As much as he was tempted to dismiss the possibility, the truth was, Marco did find himself being misunderstood at times. His friends sometimes called him anti-social, a kill-joy when it came to entertainment. He liked to have as good a time as the next person, but he thought it foolish to waste his time and money on partying when he had more important things to invest in, such as his education and career. His own parents misunderstood him. They thought his decision not to have a serious relationship with a girl until after he was finished with college was because women intimidated him. In fact, it was a rational choice based on finances. He loved women. Of course! But he wanted to be able to meet his own standards of being a good husband should he marry. That meant having a steady job and a decent bank account. It was also true, he admitted to himself, that he was picky about what kind of woman he would consider as a potential mate. He had his own expectations of a wife that included, not subservience, but teamwork, respect, and devotion.

A good five minutes later, convinced by Dolphus's assertion that Aarika might likewise be a victim of misunderstanding, Marco returned to the dining room. Aarika was nowhere to be seen. Retracing his steps to the lobby, Marco asked the front desk to telephone the girls' room, but no one answered. Perhaps Aarika, he thought, feeling guilty for her spiteful comment about Poppy, was out looking for her sister.

Marco ventured out of the hotel. Crossing via Gennaro Capriglione, he scanned the bistro tables on the crowded patio of Hotel La Fioriere, but seeing no sign of Poppy or Aarika, he kept searching. Having no better luck at the bustling Bar del Sole next door, he skirted Chiesa di San Gennaro, past knots of old locals sitting on benches lining the piazza, gossiping, smoking cigarettes, and people watching. Occasionally, he had to flatten himself against a building to avoid getting hit by the countless scooters and cars clogging the street. Coming to a fork in the road, he decided to ascend via Guglielmo Marconi. It was such a steep incline he had to stop midway to catch his breath. The thick, salty air smelled of sun-ripened tomatoes, fresh basil, and arugula mingled with lemon zest. Praiano's streetlights blinked on, casting a honeycombed glow over the nearly perpendicular village. Resuming his climb, he reached yet another fork in the road. He turned left, navigating the switchbacks of via Piazza San Luca until he finally emerged onto a large, tiled piazza on a level plateau near the entrance to the church of San Luca Evangelista.

There, sitting on a single bench on the edge of the vacant square with her back to him, not ten feet away, was Aarika. Her hands rested sedately on her lap as she gazed at the twinkling lights of distant Salerno jutting out into the sea in a broad band to the south. In the soft amber gleam of a nearby streetlamp, her hair was filigreed gold. Gone was any semblance of aloofness or superiority. To the contrary, she exuded a calm poise, an eternal weightlessness, as though she was some sort of mythical creature harvested from the great deep and set out for all the world to see. Never in a million years would Marco have expected to have his breath taken away by the sight of Aarika Geller in solitary contemplation. But in truth, that's exactly what happened. She looked so childlike sitting there, so completely vulnerable—so *angelic*—that he didn't dare approach her for fear of breaking the spell. He was, quite simply, inexplicably undone at the sight of her. Taking a deep breath, Marco pulled himself together and walked quietly toward her. Sliding onto the opposite end of the bench, he said, "I see you've found the perfect spot."

"Incredible, isn't it? I feel like I'm sailing with Ulysses." Reverently, Aarika whispered, *"I cannot rest from travel: I will drink Life to the lees . . ."*

Stunned, Marco picked up her cue. *"And this gray spirit, yearning in desire to follow knowledge like a sinking star . . ."*

"There lies the port," continued Aarika, skipping ahead in the poem. She pointed to sailboats below them bobbing like bath toys in Praiano's softly illuminated bay. *"The vessel puffs her sail. There gloom the dark broad seas."*

"Old age hath yet his honor and his toil . . ."

"Death closes all; but something ere the end, some work of noble note, may yet be done . . ."

"The lights begin to twinkle from the rocks," added Marco, *"the long day wanes; the slow moon climbs; the deep moans round with many voices . . ."*

"Come, my friends, 'tis not too late to seek a newer world . . ."

"For my purpose holds to sail beyond the sunset, and the baths of all the western stars, until I die . . ."

Aarika closed her eyes. *"Though much is taken, much abides; and tho' we are not now that strength which in old days moved earth and heaven; that which we are, we are . . ."*

"*One equal temper of heroic hearts, made weak by time and fate . . .*"

"*But strong in will to strive, to seek, to find, and not to yield.*"

A long, static silence passed between them before Aarika said, "It's not every day I find someone who can quote Tennyson."

"I could say the same," said Marco. Not trusting the avalanche of emotions overtaking him, he struggled to keep his reply casual. "I'm rather surprised you like poetry. I wouldn't have guessed it."

"Really?" Aarika lifted her head and stared at the stars. "I find it . . . therapeutic. One of my English professors in college was a Tennyson admirer. He made us memorize several poems. *Ulysses* seemed perfect tonight. And you, Marco?" she asked, turning back to him. "Did you learn Tennyson at your university?"

"Actually, I'm earning my master's degree in business and finance, but I greatly admire the arts. I took it upon myself to read Tennyson in secondary school when I was studying English literature. It's always been my favorite poem."

"Well," said Aarika, "I wouldn't have guessed you'd be pursuing a business career, not if you say you love the arts. But then, Domenico told us you're very smart. He said you could be anything you set your mind to. He even told us you wanted to be a priest when you were young."

"Most altar boys imagine they will be priests one day."

"You decided against it. Why?"

"I realized I love life too much to give up the things that would be expected of me." Leaning closer to Aarika, he added, "I have learned much from my parents' business, and with my degree, I hope to have a successful business myself some day in a field I am passionate about."

"Such as?"

"Who knows? Owning my own travel company or newspaper, managing a museum or an art gallery, or . . ." Marco swept his hand over his head. "The sky's the limit."

"You're quite the Renaissance man, Marco. I envy your dreams."

"What are your dreams?"

Aarika stiffened. After a long hesitation, she replied, "I don't allow myself to dream."

Marco was about to ask her why when Poppy's voice rang out from the edge of the piazza. "Hey, there you guys are! Do you realize there are even better views above us?" Plopping down between Marco and Aarika, she pointed above and behind them. "There's a church called Chiesa di Costantinopoli right up there, where supposedly, during the day, you can see all the way to Positano and Capri. I'd love to see it."

Marco peered in the direction Poppy indicated. He could barely make out the church looming over them from its nest-like perch atop a sheer escarpment.

"How about promising me a hike up there tomorrow, Marco?" said Poppy.

Aarika cleared her throat and stood up. "I'm going to go back to the hotel." Without waiting to see if Poppy and Marco wanted to go with her, she set out across the piazza.

"Wow," said Poppy, staring after her sister. "Did I interrupt something?"

Marco stood up. "We need to go. Neither of you should be out by yourselves at night."

Poppy rose to her feet, but immediately pulled Marco to her side so that he would be forced to walk at her pace. "Hang back with me for a while so we can talk."

"About what?"

"Aarika. What exactly do you think it is about me that she hates so much?"

"Hate is a strong word."

"Okay. What is it about me that she doesn't like?"

Marco wavered a moment before saying, "You two seemed like you were getting along better today than you have since you arrived."

"Well, I guess we did kind of have a breakthrough of sorts last night. It was the first time Aarika and I have really talked. You know, like, girl talk." Poppy pinched Marco's bicep. "Thanks to you, Marco."

Marco raised an eyebrow.

"After your little fashion lecture last night," explained Poppy, "we both felt you needed a wake-up call about the fact that it's the twenty-first century. We just couldn't agree on how to go about doing it. I wanted to play some tricks on you, but Aarika thought it was stupid and wouldn't go for it."

Marco attempted to describe himself as being a perfectly modern man, but Poppy hushed him.

"Don't bother," she said. "It won't do any good. Anyway, it was definitely a start for Aarika and me. I think I caught a glimpse of what having a sister could be like. But then, look how she treated me just now. She walked away like I had the plague or something."

"Perhaps you misunderstand her. There are two sides to every story."

Poppy came to a halt. "Granted, maybe I do misunderstand her. But Aarika's intimidating. On top of being cold and withdrawn, she's also beautiful and smart. Trust me, Marco, that combination is intimidating to other women. Of course, that's not to say I'm jealous of her. I'm not. I have my own good qualities . . ."

"Let's keep moving." Pulling Poppy along by the elbow, Marco changed the subject. "I know it's none of my business, but I'm curious. How did your trip here to Italy come about?"

"My mother arranged it with Dolphus."

"Why?"

"Because while contacting Dolphus was the last thing my mother wanted to do, she knew she had to do it for me, and also to 'gain deliverance' for herself. Her words, not mine."

Marco's face registered confusion.

"Let me put it another way: my mother sent me here hoping to get some closure in her life, and in return, I was hoping to get some closure in mine."

"Why did your mother go to America in the first place, and leave Aarika behind in Germany?"

"All I know is that when my mother was eighteen, she attended a university in Berlin where she met Aarika's father. It's also where she met my dad. Three years after having Aarika, she was back in the States, pregnant with me. My mom's strong in many ways, Marco, but when it comes to her past she's fragile as an egg. She acts like she'll crack under the pressure of talking about it whenever I try to bring it up. I thought maybe I could pry some information from my dad, but she's apparently kept a lot from him too, and he's not the most communicative person in the world. I know mom's banking on someone filling in the details for me while I'm here so she's spared all the drama fallout. She probably figures by the time I get back home, whatever skeletons I've dug out of her closet will be old news."

"Your lives are beyond my comprehension," muttered Marco, not knowing what else to say. Seeing Aarika waiting for them at the bottom of the hill, he quickened his pace.

Hurrying to get a few more words in, Poppy gushed, "I didn't even know I had a sister until a few months ago. My grandmother mentioned it before she died, when my mother and I were with her in the hospital. She said, 'Sharon'—that's my mom's name—'promise me you'll do right by Aarika. You can't pretend she doesn't exist. She's your daughter, for God's sake.' I only found out about Dolphus after my grandparents' estate was settled. They had left a small inheritance to Aarika and had hired an attorney to locate her. He tracked her down in Passau. That was in June. When my mom called Dolphus, he extended an invitation for both of us to come here and connect with Aarika. Of course, she wouldn't come . . ."

Aarika, just a few yards away now, eyed them suspiciously as they approached. "I almost went on to the hotel by myself," she said. "I was getting tired of waiting for you two."

"Marco and I were just talking," twittered Poppy, letting go of Marco's arm. "About life."

"And whose life were you discussing?"

Poppy feigned innocence. "I don't know what you mean, sis."

Aarika hitched her purse over her shoulder and resumed walking briskly toward the hotel. "Has anyone ever told you that you're immature, Poppy?"

"Quite the opposite, Aarika. Back home, I'm told all the time how mature I am. Most American girls my age spend their free time partying. I spend mine traveling overseas to get to know my sister. What excuse do you have?"

"Sorry?"

"What's your excuse for being so childish, Aarika? You're older than me. I was expecting to find someone a lot more mature. Instead, I find an aloof snob who can't handle having her prima donna life upset by her baby sister." Poppy's voice suddenly rose an octave. "Is it because I'm American? Is that why you're shutting me out? Or maybe you're jealous of me because I live with mom and you don't. What is it, Aarika?"

"Stop it, both of you," barked Marco. "If you can't get along for any other reason, think of Dolphus. He has invested much time and money to bring you two here in the hopes of facilitating your reconciliation. He doesn't need any extra stress on this trip."

The mention of Dolphus silenced Aarika and Poppy. Marco could tell by the expressions on their faces that they were already regretting the accusations they had leveled at each other. The three of them continued walking, reflective and subdued, until they reached their hotel. Marco paused before entering to retrieve their room keys from his pocket.

As he did, from the patio of Hotel La Fioriere opposite them, a group of men about Marco's age called out to Aarika and Poppy. "Hey! *Ragazze grazioso*! The night is still young. Let us show you a good time!"

Marco's head jerked up. Grabbing the girls' arms, he pulled them into the hotel lobby. "Take my advice," he said, "and don't have anything to do with men here. Do you understand?"

·8·

The Isle of Love

THE FOLLOWING MORNING, Dolphus was the first to show up for breakfast, seating himself at a table on the hotel's bougainvillea-framed patio facing Praiano's bay. By the time the others joined him, he had already eaten. Asking the waiter to bring him another cappuccino, he then turned to Marco. "What is the agenda for today?"

"I thought we could take a trip to Capri." Marco felt Aarika's eyes on him, but refused to look at her.

"Sounds most excellent to me," chirped Poppy. "Any hiking trails on the island?"

"There are several, according to this pamphlet." Marco held up a colorful brochure with the heading *"Bella Capri"* emblazoned across the top.

The waiter brought Dolphus his coffee. Lifting the cup to his mouth, Dolphus asked, "Should we take a ferry to the island or hire a boat?"

"Considering yesterday's drive, I think we should take the bus to Sorrento," replied Marco. "We would need to leave here at eight to catch it. From Sorrento, we can take the ferry to Capri."

"Let's do it," said Poppy. "But one thing, Marco. Just

remember Aarika and I don't need you hovering over us today, telling us who we can talk to. Right Aarika?"

Aarika nodded in agreement.

"If by hovering," said Dolphus, "you mean watching out for you, it was I who asked Marco to chaperone you on this trip." Sheepishly, he added, "I was cautioned before coming here that I should be vigilant in this regard."

"By who?" asked Aarika.

Dolphus turned his head sideways. "Eh?"

"By who?" she repeated. "And don't pretend you're deaf, Opa."

Dolphus rubbed his ear, as though it were plugged. "If you must know, it was one of my friends in Germany."

"Your friends are ancient." Aarika rolled her eyes. "Besides, Opa, I'm twenty-four years old. Remember?"

"But it has nothing to do with age or your ability to fend for yourself," blustered Dolphus. "It's just that you and Poppy are single, and as such, apparently . . . "

Poppy stood up. "Excuse me. May I go to my room to get ready now? I'll pretend this conversation never took place and meet you all in the lobby at eight."

As Poppy hurried out of the dining room, Aarika excused herself as well. "This is ridiculous." Scouring Marco with her eyes, she added, "I can't believe you went along with it."

Dolphus attempted to explain that Marco wasn't to blame, but Aarika turned and left before he could finish his sentence. Watching his granddaughter storm off, he apologized to Marco. "I'm sorry for getting you involved in this, Marco. It's my fault they are angry with you."

"But it is true the girls do not realize the situations they could find themselves in here," said Marco. "It is only wise for you to want me to watch out for them."

Dolphus shook his head. "I don't understand it. Why do young women these days resent chivalry? You would think they'd appreciate our desire to protect them."

"I agree."

"Now what are we going to do?" Dolphus paused to retrieve a pill from his pocket and downed it with the remainder of his blood-orange juice. "Ach! Women. I have a feeling Aarika and Poppy are going to make us pay for this fiasco today."

Marco sighed, amazed at how mercurial women could be. "There's nothing we can do except keep to our original plan," he said. "You can be sure I will watch the girls carefully. As long as they don't accept invitations to go anywhere alone with strange men, they should be fine."

"I hope you're right," said Dolphus. "Aarika's grandmother would kill me if anything ever happened to her on my watch. God rest her soul."

AT EXACTLY TEN minutes after eight, Aarika and Poppy scampered onto the crowded blue SITA bus when it rolled to a stop less than a block from the hotel. They placed their *biglietti* in the ticket machine and immediately claimed two adjoining seats in the back for themselves. Marco and Dolphus climbed on after them, seating themselves next to each other directly behind the driver. As the bus lurched into gear, Marco observed Aarika and Poppy chatting away as though they were the best of friends. Their volatile relationship astonished him. Regardless, he told himself, he should be relieved to see them getting along, even though it was at his expense. Having been outed as their chaperone, he apparently had become their mutual enemy.

Dolphus, grasping the handle bar above him to steady himself, leaned close. "Don't worry," he murmured, apparently reading Marco's mind. "The girls don't really hate you. If there's one thing I know about women: they may tell you to go away, but if you remain faithful and kind, they will invite you back into their hearts."

"And just how many women have you studied in your lifetime, signore?"

"Only one. My wife was the quintessential woman. She put up with me for many years. How she did it, I do not know."

"You don't seem like a difficult person to me," noted Marco.

"You are seeing me on my best behavior."

"I am known to be a decent judge of character. I can't be that wrong. Surely, you weren't an abusive man."

"Oh, no, no." Dolphus looked appalled. "Never."

"Well then . . . "

"I was often solitary, you see," explained Dolphus. "And given to mood swings. During those times, my wife would tell me that if it weren't for my kindness and faithfulness to her she might have given up on me. She would say it in a teasing way, but I know it was true."

"She must have loved you very much."

Dolphus smiled sadly. "There's no question of that. But I loved her far more." Signaling that he no longer wanted to talk about it, he twisted his body away from Marco and began staring toward the front of the bus.

Taken aback by Dolphus's spontaneous confession, Marco wondered what had prompted him to talk about his wife. What did being kind and faithful have to do with Aarika and Poppy? Shrugging off his curiosity, Marco devoted the rest of his time to studying maps and brochures of Capri. The bus stopped at several villages along the Nastro Verde to pick up more passengers, climbed to Meta, turned south, and less than an hour after leaving Praiano, it finally stopped at its destination in the noisy Piazza Tasso in the heart of Sorrento.

Everyone disembarked quickly, merging into the stream of tourists winding down the Vallone dei Mulini, an ancient stairway carved into a narrow ravine emptying onto Marina Piccola. Reaching the bottom, they elbowed their way through the sweaty, jostling crowd until they arrived at the ticket office. Dolphus fumbled through his wallet, looking for his credit card. When he found it, he handed it to Marco, who in turn gave it to the cashier. Gruffly, she processed their transaction and handed Marco four round-trip tickets to Capri along with four ferry schedules.

"Caremar, Pier Five," she barked, pointing to her left. "The next boat leaves in five minutes." Shooing them away with a wave of her hand, she beckoned the next group to step forward.

They traipsed down the causeway servicing the Napoli ferries in single file, and though it was not yet even ten in the morning, the heat absorbed by the cement beneath their feet and emanating from others pressing in around them was nearly unbearable. Dolphus pulled a cotton handkerchief out of his shirt pocket and wiped his forehead, muttering something about the cool mountains of Bavaria. Poppy lifted a Minnesota Vikings cap out of her backpack, put her hair into a ponytail, and positioned it strategically on her head, giving the bill a downward tug on each side to give it the appropriate American "arch." Aarika removed her sunglasses and rubbed what appeared to be fingerprints off them with the bottom of her t-shirt and then placed them back on.

Twenty minutes later, the ferry arrived. A tall, tanned attendant in Armani sunglasses and a spotless, white cotton uniform with an immaculate smile to match, descended the gangplank and unhooked the metal chain to allow passengers to begin boarding. His nametag read, *Sig. Gino De Luca*. Marco stepped aside to allow Dolphus and the girls to ascend first. He noticed that Gino craned his neck to watch Aarika and Poppy walk up the ramp, peering over the top of his sunglasses to get a better glimpse of them. Once the boarding was complete, the ship sounded its departure horn and steamed out into the Bay of Naples, shimmering turquoise beneath a cloudless, cobalt-blue sky. Marco and Dolphus settled into seats in the ship's midsection, while Poppy and Aarika scaled the steps to the top deck.

Halfway through the crossing, Marco got up to stretch his legs. He spotted the girls leaning over the service bar near the ship's bow, conversing with Gino De Luca, who was clearly impressing them with his effusive Italian charm. Marco debated joining them, but realized they'd consider it intrusive, given that they knew Dolphus had asked him to keep an eye on them. Returning to his seat, Marco found Dolphus immersed in people-watching. When a crippled old man, accompanied by an equally feeble wife, hobbled by with the aid of a cane, Dolphus's face fell. But when a sprightly, well-dressed Italian about his age—escorting a much younger, attractive woman—politely sped around the first teetering couple, Dolphus lit up.

Studying Dolphus's reactions, Marco couldn't help but wonder yet again what was going through the German's mind. Was he struggling with his mortality? Was he grappling with the reality of aging; torn between surrendering to its inevitability or defying it by drinking life to the lees? Then, in a flash of revelation, Marco realized that although both might be true, there had to be something more than age and health troubling Dolphus, something more than the loss of his wife and worry about Aarika. He couldn't put his finger on it, but in Dolphus's conflicted countenance, Marco saw regret, denial, and unresolved remorse.

The ferry shuddered and lurched, startling Marco out of his reverie. An announcement in Italian and a variety of other languages instructed passengers to prepare to debark. Getting to his feet, he gathered up his brochures and placed them in his backpack while Dolphus stood up and stretched.

"I declare, Marco," said Dolphus, with renewed vigor in his voice. "I suddenly feel twenty years younger!"

"Really?" Noting that Dolphus's eyes were still trained on the dapper Italian man and his younger female companion, Marco smiled. "My cousin Bianca says to possess the wisdom of age combined with the energy of youth is to have the world at your feet."

"I like Bianca," replied Dolphus, his chest expanding with promise. "She is an exceptionally wise woman."

THE MAGIC OF Capri, they all soon discovered, wasn't to be found in its Marina Grande, clogged with lumbering ferries, sleek hydrofoils, extravagant yachts, bobbing sailboats, fishing vessels, dinghies, Jet Skis, and every other imaginable watercraft. Nor was it evident in the village's gauntlet of overpriced gift shops and streets brimming with scores of tour guides and vendors hawking their wares.

Marco, like Dolphus and the girls, succumbed to the charms of the Isle of Love when they ascended to the island's upper reaches via a public funicular, and then proceeded by bus to the town of Anacapri. Debarking at Piazza della Vittoria, they ventured down via Orlandi—past gardens and villas, gushing fountains, and inviting cafés and boutiques—to Piazza Diaz, where they sat down on a long, tiled bench near the Chiesa di Santa Sofia to rest and get their bearings.

Slipping her sandals off, Aarika rubbed her feet together. "All this traveling to get here was worth it, I'd say."

"Yep," agreed Poppy. "It's beyond beautiful."

Since it was almost noon, Marco recommended they buy some groceries at the local *alimentari* and eat lunch at their leisure. He listed a number of sites they could see in the area and things they could do, one of which was to hike to the lighthouse at Punta Carena.

"I'm game," said Poppy, turning to Aarika. "What about you?"

Aarika glanced at her grandfather, concern on her face.

"Well," said Marco, "I was thinking that in this heat, a hike might be too difficult for Dolphus. If hiking is what you'd like to do, one of us could stay here with him."

Lifting her hand in the air, Aarika agreed. "I'll stay with Opa."

But Dolphus would have none of it. "I am perfectly able to hike with everyone," he barked. "*Guter Gott*, Marco, what do you think I do with my time in Passau? We Germans are known for our love of walking. Have you not heard of our *Volkssports?*"

"Vaguely," lied Marco.

"Let's just say this," said Dolphus, in all seriousness, "I'm probably in almost as as good shape as you are."

It took all of Marco's willpower not to laugh. The silver-haired Italian Don Juan on the ship, he thought, must have really impressed Dolphus. He sized up the old German—his creviced face, his knobby knees poking out from below his khaki shorts, his hairless legs, and bushy eyebrows—and saw in his piercing eyes a tenacity and resilience that belied his looks. "You may very well be in good physical condition, Herr Geller," conceded Marco. "But remember, you are on heart medication, and in this heat everyone's health is at risk."

Against Aarika's objections, Dolphus leapt to his feet. "Bah! How long of a hike is it to the lighthouse?"

Marco rifled through his maps. "This trail map indicates a half hour. We start out on via Nuova del Faro and then take any number of different *fortini* trails, depending on where we want to end up. The lighthouse is just one of the destinations."

Marco was still talking when Dolphus powered-walked away. He looked up to see the German racing toward the *alimentary* with Poppy in tow and Aarika at her grandfather's side protesting his recklessness. Grumbling to himself, Marco gathered up his maps and brochures and stuffed them into his backpack. By the time he caught up with the trio, they were already standing in line at the checkout counter, their arms loaded with wine, plastic cups, salami, bread and cheese.

"Come, Marco," bellowed Dolphus, bursting out of the store a moment later like a bull released from its pen. Analyzing the lay of Piazza Diaz, he added, "Which way to the lighthouse?"

Marco nodded to his right. "I think we catch via Nuova del Faro that way."

Without waiting for Marco, Dolphus sped off again, the girls in his wake. As he hurried to catch up with them, Marco caught his reflection in a storefront window. What he saw was a young olive-skinned man of average height and weight with thick, shiny black hair and pale denim blue eyes. His face was smooth and angular, almost sculpted, he had been told, with a five o'clock shadow fanning his cheeks and chin. He was in the prime of his life, and the realization made him quicken his pace.

No old man is going to beat me to Punta Carena.

THEY NEVER MADE it to the lighthouse.

The *fortini* trails were so intertwined and varied, the foursome rambled about for a good hour before finally settling down to eat their lunch on a windswept promontory beneath an ancient grove of olive and myrtle trees. Their picnic spot overlooked a secluded cove where a white catamaran bobbed on sapphire waves, blocked in on three sides by sheer limestone cliffs. From their vantage point, it appeared as though the bronzed bodies diving off the ship's side were slivers of living saffron. Eventually, an immense silence—the kind that exists only on an island or far out to sea—lulled them into a state of near bliss. As they basked in their surroundings, Aarika tore off chunks of bread and passed them around while Dolphus pulled a pocketknife out and began carving the sausage and a large round of belicino cheese.

Marco noticed Dolphus's hands were swollen. Concerned, he asked, "Are you all right?"

"Couldn't be better," replied Dolphus. "I haven't felt this invigorated in a long time."

"I'm surprised you don't go hiking at Domenico's," said Marco, uncorking the wine. "There are many trails in the hills above his fattoria. I'll show you some when we get back."

Dolphus's knife froze in his hand, as did the expression on his face. "Why would I want to do that?"

"Opa," said Aarika, surprised. "You just said this hike made you feel good. Why, then, wouldn't you want to hike in Domenico's hills?"

"I don't holiday in Tuscany to go hiking," stammered Dolphus.

"What *do* you come here to do?" asked Poppy, innocently.

"I suppose you could say Italy is a sort of pilgrimage for me," mumbled Dolphus.

Marco was tempted to ask him what he meant by "pilgrimage," but Poppy changed the subject. Pointing to a limestone outcropping in the distance, she asked, "Does anybody want to go down and check out the view from there with me?"

Dolphus folded the blades of his knife together, slipped it back into his pocket, and carefully began re-wrapping the remaining cheese and salami in their original waxy coverings. "I think I'll stay here and take a little nap."

"I'll stay with Opa," said Aarika.

Still worried by the swelling he had noticed in Dolphus's hands, Marco decided he should remain with the Gellers.

As soon as Poppy was gone, Dolphus checked his watch. "It's ten after two," he said. "Wake me up in fifteen minutes would you, Aarika?" Selecting a shady spot a short distance away, he lowered his body down into a soft bed of leaves and moss, and within minutes he was snoring.

Marco, meanwhile, nestled back against the trunk of an olive tree and closed his eyes. Not because he was sleepy, but because he was—for the second time in twenty-four hours—finding himself rattled by Aarika's physical proximity to him. He felt her complex spirit pulling him toward her and feared her presence would overpower his self-control. But within moments of closing his eyes, he heard Aarika whisper close to his ear.

"Thank you for staying with me to keep an eye on Opa, Marco," she said. "I don't know what to do when he gets these surges of energy. I worry so for him. He's all I have left."

Aarika had scooted directly next to Marco. He could feel her hot skin on his bare arm. The sensation caused him to break out in a sweat. Keeping his eyes closed, he said, "Dolphus is all you have left? I know your mother has been gone a long time, and I know your grandmother recently passed away, but what about your father? Where is he?"

"He died when I was young."

Marco's eyes opened slowly. He turned to face her. "I'm sorry, Aarika. I didn't know."

Aarika explained that her father's death was an accident, that he had died while cleaning his gun. Bringing the conversation back to her grandfather, she smiled weakly. "I have never seen Opa as relaxed, or as energized, as he is here in Italy." She paused to take in the spectacular panorama spread out before them and added, "I'm beginning to see why."

Disarmed, Marco stared at Aarika's profile, her expression transparent as glass, and his heart leapt.

"Marco?" she asked.

"Si?"

"I need to be assured that you have my grandfather's best interests at heart."

"What do you mean?"

"I'm aware of the animosity that still exists between my

country and yours. I hear the snide comments whispered behind my back, and Opa's, when we're at the beach or shopping or eating out. Of course, I am confident that Domenico respects my grandfather despite the difference in our nationalities and would never do anything to hurt or betray him. Can you promise me that I can trust you as well?"

"What kind of man do you think I am?"

"I don't know you well enough to think anything."

"Have you ever seen me be rude or disrespectful toward your grandfather?" asked Marco.

"Please, I'm simply being honest with you about what I've seen and heard since I've been here—the hatred in some people's eyes when they look at us."

"This is not meant to be an excuse, Aarika, but you must understand what German soldiers did here during the war. It is true many of my countrymen still remember the atrocities as though it were yesterday. Who am I to judge if they have not been able to forgive and forget? I can say, however, that your grandfather has elicited my respect and I can promise you that you can trust me with his welfare."

"*Mille grazie,*" said Aarika, in broken Italian. She slid her hand up Marco's forearm, causing a jolt of energy, like static electricity, to prickle over the top of his skull.

Lowering his head, Marco drew his face so close to Aarika's that he could make out the downy blond hairs fuzzing along her cheeks. "You're welcome," he whispered.

No sooner did Marco and Aarika's noses touch, than Dolphus woke with a start. His hands momentarily flailed over his face as though brushing away a nettlesome dream. "Time to start heading back to town, don't you think?" he called out.

Aarika pulled away from Marco upon hearing her grandfather's voice and rose to her feet. "Yes, Opa. We should probably start gathering up our things," she said.

Moments later, Poppy returned from her hike. Taking note of Marco and Aarika's awkward mannerisms and flushed countenances, she said, "Okay, what did I miss out on this time?"

Marco, however, was in no mood to indulge Poppy's curiosity. Instead, he hoisted his backpack onto his shoulder and barked, "Let's go!" before setting out ahead of everyone else. As he sped away from Poppy and the Gellers to get far in the lead, he chided himself for letting his heightened emotions get the better of him. *What just happened back there with Aarika and I? It makes no sense to feel the way I do for her. I've got to get myself under control.*

"Wait up!" Poppy yelled, jogging to catch up with Marco. When she finally reached him, she said, "I thought you should know I'm still peeved with you."

Distracted by his musings on Aarika, Marco blinked and said, "Peeved?"

"The whole chaperone thing."

"I'm only doing what I was told."

"Sure. You don't have a macho bone in your body."

"I don't," said Marco. "I'm just a realist."

"A realist from the nineteenth century. C'mon, Marco, you're our age. You should have assured Dolphus that watching us wasn't going to be necessary."

Marco shrugged.

"After all, I'm looking to be your friend," said Poppy. "Not your responsibility."

"Okay."

"Okay? As in, okay we're friends?"

When Marco simply nodded in reply, Poppy pouted. "Your enthusiasm is encouraging," she said. "I can see our friendship will go far."

"What do you expect me to say?" asked Marco. "The fact is, I'm getting paid to do what Dolphus asks me to do, which right now includes safeguarding you and Aarika. I'm sorry if that upsets you."

"Fine. I get it," replied Poppy. "All I'm saying is, I hope you will consider me as a potential friend. Or is dealing with Americans too taxing for you?"

"Of course I like Americans." Marco paused. "Why would you say that?"

Poppy shrugged and looked over her shoulder at Aarika, who was coming up close behind them with her grandfather. "Because you always hold me at arm's length. Unlike my sister."

Marco's mind reeled at her accusation. He would definitely have to try harder, he decided, to mask his feelings for Aarika. On the other hand, Poppy's persistence in pursuing a friendship with him was, he had to admit, quite flattering. Despite the intensity of her personality, he actually found Poppy's American quirks not just entertaining, but often admirable. In some ways, Italians and Americans were much alike, and considering Poppy's candor and tenacity, he decided she deserved a more complete answer from him.

"I'd like to be your friend, Poppy," he said. "You might find we have more in common that you imagine."

Poppy beamed. "Oh, I *know* we do."

From that point on, until they reached Anacapri ten minutes later, Poppy and Marco walked side by side, deep in conversation, while Aarika, straggling behind them with her grandfather, cast prying glimpses their way.

Later that evening, around midnight to be precise, after a long supper and a short rest, Marco found himself escorting Aarika and Poppy to The Africana nightclub in lower Praiano. Situated within two overlapping caves skirting the sea, the place throbbed with the primal rhythms of a live band. The unique dance floor featured a colorful mosaic of glass with views of the water below. Artificially illuminated stalactites and stalagmites adorned the walls, lending a surreal aura to the semi-subterranean club. Marco swirled golden *Greco di Tufo* in his wine glass and smelled its unique, fruity bouquet before turning his attention to Poppy and Aarika, who were writhing around in the center of the dance floor with two male admirers.

Suddenly all of the musicians stopped playing except for the saxophonist, who, taking center stage, began playing a slow, soulful tune on his instrument. Dance partners, who just moments ago had been gyrating wildly, now hung on each other, swaying like tangled sections of seaweed bowing in an ocean current. Poppy, Marco noticed, was glued to someone who looked to be a local. The man played with her hair as they rocked back and forth, their heads touching. Near them, Aarika had molded herself into the arms of a tall, tanned, muscular blond. A tourist, Marco reasoned, most likely German from the looks of him.

When the song ended, the girls returned to the table, their partners tagging behind them. Poppy settled into a seat directly opposite Marco, pulling her devotee into the chair next to her. He proudly introduced himself as Beppe from

Praiano, as Marco had guessed. Aarika, plopped down at end of the table. Her Teutonic companion dragged a chair up next to her and ordered a drink.

Beppe slid his arm over Poppy's shoulder. With his other hand he fanned the air directly in front of him, as though he were on fire. *"Fa caldo qui, o è perchè ci sei tu?"*

Poppy looked at Marco for the interpretation.

Frowning, Marco said, "Your friend says, 'Is it hot in here, or is it just because you are sitting next to me?'"

Poppy threw her head back and laughed, causing Beppe to do the same. When their laughter subsided, Aarika introduced her acquaintance. "Meet Holger, everyone," she said. "He's from Berlin."

Marco sized Holger up as being educated, thirty-ish, and wealthy. His roving eyes and self-absorbed mannerisms were a sure indication—to Marco, at least—that he was the kind of man who expected his flirtations to earn him a one-night stand, unlike Beppe, who seemed to be flirting with Poppy for the sheer joy of it, regardless of the outcome.

Holger sensed Marco's disapproval and when the band revved into the next song, he wasted no time in dragging Aarika back out onto the dance floor, away from Marco's menacing eyes. Beppe and Poppy, on the other hand, decided to sit the song out.

Leaning over the table, Poppy hissed, "Stop it, Marco."

"Stop what?"

"Scaring men away. I saw the way you just intimidated Holger."

"I don't care who you two dance with."

"Well, you're acting like an old grouch," insisted Poppy. "I think you're just jealous because no one's paying attention to you."

Marco chafed at the accusation. "I have been sitting here alone this evening because women are afraid to approach me thinking I am with you or Aarika."

"Do something about it then," said Poppy. "Have some fun. Aarika and I aren't going anywhere."

Accepting the challenge, Marco stood to his feet. "*Va bene.* Tell Aarika that when you're both ready to leave, you must let me know." Then, making his way to the bar, he claimed a stool and ordered a glass of Chianti from the bartender. Within minutes he found himself surrounded by several women vying for his attention. One of them eventually succeeded in getting him to dance with her, the result of which was a tango so flawlessly performed that every person on the dance floor stepped back to observe them. Marco and his lady bowed to the sound of thunderous applause when the song ended and promptly returned to their seats at the bar.

Poppy and Aarika, who had witnessed the spectacle from the sidelines, excused themselves from Beppe and Holger and approached Marco. His dance partner was still draped over him, her red dress hugging her curves like the skin of a ripe Roma tomato.

"I see you took my advice seriously, Marco," said Poppy, her hands on her hips.

"Oh, this is Pia," explained Marco, coolly. "She's on holiday from Lucca, only a twenty-minute drive from where I live. We discovered we have mutual friends in Querceta and Strettoia. She even knows where my parents' shop is. It's a small world, no? And she's an amazing dancer, is she not?"

"*Ciao,*" said Pia, barely acknowledging Aarika and Poppy's presence. Opening her purse, she retrieved a pen, and taking a napkin from the bar, she jotted something on it and then slipped it into Marco's shirt pocket, letting her fingers linger on his chest.

Aarika whispered something to Poppy, both of them casting furtive glances toward Holger and Beppe, who sat waiting impatiently for their return. Then, taking a step forward, Poppy tapped Marco on the shoulder. "We're ready to go back to the hotel."

"That's too bad, because I'm not ready yet," retorted Marco.

"Tomorrow's our last day here," pleaded Poppy. "There's a lot we want to do and see, so please, let's go."

Sighing, Marco whispered something in Pia's ear. Then, he pulled her hand to his lips, kissed her fingers, and allowed her hand to linger a moment in his before making an exit. Stepping out of the club with Aarika and Poppy at his heels, he inhaled the fresh night air.

I hate to admit it, he thought, *but revenge is sweet when delivered on a platter like Pia.*

·9·

What Men Think

AARIKA SLEPT FITFULLY that night, waking up the next morning with a raging headache. "I don't feel well," she announced at the breakfast table over a plate of untouched food. Even though the patio where they were sitting was shaded, she covered her bloodshot eyes with a pair of mirrored sunglasses that reflected the sun's glare off the sea, and popped several round pink pills into her mouth.

Dolphus leaned over to touch her forehead with the palm of his hand.

"I'm fine, Opa. Really. I don't have a fever."

Marco, his face buried behind a copy of the day's *Corriere della Sera*, addressed Dolphus as though the girls weren't there. "Poppy and Aarika both look unusually tired. Perhaps they should stay at the hotel today and rest."

Poppy scowled. "Perhaps you should take your own advice, since you were the one we had to drag away from the club last night. Right, Aarika?"

Aarika rubbed two fingertips between her left temple and ear and moaned softly.

Crossing his arms, Dolphus said, "I have no idea what you all are talking about, and quite frankly, I don't want to know. Marco, what are we doing today?"

Marco peered over the top of the newspaper. "We can drive south and tour Ravello and Salerno . . ."

Both girls shook their heads. "That's too far," they groaned.

"Or," continued Marco, "we can spend the day here in Praiano."

"Bingo," said Poppy. "That's my vote."

"Yes, let's stay here," agreed Aarika.

"What about you, Marco?" asked Dolphus. "Is there somewhere special you would like to go?"

Marco folded the newspaper and set it down next to his plate. "I met a girl from Lucca last night when I escorted Aarika and Poppy to The Africana. She is holidaying in Praiano as well. We have very much in common. I would like to stay here also, in the event I might see her again."

"Well then," said Dolphus. "It's final. A tour of Praiano it shall be."

Fortunately, the weather their last day on the Amalfi Coast was glorious. The air was fresh and clear due to a minor squall that had blown in just before dawn. By the time the four of them set off from the hotel, it was sunny and seventy-eight degrees. According to the weather report out of Naples, the temperature was only supposed to reach ninety; at least ten degrees cooler than they were accustomed to.

They began their tour of the village by climbing a narrow stairwell consisting of hundreds of steep steps, which ultimately led them to the same small piazza where Aarika and Marco had recited *Ulysses* together. Putting the memory out of his mind, Marco pressed ahead. He turned right, down an open-air corridor leading to the Chiesa di San Luca

Evangelista. The exterior of the church showcased several mosaics, including a scene depicting its moniker and the town's patron saint, the Apostle Luke, hovering angel-like over the waters of Praiano's bay. After admiring other features of the *chiesa*, Poppy suggested they climb higher yet and check out Chiesa di Costantinopoli, the church with the unparalleled views of the coast.

Poppy took the lead this time, navigating a network of winding stairs set into a vertical incline blocked by high stucco walls and dense vegetation. Eventually, they found themselves in another piazza, only this one was completely devoid of any people. In solitary awe they stood spellbound in front of Chiesa di Santa Maria di Costantinopoli, gazing out at the jagged curves of the wild Sorrentine peninsula, with the rugged Lattari Mountains overshadowing Positano to the north, and the calm, blue sea emptying into the western horizon like an enormous infinity pool. It was Marco who eventually broke the silence by proposing they go inside the church. But as they neared the entrance, Dolphus stopped abruptly, his face pale.

"I'll wait outside," he said.

"Opa, are you okay?" asked Aarika. "I can stay with you."

"No, no, you go on," replied Dolphus, indicating a spot at the edge of the piazza where he would wait for her. "I'll be fine."

Poppy removed the lens cover from her camera. "On second thought, I think I'll pass too. There are some great shots I want to take from this viewpoint."

As Poppy struck out to a nearby promontory to take her pictures, Marco extended his hand in front of Aarika and said, "Shall we?" Together, they stepped into the church's vestibule and removed their sunglasses before making their way down the main aisle toward the raised marble altar. A sacred hush descended over them as they viewed the multiple frescos and paintings adorning the ceiling and walls. Finally, turning to retrace his steps, Marco glanced out one of the church's west-facing windows. He saw Dolphus sitting forlornly on a retaining wall, his spine bent and his shoulders sagging as though carrying a huge weight. The German's bearing was so drastically different from the day before when he had reveled in the sights and sounds of Capri, Marco couldn't help but think something must be wrong.

Aarika came alongside Marco. Following his gaze, she asked what he was looking at.

"Your grandfather," he said. "Is he *Cattolico?*"

"Yes, he is Catholic. We both are. Why?"

"Because he seemed afraid to come in this church."

Aarika dismissed the idea, and continuing toward the exit, she said, "He's just tired."

But as they lingered on the front steps of the *chiesa,* Marco saw something they hadn't noticed when they first entered the church: a memorial plaque commemorating Praiano's fallen soldiers. Marco pointed to it. "This is what may have scared your grandfather away."

"Why would you say that?"

"Notice the special recognition of soldiers who lost their lives in World War II," said Marco, his finger resting on the engraving along the top right corner of the stone plaque.

Aarika set her jaw and turned to leave, but Marco reached out to stop her. "What's wrong?" he asked.

"Don't jump to conclusions about my grandfather, Marco. You promised I could trust you to have his best interests at heart, remember? And just so you know, any discussion about the war is off-limits."

"How can it be off-limits?" argued Marco. "The war has affected everything you see here in Italy today."

"As it has in Germany," countered Aarika, her voice thick with emotion.

"All right," agreed Marco. "I'll honor your request. No talk about the war. But in the end, Aarika, you must realize it is truth that sets us free."

THE HIKE BACK down to the piazza at San Luca Evangelista was long enough that by the time the Geller party stopped to order lunch at an outdoor pizzeria overlooking Marina di Praia, Dolphus was himself again, and Marco and Aarika had put the topic of war behind them. In fact, they were all so invigorated by their walk and the fabulous weather, that after they finished their lunch they spent a good hour indulging in light-hearted conversation. Eventually, the topic turned to how to best spend the rest of their afternoon.

Poppy pointed to the marina far below them. "There's Praiano's public beach. I heard it's a great swimming spot."

"Who told you that?" asked Marco.

"Beppe. You know, from The Afrikana last night."

Aarika, whose headache seemed to be completely gone now, agreed that a swim sounded great. "Would you be up for it, Opa?" she asked.

"*Ja*, sure. Whatever you girls want to do."

Having reached a consensus, they paid their bill and returned to the hotel. They arrived so sweaty and hot they couldn't change into their bathing suits fast enough, and when they met up in the lobby half an hour later, they were dressed for the beach and anxious to get going. Aarika wore her lime green two-piece bathing suit beneath a sheer white cotton caftan, while her feet were clad in bright orange, ankle-strapped Birkenstocks. With a beach towel draped over his shoulder, Dolphus sported navy swimming trunks that reached to the middle of his knees and a pair of sturdy leather sandals. Wearing plastic flip-flops, Poppy concealed her suit beneath a stars-and-stripes motif t-shirt and faded denim cut-offs. A white linen shirt paired with khaki slacks set Marco apart as the only Italian in the group.

"Do we pass the Italian fashion test, Marco?" asked Poppy. She spread her arms out, performing a pirouette for him.

"You won't embarrass yourselves," he replied soberly, "but everyone will know where you're from."

Poppy stuck out her lower lip. "What do you mean?"

Marco pointed to Aarika's Birkenstocks and said, "Germany." Then he pointed to Poppy's t-shirt. "America."

Poppy tossed her head. "Oh, who cares? C'mon let's go."

Spilling out of the hotel, they hustled down the main street to the nearest bus stop and climbed on the blue SITA heading south. It was a quick ride to the marina, nestled at the base of a steep ravine separating Praiano from Furore. When they arrived at their destination, they filed past a dozen tiny fishermen's homes and a few bistros and shops before reaching the rocky beach. Quickly, they claimed a spot on a flat ledge overlooking a semi-circular swimming hole that emptied directly into the small bay.

The girls had just stripped down to their suits when they heard a man shout, "Poppy!"

Shading her eyes with one hand, Poppy peered out over the water in the direction of a fishing boat anchored halfway between them and an outcropping of rocks. The rocks formed a miniature island at the entrance to the bay. "Beppe!" she yelled, waving wildly.

Beppe's mahogany arms and shoulders glistened as he swam sleek as a bullet toward them. Within seconds he was lifting himself out of the water and shaking his body off in front of them like a wet dog. Following a brief introduction to Dolphus, Beppe suddenly pointed to a figure approaching them from the beach. "Gino!" he shouted. "Come! I told you we might see the Americana and her *Deutsch* friend again before they leave!"

As Gino drew close, Marco saw that it was Gino De Luca, the attendant on the Capri ferry. Wearing black speedos and carrying a towel, Gino opened his arms wide to Aarika and Poppy. "It is fortunate I have the day off today," he crooned. He winked in Marco's direction and added, "It is a small world, no? Beppe and I are good friends! Would you ever have guessed it?"

The girls laughed at Gino and Beppe's enthusiasm and then one by one, like jets lined up for take off, the four of them took running leaps into the sea.

While the girls and their partners frolicked in the water, Dolphus turned to Marco. "Will you be joining them?" he asked.

"Definitely not," said Marco. "You?"

Dolphus studied the girls, now being tossed high into the air by their swim mates. "Not yet. I'll keep you company for a while." Spreading his towel out on the ledge where it butted up to the vertical face of a large boulder, Dolphus sat down. He pulled a tube of sunscreen out of Aarika's beach bag lying open next to him, and slathered some of the lotion on his legs and arms.

Marco settled down cross-legged near Dolphus. Figuring he owed him an explanation, he said, "The girls met Beppe last night at the club I took them to. Trust me, Signor Geller, nothing happened. And Gino, as you know, they met on the ferry yesterday."

"I'm not worried," said Dolphus. "Yet." He placed the sunscreen back in the bag and then continued watching the girls play a dunking game with Gino and Beppe. "At Domenico's," he continued, "it was easy for Aarika and Poppy to avoid each other. But coming here, as I thought, has been good for them. Here, they must share a room. They are forced to spend time together. And now, they have found a common reason to laugh and be themselves."

Marco nodded in half-hearted agreement. Although, their holiday had clearly brought Aarika and Poppy closer together, their "common reason" for having fun at the moment involved two charming and spirited Italian men.

"This holiday has also been good for you and me, Marco," said Dolphus.

"How so?"

Dolphus wagged his finger at Marco and then back at himself. "I feel like I know you better, and you—I hope— understand a little more about me."

"I understand that you love your granddaughter," replied Marco. "And I see that you have the utmost respect for my cousin Domenico. But if you'll allow me to be honest, it is still a mystery to me why you choose to come to Monte Montignoso every summer."

Marco didn't expect an answer and when Dolphus didn't reply, the two men fell into silent contemplation until Aarika suddenly bobbed up out of the water close to them. Gino rose up alongside her and placed his arm around her shoulder.

"Opa and Marco," she asked, her elbows resting on the rock. "Why aren't you swimming?"

To Marco's amazement, instead of replying, Dolphus

bounced up, ripped off his shirt, stepped to the edge of the rock and dove into the water next to Aarika with the grace and agility of a professional diver.

Aarika then grabbed hold of Marco's foot. "Aren't you coming too?"

Marco reached down and removed her hand. "I think I'll pass." But no sooner had he declined, than a sultry voice called out, "Marco! Marco Bertozzi!"

Pia swam up alongside Aarika in mermaid fashion, her long, lustrous hair cascading down over one shoulder and her face shimmering as though she'd been immersed in liquid crystals. Gino and Beppe gaped at her approvingly. "I was hoping I'd find you here today, Marco," she said. "Come. Swim with me."

Like Dolphus, Marco didn't hesitate. Rising to his feet, he removed his shirt, stripped down to his trunks and slid into the water next to her. In one fluid motion, Pia maneuvered herself behind Marco, wrapped her arms around his shoulders, and whispered something in his ear. Marco looked directly at Aarika, treading water with Gino just a few feet away, to gauge her reaction. He took perverse pleasure at the shock registered on her face. *Well,* he thought, *what do you expect Aarika? L'amore domina senza regole.* Love rules without rules.

And with that, Marco and Pia glided away toward the little island on the other side of the fishing boats.

A DAY OF hiking and swimming had proved exhausting, so by the time everyone gathered in the hotel dining room that evening, they were ready to settle into a long, leisurely dinner. Aarika had made a grand entrance, looking cool and serene in a kiwi-and-mango striped sundress. Her hair, bleached nearly white from several full days in the sun, contrasted sharply with her tanned skin. When Marco held her chair out for her he detected the scent of fresh laundry, a smell that, without fail, always took him back to his childhood. Poppy, he noticed, as he held a chair out for her, was dressed more casually in a short denim skirt and white sleeveless blouse. Large gold hoop earrings protruded through her thick, curly red hair. Her skin, unlike Aarika's, had burned rather than tanned, resulting in a band of deep pink splashed across her freckled nose, cheeks and shoulders. He marveled yet again at the many differences between the two sisters.

When the girls were seated, Marco sat down, placed his linen napkin on his lap and picked up his menu. He couldn't concentrate, however, because scenes of the beach that afternoon kept tugging at him. He felt a rush of remorse at having taken advantage of Pia's flirting. He really could care less about her. What galled him was the fact that he had never before experienced the emotions of jealousy and vindication, and now that he had, he found it not only regrettable, but also terribly disconcerting. How was it that Aarika—a cheeky, complicated German girl he hardly knew—continued to get under his skin? Finally deciding on a menu choice, Marco placed his order along with everyone else and made small talk until the first course was served. As the wine flowed and the evening wore on, they were all lulled into waxing nostalgic.

Poppy initiated a round of toasts. "To Compania," she said. "Praiano, Capri, Costiera Amalfitana . . . all of it!"

"*Prost!*" chimed Dolphus and Aarika together.

Marco offered the next toast. "To Dolphus, for his generosity in bringing us here."

"Please, it was nothing," Dolphus protested. "While I'm yet alive, it is my pleasure to create good memories for others. What is a little money if I can do that?"

Aarika raised her glass, her eyes trained on Marco. "I'd like to make a toast," she said. "To Marco, for putting up with us. Especially on the drive here."

"Hear, hear!" Poppy tipped her glass toward Aarika's.

Dolphus, suddenly serious, proposed the last toast. "To Aarika and Poppy," he said, his voice cracking, "sisters I never thought I'd see together, much less see getting along so well."

Marco thought he saw tears pool in both girls' eyes and the sight of it gave him an odd, mixed sense of compassion and accomplishment. All in all, he thought, this short holiday had been a success. There had been no major catastrophes and Aarika and Poppy actually seemed to be getting along better. Dolphus had guessed that the sisters, forced into sharing a bedroom at the hotel, might make headway in their relationship during their stay in Praiano. He appeared to have been right. In that moment, their glasses raised to each other, tucked away in an exotic enclave of palm trees and jasmine, Mediterranean moonlight, and gentle sea breezes, it seemed as though the four of them were suspended in time, in a bubble of protection isolated from the real world.

Had Bianca Corrotti been supping with them in Praiano, however, she would have come to a different conclusion. She would have noticed the unspoken fears and the suspicious stares that passed between the sisters when they thought no one was looking. Indeed, Bianca, true to her prescient inclinations, would have seen their secrets.

· 10 ·

How Deep Sisterhood

BEFORE MARCO ARRIVED back home from his trip with the Gellers, Domenico and Mariella stopped by my house to ask a favor. Their wedding anniversary, they reminded me, was next week and they had made reservations to spend the night at a romantic villa in Florence.

"But," said Domenico, "the problem is, Marco called to tell me that as they were checking out of their hotel in Praiano, Dolphus made a last-minute decision to stay Saturday and Sunday in Rome before returning. So, Bianca, would you mind preparing a meal for the Gellers on Monday night while we are in Florence? We will be back on Tuesday."

"Of course," I told him, happy for the opportunity to hear all about the Gellers' holiday.

Besides, I was anxious to see Aarika and Poppy again. Having sisters myself, I am naturally drawn to those two girls. Parents and grandparents pass on in due time. Marriages can go sour. Even the strongest friendships sometimes dissolve. But sisters, if they remain, are as durable as diamonds. Mine are my best friends. Oh, we've had our disagreements, my sisters and I. And there were times we didn't see each other as much as we should have, or could have. But in the end, now that we are old, widowed, and alone, we treasure one another.

So now here it is, nearly three o'clock Monday afternoon, and Domenico and Mariella are enjoying each other in Florence. My patio needs sweeping and I haven't even started preparing my *zucchine ripiene and pollo fritto alla Toscana*. The heat has ripened my garden tomatoes faster than I could pick them, wilted my arugula, and turned my house into an oven. Worse yet, my last pair of nylon stockings has snagged and I have no time to get a new pair before the Gellers and Poppy and Marco arrive in less than three hours.

Why, I ask myself, do I make promises that seem impossible to keep?

Because I believe in miracles. Of course.

"*Basta*," groaned Marco, holding both hands up against his ribcage. Enough. Domenico might bake the best pizzas in Versilia and be one of the most respected cooks in the region, but Bianca, in his estimation, came in a close second. Not only was her succulent *pollo fritto alla Toscana* superb, she had made enough to feed everyone twice over.

Dolphus, Aarika, and Poppy also declined another serving. "You warned us we must save room for dessert, Bianca," Dolphus reminded her.

Helping Bianca clear the table, Marco followed her into the kitchen and began loading the dishwasher. "Dinner was delicious," he said. "I was getting tired of eating out on our trip."

"There's nothing like home-cooked food." Bianca stole a look out the kitchen window facing the patio where Aarika and Poppy were sipping wine and talking. "I see your trip to the Amalfi went well."

"Surprisingly, yes," agreed Marco. He knew Bianca well enough to know this was her lead into a conversation she hoped would provide her with more information.

"I especially notice Aarika and Poppy seem to be getting along better."

"Very perceptive, Bianca." Marco hooked up the hose to the vintage dishwasher and proceeded to fill the dispenser with soap. He then pushed a series of buttons. There was a "click" and the sound of surging water in the pipes before the motor kicked into action. "Can I help with anything else?" he asked.

Bianca put one hand on her hip and the other on her forehead. It was clear to Marco she was thinking of how to stall him, how to keep him inside the house with her so they could continue talking in private. "Actually, there is something you can help me with," she said. "Would you mind getting out the bowls and spoons for dessert?"

"Sure. What are we having?"

"Gelato—from Arcobaleno."

"Ah, my favorite gelateria!"

While Marco counted out bowls and spoons and set them on a tray, Bianca played with her apron. "I notice you seem to be less . . . bothered by Aarika," she ventured.

Bianca's attempts to disguise her curiosity were failing miserably, thought Marco. "I suppose so," he replied.

Throwing her hands into the air, Bianca exclaimed, "Oh! How could I forget? I have some Prosecco in the cellar that Domenico gave me several months ago. Would you mind accompanying me, Marco? My knees have been bothering me this week."

"Just tell me where it is," said Marco. "I'll get it for you."

"No, no. You would never find it. I must go with you."

Marco took Bianca's hand, guiding her toward the cellar door. "Carefully now," he warned, as they inched down the steep steps.

Bianca's basement served two purposes. Half of it was built as a walk-out living area, with a fully-equipped kitchen, and a small bathroom and bedroom, which she used in the wintertime to save money on heating. Though paneled with wood, several large windows facing south made it a bright, cheery apartment. The other half, in which Bianca and Marco now found themselves, served as the Bertozzi family's wine cellar. It was at least ten degrees cooler than upstairs, even cooler than the adjoining apartment, and smelled of fermented grapes, oak barrels, mountain berries, ripe apples, and a variety of spices. Wine bottles in all shapes and sizes lined the walls. Some were filled and corked and others were empty, but all were arranged in a specific pattern known only to Bianca. The cement floor was stained purple with years of spilt pulp from the grapes. Errant spider webs, gray and gauzy in the half-light, stretched between the massive floor beams above their heads.

Bianca went over to a far wall and carefully inspected several rows of wine before selecting a bottle. "Here it is," she said. "I've been saving it for a special occasion. I would say when sisters discover each other, it is *molto speciale*, no?"

"It most certainly is," agreed Marco. He waited as she dusted off the Prosecco with the edge of her apron.

She handed the bottle to him. "How did it happen?"

"How did what happen?"

"Aarika and Poppy. What made them start liking each other?"

"To be honest, I think it was because they felt the need to band together against Dolphus and me."

"They formed an alliance?"

"Exactly."

"Why?"

"Well," Marco explained, "they are beautiful women, no? Dolphus was concerned about the men who would be attracted to them while we were in Praiano and asked me to watch them carefully. When they found out, they were very angry with us."

"Italian men love beauty," smiled Bianca. "I'm sure it was a challenge for you to keep them away from the girls."

"Of course, but . . ."

"But other men's appreciation is not acceptable when it is a woman you care about."

Marco didn't expect this. Bianca's blunt assessment hit him square in the chest. He tucked the wine bottle under one arm, pulled the chain on the ceiling light above them, and escorted Bianca from the cellar. As they ascended the stairs, Bianca said, "Don't worry, Marco. Your secret is safe with me."

"There is no secret," he replied. "As a matter of fact, I met a woman in Praiano. Her name is Pia. She is from Lucca, if you can believe it."

"Oh?"

It maddened Marco the way Bianca could see right through him.

"The important thing is," continued Bianca, "Aarika and Poppy have found something that connects them, outside of their past. They may not be best friends yet, and no doubt there will be many things that will test their relationship, but the healing has begun."

When they reached the top of the steps, Marco waited as Bianca caught her breath. Once she had composed herself, she handed him the tray of bowls and spoons, and together they returned to the patio. While Bianca prepared the dessert, Marco extracted the cork from the bottle of Prosecco, and as he did, it struck him that there were similarities between wine and relationships. Winemaking was a long process at the mercy of a variety of conditions, such as weather and timing and the quality and composition of aging materials. Once the wine was bottled, and as long as it remained so, it was safe, protected from consumption, a product to be admired for its mystery and its contents only dreamed about. Uncorking a bottle of wine forever changed that dynamic; it presented a risk of exposure. The mystery was revealed and, like it or not, there was no going back.

As he began circling the table, pouring Prosecco into each person's glass, Marco wondered if he was ready to take a risk. To be so vulnerable with a woman was beyond his experience and imagination. The very thought terrified him. Coming up behind Aarika, he leaned down to pour wine into her glass. His arm brushed against hers. *I cannot fall in love with Aarika Geller,* he thought. *I don't care how beautiful she is or how much her unbelievably soft skin and great expressive eyes make me melt. Surely, there are too many differences working against us.*

When he finished filling everyone's glasses, Marco sat down, taking his seat next to Aarika. She turned to him and raised her wine glass to his. Then, leaning in close, she whispered in his ear. "What a wonderful evening this has been, Marco. And this wine is delicious. *I will drink Life to the lees.*"

Marco, his resolve waning, replied with another line of Tennyson, "*That which we are, we are, Aarika.*"

Aarika touched her glass to his. "Indeed, Marco. Here's to opposites with the same love of poetry . . ."

"And wine," added Marco.

Laughing, Aarika nodded. "And nature."

Marco trained his eyes on Aarika, just inches away from him. "And beauty."

Aarika blushed and turned away from him, and at that moment Marco knew he had just allowed his heart to be uncorked.

By the time everyone had finished their gelato and enjoyed a second round of Prosecco, the bright ceramic clock above the stove in Bianca's kitchen read eleven fifteen. Dolphus was in the midst of thanking Bianca for the meal when Poppy exclaimed, "Oh, Bianca, I forgot. May I use your telephone? I promised my mom and dad I would call them when I got here, but there's no phone service at Domenico's and I've been so busy, I totally spaced it out."

Marco interpreted for Bianca. Nodding vigorously, Bianca said, "*Si, si, non problema!*"

Poppy retrieved a calling card from her purse and handed it to Marco. "Can you get it set up for me?" she asked. "I would never be able to figure out what the operator is saying."

Marco picked up the receiver of Bianca's vintage yellow Olivetti dial phone and went through the myriad steps required to place the call. When he heard ringing on the other end, he handed the phone to Poppy. Aarika, meanwhile, stood just inside the kitchen door next to her grandfather, her eyes riveted on her sister. Seconds later, a high-pitched voice coming out of the handset echoed through Bianca's kitchen.

"Poppy? Is that you? I can hardly hear you."

"Yes, mom. It's me," shouted Poppy. "How are you? Yeah, yeah, I'm fine. Sorry I haven't called before now, but with the time zone difference and everything . . . what? What did you say?"

The foreign voice from America droned on, Poppy occasionally bobbing her head in reply.

"We just got back from the Amalfi Coast," said Poppy. "We were only there for a few days, but it was so amazing. You would have loved it, Mom. Did you get my postcard? Yeah, I know, six weeks is a long time, but it's going really fast."

Poppy paused. Her eyes darted to Aarika. "She is. She's right here. You do? Well, Mom, I don't know . . ."

With an expression of regret, as though she was only now realizing the awkward situation she had created, Poppy placed her hand over the mouthpiece and said, "Aarika, Mom wants to talk to you."

Aarika shrank back. Tugging at Dolphus's arm, she turned and walked away with him in tow. Poppy dropped the hand she had used to cover the mouthpiece of the phone. "I'm sorry, Mom. She's not ready."

A few more moments passed with Poppy saying repeatedly "I'm sorry" and "I don't know what to say" and "Yeah, I know, Mom." An automated voice interrupted the call, warning that there were only five minutes left on the calling card.

Poppy scanned the room to be sure Aarika was gone. Lowering her voice, she said, "Yes, Mom, Aarika is beautiful. I'll try to send you some pictures. Mom, like I said, I don't think she's ready yet. I've gotta go now, so tell Dad I love him. What? Okay, yes, I'll tell her. Bye."

The sound of the telephone receiver being set back in its cradle fell heavy in the silent kitchen. As Poppy picked up her purse and prepared to go out to the car, Bianca reached out and hugged her. She said something in Italian, asking Marco to translate for her.

Turning to Poppy, Marco said, "Bianca says you may use her telephone anytime. It is important, she says, for daughters to talk with their mothers. She also says she wishes she could pick up a telephone and talk to her mother, but there are no telephones in heaven."

Poppy smiled sympathetically at Bianca and returned her hug. "Ask her if she can be my mother while I'm here if I find that I need one."

Marco didn't bother interpreting. "All Italian women are mothers," he told her. "If you need a mother, you can come to Bianca, or Mariella, or my mother. They will all help you."

A shadow passed over Poppy's face. She nodded and stepped past them out of the kitchen.

Marco sighed. Leaning over, he kissed Bianca good-bye and thanked her for the evening. Glumly, he added, "I'm not looking forward to the drive back up to Domenico's. And just when I thought things were improving too."

OUTER SPACE COULDN'T have been emptier than the vacuum in the car on the drive back to the fattoria. Marco began humming under his breath in an attempt to lighten the mood, but it sounded forced and out of place, so he stopped.

Poppy was the first to eventually speak. "I'm sorry, Aarika," she said. "I should have thought about you when I called Mom." When Aarika didn't reply, she added, "It's just that I had promised her and my dad that I would call as soon as I got here and never did. Believe me, I didn't have any ulterior motives in making the call from Bianca's tonight."

"I never want to speak to your mother," said Aarika. "You can tell her that the next time you talk to her."

"That's fine, if you're sure that's the way you want it." But the way Poppy said it indicated it was anything but fine.

Marco glanced over at Dolphus. His eyes were closed as though he were sleeping, or thinking, or remembering something unpleasant.

Another few maddening moments of silence passed as they ascended the last, lonely stretch of the mountain road. Marco downshifted through the first series of switchbacks. When the road evened out again, Poppy said, "Mom asked me to give you a message, Aarika. Do you want to hear it or not?"

Again, Aarika didn't reply. But Poppy, instead of letting it rest, blurted, "She said to tell you, 'It's not your fault.'"

Dolphus, who had appeared not to be paying attention a moment before, gasped. It was a quick intake of air followed by a slight, tremulous cough. Marco noticed too, that his hands, which had been resting atop his knees, tightened into fists.

· 11 ·

Babsi

Tuesday began auspiciously. Domenico called Marco early in the morning to say he and Mariella were back from Florence and would be by in the late afternoon to prepare dinner for the Gellers. Would Marco, he asked, be sure to take some rolls and croissants over to them for breakfast, take them swimming if they wanted, and get them some lunch? Domenico rattled off a few other odd jobs he needed Marco to do on the property, and then finished the call by asking, "Is there anything I need to know—anything new with the Gellers since your holiday in Praiano?"

"No," said Marco, "everything's fine."

"*Bene, bene.* I am anxious to hear about your trip. Well then, see you later. *Ciao.*"

Marco, who was still in bed when Domenico had called, hustled as fast as he could to get ready. Ten minutes later he left his house with his mother's kiss still fresh on his cheek and her suggestion to stop at a certain bakery in Strettoia for the requested croissants ringing in his ears. When he finally arrived on the mountain it was nine o'clock. It was so hot already that packs of flies were buzzing in thick black circles above the orchards, and the neighbor's chickens and roosters were napping, limp-feathered, in the shade of their coops.

Marco knocked loudly several times on the door to the fattoria before Poppy finally opened it, her eyes blinking as they adjusted to the light.

"Why are you here so early?" she asked.

"It's nine o'clock," replied Marco, as though the hour spoke for itself.

"That's what I said. It's early."

Stepping around her, Marco placed the box of *cornetti* and other pastries on the table. "I'm not here any earlier than Domenico usually is when he comes by for breakfast."

"I suppose so," yawned Poppy.

Marco searched about for the large stainless-steel espresso maker, found it, and began filling the chamber with freshly ground coffee. "Where's everyone else?"

"Sleeping, I would imagine." Poppy plopped down on the nearest chair. "Aarika and Dolphus were both awake a lot last night."

Placing the coffee on the stove, Marco looked for a match. He found one and held it beneath the pot until a sharp blue flame flared out of the burner. "How do you know?" he asked.

"I kept hearing noises all night. One time, I got up and saw Aarika and Dolphus talking together in the living room. Another time, I looked out the window and Aarika was walking around in circles in the front yard while Dolphus sat at that stone table under the tree." Poppy stretched and yawned again. "Who knows what's eating them? Maybe they're still mad at me for calling my mom last night."

The smell of fresh-brewed coffee filled the kitchen. Marco placed some napkins and cups on the table and poured some milk into a small pitcher. He opened the box of croissants and offered one to Poppy, who proceeded to devour it.

"*Guten Tag.*" Dolphus materialized in the doorway, his

hair a mess and his clothes crumpled as though he had slept in them. "I thought I smelled coffee." He walked to the table, picked up a roll, and mumbled, "Why are you here so early, Marco?"

Poppy snickered.

"I brought breakfast over," said Marco. "Domenico asked me to see if you would like to go to the beach today."

Aarika, her eyes swollen, stepped into the house. "You can all go to the beach if you like," she said. "It's too hot. I'm staying here." Like Dolphus, her clothes were badly crumpled and looked as though they'd been slept in. From the sheen on her face and arms, it appeared she had been out for a walk already.

"Sleep well last night, Aarika?" asked Poppy.

"I slept fine, thank you."

"Really?" Poppy retorted. "It must have been ghosts I heard roaming around in the wee hours of the morning then, if it wasn't you."

"I wasn't roaming around."

Poppy finished the last bite of her croissant and licked her fingers. "Could have fooled me."

Put off by Poppy's sarcasm, Aarika snapped, "Well, excuse me, but some people have other things on their minds besides their mothers in Minnesota."

"Is that so?" Poppy rose to face Aarika. "For your information Miss High and Mighty, most people have a real beating organ in their chest instead of a set of Wusthof knives where their hearts should be."

Dolphus ordered both girls to stop and sit down. "It's time, Aarika," he said, in a surrendering but authoritative tone. "Poppy deserves to know."

Catching the look of sheer horror on Aarika's face, Marco

decided he should go outside and do some work, but as he made a move to leave, Dolphus asked him to stay with them.

"This will be very difficult," explained Dolphus. "We may need a translator to interpret some German into English for Poppy." Noting Marco's reluctance, he added, "I hope you don't mind, Marco. We—I—will need your support."

Marco gritted his teeth and complied, taking up a seat at the table next to Poppy while Dolphus sat down next to Aarika.

Four hours later, he was eating lunch at Bianca's, telling her what happened.

After leaving the mountain, Marco stopped by my house to say his mobile wasn't getting service and to ask if he could use my phone to call Domenico.

"A situation has arisen with the Gellers," I overheard Marco say. "I can't go into detail right now on the phone, Domenico. It is too complicated. I would need to talk to you in person. But Dolphus has asked that you deliver their evening meal and leave it in the casala, not the fattoria, rather than preparing and serving it on site tonight. He and Aarika and Poppy may not have an appetite, but if they get hungry, they can at least eat when they are ready."

I could tell Marco was distressed, so after he hung up, I asked him to stay for lunch. To my surprise, he agreed.

What he told me about Aarika and her family, and what transpired at the fattoria this morning, troubled me greatly.

The Story of Aarika and Her Sister
As told to Bianca by Marco Bertozzi

DOLPHUS GELLER AND *his wife had one son: an only child named Conrad. Smart, handsome, and strong, he was their pride and joy. When Conrad was eighteen, he enrolled at a university in Berlin. It was 1975 and Germany was still a broken and divided country. East Germany was separated from the west. The older generation of Germans was ashamed of—and continuing to deal with—the aftermath of World War II, and German youth distanced themselves from their elders via a culture of rebellion, drugs, and "free love," as they called it.*

Conrad changed radically his first year at university. He experimented with a variety of illegal drugs and dropped out of school without telling his parents. Dolphus and his wife, after not hearing from their son for weeks, became worried. When all their efforts to contact him failed, they went to Berlin, having no idea where he might be. They found him penniless, living in a commune with a girl named Sharon, an American student who had been studying in Berlin at the same university. Both of them had dropped out of school and both of them, according to Dolphus, were drug addicts—Conrad primarily to heroin and Sharon to alcohol and barbituates. It was so bad, said Dolphus, he and his wife were forced to take legal measures to get their son help.

While Conrad was receiving treatment in a hospital, Sharon —who had apparently had a falling out with her own family in America and didn't want to be separated from Conrad—moved in with the Gellers at their invitation. Their hope, as parents, was that both Conrad and Sharon would receive all the help they needed, do the right thing, and make a fresh new start on life. After two weeks, Conrad was transferred to a drug rehabilitation center in nearby Passau where he stayed for nearly a month. The day following his release, he and Sharon were married in a small ceremony at the town hall. Sharon was pregnant. Dolphus and his wife would have preferred they had been married in the Church, but under the circumstances . . .

Determined to make a go of their lives, Conrad asked if he could work on the farm Dolphus had inherited from his father and continue to live with them while he saved money and plotted his future. Dolphus agreed and welcomed his son and new wife with open arms. Although it seemed to go well at first, there was a restlessness about Conrad that Dolphus had never seen before—a disjointedness or dissatisfaction with his existence, as though his son was searching for a missing piece of the puzzle he felt his life had become. Part of Dolphus suspected that his son's mental condition had roots in Germany's postwar identity crisis. The shame and guilt of having enabled Adolph Hitler to pervert an entire chapter of their national history rested almost as heavily on Conrad's generation as it did on Dolphus's.

Sharon and Conrad stayed on the farm until the baby was born. They named her Aarika. She was, Dolphus said, the most beautiful baby they had ever seen. Happy and content, she was one of those infants who slept well and rarely fussed. She was perfect in every way and they adored her. When Aarika was twenty months old, however, Sharon announced she was pregnant again, and several weeks later, saying it was time they struck out on their own, Conrad made the decision to move his family off the farm. They found a small apartment in Passau, and though it wasn't far away, the grandparents—while trusting it was for the best—struggled with being separated from their son and granddaughter, whom they'd grown deeply attached to.

Aarika's sister, a downy-haired, flaxen-skinned girl named

Babsi, was born on a cold, bleak winter day in early January. It was a difficult birth for Sharon, especially considering she had already been struggling with an unexpected bout of homesickness over the holidays to the point of depression. Living in their own apartment in Passau also meant Sharon didn't have the same ready help from Conrad's parents that she had relied on while they had lived on the farm. The falling out she had had with her own family in America had been thawing ever since Aarika's birth, and now Sharon's parents were begging her and Conrad to move to Minnesota.

At this point, Dolphus and his wife, noting that Sharon wasn't bonding with Babsi, offered to take two-and-a-half-year-old Aarika into their home for a few days to give Sharon the opportunity to become more closely attached to her new baby. Sharon accepted their offer. But as days turned into weeks, Conrad and Sharon became alarmingly distant and secretive. Conrad stopped working on the farm to pursue a business opportunity in town. What the "business" was exactly, he was not at liberty to say, but he asked if Aarika could stay on the farm a bit longer until they got back on their feet financially.

Soon, Conrad and Sharon began insisting Dolphus and his wife call before bringing Aarika over to visit Babsi. Troubled by the turn of events, Dolphus confronted his son, telling him in no uncertain terms that Aarika could no longer stay at the farm without one of her parents in attendance. It was only right that Conrad begin acting like a father to her, he said. By laying down the law, Dolphus hoped his son and daughter-in-law would become more responsible.

The opposite proved to be true. Sharon and Conrad came to collect Aarika from the farm and refused to let her see her grandparents again. Within months, Conrad and his wife became friends with some of Passau's more questionable characters and soon they were drinking and doing drugs more than ever before. Worse yet, they were partying at home or going out when Aarika and the baby were sleeping.

In March of that year the unimaginable happened.

Conrad and Sharon left the house one night to meet up with acquaintances at a bar near their apartment. Before leaving, they placed both Aarika and the baby in their bed. Sharon would later say that she often let Aarika sleep with her and Conrad, and that on that particular night, because it was so cold, they reasoned the sisters would be warmer sleeping together for the few hours they assumed they would be gone.

"Both the girls were asleep next to each other when we left the house," Sharon told the police. "We thought they would be perfectly safe."

But, when the couple returned home that night, at least four hours after they'd left, they found Aarika on top of the baby, completely covering her.

Babsi was dead.

"Caro Dio!" I cried, when Marco finished telling the story. "What happened?"

"All I know is the baby died of suffocation." Marco wiped his mouth with his napkin, stood up from the table, and carried his dishes to the sink.

"How did the girls react?" I asked.

"Aarika, who already knew the story, sat through its telling hard as stone. But when Dolphus got near the part about her parents going to the bar and leaving her in bed with her baby sister, she jumped up and began pacing around the kitchen, mumbling loudly to herself and brushing her arms as though spiders were crawling on them. Dolphus backed off from finishing the story for a long time until she settled down."

"And Poppy?"

"She was astounded. It was the first time she'd heard about her other sister. Basically, the only thing her mother had conveyed about her earlier life in Germany was that she had been 'messed up.' Sharon claimed Aarika grew up with her grandparents in Germany because Dolphus was awarded custody of her when his son died, but she never told Poppy why that was so."

"When did Dolphus's son die?"

Marco finished rinsing the dishes and sat back down at the table. "I need to talk to you about that," he said. "I left because they said they wanted to rest for a while and then resume talking this afternoon. Dolphus insists on continuing the conversation with Aarika and Poppy. He believes now is the time to resolve everything with the girls."

"He is probably right."

"He asked me to return to the fattoria around three. It was terrible this morning, as you can imagine, which is why Dolphus and I have a favor to ask of you."

"But of course. Anything."

"Dolphus asked what I thought of bringing a woman back with me this afternoon. He feels a motherly presence might help the girls. It would help him, and me also, because we don't know how to respond to the girls' emotions. It's . . ."

"Awkward?"

"Very."

"Can't Mariella go? Domenico's wife is wonderful with young girls. I am so old."

"Mariella can't. She took her mother to Livorno today to visit family there. You are not too old, Bianca."

"But, what would I do? I won't understand anything they say, and they won't understand me."

"Just be yourself," said Marco. "I'll translate for you when needed. You may not realize it, but you have been a great comfort to many in your life."

"Well, if you say so."

"I say so." Marco bent down and kissed me. "You being there this afternoon might make all the difference in the world."

· 12 ·

The Story of Flying Robert

By the time Marco and Bianca arrived at the fattoria, an eerie stillness had descended on the place. The grounds were devoid of any sound or movement. There was no birdsong gracing the air, no fluttering leaves, no muffled stirrings of neighbors puttering about their vineyards or gardens— only the whishing of blood in their own ears as they listened intently for any sign of life.

"We'd better see what's going on," said Marco.

They checked the lower floor of the casala first, where guests were apt to retreat when they needed their privacy. When they found no one there, they moved on to the fattoria. Stepping through the open French doors, they discovered Dolphus lying on the sofa, his eyes closed and his hands crossed over his chest. Marco leaned down over him to make sure he was breathing. The German opened his eyes in surprise.

"Sorry," said Marco. "I was just making sure you were all right."

Noticing Bianca standing behind Marco, Dolphus stood up and said, "Thank you for coming, Bianca. It is very kind of you."

Bianca nodded. "Where are the girls?"

"Aarika went for a walk. Poppy is in the casala, in the little bedroom upstairs. She wanted to be alone for a while." Moving to the open doorway, Dolphus surveyed the premises and then motioned for Marco and Bianca to sit on the sofa. Pulling a chair up next to them, he said, "I'm glad we have a moment to talk in confidence."

Even though Dolphus no longer farmed the land he lived on—it was leased to a neighbor—he still bore the hands of a laborer: broad, rough, and calloused, with short ridged nails that resembled miniature washboards. He laced his gnarled fingers nervously together and then unlocked them, sliding the fingers of one open-fisted hand over the fist of his other.

For an otherwise stoic German, thought Marco, Dolphus's actions spoke volumes.

Bianca reached out and placed her hands over Dolphus's. "It will all work out the way it's supposed to," she said in Italian, as Marco interpreted. "You're doing the right thing."

"I hope so," replied Dolphus. Bianca's touch seemed to have a calming effect on him. "I take it Marco told you the story."

"Only until the baby died."

Dolphus slouched forward. "Aarika has always blamed herself."

"Nonsense," said Bianca. "There was nothing at all deliberate in what happened. Her parents should have known better."

"Her parents were not in their right minds at the time."

"*Certamente.*"

"Still," he continued, "even though Aarika was only three years old, she claims she not only remembers her sister's lifeless body and her parents' panic when they found her, but the funeral as well. What disturbs me is that some of the details she recalls are accurate: her description of Babsi's corpse, her mother not attending the wake or the Mass, the storm that came up suddenly at the cemetery, Conrad breaking down in tears as they lowered the tiny casket into the earth. Aarika has even described to us how we were dressed the day of Babsi's funeral. I wore a black wool overcoat and fedora. My wife wore a brown fur coat and hat with a gold comb in her hair. It is hard to believe she could recall these details from such a young age, yet our doctor assured us it is quite possible, and although those memories torment her, they are, unfortunately, just the tip of the iceberg."

Bianca folded her index finger over the tip of her thumb and held it up near her lips. "No doubt, the baby's death tore Aarika's parents apart."

"Oh, yes," replied Dolphus. His face turned ashen. "It destroyed our family. The problem is, I haven't been completely honest with Aarika about some of it. I fear if I don't tell her soon, she'll eventually find out from someone else. Sharon knows what really happened to Conrad."

"Are you sure you should pursue it, considering how difficult it was for Aarika this morning?" asked Marco.

"This morning was actually hardest on Poppy, I think," said Dolphus. "You see, she knew nothing about having another sister, nor did she seem to know much about her mother's life in Germany during that time. Certainly, it wasn't easy for Aarika to revisit Babsi's death, but it is something she's lived with her entire life."

Dolphus waited until Marco was finished interpreting for Bianca before adding, "This morning was difficult for Poppy because her perception of her mother has changed, but this afternoon Aarika's perception of her father will change. I have kept this secret for too long," he concluded. "Sharon was brave enough to risk her relationship with her daughter by allowing her to come here and be with us. I can do no less."

Approaching footsteps stilled their talk. Poppy entered the room cautiously, her eyes red and her face puffy. When Bianca stood up to greet her, Poppy ran into her arms.

"There, there," cooed Bianca, in Italian, letting Poppy cry and snivel on her shoulder.

"How could she not tell me?" sniffed Poppy, pulling away so she could swipe at her nose with a Kleenex. "All these years and I never knew I had another sister who died before me. Did my mother think I'd hate her if I knew the truth?"

Marco brought a chair out of the kitchen and placed it next to Dolphus while Bianca motioned for Poppy to sit down next to her on the sofa. A movement near the driveway drew their attention outside. They saw Aarika ambling along the stone-and-mortar wall separating the grounds of the fattoria from the road. She stopped, opened her purse, took a small object out of it, and held it to her lips. Then, putting it back, she slung her purse over her shoulder and continued toward the house, her arms hanging limply at her sides.

"Poppy, this revelation hasn't affected your feelings for Aarika, has it?" asked Dolphus urgently, as Aarika drew near. "I hope you will be able to erase the image from your mind of her smothering your sister Babsi."

Poppy stared at Dolphus, her eyes still watery. "That image never entered my mind. Will *you* ever be able to erase it from yours?"

Aarika entered the living room just then, and scanning the sober faces gathered around she said, "What's going on?"

"It's time to continue where we left off this morning," replied Dolphus.

"I thought we were done talking," said Aarika.

"I asked Marco to come back this afternoon so we could resume our conversation." Dolphus nodded toward Bianca. "And Bianca was kind enough to come with him to provide maternal support."

Aarika lashed out at Poppy as though she assumed it was she who wanted to talk some more. "If you have a problem with our sister's death, Poppy, we can talk about it later. I've had enough for one day."

Indignant, Poppy crossed her arms. "There you go, Aarika, jumping to conclusions again. I have no idea what your grandfather wants to discuss."

Dolphus pointed at an empty spot on the sofa next to Bianca. "Sit down, Aarika," he ordered. "I know this morning was difficult, but we must press on so that no stones are left unturned."

After Aarika was comfortably seated, Dolphus barreled ahead. "As you can imagine, Babsi's death was just the beginning of problems for our family." Then, clearing his throat, he asked Aarika point-blank, "What do you remember of your mother following Babsi's death?"

Apparently taken aback by the question, Aarika took a few moments to reply. "Very little," she said, finally. "Other than in hindsight, I felt like she acted as though she wanted nothing to do with me. Of course, Opa, I lived with you and Oma after Babsi died, not with her."

Dolphus put his hands together as if in prayer. "But, do you recall your mother's visits to see you?"

Aarika squirmed.

"You were three years old, Aarika. You remember other things, but you don't remember your mother's attempts to reach out to you?"

"What's your point, Opa?"

"Before we go on to discuss your father, I simply want to establish the fact that your mother tried to repair her relationship with you. So, I'll ask you again: Do you recall your mother's visits to the farm?"

"Somewhat."

"And?"

"I remember that whenever she picked me up she would stiffen and put me back down. It seemed like she couldn't stand being around me. She never stayed very long."

Dolphus tried to suggest to Aarika that the negative impression she had of Sharon's visits might all be in her mind, but she was convinced otherwise.

"Why are you defending her, Opa?" she asked. "You know very well she abandoned me because she was selfish, weak, and unfit to be a mother."

Poppy interrupted her. "Wait a minute, Aarika. You forget this is my mother we're talking about too. She's not selfish. As for being weak, what do you expect? I always wondered why Mom was so emotionally detached at times, and so tight-lipped about her past, as though she never had one. I mean, have any of you thought of the effect Babsi's death had on her?"

Bianca, sensing the tension between the sisters, placed a hand on each girl's knee and squeezed. Immediately, they stopped squabbling.

"Your father?" asked Dolphus, his voice husky. "What do you remember of him, Aarika?"

Aarika hedged, her grandfather's unusual request again catching her off-guard. With slow deliberation she said, "He was big . . . and strong. He was very handsome and very quiet."

"What do you mean by 'strong,' Aarika?"

"I remember him working on the farm: digging, driving tractors, cleaning stalls. I remember he liked to fish and hunt too."

"Yes," Dolphus agreed, a faraway look in his eyes. "That he did."

As an afterthought, Aarika said, "He was much taller than you, Opa."

"Yes, I sometimes forget what a large, strong man Conrad was." Dolphus closed his eyes and mumbled, "How unfortunate my son's soul was not equal to that strength."

"Sometimes," continued Aarika, not catching her grandfather's last comment, "he would read to me before I went to bed. My favorite book was *Der Struwwelpeter*, the story of '*Die Geschichte vom fliegenden Robert.*'"

Dolphus opened his eyes. "Ah! 'The Story of the Flying Robert.' Your grandmother used to read that story to your father when he was a little boy. It was his favorite also." Cryptically, he asked Aarika if she'd ever suspected that all was not as it seemed with her father despite her positive memories of him.

"How so?"

"Your mother wore her heart on her sleeve," he explained. "Sharon was who she appeared to be, whatever you may think of her. Your father, on the other hand, was—as you said—quiet. Perhaps you cherish the times he read to you because he barely spoke otherwise. Perhaps you overcompensated for your mother's rejection by assigning attributes to your father that weren't, well, realistic. Your father was strong in his body, but his mind was . . . much like Flying Robert in *Der Struwwelpeter*. Like Robert, Conrad chose to go out into a terrible storm rather than stay safe and secure with his family, and like Robert, he paid for his poor decision when the wind caught his umbrella and carried him away to his destruction."

"You're speaking in riddles, Opa."

Marco's rapid-fire translating skills had been utilized throughout the conversation—some German here, some English and Italian there. But now, no one needed an interpreter to understand that Dolphus was beginning to break emotionally as he struggled to speak.

"Your father didn't die because he was cleaning his gun, Aarika. We let you think it was an accident because we wanted to spare you any more sorrow than you had already suffered. I don't know why I thought telling you a falsehood would be better than the truth. I was wrong to think so. You would have found out eventually, so I decided it would be preferable for you to hear it from me first." Dolphus took a deep breath. "Your father killed himself, Aarika."

Aarika shook her head angrily. "That's not true. He couldn't have. *Vater* had you and Oma. He had me. Why would he take his own life? It doesn't make any sense."

"I found him in the barn . . ."

Aarika wouldn't let her grandfather finish his sentence. "You don't know that it was suicide," she said. "Someone who had a drug vendetta against him could have shot him and made it look like a suicide, or maybe Father really was cleaning his gun like you always said he was."

"He left a note." Dolphus leaned forward and pulled his billfold out of his back pocket. Slowly, he opened it and gently removed a yellowed square of paper. In painstaking German, he read: "*Since Babsi died, my life is unbearable. In truth, I am to blame. I was the one who insisted we go out that night and leave the girls alone. The stares and the rumors and whispers in town follow me everywhere. No one will hire me. I have lost hope that I will ever be free of the demon in me that cannot say 'no' to my addictions. My marriage is over and I am left a failure: as a father, a husband, and a son. It is better that I go now and spare all of you my shame. Vater and Mutter, I know you will take good care of Aarika. Please always love her for me, and if you can, forgive me."*

Aarika sat in shock as Marco, in hushed tones, interpreted the letter for Poppy and Bianca. Dolphus didn't look up; he simply stared at the piece of paper in his hands, his lower lip trembling. After several moments, he refolded the letter, placed it back into his wallet, and retrieved a clean handkerchief from his pocket to wipe his eyes and blow his nose.

A considerable amount of time passed before anyone attempted to speak. Poppy ventured the first question. "Were my mother and Conrad still married when he died?" she asked.

Dolphus stared intently at Poppy until she blurted, "Yes, I know my mother was pregnant with me when she left Germany, Dolphus. Apparently my dad was an acquaintance of hers at the university, where he was a summer student."

Directing his reply to both Poppy and Aarika, Dolphus nodded. "It is not for me to judge Sharon or her relationships at the time of the breakdown of her marriage to my son. I will say this: we were all stunned by the news of another pregnancy. Some ridiculed her for it. Many condemned her. But then," Dolphus held his palm toward Poppy and smiled weakly, "you were the result, so what did they know?"

"As far as Sharon and Conrad's marriage," he continued, "Sharon had already returned to America and started divorce proceedings. To her credit, she was determined to get clean, especially when she found out she was pregnant with Poppy. She told us that she wanted to start an entirely new drug-free life and that as long as she was with Conrad she didn't believe it was possible. Knowing the extent of my son's addictions and the depth of his depression, perhaps she was right. Several days before Conrad shot himself, he received documentation that the divorce had been finalized. A letter from Sharon followed in which she confessed to being tormented by guilt for Babsi's death. She claimed she 'deserved to lose Aarika' as judgment for her 'inexcusable neglect.' In order to attain a quick divorce, Sharon granted Conrad full custody of Aarika. There was no custody battle between them."

Aarika, her hands clenched into fists, hissed, "What was my mother's reaction to the news of *Vater's* death?"

"We never heard from Sharon again," said Dolphus. "That is, until recently when she called about Poppy coming to Italy. Your grandmother and I should have taken the iniative to contact her, but we allowed our grief and anger to obliterate everything from our son's past. Everything of course, but you, Aarika. We wrongly assumed that it would be better to protect you from knowing the status of your mother's life. We didn't bother to find out what happened to the baby Sharon was carrying when she left Germany. We didn't care whether or not she had remarried. After all, if Sharon had indeed conquered her demons and was a happily married wife and mother, we feared it would only pour salt into our wounds. I am ashamed to say, we didn't even know if Sharon was still alive or not, until I received her call. The truth is, after speaking with her, I actually found myself happy and thankful that she had survived what Conrad could not. If only my wife could have received that assurance before she died."

Her face pale, Poppy rose from the sofa and announced

she was retiring to the casala. "I need my space," she said. "So, if you don't mind, I'd prefer to be left alone the rest of the day."

When Poppy was gone, Aarika stood to her feet. Unsteadily, she took a step toward Marco, reaching for his elbow for support. "Would you take me somewhere?" she asked. "Anywhere. I just need to get away from here for awhile."

"I understand," said Dolphus, giving Marco his approval to assist Aarika.

Marco conferred with Bianca and then turned to Aarika. "I have to take Bianca home. She has invited you to come with her."

"Would she mind if I spent the night? I could pack quickly."

Again, Marco spoke first with Dolphus and then Bianca. As soon as Aarika heard Bianca say, "*Si, si,*" she excused herself and went to her room while Marco and Bianca prepared to leave.

Dolphus, looking exhausted, remained seated in his chair. "I am greatly indebted to both of you," he said. "Your translations, Marco, helped to eliminate any confusion or misunderstanding that could have arisen today. And, Bianca, I know the girls were calmed by your presence."

Pausing to check the time on his wristwatch, Dolphus added, "No doubt, Domenico will be here soon to deliver dinner. I hope to be sequestered in my room before he arrives. Would you do me one last favor, Marco, and ask him to leave the meal in the refrigerator in the casala? Perhaps, if our appetite returns, we can eat it later. Also, would you explain to Domenico what has transpired? He deserves to know why we are behaving so rudely as not to eat dinner with him tonight, after all the work he has taken to prepare it."

"*Naturalmente,*" said Marco.

"And Marco?"

"*Si?*"

"Conrad used my gun to kill himself." Dolphus blinked, as though he had been daydreaming and was just waking up. Noting the surprise on Marco's face, he hurried to add, "But, that's a different story for another time."

· 13 ·

Tempest Dreams

From his bedroom overlooking Monte Montignoso's vineyards, Dolphus heard Domenico pull up in his car and cart some food into the casala. He was tempted to intercept him to ask if they could sit down and talk for a while, but he was still struggling to maintain his composure. Besides, what purpose would it serve? Hearing Domenico leave the casala a few moments later and go back to his car, Dolphus realized he had other reasons for avoiding his Italian host. Usually, Domenico never talked of the war. But this summer he had already said several things that had raised red flags.

On Dolphus's very first day in Tuscany, Domenico had said, "You were on Monte Montignoso during the war, Dolphus. Of course, I doubt you would have even noticed this tree we're sitting under when you were here. It is ten times the size now as it was then. My grandfather planted it when my father was a young man. When I was a little boy I used to play in it for hours on end. It seemed huge at the time, but then it was surely no more than fifteen or twenty feet tall."

Domenico's comments had been innocuous enough. There was no way he could have known about Dolphus's experiences on the mountain so long ago. How could he? Aside from other German soldiers and a couple of women trying to escape when his battalion stormed the hill, Dolphus hadn't seen a living soul anywhere. Still, the conversation had made Dolphus uneasy.

Then, just the other day, Domenico had said, "See that house below us with the swimming pool, Dolphus? It was a pile of rubble fifty years ago, but Luca Gabrelli has done a fine job of restoring it. His grandmother was killed here. But, oh, forgive me. I probably shouldn't speak of such things."

That comment had hit much closer to home. Domenico knew of an old woman who had been killed on the mountain near the fattoria during the war? What if Domenico suspected something? What if, in reality, Domenico was hoping to pry personal information from him? With the past already weighing heavily enough on his mind, Dolphus watched with relief as Domenico drove away. Then, even though it was only six o'clock, he took off of his outer clothing and crawled into bed.

Too hot to suffer even a sheet over him, Dolphus laid exposed on top of the mattress, staring up at the antiquated whorls in the plastered ceiling above him until, eventually, he dozed off. As a bank of clouds rolled in off the Ligurian Sea and accumulated along the crest of the Carraras, he fell into an abysmal sleep, a prisoner in a dream of his own making.

The images began innocently enough: carefree days fishing the River Inn as a child followed by pre-war vignettes of idyllic family dinners on the farm, his older sisters and their husbands sharing their new babies and babbling toddlers with doting grandparents. He could see his parents, still relatively young, healthy, and strong, standing outside his school smiling, telling him how proud they were of his excellent grades. But then the sedate scenes morphed into a surreal montage of jarring recollections extracted from Passau, Vienna, and Italy.

"Mater, don't cry. Vienna isn't far." Dolphus stood at the Passau train station saying good-bye to his weeping parents. "I'll be safe with Ralf. I'm part of the Wehrmacht now. I must do my duty." Tearing himself away from his mother, he boarded the train departing for Austria and leaned out the window to wave a final farewell to them. "I'll write!" he yelled. "And I'll be home before you know it!"

On the train, Dolphus opened his satchel and pulled out a gun. It was a C96 semi-automatic "Broomhandle" Mauser; a gift from Ralf. His cousin had used it to kill Russians on the Eastern Front. Ralf's voice flooded his brain: "Don't just sit there, Dolphus. You need to train in a fraction of the time it usually takes recruits to prepare for battle."

Dolphus gazed at the other passengers in the railcar. Ralf was nowhere to be seen. "But Ralf," he called out, "I've never used a handgun. I'm a farmer. I'm only familiar with rifles."

An invisible hand—he knew it was Ralf's—grasped his. It forced both his hands around the handle of the gun. Panicking at his loss of control, Dolphus fought against the force, but it was futile. He watched in horror as he raised the gun and pointed it at a young mother sitting across the aisle from him. He felt his finger place pressure on the trigger. He closed his eyes. The explosion in his ears rocked him, and then . . .

He was with Sabine in Old Vienna, walking in circles. She looked so beautiful, so captivating, he wanted to duck into every café, every nook and crevice with her to spend eternity. But he could barely speak to her. She was a complete stranger. So he continued going round and round the city's inner ring with her until, suddenly, he stumbled and fell. Sabine reached for his hand.

When he stood up, he looked down to see that he had tripped over, not one, but five lifeless bodies.

"They're dead," whispered Sabine.

Dolphus whipped out the gun Ralf had given him. "We'll see," he said.

Bending over, he gently turned over the first body. It was a woman whose cherry-red lips, bleached hair, and sequined gown he vaguely remembered. Her cold eyes confirmed she had no life in her.

The next two bodies were women as well. One was old; the other was young. Their dark looks indicated they were foreign born. With the tips of two fingers, he tenderly closed their sightless eyes.

The fourth body was a male lying face down in a pool of blood. Seizing him by the shoulder, he lifted the man partially off the ground and when he recognized who it was, he let out a scream. It was the victory shout of a warrior heard at the end of a bloody battle in which only two opponents are left facing each other to the death. Clenching his jaw, he let the body drop back to the ground with a thud.

Reaching for the fifth and last body, Dolphus froze. There was something painfully familiar about the young man whose face was obscured from him. The sandy hair. The smell of hay and earth and thwarted dreams. Suddenly, the gun fell from Dolphus's grip. It rolled crazily across the man's abdomen and into his dead hand, outstretched at his side.

Dolphus felt Sabine's hands on his shoulders, dragging him away from the dead bodies.

"Run," she said. "You must get as far away from here as you can, Dolphus. You could be next."

"Where can I run to?" he asked. "The world will be my prison."

"I'll tell you of a place," she replied. "But not yet. First you have to hide. Then you have to find me again."

"But my gun! I have to get it back before it kills someone else!"

Writhing on top of his sheets, Dolphus shouted, "My gun! Where is it? Where's my gun?" His desperate cries fell flat in the dark, empty fattoria.

Lightning bolts began sizzling across the black sky, followed by great claps of thunder that echoed off the marbled peaks, roaring down along the foothills until they shook everything in their path. Dolphus sat bolt upright in bed, half-asleep and drenched in sweat. His eyes darted wildly about the shadowed room, but all he remembered seeing after the storm passed was the last image in his dream. That of a young man holding the gun Ralf had given him in his dead hand, and Sabine screaming at him to run.

Dolphus wasn't the only Geller tormented by dreams that evening. A few miles away in Bianca's villa, his granddaughter suffered her own nightmares. It came as no surprise to Bianca, who had always believed certain Tuscan storms have a unique smell associated with them—a mingling of fish and earth and air, laced with the primeval groaning of mountains and sea—that adversely affect people's dreams. Sometimes, she said, the tempests would cause animals to react in a bizarre fashion. Dogs cowered and howled, cats chased their tails, and rabbits danced on their hind legs.

Regardless, Aarika made such a commotion during the night, Bianca had to call Marco to come to her aid. By the time Marco arrived, however—about eleven to be precise—the crisis was over. All that was left for the three of them to do was sit down at the kitchen table and discuss what happened while Bianca served up some warm spiced milk and biscotti.

After a good deal of encouragement, Aarika hesitantly recounted her nightmare. It started, she explained, with her as a child happily playing with dolls on her grandparents' farm. Seconds later, the dolls' faces turned into people she knew. The face of one, which she recognized as her mother, was grotesque. Its skin had petrified, its lips were coated with blood and its eyes stared back at her, infinitely empty. Terror-stricken, she hurled the doll as hard as she could against the nearest wall, but when she did, its head separated from its body and began bouncing round and round the room. The lips on the doll moved the entire time, shouting accusations at her: "Murderer! Child Killer!"

Aarika seized the doll's head and squeezed it to get it to stop, but to her horror the eyes popped out of their sockets. Not only did it not silence her mother's voice, but the eyeballs—which looked like two marble-sized hail stones—were now bouncing on the floor along with the head. Using her hand in defense, she batted at them until finally the eyeballs flew up into what should have been the ceiling, but in her dream was an opening into the night sky. The eyes disappeared into, and then mingled with, the stars. Shocked, Aarika stared at the vast Milky Way, trying to determine which two among the billions and billions of stars might be her mother's eyes still watching and condemning her.

Then, said Aarika, "I heard a child call my name. I looked down near my feet and saw that one of the other dolls had turned into Babsi. At first she jabbered and babbled at me incoherently, but within minutes she was crying so frantically she began choking. In my dream, as Babsi gasped for air, I thought I could resuscitate her."

Aarika described how she sprang into action, pulling the baby doll's face toward her so that she could breathe life into its mouth. But when Babsi's cries stopped altogether, she placed both her palms on her chest and pressed so hard the doll shattered into pieces. Frantically, she tried to pick up her sister's toes, legs, fingers, nose, ears, and other body parts, but no sooner would she gather them together than they would fly out of her hands in different directions until it was clear she would have to hunt throughout the cluttered room to find them.

"I thought surely," said Aarika, "that all I would have to do is retrieve each of my baby sister's dismembered parts, put them back together, and Babsi would be alive again. Yet the more I dug and scratched under tables and through drawers and cupboards, the more I realized it was hopeless."

Aarika paused, trembling from the effort to recall her dream. Dark circles tainted the crescent of skin beneath her eyes. Bianca prepared another cup of warm milk, and after handing it to Aarika, she admonished her to continue.

Holding the warm cup in both her hands, Aarika took a deep breath and said, "Another doll on top of the dresser called out to me. I recognized her as my grandmother. 'What about me?' she cried. 'Why do you care what your mother thinks? I loved you as much as any mother could have loved a daughter.' Then she shouted, 'Hurry to the barn, Aarika! Your father can still be saved if you get there in time. Tell him not to do it! Conrad won't listen to Opa and I, but maybe he'll listen to you!'

"I raced to the barn as fast as I could, but in my dream I was getting nowhere. Just when I felt like I would collapse from the effort, I saw the barn's great double doors open, and there, right in front of me, was my father holding a gun to his head. In his other hand, he held an envelope. He looked me straight in the eye and said, 'Now you know the truth, Aarika. Your mother wants to start a new life without us. She's found someone else and is pregnant with his child.' Then he threw the envelope at me. 'I've failed everybody, including myself. Life is no longer worth living. I'm not even worth remembering, Aarika. I was never meant to be.'

"Before I could respond, there was an explosion and he was dead, sprawled sideways on the barn's dirt floor, blood streaming out of the side of his head. One moment I was frozen, unable to move, and the next I was kneeling over his body, my eyes closed, screaming for help. After what seemed like ages, I opened my eyes. My father's body had disappeared, and in its place was a small pile of gray ash."

The kitchen fell quiet. Aarika set her empty cup down on the table. "The last thing I remember," she said, "was turning around and seeing Poppy standing in the doorway of the barn. I was filled with such rage when I saw her, I stooped down and picked up the gun my father had used to kill himself. I pointed it at her and screamed, 'You and my mother are the reason my father killed himself!' But when I looked into Poppy's eyes, I couldn't pull the trigger."

"And that was the end of your dream?" asked Bianca.

A groan escaped from Aarika's throat. "When I couldn't shoot Poppy, I turned the gun on myself."

Clicking her tongue on the roof of her mouth, Bianca hurried to soothe Aarika. "That would explain your panic before waking up."

Aarika embraced Bianca. "I'm so sorry if I hurt you when you came into my room," she sobbed. "I was still half-dreaming and didn't know it was you, Bianca. I thought you were Poppy, trying to wrestle the gun from me."

Marco, who had been following Aarika's account of her dream as he translated, looked startled. "Bianca, are you hurt?" he asked.

Dismissing his concern, Bianca said, "I've had far worse things happen in my life than a young girl slapping me in the face because she's trapped in the middle of a nightmare." Then she held Aarika out at arm's length. "Back to bed with you now, child," she said in Italian. "You need your rest."

Aarika protested. "I'm not tired. Besides, I'm afraid to go back to sleep."

"There's nothing to fear any longer, I promise you. The worst is over." Guiding Aarika into the bedroom, with Marco at her elbow, Bianca tucked her into bed. "I've prayed a blessing over your room. You'll sleep fine now," she told her, before switching off the light and stepping into the hallway. "*Buonanotte.*"

"*Gute Nacht,*" replied Aarika.

Marco lingered a moment, and as he finished interpreting Bianca's final words to Aarika, she reached for Marco's hands. "*Danke,* Marco," she said. "Please don't go yet. I feel so safe with you here."

Lowering himself on one knee so he could see Aarika better in the darkened room, Marco whispered, "You need to sleep, Aarika. I'll do my best to keep you safe. I promise you."

Aarika squeezed his hand, like a child might cling to a parent. "I guess I'm not as strong as I thought I was. I wish I could approach life like you do, Marco, and not worry so much about what's been and what will be."

"None of us are as strong as we think we are," said Marco. "That's why we need each other. And believe me, everyone worries about what's been and what will be, whether we act like it or not. Good night, Aarika. Sleep well."

With that, Marco rose to his feet, closed the bedroom door and returned to the kitchen. He drank the rest of his spiced milk and then checked his watch. "Sorry," he apologized, "but I have to go soon, Bianca. Are you sure you're okay?"

"I'll be fine," she replied. "I probably shouldn't have bothered you tonight, Marco, but I was afraid Aarika might hurt herself. I was worried I wouldn't be strong enough to stop her."

"What exactly did she do, if I might ask?"

"Well, there was a lot of groaning and moaning coming from the bedroom at first. I thought it was harmless, just her talking in her sleep. But I knew something was wrong when she began screaming. Even then, I hesitated going in to check on her. But soon other strange noises followed, so I crept into her room and saw her sitting up in bed, her eyes wide open, and her hands flailing wildly in the air. I tried to calm her, but her shrieking intensified and she began wrestling with me. That's when I tore myself loose from her and called you."

"Do you think . . . ?"

"Yes," said Bianca. "I think in her dream, she had just shot herself."

Marco shook his head.

"It's tragic, I know. My heart breaks for her."

"It's a catastrophe," said Marco, rising from the table and making his way to the kitchen door. "And to think that their stay here is barely half-over! The Gellers and Poppy leave to go back home on the fifteenth of September. The first of September isn't even till next Saturday. Considering today's events, I fear what the second half of their holiday will bring."

"No need to think the worst, Marco. But it is strange that

all three of them seem to be confronting their demons here in Italy this summer, no?" asked Bianca.

"What demon is Dolphus confronting? None of this was news to him. Unlike Poppy and Aarika, he knew about Babsi's and Conrad's deaths and why Sharon went back to America."

"Yes, but Dolphus kept these things a secret all these years and only today has he shared them. I suspect now that these secrets have been exposed, others will follow."

"Secrets? Like what?"

"I'm not sure yet," replied Bianca, touching the tip of her nose with her index finger. "I'm just convinced there are more. Not only that, but I sense we may play a role in the Gellers' deliverance and reconciliation. Especially Domenico."

"Why Domenico?"

"In addition to being a great host, he is also a superb cook. You would be wrong, Marco, to assume the art of cooking has little to do with people. Domenico knows how to take any ingredients available to him and create a masterpiece. He has the patience to wait until the right time to remove a dish from the oven, or a pot from the stove. He understands the science of balance and precision. Domenico knows exactly what to do with food—and people—and he'll persevere until the job is complete. You'll see."

"For all our sakes," Marco replied, "I hope you're right, Bianca."

$$\cdot\ 14\ \cdot$$

The View from
the Tree and the Shed

"So that's what happened," said Marco, concluding his recap of the last few days with a swat at a mosquito rooting through the hairs on his forearm.

He and Domenico were in the midst of a leisurely outdoor breakfast at the Sacchelli's primary residence in Strettoia at the foot of Monte Montignoso. Mariella was busy inside the house preparing a *café doppio*—double espresso—for each of them, while Rina, her ninety-five-year-old mother who lived with them, sat nearby in the warm sunshine mending one of Domenico's shirts. It was early Thursday morning and no one was in a hurry to do anything, as the Gellers had been encouraged to spend at least one quiet day by themselves on the mountain recuperating from their traumatizing revelations.

"Are you sure you've told me everything?" asked Domenico, reaching into his pocket and handing Marco a tube of bug repellant.

Marco slathered the smelly stuff on his exposed skin while mentally ticking off the highlights of his story. There was the dinner at Bianca's Monday night; the phone call Poppy made to her mother, which had set everything off; Dolphus's confession about his son's dysfunctional life and ultimate suicide; Poppy's reaction; and the dream that Aarika had shared at Bianca's.

"Yes, that's everything, Domenico," he concluded. "Aarika is back at the fattoria with Poppy now, though neither of them is talking much about what happened."

Domenico rubbed a clove of garlic on a piece of day-old bread and held it up to his mouth. "People handle tragedies in their own way, but it will take time. So, what is your opinion of all this, Marco?"

"*Veramente*, I've never seen a family with so many problems."

"Problems are not the domain of the Gellers alone. Every family has skeletons somewhere—even ours . . . even yours."

Not sure what his cousin was insinuating, Marco said, "Whatever skeletons our families may have, they remain buried where they belong. What is the point of digging them up?"

"Perhaps people unearth old bones because they feel there was not a proper burial for them in the first place."

Marco conceded it was a good point. "But," he said, "Aarika's not dealing with it very well. I suppose because she's a woman, it will take her a long time to get over it."

Looking up from her mending, Rina clicked her tongue. "What do you mean, Marco?"

"I mean women can't seem to let things rest."

Rina dropped her mending on her lap. "*Ah, miserabile!*" she exclaimed. "Men can be so ignorant of a woman's heart."

Mariella materialized in their midst with a platter loaded with fruit, cheese, and the double espressos. She had caught the last bit of their conversation. "For Aarika, life is *molto capriccioso,*" she said. "Very unpredictable. As a result, she has built strong walls around herself. It is sad, no?"

"*Si,*" agreed Rina, shifting her body around so she could better hear what was being said. "Also very *tipico.*"

Marco wondered what he was missing in Rina's reasoning. "Typical?'"

Rina, likewise, acted surprised that Marco would have to ask what she meant. She looked at her daughter for help in clarifying.

"You see," explained Mariella, "when someone is burdened with guilt, they struggle with how they can live with themselves. First, they try to justify what they've done, and if they can't do that, they blame someone else, or pretend nothing is wrong, or sabotage their own lives by making others hate them as they hate themselves."

"But Aarika was only three-years-old when Babsi died," said Marco. "Surely, she can't blame herself for her sister's death?"

"You and I see it that way," replied Mariella, "but it doesn't erase the reality of Babsi's death and Aarika's implication in it. When someone's life is forfeit, or changed forever because of one's actions—no matter how innocent or unintentional the case may be—it is only natural to blame oneself."

Domenico raised his finger in the air. "Just think, Marco, if you were in a car accident and a child was killed. Even if you weren't responsible for the collision, how would you feel?"

"I concede it might be natural for Aarika to blame herself," Marco sighed, "but it happened years ago. Today is today. There must be some way she can, I don't know, come to terms with it."

"Your German girl is running away from her past," said

Rina. "With a bit of love and lots of forgiveness, she will move on eventually."

"Aarika is not 'my girl,'" sputtered Marco.

"Of course not," chuckled Rina, returning to her stitching.

"Oh, of course not," twittered Mariella.

"Well, you and Aarika *have* known each other a long time, Marco," said Domenico.

"You call being acquainted as children one summer many years ago 'knowing each other a long time'?" asked Marco.

Domenico brushed aside such reasoning. "Regardless," he said, "you share common ground with Aarika in other areas, Marco. You've lost two of your grandparents, one of your cousins, and that friend of yours who drowned when you were in elementary school. What was his name?"

"Stefano Santini."

"Ah, yes. Sweet child," sighed Domenico. "Very tragic. See Marco? You understand what it is to grieve. Aarika was also raised as an only child, like you. It is not easy being an only child. Great responsibilities rest on your shoulders."

"What is your point?" asked Marco.

"Our point is," said Domenico, including Mariella and Rina in his reply, "that you are in a unique position to help Aarika and perhaps impact her future while she's here. That's all we're saying."

Picqued, Marco held his hands up as a signal that everyone's point was taken. In truth, he wanted no more talk of Aarika lest they guess what his real feelings were for her. Assuming an ambivalent posture, he changed the subject. "So, what about our current dilemma with the Gellers?"

"Considering the events of yesterday and last night," said Domenico, "we should let them decide how busy they want to be this week and take our cues from them. And as far as the possibilities in terms of sightseeing, perhaps you could take them on some short day trips to nearby areas. Nothing too extended or tiring, I wouldn't think."

"They might enjoy touring Pietrasanta," suggested Mariella. "The art school and shops there are lovely."

Domenico concurred. "Excellent idea, *mia cara*. I have some work to do on the casala tomorrow. Marco, why don't you meet me there at nine o'clock and we'll talk to Dolphus and the girls and verify what they would like to do."

"*Certamente*." Marco hastily checked the time on his mobile and then thrust it back in his pocket. Pushing his chair back away from the table, he said, "I must go. I have an errand to run for my parents." Before heading to his car, he leaned down low to kiss Rina and Mariella good-bye.

Domenico followed Marco to the driveway. Placing his hands on the car door, after Marco was seat-belted in, he said, "I keep forgetting to tell you something, Marco. Has Aarika told you how her grandmother died?"

"No. Why?"

"According to Dolphus, Aarika was very close to her grandmother. Evidently, Mrs. Geller died of cancer. Very aggressive. Colon cancer, I believe. Aarika dropped out of school to care for her the last year of her life. I only tell you, Marco, because of what you saw and heard the other day with the Gellers. Perhaps it will provide you with another piece of the puzzle to Aarika's life."

"Yes, it does," admitted Marco, moved with compassion for Aarika. The fact that she had sacrificed her own education to care for her grandmother spoke volumes about her character, and he found himself not being surprised that she had not spoken about it to him.

Stepping away from the car, Domenico held his finger

to his forehead in a farewell salute. "I should have told you before, Marco. It just kept slipping my mind."

"I'm glad you remembered."

"So am I. *A domani*, Marco."

Starting the car, Marco proceeded to back out of the Sacchellis' driveway. He could barely keep his emotions in check, for with absolute certainty—within the span of just the last twelve hours—he had come to accept the fact that he was in love with Aarika Geller. *Caro Dio!* There were so many obstacles and unknowns and loose ends in their relationship, how was it possible they could ever come together?

Yet, despite the apprehension that was part and parcel of his affection for Aarika, the pull he felt toward her was irrationally, irrevocably real. It was relentless and inescapable, like the gravitational lure of the moon on the earth's tides. Contradictions clawed at his mind and toyed with his heart. He felt hopeful and hopeless at the same time. Resolute and terrified.

This, he thought, his stomach doing a flip, *must be what true love feels like.*

Domenico woke at four thirty the next morning. Though it was the middle of the night, and despite every window in their bedroom being open and the ceiling fan operating at full speed, there was no relief from the heat. Knowing sleep was impossible, he climbed the stairs down to the kitchen, flipped the switch on the box fan wedged into the windowsill, and made himself a cup of espresso. Tuning his radio to a station broadcast out of Pisa, he heard the weatherman predict it would be the hottest day of the year yet, with temperatures possibly reaching 104 degrees. The threat of thunderstorms was also forecast, lasting from late morning through the evening hours. At six o'clock, Domenico ventured outdoors, where a thermometer nailed to his garage read eighty-six degrees. An hour later, itching to do something constructive before the heat made physical labor impossible, Domenico decided to drive up the mountain to the casala.

Of course, he realized he would have to be careful not to wake anyone up in the fattoria. He figured he would keep a low profile by parking his car near his lower vineyard, where he could check on the status of the vines and the soil and the retaining walls. Surely, when he was done with all that, it would be close to the time Marco was supposed to show up.

By eight thirty, however, he was finished, and with time to kill he decided to hike up to the shed next to the casala to check on supplies. He didn't realize how tired he was until he stepped inside the ramshackle structure, where it was dark and refreshingly cool. Spying some sacks of grass seed stacked in the corner, he deemed it the perfect spot for a nap, and seconds after nestling down in them, he was snoring.

He was five years old again, perched on a branch of the chestnut tree overlooking the fattoria. Even as he dreamed, he realized this dream was a continuation of the one he'd had a few weeks ago. In fact, it picked up where the last one had left off. From his vantage point up in the tree, he could see his father, mother, and their neighbor, Signora Gabrelli, frantically deliberating what to do as German troops approached. Every few seconds, Orazio, his father, would glance up at him with his finger to his lips and motion for him to climb higher.

Domenico obeyed, scaling several more branches until he was well hidden below the crown of the tree. He could hear the rumble of hundreds of German tanks, boots, and motorcycles getting ever closer. Sporadic gunfire popped and echoed all around him. Through scattered openings in the leaves, he could see large patches of sweat soaking through the back and armpits of his father's shirt. He watched the color drain from his mother's face as her husband insisted they must separate. Then, lurching forward, Orazio made an executive decision. At his command, Elvira got on the other side of Signora Gabrelli and together they lifted the old woman under her arms and carried her behind the house. Mystified, Domenico watched the three of them escaping through the low-lying foliage bordering the forested, rock-strewn hillside.

Fearing they had left him behind by himself, Domenico panicked. He debated climbing down from the tree to follow his parents, but his father had explicitly ordered him to stay where he was. As he struggled with what he should do, a military vehicle backfired near their vineyard. Domenico shut his eyes, and wrapping his arms tighter around the branch he was stretched out on, he clung to it for dear life.

"*Pater noster, qui es in caelis, sanctificetur nomen tuum,*" he repeated over and over to himself. His mind was so engrossed in reciting the Lord's Prayer, the only prayer he knew by heart, he saw and heard nothing until a touch on his back made him jump. Before he could turn to see who it was, he felt an arm encase him. A rough hand covered his mouth. In his ear, his father whispered, "Do not move, son."

Just then, two motorcycles, enveloped in a cloud of gray dust, came to a screeching halt behind the wall separating the driveway from the Sacchellis' home. The riders disembarked before their kickstands were fully deployed. Stealthily, they crouched down and then scurried along the wall to get as close to the fattoria as possible. They were so near the tree now, Domenico could have dropped a chestnut and hit them.

"*Dieses haus. Das ist gut,*" grunted one of the soldiers, pointing to the house. He removed his helmet, placed it on the butt of his rifle, and lifted it slowly over the top of the wall. When no one shot at it, he tossed it on the ground next to his motorcycle. The other soldier threw off his helmet too, both of them revealing heads full of damp light-colored hair and foreheads glistening with perspiration. Domenico was struck by the similarities between the two men, as though they could be brothers.

The taller of the two shouted to his companion, "Dolphus! Check the perimeter. I'll search the houses."

Strangely enough, although the command was spoken in German, Domenico, in his dream, understood what was being said. Terror caused his blood to pump through his veins like firing pistons. With the added weight of his father pressing against him, his breathing became more labored. Not only was he worried he would involuntarily gasp for air and thus draw attention to themselves, he also realized that beads of sweat from his father's overheated body were dripping onto the ground below the tree. Undoubtedly, if one of the Germans came and stood directly beneath them, they would be discovered.

Meanwhile, the taller German was still hunkered down near his motorcycle. He signaled to some additional troops who had paused at the end of the driveway, motioning for them to continue their ascent and commandeer other homes further up the mountain. Then, his gun drawn, he leaped over the wall and ran in a zigzag fashion toward the fatto-ria. Using great caution, he entered through the kitchen door, which had been left wide open. Five minutes later he emerged, a hunk of Elvira's still-warm bread sticking out of his mouth. Domenico swallowed hard. He was keenly aware that the freshness of the bread had betrayed the fact that the owners of the house had either just fled or were hiding nearby.

Creeping stealthily along the exterior of the house, the soldier paused before darting toward the shed. Once there, with his back against the wall and his pistol raised, he edged his way along until he was positioned next to the door. Then, lightning fast, he swung around and kicked it open.

Knowing the soldier would not find anyone there, Domenico switched his attention to the soldier called Dolphus, who was in the process of combing the rugged hillside behind the house. Through an opening in the leaves the size of a man's shoe, he could see that the soldier's gun was drawn as he searched through the bushy undergrowth, and that he was also getting dangerously close to where he guessed his mother and Signora Gabrelli were hiding.

Suddenly, the other German stepped back outside the shed, his gun lowered. "Dolphus!" he yelled. "Both buildings are clear." Turning his gaze in the direction of the chestnut tree where Domenico and his father were hiding, he began to make his way toward them.

Domenico couldn't believe his eyes. The German, unzipping his pants as he drew near, was going to relieve himself on their tree. But just before he reached them, a woman's scream pierced the air. An expression of anticipation, almost animalistic, spread across the soldier's face. "Dolphus?" he called out again, turning in the direction of what now sounded like another woman wailing loudly. When there was no answer, he zipped his pants back up, and like a blood-hound, followed the scent of prey behind the house and up the mountainside toward the muffled cries that continued to come from amidst a scattered pile of large boulders.

Domenico felt his father's body lift, as though he was going to climb down the tree and go to their rescue, but Orazio stayed where he was. They both watched, horrified, as the soldier met up with Dolphus. The tall German, his legs spread apart and his gun aimed at the woman hidden from sight, pointed to the tip of his boots. *"Hier!"* he motioned. "Both of you!"

At his command, Elvira and Signora Gabrelli stood up and stepped forward into full view. Trembling with fear, they faced him. When Signora Gabrelli began hysterically begging for mercy, he ordered both women to their knees. "Who else is here with you?" he bellowed in broken Italian.

The acoustics were such that Domenico could clearly hear his mother swear that there was no one else with them. In her frailty, Signora Gabrelli reached out and grasped the German's legs for support. "She tells the truth," she cried.

"I don't believe you!" Without warning, the soldier struck Signora Gabrelli with the butt of his pistol, knocking her off her knees. Screaming in pain, she raised herself on her elbows and scooted away from him, retreating behind a large rock.

Dolphus, up until this point appearing to be indifferent, spoke up. He and the other soldier had been speaking in simplistic, broken Italian, apparently so that the women would understand what they were saying. Calmly, he explained to the other soldier that the women were probably telling the truth, but his partner ignored him. Instead, he turned to Elvira and shoved the nose of his gun into her temple. "On the count of three," he yelled excitedly, as though he was going to surprise her by pulling the trigger before he got to three. Elvira took several steps back. Now she and Signora Gabrelli were both out of Domenico's range of vision.

"*Eins, zwei . . .*"

"Please, Ralf. Let me take care of it," shouted Dolphus. His voice was insistent as he placed his hand on the other soldier's arm. "Trust me, I can make them talk."

Ralf hesitated. "All right, Dolphus," he said finally. "You need the experience. Let's see what you can do." Walking back to his motorcycle, Ralf retrieved a cigarette while Dolphus disappeared behind the boulders concealing the women. Lolling around his bike, Ralf peered up the hillside with the eyes of a hunter. He was so close to the chestnut tree, Domenico could make out a bright red scar on the side of his face.

"I know what you're up to, Dolphus!" yelled Ralf, grinning widely. "Make short order of the young one and let me have her when you're finished!" But a moment later, two shots rang out in succession and Ralf, tossing his unfinished cigarette to the ground, raced back up the hill.

Dolphus emerged, meeting Ralf halfway between the outcropping of rocks and the fattoria. "It was pointless," he said, shaking his head. "They wouldn't talk."

"Idiot! I didn't get a chance to . . . " Ralf removed his holster, and handing it to Dolphus, he sauntered toward where the bodies of the women lay. As he neared them, he turned to Dolphus and barked, "Do you want to watch?"

Instead of answering, Dolphus set out after Ralf.

And then, abruptly, the dream ended.

Domenico started, completely disoriented, his head jerking backward and his legs flopping like a fish on a hook. A distant peal of thunder heralded the approach of a storm, adding to the uncanny sensation that he was sandwiched between the past and the present.

Reflecting on the dream, Domenico recalled that although his father had covered his eyes the moment Ralf disappeared behind the boulder, years later he told him what happened. In essence, after a frenzied series of growls and grunts and groans, both soldiers emerged with their shirts wrapped around their heads as makeshift tourniquets, making it impossible to tell who was who. Both had head wounds bleeding bright red through the army-issue brown fabric. One of them was unconscious. The soldier with the lesser injuries carried the other soldier down the hill. Looking about the property, he made his way to the shed. He opened the door and tossed his unresponsive comrade in, making sure to latch the door on the outside in a way that would make escape difficult, if not impossible. Then, heaving from the exertion, he mounted his motorcycle and revved off—not in the direction the other troops had gone—but down the mountain.

After the German left, and his father allowed him to open his eyes, all Domenico remembered was climbing down the tree, checking the shed to make sure the latch on the door was firmly in place, and then racing up the hill with his father to see what had happened to his mother and Signora Gabrelli.

Domenico, still groggy from his nap, heard Marco's voice call out from the other side of the shed's door. "Aarika! Over here!"

Storm clouds were advancing toward the mountains, but there was still enough morning sunlight in the eastern sky to illuminate Marco's profile, which Domenico could make out through a wide vertical gap in the shed's splintered door. Debating whether he had time to get out of the shed before Aarika arrived, he realized he was trapped when he heard Aarika say, "I saw you waving at me. What is it, Marco?"

"I need to talk to you," said Marco. "Alone."

"About what?"

"I was concerned about you last night at Bianca's."

Aarika tucked her hair behind her ears and said, "I appreciate your concern, but I feel much better today, Marco. Thank you."

Marco took a step toward her. "Domenico told me how your grandmother died. I'm so sorry."

Domenico detected fear and suspicion in Aarika's voice as she replied, "I'd better go back to the fattoria." He was familiar with reacting to the death of a loved one by not wanting to talk about it and empathized with Aarika's evasive response.

Marco reached out to stop Aarika from leaving. "Please stay with me a minute," he asked.

What Aarika did next, surprised Domenico greatly. She buried her face in her hands and began to cry. He watched with fascination as Marco gently consoled her, using Italian phrases of comfort that a father would use with a child.

"I don't know what came over me," said Aarika, dabbing her eyes.

"You don't need to apologize," said Marco.

"You'll think I'm weak."

"Spoken like a true German."

Aarika seemed to appreciate Marco's attempt to lighten the mood. Smiling, she said, "Don't tease. It's important to me to be strong."

"The fact that you cared for your grandmother the way

you did proves how strong and compassionate you really are." Marco opened his arms wide to Aarika. "It's important for me to be strong too. For you."

Domenico watched Aarika fall into Marco's arms and heard the door of the shed groan under Marco's weight as he braced his shoulder against the door for support. For a moment, Domenico feared the pressure would force the door open and he would be discovered.

"You must know how beautiful you are," murmured Marco. "Inside and out. I've wanted to tell you for so long."

"How long?" whispered Aarika.

"Now you're teasing me."

"No," she said. "I really am curious."

"Since Capri, when I saw you sitting alone in the piazza, when we recited Tennyson together."

Aarika tapped her knuckles on Marco's chest. "But you acted like you didn't care about me in Praiano."

"Believe me, I cared."

"Believing is hard for me to do," said Aarika, her voice suddenly glazing over again with fear.

"It's easy enough when you care for someone as I do for you."

"But that's the problem, Marco. Caring is easy for you because you're full of confidence. It's in your nature to be affectionate and to see the world in black and white." Struggling with her words, Aarika added, "My life isn't as neatly packaged as yours. I don't trust or understand my emotions. I think that's why they neufuse me. Right now, it's all I can do to convince myself that your infatuation with me isn't based on pity, or the fact that you're simply looking for a summer fling."

"You can't be serious, Aarika," said Marco, offended to the

point of raising his voice. "You are not an infatuation. If I pitied you, would I be baring my soul to you like this?"

Oblivious to Marco's assurances, Aarika asked, "How can you really be serious about an orphan girl from rural Germany with a pathetic past and a rejection complex, who can't tear herself away from her grandfather? I'm no match for someone as bold and full of life as you, Marco. I'm fearful, opionated, and set in my ways." Lowering her eyes, she added, "But then, I guess that's what happens when you're raised by your grandparents."

"I'm thankful your grandparents raised you as they did. It's what made you who you are. I think of you as simply being wise beyond your age." Marco rested his hands on Aarika's shoulders and waited until she finally raised her eyes to him. "I love you, Aarika Geller," he whispered.

"What about the girl from Florence? The one you danced with at the Africana in Praiano?"

"Pia?"

"Yes, Pia."

Marco grinned. "I just wanted to show you that some women found me desireable, since you didn't seem to."

"Ah, you admit you were trying to make me jealous."

"I could say the same about you," scolded Marco.

Squaring her shoulders, Aarika took a step back. "Marco, we've got to stop this before it goes any further. When I'm with you like this it feels *great,* but we both know it won't work."

"Of course it can work, Aarika. What are you saying? It feels great between us because we're meant to be together."

Aarika turned her face away. "Even my own sister would be a better match for you than me, Marco. As a matter of fact, the more I get to know her, the more I wish I was like her. I don't know if it's because Poppy's American, or has a different father than me, or was just born the way she is, but I envy her carefree personality. But with me being German and you being Italian on top of everything else . . ."

As Marco tried to convince Aarika that she was being irrational, Poppy's voice rang out. "Marco, where are you? I can hear you out here somewhere."

Aarika tipped her head in the direction of Poppy's approach and whispered, "I'm so sorry, Marco."

No sooner had Aarika walked away from him, but Poppy appeared in her place. Jabbing her thumb at her departing sister, she said, "I feel like I'm always interrupting something between you two. What were you talking about?"

With a long face, Marco muttered, "*Il nostro amore.*"

"Love!" Poppy's mouth fell open. "Really?"

"Yes, love."

"What did she say?"

Marco peered over Poppy's shoulder at Aarika's receding form and gave a forlorn shrug.

"No way." Poppy followed his gaze. "Are you telling me the feeling's not mutual?"

"Oh, she loves me," said Marco, defensively. "I am sure of it. She's just afraid to admit it."

"Aarika's never said anything to me, of course, but I can tell she's attracted to you. Should I be jealous?"

Marco dismissed Poppy's quip with a low laugh before turning the conversation around. "I haven't had a chance to ask you how you're doing, Poppy," he said. "It must have been very difficult for you the other day."

Poppy reached into her hair, grabbed a coppery corkscrew

curl, and pulled on it until it went straight between her two fingers. "Yeah, it's been pretty weird. I wish I could forget the whole thing."

"Is that possible?"

"Well no, but . . ."

"I'm not sure why Dolphus felt he needed to expose your mother's past to you," said Marco. "For your sake, I'm sorry he did."

Continuing to play with her hair, Poppy said, "In a weird way, Marco, I'm not. Although I have to admit, when I found out just how messed up my mom had been, I was tempted to call her and tell her what I'd found out. I mean, why didn't she tell me that I'd had another sister who had died? Because of her neglect, no less?

"But then," Poppy rushed on, "I realized she didn't tell me because she was probably ashamed and afraid I would judge her for it. Which, of course, was exactly what I was doing. Honestly though, it's made me have more empathy for Aarika. At least I've had a relationship with my mother all these years—that kind of minimizes whatever happened in the past. Aarika has nothing *but* the past."

A blinding crack of lightning, by the looks of it less than a mile away, caused Poppy to jump into Marco's arms. A deluge immediately followed—such a blinding torrent of rain, it forced both of them to seek shelter in the shed. There, to their utter amazement, they found Domenico asleep in the corner, groaning softly.

When the next bolt of lightning struck, even closer this time, Domenico leaped up, acting as though he was startled out of his wits. Rubbing his eyes, he exclaimed, "What? What? Oh, these Tuscan storms. What nightmares they're giving me! Is that you, Signorina Poppy? Ah, yes, now I remember why I'm here. Shall we discuss touring Pietrasanta tomorrow?"

Marco's accusing glare told Domenico that he could not be duped so easily. The rain stopped as quickly as it had begun, so politely dismissing Poppy from the shed in order to talk privately with his cousin, Marco lent Domenico a hand and helped lift him off the sacks he'd been napping on. "Now you know I'm in love with Aarika," he said. "You heard everything."

Domenico apologized for eavesdropping, insisting it couldn't be helped. Then, brushing off the seat of his pants, he said, "I don't believe it, Marco. I thought you might be attracted to Aarika. But love? How did it happen?"

"It happened because you hired me to be the Geller's translator and guide this summer."

"Is that giving me credit or blame?"

"Only time will tell."

"Well, what do you think, Marco? Surely you have an idea if she will reciprocate. Love is a straightforward enough affair."

"Not with Aarika Geller, it isn't. But perhaps tomorrow when we go to Pietrasanta I can talk with her again. I'm confident that, with time and patience, she will succumb to her feelings for me."

Domenico gave Marco a comforting pat on the back. "Well, be forewarned that pursuing love with a foreign woman will have its challenges. There is no doubt of that. But if Pietrasanta doesn't provide an atmosphere for love to blossom, nowhere will."

· 15 ·

Almost in Pietrasanta

"Here, in the medieval town of Pietrasanta," said Marco, reading from his guidebook, "otherwise known as 'Little Athens' for its abundance of statuary and marble studios, one can also find an ancient Etruscan cemetery, Roman-era quarries, and monuments to its native son Giosuè Carducci, Italy's poet laureate."

The group of five paused in front of the Cathedral of St. Martin, where Marco recited more historical facts. Then, leaving the Piazza del Duomo, he led the way down Via Mazzini to the Museo dei Bozzetti. As they meandered through the town's deep streets and alleys, he was acutely aware of the fact that Aarika was avoiding him and was at a loss as to what to do about it. She had spent the entire twenty-minute drive in the car absorbed in a magazine and was now deliberately lagging behind so she wouldn't have to speak to him. Several times, he tried initiating a conversation with her, but to no avail. Every overture he made was rebuked or met with indifference.

Stepping into the serene interior of the centuries old Cloister of St. Augustine, which housed the museum, Marco found a niche where his voice could be heard above the din of tourists milling through the gallery.

"Museo dei Bozzetti—or the Museum of Sculptors' Models—hosts collections by sculptors from the nineteenth century to the present day," he began, employing the tone of an instructor. "You remember Fernando Botero's famous statue, *The Warrior*, which I pointed out to you when we entered town near Piazza Matteotti?"

"The fat, naked centurion?" quipped Poppy. "How could we miss him?"

Marco pressed on. "Botero, a Spanish Colombian who studied here, is only one of hundreds of world-renowned artists who have called Pietrasanta home."

Domenico called out, "Marco, remember this is where my mother-in-law's uncle, Egisto Bertozzi, learned his art, at the Stagio Stagi Art Institute. His brother Francesco studied here also."

"As you can see," continued Marco, barely acknowledging Domenico's comment, "We are currently standing beneath the external *loggia* of the museum's ground floor. We will begin here and then proceed to the upper *loggia* where you can view preliminary models—made from paper, or in the form of clay, plaster, cement, fabric, or Styrofoam—that the sculptors crafted before creating their masterpieces. You will find these prototypes quite beautiful in their own right. The models are called *bozzetti* in Italian, giving the museum its name. Because the French word for the models is *maquettes*, you will also hear this institute being referred to as Museum of the Maquettes. Now, if you will follow me."

Quickening her pace, Poppy caught up with Marco. "Slow down," she said. "What's the rush?"

"No one appears to be interested in art today," he complained.

Poppy glanced over her shoulder at Aarika, intently study-ing a headless female torso carved from cement. Pointing to her, she said, "Your little *ragazza* appears interested."

Marco allowed himself a glimpse of Aarika. Once he did, he couldn't take his eyes off her.

"Look how close she holds her purse to her body," said Poppy. "Ever notice that?"

"Her purse?"

"She takes it with her everywhere."

"You're exaggerating."

"I'm not, trust me. She even sleeps with it. Every night. I'm telling you, it's weird. I looked in it one of the few times she left it around unsupervised," said Poppy, "but I didn't see anything out of the ordinary."

"You invaded her privacy?"

"Of course. She's my sister."

"Sorry?"

"Oh, for heaven's sake," snapped Poppy. "Are you even lis-tening to me? Just go over and talk to her, why don't you."

"I've tried."

Linking her arm through Marco's, Poppy said, "Well then, forget about her. Come on, show me around."

Separating themselves from the others by moving to the opposite end of the *loggia*, they circulated through the maze of *bozzetti*. Every so often, Marco snuck a peek at Aarika.

"She's got nerves of steel," Poppy warned him at one point, catching him in the act.

Speaking more to himself than to Poppy, Marco mut-tered, "How can she believe things won't work out between us unless she gives us a chance?"

"Maybe she's afraid."

"Of what?"

"Of being responsible for anyone else's happiness or sanity. Look at her life; it's a case study in misfortune. I mean, she believes she's had a negative impact on every close relationship she's ever had. As a matter of fact, based on the odds, I wouldn't be surprised if she fears Dolphus will be her next victim."

As they spoke, Aarika unexpectedly appeared, skirting around them so she could join up with her grandfather and Domenico, who were advancing to the next level of the museum.

"What is it about her you find so attractive anyway?" whispered Poppy, when her sister was out of earshot. "I mean, yeah, she's beautiful. But what else?"

"She's sensitive, caring, and smart, among other things." Marco slipped behind a life-sized statue of two fishermen gathering their nets in order to get a better of view of Aarika without her seeing him. "See the way that shaft of sunlight she's standing in makes her hair shimmer like . . . " Marco whisked his hands in the air searching for the perfect word.

"Uh, pearls?"

"Exactly! And notice how she carries herself? Tall and erect, yet with movements as fluid as . . . "

"A *queen*?"

"Yes!"

"Enough, Marco. I get the picture," sniffed Poppy. "Well, I'd be lying if I said I wasn't beginning to warm to Aarika myself. She's been making more of an effort to be nice to me, for sure. But a few weeks ago? I thought she was a heartless pain in the neck."

Marco, seeing that Aarika had now joined Dolphus and Domenico and was beginning to climb the steps to the upper *loggia*, motioned for Poppy that it was time to move on. Taking their time, they wound their way through the cloister's Romanesque arches.

"What is Aarika's . . . I mean, your mother like, Poppy?"

"*Our* mother is beautiful. Blond. Aarika looks a lot like her, whereas unfortunately, I look like my dad."

Marco touched his temple. "How is your mother in here?"

"Mentally? She's very private, given to brooding sometimes. A little quirky. But she's really smart. She speaks several languages. German, of course. I guess you could say she's a study in contradictions. There's a dark side to the face she lets the world see. It doesn't show itself very often, but when it does, she checks out." Poppy emphasized her point by circling her finger over her ear. "You know, she goes somewhere no one else is allowed."

"Do you think she will still have her black moments when you return home, now that she knows you know the truth?"

"I suspect they'll be fewer and farther apart." Turning to climb the steps behind the Gellers and Domenico, Poppy added, "But then again, perhaps it depends on if Aarika can ever forgive her."

THE DREAM DOMENICO had in the shed yesterday had stayed with him, as fresh and vivid in his mind as if he'd memorized every detail. Now, as they were finishing up their tour of Pietrasanta with an early evening meal at Il Gatto Nero, Domenico couldn't shake the feeling that it might be time to talk to Dolphus about the war.

Though it was too light for the streetlamps to come on yet, it was still dark enough that the waiter lit candles on their table before seating them. As they were all determining who would sit next to whom, Aarika suddenly changed her mind and announced she was going to stroll around town and do some window-shopping. She would fend for dinner herself, she said, and would meet them back at the restaurant in two hours. Dolphus protested, but Aarika simply kissed him on the cheek and left without another word. After she disappeared, Poppy insisted that she would prefer to go to the Bar Igea next door to get a drink and a slice of pizza and then do some shopping before the stores closed. Marco, at her request, agreed to accompany her. That left only Dolphus and Domenico seated at the table.

"Well," said Dolphus. "It looks like it's just you and me, Domenico."

"Evidently." Domenico held up two of his fingers at the waiter to indicate the change in the size of their party.

Dolphus removed a large white napkin from beneath his knife and fork and set it on his lap. Glancing at the menu, he asked Domenico what he would suggest.

"The food here is good, but nothing special," said Domenico. "You might like their pizza."

Dolphus laughed at the idea. "Why would I order pizza here when I can eat your pizza at the casala? There is no comparison. It's one of the reasons I keep coming back here every summer. Or didn't you know?"

Domenico thanked him for the compliment. Then, nonchalantly, he asked, "What else brings you back every summer?"

"Haven't I told you before?"

Domenico fumbled with his menu. "My memory isn't what it used to be."

"We Germans have always loved Italy for the art and music, the climate, the sea, the history . . ."

As Domenico listened patiently, the waiter returned to take their order. "I think I'll order the *pappa al pomodoro*," said Domenico. "I've heard it's delicious."

"I'll have that also," said Dolphus.

The waiter jotted down their requests, retrieved their menus, bowed, and left. As soon as he was gone, Domenico cleared his throat. "I've always wondered about your name, Dolphus," he said. "Is it a common name in Germany?"

"Yes. Or, at least, it was more common in my generation. It is probably like your Francesco or Roberto here in Italy."

"Oh," said Domenico, disappointed that one of the clues to Dolphus's identity had just been thwarted by commonality. "Dolphus sounds more Latin than German."

"It's an old German name. I think it means 'noble, majestic wolf.'"

"Ah. Adolph wouldn't be from the same root word, would it?"

Dolphus's upper lip twitched. "I believe it is. What does your name mean, Domenico?"

"My mother said it means, 'Belongs to God.'"

"If that's the case," said Dolphus, soberly, "you are a lucky man."

"I have been protected many times in my life, it is true."

The waiter arrived with a basket of warm bread and olive oil, as well as two glasses of Chianti. After dividing the bread between them, Dolphus noticed distant lights flickering in the rose-tinted hills to the east. Pointing at them, he said, "What town is that, Domenico?"

"It is Valdicastello. You have heard of it?"

"I don't believe so."

"What about Sant'Anna di Stazzema?"

"No. Why do you ask?"

"There is a village below Valdicastello called Capezzano di Pietrasanta; not far from here. It is where my family fled when the homes on Monte Montignoso were confiscated. Starting in Sant'Anna di Stazzema, the Germans massacred nearly six hundred of my countrymen, leaving a mountain of corpses. Then they moved down the valley, hanging people from bridges and shooting everyone in sight in Valdicastello and the other villages. They herded the townspeople into stables and churches and barns and burned them down: men, women, and children. My parents and I were among the fortunate few who barely escaped with our lives."

When Dolphus, his head lowered, said nothing, Domenico added, "I hope I haven't spoiled your meal, my friend."

An awkward silence stung their conversation. Dolphus placed his hands on his lap and looked at Domenico. "No more than I have spoiled my own life over my remorse for what happened here during the war to your people."

"*Questa!*" The waiter materialized at Domenico's elbow with two steaming bowls of *pappa al pomodoro*. Placing one in front of each man, he bowed slightly. "*Buon appetito.*"

Wasting no time, Dolphus tasted the stew. "Mmm. Delicious," he said. "Very good choice, Domenico."

Domenico debated whether he should bring the conversation back to the war, but decided against it. The Gellers would be in Italy for fifteen more days. Hopefully, between now and then, a better opportunity would present itself.

THE RIDE HOME from Pietrasanta that night was, on the surface, non-eventful. Dolphus and Poppy joined Aarika in shutting out everything except their own thoughts. Even Domenico, whose droll charm typically went into overdrive after sunset, barely said a word. Marco had only opened his mouth twice: once to shout at, and the other to criticize, drivers he considered inept. He didn't even say good night when he dropped Domenico off at his house. They simply grunted an obligatory farewell to each other

But Dolphus was silent because he had finally guessed what everyone else knew. Marco was in love with his granddaughter. He had come to the realization after he and Domenico had finished eating in Pietrasanta, when Marco began fretting over Aarika because she was late meeting back up with them. When Aarika finally returned to the restaurant, Marco had been unable to conceal his relief.

Yes, thought Dolphus, *it appears Marco may be smitten with Aarika. But how does she feel about him?* It was a disturbing, unsettling question. A union between two such different cultures sharing an acrimonious history was a serious matter. *Poppy is leaving September tenth,* he reasoned. *Perhaps I should cut short our stay and leave then as well. The less time here in Tuscany, the fewer opportunities there will be for Marco to pursue Aarika.*

As Marco drove through the gate to the fattoria and coasted down the driveway, Dolphus continued brooding. *But then, what if this is my last summer in Italy? What if the doctor wasn't completely honest with me about my disease and it's worse than he's led me to believe? What if I dodge one bullet, only to meet another kind of death—an accident, the loss of my mind, or a far more crippling disease? If that were the case, I would definitely want to stay here until the last possible moment.*

Fear and resolve gripped him. *If this is my last summer here, I have to make the most of it. I must watch Aarika carefully, so she doesn't fall prey to her emotions. Right now she's reeling from the news of her father's suicide and struggling to come to terms with Poppy. The last thing she needs is to overreact, throw caution to the wind, and make a mistake she'll live to regret. She needs my protection. Yes, that's exactly what she needs.*

Marco pulled up to the front of the fattoria, letting the engine idle as he got out to help Dolphus and the girls with their things. Dolphus took special note of the young Italian's body language around Aarika. He watched as Marco placed his hand on the small of Aarika's back when she bent over to retrieve a sack from the back of the car, and frowned darkly when Aarika allowed Marco's hand to remain there as he escorted her to the fattoria.

Following Marco and the girls into the house, Dolphus struggled with the new reality he was facing. *So, it's not my imagination,* he thought. *There is something going on between them. This is not good. Not good. There must be a way to nip this in the bud before it gets out of control.*

· 16 ·

Turning the Tables

S ATURDAY, THE FIRST of September, brought with it a noticeable change in weather. The humidity was still high, but the relatively cooler temperatures lent a hint of fall to the air. The moderation was enough to set off thoughts typical of the seasonal transition.

For Aarika and Poppy, decisions about their future began to weigh on them. Poppy was halfheartedly set to enter her third year at the University of Minnesota. Without a clear idea of what she wanted to do with her life, she wasn't looking forward to another year of boring lectures and cramming for tests. Aarika, having suspended her education to help care for her grandmother before she died, had discovered she did not have the heart to pursue a career in the medical field, as she initially had. She vacillated between continuing her education in a different field, such as teaching or language arts, or getting a job in training as a legal assistant at a law firm in Passau. Dolphus was encouraging her to do the latter as he was good friends with the head of the firm, a man whose grandson had been expressing an interest in Aarika for some time.

Unlike the girls, Marco was thrilled at the prospect of

being a year closer to his goal of becoming a private business owner. He spent an hour after waking on the morning of September 1st figuring out his finances. Domenico would pay him for his services on the fifteenth, after the Gellers vacated the fattoria. With that money, his scholarship, and the money he had saved earlier in the year working part-time at a pizzeria near his university, he reasoned he would have enough to cover his bills and then some, plus enough to buy something special for Aarika before she left. A gift that would demonstrate how much, and how deeply, he cared for her.

After eating a light breakfast, Marco swung by his parents' hardware store to pick up a box of nails and a roll of duct tape for Domenico. With their conflicting schedules—him arriving home late most evenings and them at the shop early every day—he had spent little time with his parents this summer. Therefore, it was no surprise that Marco's mother, upon seeing her son step into the store, left the customer she was helping to talk to him.

"Marco!" she exclaimed, kissing him on the cheek. "What brings you here?"

"I'm on my way to the fattoria to pick up the Gellers and take them to the beach," said Marco. "I need to pick up an order for Domenico first."

Shouting at her husband to get Domenico's order ready, his mother scuttled Marco into the back of a dead-end aisle overflowing with plumbing and electrical supplies. "Why do you look so tired, Marco?" she asked. "Did you not sleep well last night?"

"I'm fine."

"Are you feeling ill?"

"I'm fine, Mama."

Marco's mother placed her hands on her hips and studied him closely. "Who's the girl?"

Peering over her head at his father, who was approaching them with the box of nails and tape, Marco said, "You know me better than that, Mama. I don't have time for relationships."

She stared at him disbelievingly. "Humph."

"*Buongiorno*, son," said Marco's father, stepping between them.

Marco's mother crossed her arms. "Marco is hiding something from us."

Grabbing the supplies from his father's hands, Marco squeezed past his parents, warning them it was possible he might be late getting home that evening as he wasn't sure yet what the Gellers would require of him after dinner. "So, don't wait up for me," he called out as he left.

"We never do," mumbled his father.

Had Marco lingered in the store before racing off, he might have overheard his mother declare to her husband, "All I can say is, it better be the American girl he has a crush on. Nothing would ever come of a having a girlfriend in America. It's too far away. But a *ragazza* in Germany? Now that would be a different story entirely."

SINCE THE MORNING in the shed, when he had overheard Marco pour his heart out to Aarika, Domenico had told no one but his wife about what he'd seen and heard. But, of course, Mariella had already guessed Marco's feelings for Aarika. It was hardly news to her, she said.

"And what do you think of it, Domenico?" she had asked him.

Domenico had admitted he'd been shocked at first to discover Marco was in love with Aarika, but said he'd formed no opinion yet, other than Marco had better think very carefully about what he might be getting himself into if Aarika were to return his love. "Language, culture, history, prejudices; there would be so many hurdles to overcome," he told Mariella.

Now Mariella was bringing the subject up again as she cleared breakfast dishes from the table. "Have you noticed Aarika warming yet to Marco?"

"No. But then, I have other, more pressing, things to worry about," said Domenico.

"Really?"

"I broached the subject of the war with Dolphus the other day in Pietrasanta."

"And?"

"I found out that the name 'Dolphus' is a common name for German men of his age."

"And?"

"He also asked about Valdicastello. We could see it from the restaurant we ate at. You should have seen his face when I told him what happened there during the war."

"I can imagine it was awkward for him. Being German, I'm sure he was ashamed. But that's all you learned, Domenico? You didn't use the opportunity to ask more questions?"

Domenico muttered something under his breath about her not possibly being able to understand and ducked outside to putter around in the yard. Mariella followed him out the door.

"Believe me, Domenico, I do realize how difficult this must be for you," she said. "But after all these years of renting to Dolphus, can't you just come out and ask him?"

"Ask him what? That's the problem, Mariella. Do I say, 'Oh, by the way, Dolphus, when you were here on the mountain during the war did you happen to hear anything about my mother being attacked by Germans behind our house?'"

"It sounds like a reasonable question to me."

Domenico's lips puffed out like a blowfish. "Sure it's reasonable, unless . . ." Domenico turned away from his wife and busied himself rearranging some potted plants on their patio.

"Unless," said Mariella, stepping around him, "Dolphus's answer is yes. That's what you're afraid of Domenico, isn't it? If Dolphus knows what happened, then he knows other things. Details. Names. Then what? Where do you go from there?"

Domenico stopped what he was doing and found a lawn chair nearby. He lowered his body into it, saying, "You're right, Mariella. I am afraid of the consequences. And the older I get, the more I struggle with whether it's even worth it anymore to find out the truth."

"Well," said Mariella. "You should ask yourself how many people you know personally who were on the mountain during the war that can give you the information you need."

"Other than Dolphus, none."

"So, if you end up not broaching the subject with Dolphus this summer before he leaves, will you regret it?"

Domenico, his face lined with apprehension, shrugged. "There's always next year I suppose."

"Is there?" countered Mariella. "What if Dolphus dies and never comes back? He's getting old. What if his mind starts going and he can't remember anything? And I could say the same of us. We're not getting any younger. Can you live with the consequences, Domenico?"

Domenico knew only too well what it was to live with the consequences of his actions. Years ago, when he had first started letting his fattoria as a holiday rental to Dolphus, a firestorm of criticism had engulfed him. How dare he, their neighbors fumed, rent to a former German soldier who had been on their mountain during the war? He was accused of being a traitor. Some were so furious they never spoke to the Sacchellis again. Even members of their own family continued to be outraged that he showed preference to Dolphus over other possible renters.

Domenico reminded Mariella of those years. "I'm more than capable of living with the consequences of my actions," he concluded.

"Yes, you are," she smiled. "You told all your critics that you were simply turning the table on the Germans. That did the trick for a while. But we *did* need the money at the time and Dolphus had it to spend. He's been money in the bank for us ever since, and that's the truth."

Domenico returned his wife's smile. "It certainly shut everyone up, didn't it?"

The sound of a car entering their driveway caused the two of them to turn. "*Buongiorno*, Marco!" they called out together.

Marco stayed in the car. He leaned out the window, a box of supplies in his hand for Domenico. Raising his voice above the hum of the engine, he asked, "Do you have any idea what the Gellers want to do this afternoon when they're done at the beach?"

Domenico explained that Dolphus had told him he would like to see Aarika and Poppy be more actively involved with each other again. "He noticed the girls got along much better when you holidayed on the Amalfi. He believes it was because they were forced to do things together."

Marco concurred that was probably the case.

"And also," said Domenico, winking, "Dolphus said in Praiano they found something in common they both liked."

Marco was about to ask Domenico what that was, and then it dawned on him. Narrowing his eyes, he said, "Men."

"What else?" Domenico slapped Marco on the forearm. "That's why he wants to take them to the *festa* tonight."

"And back to my original question," mumbled Marco. "What do they want to do after the beach this morning?"

"They would like to go to lunch somewhere in Forte dei Marmi and then the girls mentioned they would like to do some shopping afterward. When they're done, you can take them back to the fattoria to get ready for the *festa*. If you have them at the fairgrounds by eight, they can eat dinner there. Mariella wants to go too, so perhaps we'll see you tonight, eh?"

"Great," grunted Marco. "I'll be chaperoning Poppy and Aarika again."

"And translating," replied Domenico. "And making sure they don't get taken advantage of because they are tourists when they go shopping."

Shifting into reverse, Marco checked the rearview mirror, turned his head, and began inching out of the driveway.

"Wait a minute," Domenico called out, racing to catch up with Marco before he reached the road. "I was up working in the vineyard this morning when Dolphus told me of a possible change of plans. He said he and Aarika might go back to Germany on the tenth, when Poppy flies back to America, instead of on the fifteenth as they had originally planned."

Marco slammed on the brakes. The look on his face, a mix of shock and immense disappointment, made Domenico realize this wasn't just a fleeting summer romance as far as Marco was concerned. He was truly, seriously in love with Aarika.

Tapping Marco's shoulder, Domenico said, "It's never easy to say good-bye to people who grow on you, like the Gellers."

Marco nodded, and as he stepped on the accelerator he said, so softly that Domenico wasn't sure he heard him correctly, "But I'm not willing to let good-bye be an option yet."

· 17 ·

Clandestine

WHILE AARIKA AND Poppy shopped the trendy boutiques of Forte dei Marmi with Marco in tow, Dolphus opted out by sitting in the shade of a *pino* tree on a bench in Piazza Marconi. He was reading *Der Spiegel,* a day-old copy he had picked up in a nearby *tabacchi* shop, and was absorbed in an opinion piece about the recent G-8 gathering in Genoa and all the threats made by Osama bin Laden to assassinate George Bush, who had attended the meetings. Versilia had been abuzz in July, just before Dolphus had arrived there, with the fact that the President of the United States was flying north over their beaches every day in a military helicopter on his way to Genoa from a secure location near Pisa.

Dolphus finished the article, folded the paper neatly and set it next to him. Yes, change seemed to be the order of the day, what with globalization, the birth of the EU and a common currency set to take place soon. Traditional Europe as he had known it, or at least as his parents and grandparents had known it, was undergoing a monumental transformation on many levels. He wondered how he, to whom change had never come easily, would adjust to it. Financially, would he be able to continue coming to Tuscany, or would the euro make staying in Italy too expensive?

"Oh well," he mused, draping his arm over the back of the bench, "I shouldn't be entertaining such negative thoughts on such a beautiful day."

But even as he stared up through the trees at the soft-blue sky, and listened to the bustle of people going about their lives in security and peace all around him, Dolphus just couldn't shake the spector of saber rattling going on around the world. How could he? The slightest suggestion of armed conflict gave him palpitations, not because he was a coward, afraid to defend his family and country from harm, but because he was afraid of what war would do—what it already had done—to him. Simply reading the article on Al-Qaeda in the paper had made his stomach queasy. The world couldn't afford another world war. Nor could he.

His mind wandered to the past, and before he knew it, he was a renegade Nazi soldier fleeing the *Wehrmacht*, racing down Monte Montignoso on his motorcycle, darting in and out of German troops still storming the mountain. The first day after he had left Domenico's, following his altercation with Ralf, he had ridden in what seemed like circles, without any maps or sense of direction other than knowing the sea was to his west and enemy troops were positioned less than two miles from the base of the mountain. When he finally ran out of gas, he ditched the bike, escaping with his gun and backpack into the woods east of Pietrasanta. He spent nearly a week hiding in caves and burned out logs, drinking from mountain streams and rainwater puddling on rocks. Facing starvation, he began hunting for food and clothing to replace his Nazi uniform.

Mental snapshots of those weeks he spent hiding shuffled across his field of vision. He saw the bodies of an Italian man and his family butchered inside their farmhouse.

He watched himself tearing the bloody clothes off the dead man's body, watched as he clubbed chickens, rabbits, squirrels, and rats to death to keep himself alive on his subsequent trek north. More than a month of living in Italy's forests and mountains reduced him to a scarecrow of a man.

At times, he fell into delirium, imagining the entire *Wehrmacht* army was hunting him down. His gun and ammunition were always hidden on him, ready to use at a moment's notice. Dependent on aid from locals, he had been faking deafness and the inability to speak. Fortunately, having blue eyes and light hair was not uncommon in northern Italy, or his looks might have given him away.

Because he hoped to somehow return to Passau, even though as a deserter he would be executed immediately if caught, he spent his down time devising elaborate stories in his defense. He was the lone survivor of an ambush, became disoriented, and was trying to find his way home, or he'd been injured in battle and was suffering from amnesia. If all else failed, he reasoned he could assume a new identity, or lay low in an obscure Bavarian town and go back to the farm after the war was over. But as long as he was still in Italy, Dolphus Geller's primary mode of survival was pretending to be a deaf-mute in search of work.

Winter had already set in when he found himself just south of Milan. A farmer who had given him temporary shelter suggested—by way of a crude map drawn in the dirt and equally simplistic sign language—that Dolphus should continue on to a region north of Milan called Franciacorta. Apparently many winemakers there employed help without asking many questions. Dolphus reasoned it might be worth pursuing. Not only would he be closer to the border, but he could find work for a few days, allowing him time to figure out how best to get back into Germany. That, and he'd probably have a decent bed and be fed well, all without drawing attention to himself.

As Dolphus was contemplating the idea, the farmer used his finger to write the name "Cavalleri" in the dust.

"Try and find Signor Cavalleri's vineyard if you can," said the farmer. "Not only is he well-known and admired throughout Lombardy for being generous to the poor, he is also a relative of mine. A very distant one. I would tell you to tell him Renzo of Rozzano sent you, but . . ." The farmer hurriedly swept the Cavalleri name away with the palm of his hand. "You can't speak."

Making a slicing motion across his neck, the farmer also warned Dolphus that times were treacherous, telling him he would do well to travel at night on secondary roads to escape undue attention to himself. "These days," he said, gesticulating wildly, "no one is safe. *Capisce?*"

Dolphus did understand, and before sunup the next morning, armed only with his satchel, a thin blanket, and a tiny piece of paper with the name "Franciacorta" scrawled on it, he headed out in search of the Cavalleri winery. After walking for nearly an hour, a small rickety delivery truck loaded with sacks of maize picked him up. Dolphus showed the driver the slip of paper indicating his destination and several jarring, uneventful hours later, the truck pulled over to the side of the road and stopped.

"Franciacorta!" the driver shouted, his arm waving out the window as a sign Dolphus should get out.

Hopping down off the bed of the truck, Dolphus raised a hand in thanks. In the bright, pre-dawn moonlight, he could make out rolling vineyards stretching in every direction. He waited until the truck pulled away and continued its climb toward the mountains before setting out again. As he stumbled along, Dolphus paid attention to the signs posted at the bottom of each vineyard. Soon, he was so cold, hungry, and exhausted, that he debated giving up his hunt for the Cavalleri estate.

I'm sure one vineyard is as good as the next, he reasoned. *But then again, it would be foolish to go knocking on doors at this early hour. Better not stop quite yet. I wish it would get light soon.*

Three things happened next, nearly simultaneously, that resolved Dolphus's dilemma. First, a lone lorry pulled up behind him, stopping just long enough for one of its occupants to yell out at him, *"Fascisti! Pericolo!* Danger—get out of the way!" Then as the truck sped away, Dolphus—not imagining what the warning might be about—made out the name "Cavalleri" painted in large white letters on a carved wooden sign to his left, less than fifteen feet away. He took two, maybe three steps toward it before noticing a concentrated glow of light gathering at his back, its growing intensity casting Dolphus's shadow onto the road. He turned around to see where the light was coming from, and as he did, he had to shield his eyes from the brilliance of multiple headlight beams flashing around the bend in the road less than a mile behind him. At the exact same time, the ground beneath Dolphus's feet began to shake, and in an instant, he recognized it as the thunder of a military convoy. Without question, a German one.

Adrenline surged through Dolphus as impending danger bore down on him by the second. Beyond the Cavalleri sign, he could barely make out a large home situated on what appeared to be a palatial estate set above the vineyard. Long rows of vines, half-buried in snow, were planted vertically from the road up to the house. Gathering every ounce of strength he had, Dolphus ran for his life up the hill. The incline was so slippery, he had to stop halfway up and fall prostrate on the snowy ground to avoid detection as the convoy rumbled by. It wasn't until the taillights of the last vehicle disappeared that Dolphus dared to ease his shivering body out of the snow. At a loss as to what to do next, he finally decided it was best to tempt fate and inquire for shelter at the estate immediately.

Setting out again, he continued trudging until he rounded the top of the hill. There, behind the darkened main house, he spied a guesthouse or servants' quarters, with a gas lantern burning in the window. He stumbled toward it, and reaching it, he stood on his toes and peeked in the window. Through a thin curtain, he could make out a middle-aged woman in a bathrobe, her hair pulled up into a bun, standing over a stove in the kitchen. Taking a deep breath, he edged his way to the door and knocked. Several minutes passed before it opened. It was locked with a chain, so the only thing Dolphus could see through the narrow opening was a small section of a woman's face peering suspiciously at him.

"*Que?*" barked the woman.

Dolphus grunted, pointing first to his mouth to indicate he couldn't speak, then to his ears to indicate he couldn't hear, and finally to his belly as a sign he was hungry. The woman opened the door a bit further, her eyes glinting at him. Dolphus grunted again, but this time he pulled his blanket tightly around him and set his teeth to chattering. He didn't have to feign shivering uncontrollably; it was so cold he could no longer feel his fingers or toes.

Stepping back, the woman unlocked the door and opened it. Dolphus saw that in her hand she held a meat cleaver. She pointed it toward the fireplace. "Go!" she said in Italian. "Get warm while I make some tea." Brandishing the knife, she added, "And if you even think of harming me, I'll be sure you have no hands left to touch anything ever again."

Dolphus knew enough Italian to know he was being threatened, but stared at the cleaver as though he hadn't understood a word she said.

Grumbling under her breath, she grabbed him by the elbow and led him to an overstuffed armchair by the fire where he sat down and tried to get warm. The woman stood over him, her arms crossed, staring at him. Finally, she set the meat cleaver on the counter. "My name's Mariesole," she said. "I'd ask you what your name is, but obviously you can't speak. And since you can't hear me either, I may as well talk in English. It's my mother tongue, if you can believe it."

Retrieving two matching cups and saucers from a cupboard, she proceeded to put a pot of water on the stove to boil. "I suppose you were part of that racket on the road that woke me up a bit ago? Well, no matter. Like it or not, I guess we're all where we're supposed to be, although what I wouldn't give to be back in Chicago right now. I'm American, you know." Mariesole smiled and held her finger to her lips. "No problem trusting you with that secret, eh?"

"I was born in Chicago, but my parents were from here," she continued. "I married an Italian longshoreman who talked me into moving back here before the war. What a mistake that was." Pausing to stare into the fire from her station in the kitchen, Mariesole whispered, "He was drafted into Mussolini's army and has been missing in action for six months. This damn war."

The whistling teakettle brought Mariesole back to attention. Deftly, she poured the boiling water into a chipped porcelain teapot and dropped a perforated cylinder filled with tea leaves in it before placing the lid back on top. Then she sat down near the fire opposite Dolphus.

Dolphus pointed in the direction of the main house.

"Oh, that's the home of Signor Cavalleri," said Mariesole. "Grand, isn't it? The signore is a vintner—the best around. This is his winery and these are his vineyards. He is a good man. I count myself fortunate to work for him. I'm his housemaid and cook."

Glancing at the clock above the mantle, which read five thirty, she added, "I usually check in at the villa's kitchen around six thirty. Signor Cavalleri is a widower, bless his heart, and has a butler who serves him coffee in the morning. That's all he usually eats until lunch. I'm just expected to feed his two children breakfast—a boy and a girl. Sweet things they are, and well mannered too. They clean up after themselves, so keeping the house clean is no problem. It's the unannounced guests who barge in here expecting royal treatment that make me want to scream."

Dolphus smiled at her dumbly and took another sip of tea, making sure his thankfulness was evident. He was confident the friendly gesture would embolden Mariesole to continue talking.

"For example," she said, "just the other day I was serving dinner, when out of the blue someone rapped at the door, yelling to be let in. Signor Cavalleri instructed the butler to see who it was. When he opened the door a Fascist thug by the name of Bruno Carditi bullied his way in. There were four others with him. One was a big-shot Nazi officer by the name of Werner Kolbe. Both men had their wives with them. Insipid little creatures they were, though the German's wife, I have to admit, looked like a Hollywood movie star."

"The fifth person in their group," she continued, "was an Italian woman who had moved to America with her husband. She had had two children with him, but then left them to come back here. Sad story, really. Her name was Armida Sigali. She was lovely too. Like me, she was also a housekeeper, but that's where the similarity ended. Working for Carditi must have been like working for the Führer himself."

"Well," said Mariesole, stretching her slippered feet toward the fire, "Carditi demanded they be given the best wine to drink, without paying for it, of course, and the whole lot of them—except for Armida—proceeded to get drunk out of their minds. They ended up playing a card game in the private wine cellar to win one of Signor Cavalleri's most prized possessions . . . some ancient grape seeds, and who do you think won the game? Armida!"

Mariesole clapped her hands. "Oh, it was rich. You should have seen the fireworks go off when that happened! An outright brawl erupted between Carditi and Kolbe. Signor Cavalleri broke it up, marched them all out to their car and sent them away. Armida, being the only sober one of the bunch, had to drive. Poor woman. I felt so sorry for her." A shadow flickered across her face. "I'm glad I wasn't in her shoes. Signor Cavalleri told me he gave her the seeds. They're worth a small fortune. That shows you what kind of man he is."

Dolphus remained stoic, fighting the urge to respond to the story she had just told. At all costs, he had to maintain his ploy of being deaf.

"Enough talk of Germans," sighed Mariesole. "Besides, what in the world am I doing talking the ear off someone who can't even hear me? I suppose that's what happens when you live alone." With a faraway look, she added, "But then, my husband always teased that I'd keep the ceiling and walls company if no one else was around to listen to my prattlings. So there you go."

A few silent moments passed before Mariesole next began applying a critical eye to Dolphus's appearance. Peering closely at him, she said, "From the looks of you, I'd guess you're from around here somewhere. Farther north maybe?"

Dolphus blinked.

Mariesole waved her hand toward the northeast. Speaking slowly, she said, "Are—you—from—the—Veneto?"

Dolphus let his eyes track the direction she was pointing, but maintained a look of confusion on his face.

Squinting, Mariesole scrutinized him a bit further, before concluding, "Well, regardless of where you're from, you look terrible. I'm going to have to talk to Signor Cavalleri about you. There should be no problem with you being allowed to stay here for a while to rest up. The signore's a good soul when it comes to helping people, and he hates the Germans, so don't worry on that count." Chuckling, she added, "Good thing you can't hear or speak. We wouldn't want that news to get out."

Mariesole glanced at the clock again and stood up. "Well," she said, "Let's get you into something dry and then get some food in you." Scooting him toward the only bathroom in the house, she handed him a towel, her husband's bathrobe, and a clean blanket. "Here, give your knapsack to me," she said, reaching for it.

Dolphus shrank back, clutching the satchel to his chest.

"No? All right then, you can keep it." Mariesole used sign language to show him she wanted him to take a bath, put on the bathrobe, wrap the blanket around his shoulders, and then come to the kitchen table where she would leave some food for him to eat.

As she was telling him what to do, Dolphus noticed a flyer

tacked to the wall in the hallway just outside the bathroom door. His heart stopped. The flyer was in German and Italian and featured a rough sketch of him in uniform with a warning emblazoned below it:

Dolphus Geller: Traitor, Deserter.
Weight: 190 lb. — Height: 6 ft.
Approximately 18 yrs.
Dark blond hair, blue eyes.
Wanted, dead or alive, for the attempted murder
of an officer of the Third Reich.

Anyone with information leading to his arrest will
receive a handsome reward.

No mercy will be shown those withholding information

Attempted murder? He could have sworn Ralf was dead when he'd dumped him in the shed on Monte Montignoso. He had checked his cousin's pulse and felt nothing.

A quick glance in the bathroom mirror assuaged some of his fears. Not only was the sketch a poor representation of him, he now looked very little like the boyish, clean-shaven soldier depicted on the flyer. His beard and moustache made him look much older than he was and his sunken cheekbones were those of a man who weighed far less than 190 pounds.

Dolphus's mind raced. While he had been on the run, Ralf had been hunting him down. The fact that his cousin had issued posters, especially in the region of Italy's northern lakes, told him that Ralf had guessed Dolphus was trying to get back over the border into Germany. This was no longer just about getting back home, Dolphus realized. It was about escaping the murderous rage of Ralf Geller.

Mariesole, having noticed Dolphus's initial shock, was quick to console him. Ripping the flyer from the wall, she tucked it inside the collar of her bathrobe. "Everyone's been forced to display one of these flyers in their home," she explained. "As though there aren't thousands of people trying to escape the Nazis. Who isn't trying to hide from the bastards? And they think we're going to hand over some young kid that actually had the guts to try and take down an officer? One of his own? Still, all I can say is, this Dolphus better not be anywhere around here. Word is that the officer he tried to kill has been looking for him down the road in Brescia. Besides, once Milan falls to the Allies, any Germans left in these parts will be dead meat."

"Ah, well." Mariesole snapped back to the present, her focus solely on Dolphus. "That scruffy beard of yours," she grunted, giving the thick hair on his chin a tug. Using sign language, she added, "I'll get a razor from Signor Cavalleri so you can shave it off tonight."

Dolphus recoiled. Without his beard and moustache, she might recognize him from the poster. It was a remote possibility, considering what a poor drawing it was of him, but using the side of his index finger he made a scraping motion along his cheek. Adamantly, he shook his head no.

"My, you're a picky one," grumbled Mariesole. "All right, never mind. Just get cleaned up. That's all I ask. While you do that, I'm going to get dressed and head over to the house. I'll see if there's something Signor Cavalleri needs done around the place to keep you busy for a while. And do you . . . ?" Pausing, she said, "Oh, forget it. You're not understanding a thing I say." And with that, she turned and walked away.

Dolphus immediately shut the bathroom door and locked

it. Turning on the faucet, he let the small cast iron bathtub fill up with warm water. When he was absolutely sure Mariesole had left the cottage to go to the main house, he tore off his moth-ridden clothes and eased his filthy body into the tub. He used a thin bar of olive oil soap to wash his body and scalp, and grabbing a stiff brush hanging near the tub, he scrubbed himself raw. Nearly an hour later, with his hair and beard thoroughly clean and his skin puckered like a newborn's, he climbed out and dried off. Feeling almost human again, he put on the wool robe Mariesole had given him and tied it around his middle. Then he picked up his backpack and wrapped the clean blanket over his shoulders.

Carefully, he opened the bathroom door. Seeing the coast was clear, he went into the sitting room, threw a couple of logs on the sputtering fire, grabbed the plate of bread and cheese Mariesole had left on the table, and returned to the chair by the hearth. Lifting the soles of his bare feet to the heat of the flames, he began to process his predicament in light of what he had just learned.

He was probably less than fifty miles from the Swiss border, he reasoned. But now, with a bounty on his head, he could no longer risk traveling even on remote secondary roads. He would have to cross the Alps on foot—a dangerous undertaking—or secure safe transportation from someone who could be trusted. Then again, if what Mariesole said was true, and Milan was going to fall to the Allies soon, German troops would be retreating as a result, making it even more dangerous for him should he be caught in their exodus. He was a wanted man. Where could he possibly escape to?

As the wheels of his mind turned, a picture formed somewhere in its recesses. Moments later, with visions of Sabine and Vienna swirling behind his closed eyes, he fell asleep. It was a sleep so deep, he didn't wake up again until Marie-sole returned at six that night to check on him and bring him dinner.

Dolphus jerked back to his senses. Marco was tapping on his shoulder.

"Sorry to wake you up," apologized Marco. "Aarika and Poppy are done shopping. Are you ready to go?"

"I wasn't sleeping," said Dolphus, standing up quickly. "I was just resting my eyes."

"Of course." Picking up the newspaper Dolphus had left on the bench, Marco asked, "Is this yours?"

"Just throw it away," said Dolphus. "Who needs any more bad news in their life?"

"Not me," mumbled Marco, tossing the paper in a nearby trash can. He noticed that Dolphus appeared somewhat disoriented. "Are you sure you're all right?" he asked.

"Yes, yes," replied the German. Then he halted and out of the clear blue he asked, "Have you ever felt trapped in something, Marco, to the point that you can't survive without help? I mean, have you ever been so incapacitated that unless someone steps in and gives you a hand—even if it's just one person, or one hand—you're doomed?"

"I know exactly how that feels."

Seeing Aarika and Poppy waiting by the car just a couple blocks away, Dolphus slowed his pace. "You have no idea of the weight I carry, Marco. At times, the pain is unbearable."

Marco whisked Dolphus beneath a storefront canopy under the pretense of showing him some watches displayed in the window case. "I, too, carry a weight I can no longer bear," Marco confessed. "As you said, sometimes all we need is one hand to save us. I need your hand and your approval, Herr Geller. I'm in love with Aarika. She knows how I feel," he added. "I've told her."

"And what was her response?"

"She seems convinced it would never work out between us."

"What do you expect me to do?" asked Dolphus. "Make her love you?"

"I believe she already does," Marco replied. "I simply want you to assure her there's nothing to be afraid of—convince her that we can be happy despite our differences."

"I'm sorry, young man, but that's impossible." Turning his back on Marco, Dolphus made his way toward Aarika and Poppy, leaving Marco wondering how love could possibly be impossible and how a man who knew the value of a helping hand was unwilling to give him one.

· 18 ·

Tango

"THIS REMINDS ME of a carnival back home," shouted Poppy. The pounding beat of a local Italian band imitating Michael Jackson's "Beat It" made it difficult for anyone to hear what she was saying.

Marco ushered the girls and Dolphus away from the sound stage into a large tent nearby, under which dozens of picnic tables and chairs had been set up. After they were all seated, Poppy repeated what she had said about carnivals.

"What is a carnival in America like?" asked Marco.

"Like this." Poppy swept her hand in a 180-degree motion. "Food, booths, games, crazy lights, rides. Although, this live music makes it a little more like a fair than a carnival."

"My daughter-in-law used to talk about something called a state fair," said Dolphus. He was so absorbed in watching throngs of people weaving through the dusty *festa* grounds that he said it more to himself than to anyone else.

Poppy glanced at Dolphus, surprised. "My mom loved the Minnesota State Fair when she was a kid. It's so weird to think she was once your daughter-in-law."

Aarika asked Poppy why she would think it was strange when, in fact, Dolphus had been the first father-in-law Sharon had ever had. But before Poppy could reply, Marco said, "I'll take everyone's order for dinner and bring it back to the table. What do you all want to eat?"

Moments later, as Marco headed to the food booths to purchase the meals, he found Poppy tagging alongside him. He leaned close to her so he wouldn't have to yell over the music to be heard. "I told Dolphus today."

"About you and Aarika?"

Marco nodded.

"So that's why he was such a grouch this afternoon," Poppy rolled her eyes. "He and Aarika had a big talk after you took us back to the fattoria."

Marco raised his eyebrows. "And?"

"Really Marco, what do you think? Dolphus has issues with you being Italian and Aarika being German."

"I shouldn't have told him," growled Marco. "It's probably only made things worse. Now he won't let me have a moment alone with Aarika."

"Still not ready to give up on her, huh?"

Marco scowled at Poppy before stepping up to the cashier and placing their order. While they waited for it to be filled, he told her in detail how Dolphus had reacted to his request for backing up his relationship with Aarika. "I have a feeling he's going to try to turn her against me," he said.

"Then I guess you'll see what kind of mettle Aarika's made of."

"Oh, there's no question Aarika is strong. You've seen how she picks up the slack whenever Dolphus isn't feeling up to a task. I have yet to see her shrink from any challenge."

"She is a hard worker," agreed Poppy. "A made-of-steel sort of girl, I have to admit. She must have gotten it from her father, or her grandparents, because our mother isn't like that."

"The problem is," noted Marco, "Aarika can be stubborn to a fault."

Poppy snorted. "You can say that again."

"She's already convinced herself a relationship with me wouldn't work, and with Dolphus taking her side, it will only strengthen her determination to try and forget about me."

When their order was ready, Poppy helped Marco carry the plates, sacks, napkins, and silverware back to the *festa* table. Domenico and Mariella had arrived in their absence and were sitting with the Gellers. After distributing all the food, Marco took the only seat left available, next to Domenico. Aarika, he noticed, was planted firmly next to her grandfather at the other end of the table. Poppy wormed her way in between Dolphus and Mariella. Everyone chatted while they ate, except Dolphus and Aarika, who picked at their food and said nothing.

The band returned from a break and started another set. This time, instead of classic rock, they began playing Brazilian tunes, the saxophonist and percussionist belting out Latin rhythms and leads that had *festa*-goers leaping from their seats and racing to the dance floor. Mariella drank the last of her wine hurriedly, pushed her plate away, and with her elbows raised shoulder level and her hips swaying, she told Domenico she absolutely must dance. Laughing, Domenico obliged. They cha-cha'd toward the band stage, their middle-aged limbs as pliable as couples half their age. Seconds later they had disappeared into the crowd.

Poppy shot Marco a "watch me" glance, and rising from her seat, she walked around to Dolphus. Squatting down next to him, she placed an arm around his neck and whispered something in his ear. Marco saw Dolphus blush like a schoolboy and shake his head twice. Poppy whispered something to him again. This time, Dolphus paused and held up one finger before rising from his seat.

"Dolphus has agreed to dance with me, everybody!" Poppy cried. Triumphantly, she grabbed his hand and dragged him in the direction Mariella and Domenico had gone.

Marco waited a few more seconds and then stood up and walked over to Aarika. She sat in a defensive position, her eyes trained straight ahead, refusing to look at Marco. Undaunted, he sat down next to her and placed his hand on her knee. Her thigh tensed under his touch.

"Why did you talk to my grandfather about me?" she asked. "Now he's upset."

"I was hoping he would help you see how irrational you're being."

"You made it worse."

"Aarika, it doesn't matter what he thinks. All that matters is that you know what is right for you."

"My grandfather is all I have left. I can't hurt him."

Marco wanted to hold Aarika in his arms so badly he felt his brain go light, as though it were levitating in his skull. "How can loving me hurt Dolphus?"

"He'd be left alone."

"He doesn't have to be alone, Aarika. He could live with us."

"Don't you see, Marco? That's just the tip of the iceberg. Think of the challenges. Where would we live . . . here? You know full well what Italians think of Germans. Or would you be willing to live in Germany?"

Marco's face fell. The idea of living in Germany had never occurred to him. He could offer no reply, because thinking about it now gave him a fleeting glimpse of Aarika's perspective.

"I told you, this will never work," Aarika said, her voice insistant. "You're a talented, smart, wonderful man, Marco. You deserve someone who can love you without any strings attached."

In the background, Marco heard the band preparing to play a new song. "Come, Aarika," he said. "Dance with me."

Despite her objections, Marco pulled Aarika to her feet. Placing himself directly in front of her, he reached behind his back and grasped both of her hands, and then wrapped them around his waist. Holding on to her firmly, he led her through a wriggling mass of revelers until they reached the center of the dance floor. There, he turned and scooped her into his arms. Holding her as close as physically possible, Marco began swaying, more to the pulse of her heartbeat than the music filling the air. Halfway through the song, he leaned back slightly so he could take in all of Aarika's face. "You're so beautiful, Aarika," he whispered. "It's killing me."

"It must be my new dress," she replied nervously, avoiding Marco's eyes.

"It's not the dress."

Marco felt Aarika's ribcage expand and contract beneath his hands as her breath quickened. "It's not just that my heart stops whenever I look at you," he continued. "I watch you when you think no one can see you. I've noticed how devoted you are to your grandfather, how tenderly you care for him and how much you love and respect him. You've warmed to Poppy too, even though it must be difficult for you. You're smart, decisive, sensitive, and strong. You've never complained about the rustic conditions at the fattoria, like some women might." Marco smiled. "And you can recite Tennyson. All the things I love most in a woman."

Blushing, Aarika locked eyes with Marco. "Can I be honest with you?" she asked.

"*Certamente.*"

"After what's happened in my life, it's hard for me to believe anyone could really love me. The truth is, I live in fear that I'll either hurt the people I love, or they'll end up leaving me. Sometimes I feel so . . . unworthy."

Marco lifted Aarika's hand to his lips and kissed her fingertips. "You earned my love just by being you," he said. "There's nothing else you could do to make me love you more than I do right now. And if you really knew me, Aarika, you'd know I never go back on a promise. When I commit to love, it's forever."

Aarika closed her eyes. "I'm dreaming."

Marco bent down, swept her hair up with his hands, and kissed her neck. "Does this *feel* like a dream?" he whispered.

"I never want to wake up," she sighed.

"We don't ever have to."

Without warning, Aarika snapped her head back. "Marco, it's more complicated than you think."

Marco gazed so deeply into Aarika's eyes she finally had to look away. "There's someone else, isn't there?" he asked.

"Not really."

"Not really?"

"There's a man in Passau, the son of a friend of Opa's. He's always liked me, but you're getting me off track, Marco. That's not what I meant by complicated . . ."

"Your grandfather is fond of this man?"

"Well, of course. He's a good person, but . . ."

"Dolphus hopes you will marry him."

"I wouldn't say he 'hopes.' Opa has always just assumed . . ."

Marco stopped dancing. "Do you love me, Aarika?"

Aarika's lips parted as though trying to formulate an answer, but nothing came out. The band segued into a tango. Immediately, Marco slipped behind her, placing one of his hands flat against her abdomen. He used his other hand to guide her free arm out at a straight angle from their bodies. Placing his lips against her ear, Marco said, "I know you love me, Aarika Geller. I can wait awhile longer to hear you tell me that you do, but tonight, at least, show me what you feel for me."

Not another word was spoken between them. Even after the tango ended, after they stepped off the stage, still flushed from the passion of their dance, and made their way back to the tent, neither of them spoke. Looking as though they were floating on air, Aarika and Marco circled the tent hand-in-hand looking for Dolphus and Poppy.

After several futile rounds, Marco ushered Aarika to the table where they had been sitting earlier and asked her, apologetically, if she would mind waiting there until he came back. "I don't want to drag you around the *festa*," he explained, squeezing her hand. "I'll find your grandfather and bring him back. Then we'll talk to him . . . just the three of us."

"*Ciao, Marco!*"

Spinning around, Marco came face-to-face with Poppy. Standing next to her was Pia, the girl from Lucca he had met on the Amalfi Coast.

"Look who's here!" chirped Poppy, her face a mask of artificial excitement. "Pia and I just bumped into each other. Small world, isn't it?"

Dressed in nightclub attire—a short skirt, a tiny metallic top, and four-inch heels—Pia lost no time in attaching herself to Marco. "Some friends of mine invited me to come and hear the band tonight," she said. "I thought to myself, 'Ah, the Viareggio Festa. Perhaps Marco Bertozzi will be there!' Did you lose my phone number, Marco? I thought for sure you would call me when you got back from Praiano."

While Marco tried to extricate himself from Pia, Poppy pointed her finger in the air and yelled, "Dolphus! Over here!"

Dolphus swooped into the tent, took note of Aarika's distressed appearance, and suggested it was time to leave. Shooting Marco a look of disdain, he added, "I'll ask Domenico to take Aarika and I back to the fattoria. You can bring Poppy back home later, Marco, if she prefers to stay here."

As Dolphus escorted Aarika away from the table, Poppy disappeared back into the *festa* crowd. Twenty minutes later, during a lull in the music, Marco found her flirting with one of the band members. He told her it was time to go and as they started toward the exit, he added, "You have some explaining to do, my friend."

"How was I supposed to know tonight was the night Aarika was going to give in to your charms?" asked Poppy. "I'm not a mind reader."

Marco pressed his foot hard on the accelerator and squealed away from the last stop sign in Strettoia. "I can't believe you found Pia at the *festa* and brought her to me when you did," he hissed.

"For the hundredth time, Marco, that's not what happened. I told you: I saw Pia in the crowd when the band started their second set. My original plan was to get Dolphus to dance with me so you could talk to Aarika alone. I begged him, but when he refused, I told him I'd seen a girl at the *festa* who liked you, and if he would dance with me, I'd bring her over to our table when we were done."

Crossing her arms, Poppy added, "You should be thanking me, Marco. At least you had Aarika to yourself for a little while. That's better than nothing."

"No, Poppy, it would have been better had Aarika and I been able to talk to Dolphus. Tonight may have been our only opportunity and now it's lost. You scared her off, that's what you did."

"Aarika needs to get over her jealousy."

Marco kicked the car into fourth gear on the final stretch of road leading up to the base of Monte Montignoso. "Aarika's not jealous. She simply took Pia as a sign she's not right for me. I know her. I'm sure that's exactly what she thought."

"Well, *I* thought you'd appreciate what I tried to do for you. See if I do you another favor anytime soon." Though Poppy said it jokingly, her voice cracked with regret.

Marco downshifted as they began scaling the mountain. "I'm sorry, Poppy," he sighed. "I know you meant well."

"Are you absolutely sure Aarika is the one for you, Marco?"

Marco bit his bottom lip. Trying to apply reason to love was all new territory for him. "Aarika and I each have a hand in our destiny. Of that, I am sure."

"What will you do if Aarika goes back to Germany and refuses to have anything to do with you ever again?"

"I can't let that happen. If she leaves here without acknowledging our love, and if I can't get Dolphus's approval, I'm afraid I might never see her again."

"Why do you say that?"

"She still lives on the farm with Dolphus. He'll make sure I can't get in contact with her."

"That's outrageous. Aarika's an adult. What's Dolphus

going to do? Monitor her e-mail accounts and check her cell phone messages?"

Marco looked askance at Poppy.

"Yeah, what was I thinking?" muttered Poppy. "He is pretty protective. He might do anything to keep her from you."

"Dolphus wouldn't have to resort to drastic measures," said Marco. "All he really would have to do is plant seeds of doubt in Aarika's mind so that she'll convince herself there was never anything between us to begin with."

"You could force the issue," suggested Poppy. "Follow her to Germany and make a pest of yourself until she gives in."

"That would just put them both on the defensive and make matters worse. I need your help, Poppy. Do you think in the next day or two you could arrange a time for me to get alone with Aarika again?"

"How much will you pay me?"

"Poppy, I'm serious."

"You know Dolphus will be making sure he's with her all the time. It won't be easy."

Steering sharply into the last curve before the fattoria, Marco set out the itinerary for the next day. He told Poppy he would be picking them up in the morning to take them to the beach. "Can you think of something to do afterward that would allow Aarika and I to be alone together?"

Poppy stifled a yawn. "Let me sleep on it."

Pulling up to the house, Marco put the car in park. Then he got out and went around to Poppy's side of the car to open the door for her.

As Poppy stepped out, she extended her hand to him. "So, I take it you've forgiven me, Marco?"

Marco gave her hand a firm shake. "Forgiven."

Poppy wouldn't let his hand go. "We're still friends?"

"Always."

"Okay, handsome," laughed Poppy. "Better shore up the rest of that Latin charm of yours for Aarika tomorrow. You're going to need lots of it."

· 19 ·

Signora Cavalleri

Having spent his childhood learning to swim on secluded beaches hidden from the cosmopolitan, well-heeled hordes of tourists descending on Forte dei Marmi every summer, Marco rarely frequented the Monte Cristo Beach Club. The clock was ticking, however; now he was desperate to be near Aarika at every opportunity. And so it was that on this particular Sunday morning, a spectacularly perfect September day, while Bianca and her sister Rina were attending Mass in Forte dei Marmi's quaint Chiesa di San Francesco, the beach club was precisely where Marco found himself. Within moments of his arrival, he was accosted by scores of locals and old friends who had come out to enjoy the beach now that the tourists had disappeared.

"*Buongiorno*, Marco! I haven't seen you all summer. Who are these lovely girls with you?"

"*Buongiorno*, Marco! I see you've been busy. Do both of these charming ladies belong to you?

"*Buongiorno*, Marco! Where have you been hiding these beauties?"

Invariably, when Marco introduced Poppy to his acquaintances they greeted her excitedly, asking her countless questions about America. Aarika, on the other hand—as soon as they heard her German accent—was dismissed with an obligatory handshake followed by a discreetly cold shoulder. The rebuffs were obvious to Marco and he was angered by them more than he could ever have imagined. But at the same time, the slights were subtle enough that he was at a complete loss as how to rebuke his friends without causing a scene or embarrassing Aarika. Indeed, for the first time in his life, Marco realized just how pervasive and prevalent the stigma attached to Germans in postwar Italy was.

When the last of his visitors finally excused themselves, Aarika, reclining on the lounger farthest from Marco, called out loudly, "I didn't realize you were so popular, Marco. It must be nice having so many people interested in your welfare."

Knowing she was being facetious, and wanting to avoid the whole issue, Marco tried to make light of it. "Italians are that way."

"I wasn't paying your friends a compliment. Busybodies and bigots are what they are." Aarika removed her sunglasses and placed them atop her head. "Are you blind, Marco?"

Poppy, lying prostrate on her stomach, her head tilted to the side, agreed with her sister. "Marco's friends definitely acted as though they liked me better than you."

"See?" said Aarika. "I should just wear a sign saying I'm German. It would save me having to go through all the humiliating preliminaries leading up to my rejection."

Marco began to protest that Aarika was exaggerating, but Dolphus, his eyes closed and his hands clasped over his belly, cut him off. "There's a reason Italians feel the way they do about Germans, Aarika," he said. "And you really can't blame them for it."

"The war's been over for nearly sixty years, Opa," snapped Aarika. "There's no excuse for rudeness. I don't care what the reason is."

Dolphus, his eyes still closed, disagreed. "We Germans still feel great shame about the war and that shame can be mistaken for smugness or superiority. Italians naturally react in kind if it's perceived that way." Rolling his head toward Marco, Dolphus opened one eye and added, "Which is why marriages between nationalities who mutually distrust each other can be a disaster for their families."

Marco bristled at the implication. "So you're saying, Herr Geller, that the solution is to marry someone based on their nationality? Love has nothing to do with it?"

"Actually, in the long run, yes," said Dolphus. "When the feeling of love wears off, it is commonality that remains."

Marco, feeling as though the conversation had become a noose around his neck, rose from his chair and approached Aarika. Extending his hand to her, he said, "Come. Let's go for a walk and talk."

"No, thank you," she replied, sliding her sunglasses back down over her eyes.

Marco waited a full minute before saying, "Have it your way, Aarika. If you change your mind, you'll have to come find me."

Poppy watched as Marco set out across the white sand and then began walking north along the surf. Standing up, she pulled a t-shirt over her swimming suit and made a move to follow him. But before racing away, she turned to Aarika and said, "You're going to live to regret this, Aarika. Just you wait and see."

After Poppy left to join Marco, Aarika got up and said that she, too, was going to go for a walk. Dolphus watched her head south, in the opposite direction from her sister and Marco, and then turned to see Mariella, along with her mother and Bianca, walking down the club's boardwalk toward him. With their nylon stockings, their simple, hand-made dresses swaying in the breeze, and the heels of their flat leather shoes clacking on the wooden slats, the three women stood out from the scantily dressed sun revelers around them like china in a Tupperware store.

Dolphus swung off his lounge to greet them. "How was church this morning, ladies?"

"Very satisfying," replied Mariella. "If you would have attended Mass with us, I'm sure you would have found it inspiring as well."

"Perhaps another time," said Dolphus, bowing slightly.

Suddenly, Mariella stood on her tiptoes and called out to a woman emerging from the cabana near the club entrance. "Here, Signora Cavalleri! We are right here!" Turning back to Dolphus, she said, "We brought a guest with us today. She called Bianca last night to see if she could meet with her and my mother about an affair that may have involved our family during the war. We met her for coffee this morning and then attended Mass together. She is a delightful woman, signore, as you will see."

Dolphus, transfixed by the sight of a beautiful, fifty-something year-old woman making her way toward them, didn't hear Mariella's last sentence.

As she drew close, the signora zeroed in on Dolphus. "*Ciao!*" she said, as Mariella introduced them to each other. Pointing to the empty chaise vacated by Poppy she asked, "May I?"

"Please," said Dolphus, his palm raised toward the lounger. As the signora set her things down next to the chaise and removed her swimsuit cover-up, he looked at Mariella for an explanation.

"The signora is staying at a hotel near here. We thought she would like to spend a few hours at the beach, so we took her back to her room after church in order for her to change clothes. Domenico dropped us off and is waiting for us in front of the club. He said Marco would be here with you." Mariella paused. "Where is Marco anyway?"

Dolphus pointed to two distant figures to their right, strolling along the beach. "They should be back soon."

"When he returns," said Mariella, "would you introduce him to the signora and tell him she is our guest? I am sure Marco will know to be attentive to any needs she may have. I assume he can take her back to her hotel when you leave here? Tell him we will explain everything to him in more detail later this afternoon."

"Of course," said Dolphus, glancing nervously at Signora Cavalleri, now stretched out like a tigress on the chaise next to his.

Waving good-bye, the three women shuffled their way along the boardwalk back to the clubhouse entrance where Domenico was waiting to take them home.

As soon as Dolphus lowered himself back onto his chair, Signora Cavalleri said, "I have been to Tuscany before, but this is my first time to Forte dei Marmi. It is wonderful, don't you think?"

"I am from Passau, in Germany. Tuscany is wonderful, indeed, signora. I come here every summer."

"How fortunate for you." Smiling, the signora said, "Please call me Elisabetta, Herr Geller."

"You may call me Dolphus."

"Ah," she sighed. "It is a perfect day, Dolphus, is it not? Where I am from, it is starting to get cooler already."

"And where would that be?"

"Franciacorta. In the mountains, near Lago d'Iseo in Lombardy."

Dolphus froze. Several moments went by, the roar of the surf blending with the swish of blood rushing in his ears. "Excuse me," he said, finally. "But you wouldn't be related to a Signor Cavalleri who owns a vineyard in Franciacorta?"

"Indeed, he was my father!" Surprised, Elisabetta asked Dolphus how he knew him.

Having begun the conversation, Dolphus now found himself in a fix. Had Elisabetta not been in possession of such mesmerizing almond-shaped eyes, volumes of predominately dark hair, and a body type similar to Sophia Loren, he would have had no problem giving her a cursory reply. Brushing her off would make him look arrogant. Telling the truth might shock her. Realizing there was no other way around the situation, he finally blurted, "I was at your father's vineyard during the war."

Elisabetta didn't appear in the least surprised, especially, thought Dolphus, considering he was German.

"The war made villains and heroes of men and women on both sides," said the signora. "Shame and suffering, my father used to tell me, were not exclusive to any one country. You would be surprised how many people of different nationalities he helped: Italians, Germans, Austrians, Poles, French. Actually, it's by reason of my father's activities during the war that I'm here."

"And why is that, signora?"

"My father met a woman from Ripa who was in very grave

danger during the last days of the war. He was hoping he may have helped save her life. Her name was Armida Sigali. She was related to the Bertozzis. I found out from Bianca this morning that she was murdered in Lago d'Iseo the same day Mussolini was shot. Very mysterious; but then, the story of her life is one of great sadness and intrigue."

"Very noble of you to care so much about her fate," said Dolphus.

"Not as noble as you think, although certainly, I cared about what happened to her. There was a sort of family heirloom involved, something my father owned that was priceless."

"In that case, I hope you find what you are looking for."

Elisabetta laughed. "Oh, after talking to Bianca and Rina this morning, I'm almost ready to give up trying to find it. My father has passed on. I was researching this Armida woman simply to put some closure on an incident from the past. It's one of the last things I felt I could do in my father's memory."

Dolphus knew he should drop it; knew he should settle back in his chaise, close his eyes, and pretend to nap. But he was thoroughly enchanted with Elisabetta. He chided himself for being foolish, for thinking that—as someone old enough to be her father—she would be even remotely interested in continuing a conversation with him. "You must have been very young during the war," he finally ventured.

"I was five years old when the war ended. Old enough to remember things I wish I couldn't remember." Her smile faded. "Did Mariella say your name was Dolphus *Geller?*"

As the memory of Elisabetta as a child suddenly burst into the forefront of Dolphus's mind, he stiffened. He stared at the signora, dumbstruck, knowing that sooner or later, either she would figure out who he was, or he would have to tell her.

·20·

Wanted

TRUE TO HER word, Mariesole had spoken with Signor Cavalleri about finding work for the deaf and mute refugee who had shown up at her doorstep in the wee hours of the morning. When the housekeeper returned that evening from her duties, she found Dolphus dressed, wearing his old clothes that had been washed and dried by the fire. He still sported a beard and moustache, but his hair—at least the hair sticking out over his ears beneath his cap—appeared to be clean.

"Sit down," she ordered, pointing to the kitchen table. "I'll have dinner ready in a minute. And for heaven's sake, set that filthy satchel down over there." Mariesole pointed to a corner of the kitchen, but when Dolphus held on to his backpack, slung securely over his shoulder as though he would never let go, she threw up her hands and proceeded to prepare supper.

After dinner was finished, Mariesole retrieved a pad of paper and a pencil and wrote down in Italian what Signor Cavalleri could offer Dolphus in the line of work. "Here," she said, shoving the paper toward him. "Since you can't hear me, you can read about the jobs you can do. The signore says there's enough to keep you busy for a couple of weeks."

Dolphus stared at the foreign language in front of him. He spoke and understood Italian better than he could read it, so he could only guess what she had written. Shaking his head, he handed the paper back to her.

"What? You can't read either?" Mariesole clicked her tongue. "I should have known. You must come from poor stock, if your folks didn't have the means of giving you an education. Back in America they have special schools for people like you."

Pulling her chair close to Dolphus, Mariesole began making exaggerated gestures. "Do good work," she mouthed slowly, drawing her hands over her shoulder as though she were using a pickax. "That way, you might be able to stay on longer than two weeks. Signor Cavalleri needs tools and machinery repaired, his fencing fixed, and debris cleared from the property."

"Do—you—understand? *Capisce?*"

Dolphus shrugged.

"Well, this should be interesting." Mariesole began clearing the dishes from the table. When Dolphus tried to help her, she shooed him away. Pointing to the threadbare couch near the fireplace, she indicated he was to sleep there for the night. From that point on, she said nothing more until, about an hour later, she brought him a blanket and bid him good night.

It had been Dolphus's intent to wait until Mariesole was asleep and then, under cover of night, sneak out of the house and head northeast in the direction of Trieste. With posters of him plastered all over the lake region, he had determined that his best bet for escape was Austria, and not Germany as he had originally planned. If he could reach Vienna, perhaps Sabine could help him. Planning the details of his escape was the last thing he remembered before Mariesole shook him awake.

"Get up," he heard her say. "It's five thirty. Breakfast is ready."

While Dolphus ate and drank the coffee offered him, he realized there was nothing he could do now but stay at the vineyard that day and work. By six fifteen, he was in the Cavalleri barn being shown what to do by Aldo, one of the liverymen—an old, arthritic Italian whose most productive years were long gone. It spoke volumes of what kind of man Signor Cavalleri must be to keep such a man in his hire, thought Dolphus.

After Aldo left, Dolphus set to work cleaning tools and blades and machine engines as best he knew how. The mindless, methodical labor transported him back to his father's farm in Passau and soon he was deep in thought, homesick for his family and friends.

Just as he began to give himself over to a relaxing sense of security in his new surroundings, a sudden movement near the door startled him. Reaching into his satchel for his gun, he ducked behind a plow and waited. Had someone recognized him and turned him in? Were storm troopers at that moment surrounding the building, preparing to mow him down the minute he stepped outside?

Then he heard a giggle. Placing his gun back in his pack, Dolphus stood up. As he did, he saw a small shadow dart behind one of the large oil drums stacked along the far wall. He approached it stealthily, and then cautiously peeked around the edge of the nearest drum. There, to his great relief, crouching on her knees, was a delicate, raven-haired girl clasping several toy soldiers in her hands. Not wanting to scare the child, Dolphus puckered up his face in a way that would make her smile. The girl jumped up and giggled again, as though Dolphus had caught her in a game of hide-and-seek, and began babbling in Italian. Dolphus pointed to his lips, shook his head and shrugged.

The little girl seemed to consider his gesture a moment. Setting her toy soldiers down on a nearby bench, she pointed to herself and said, "Elisabetta."

Dolphus pointed to himself and grunted.

Smiling, Elisabetta mimicked him by grunting as he had. She stared intently at him for a long time and then said, "English? Mariesole teach me English."

Dolphus smiled.

"I play," she said, picking up the soldiers again. "These belong my brother. Mariesole say me tomboy."

Dolphus held out his hand. Elisabetta gave him two of the soldiers. For the next five minutes or so, they silently parried their toy men against each other, the little girl making booming sounds each time they clashed.

"Me hate Germans," she said, holding up one of the toy men to Dolphus.

Dolphus raised his eyebrows. *Why?*

Pointing toward her father's house, she said, "Bad German soldier talking to Papa now. Name Ralf."

Leaning close to her, Dolphus placed his finger near his ear, as though if she said it again he might be able to understand. Elisabetta complied. "Bad soldier in house. Name Ralf."

Lightning fast, Dolphus raced to a pile of hay stacked in the far corner of the barn and dove in. Elisabetta ran after him. Throwing more hay on top of the spot she saw him disappear into, she called out, "No afraid of German. You safe with me."

Less than five minutes later the doors of the barn swung open. Dolphus heard Aldo call something out in Italian. Then he heard a voice—Ralf's—cursing in German as he entered the barn. Suddenly, Elisabetta began singing softly. Aldo asked her something, to which she replied, *"Non questa."*

Dolphus could hear guttural sounds coming from Elisabetta and guessed she was playing with her toy soldiers again. Huddled near the back of the haystack, beneath at least four feet of hay, his Mauser loaded and ready to fire, Dolphus told himself it was over. *When Ralf finds me,* he thought, *there will be no mercy. One of us will die. It will be either him or me.* Then he heard the rasping sound of a pitchfork stirring through the hay pile he was in and Ralf mumbling something about idiot Italians. The pressure in the mound began to shift and suddenly Ralf's pitchfork was within inches of him. Dolphus even thought he felt one of its prongs poke his shoe. He lay stock-still, in a cold sweat, every muscle in his body taut with terror.

Just as Dolphus was sure Ralf's next prod would pierce him, Elisabetta ran out of the barn screaming, *"Ratti! Ratti!"*

Dolphus heard the pitchfork drop on the dirt floor and listened as heavy footsteps raced toward the barn door. In broken Italian, Ralf yelled, *"Ratten?* Rats? There are rats here?"

Ralf couldn't conceal the fear in his voice and Dolphus knew why. His cousin was musophobic; he had an irrational fear of rats. Ralf might be older than him—stronger and smarter—but all Dolphus had to do when they were children was capture a rat and hold it close to Ralf, and the swaggering warrior turned into a jellyfish.

The next thing Dolphus heard was Ralf hightailing it out of the barn, yelling at Aldo to take him to the vineyard so he could search for Dolphus among the vines and other outbuildings at the edge of the Cavalleri property. Dolphus didn't budge. He remained buried in the hay until Elisabetta returned, about half an hour later. She moved so lightly, Dolphus didn't know that she was in the mound with him until two small hands parted the hay above his head.

"Signore?" she whispered.

Tentatively, Dolphus raised himself up.

"Ralf gone," she said. "You safe now."

Dolphus looked doubtful.

"Ralf drive . . . " Pausing, Elisabetta raised her elbows while twisting her wrists, as though she were starting a motorcycle. "*Brrroom, brroom.*" Pointing north, she added, "That way."

Unexpectedly, Aldo stepped into the barn and caught Elisabetta sitting next to Dolphus on top of the hay. Approaching them, he stopped when he got close enough to talk to Dolphus without raising his voice. "*Sei Dolphus Geller?*" he asked.

Dolphus almost shook his head no, but remembered he was playing deaf. He stared at the old man.

"*Lui paura dei Tedeschi,*" said Elisabetta.

"Ah," nodded Aldo. He looked at Dolphus knowingly, pointed to himself, and said, "*Anche a me*—I am afraid of the Germans too." Then, winking before he left, he led Elisabetta out of the barn to the house where he said lunch was waiting for her.

Meanwhile, Dolphus returned to his duties. Now, more than ever, with Ralf so close on his trail, time was of the essence. He reasoned he would be safe at the Cavalleris' the remainder of the day, since Ralf had just been there and moved on. But soon, his cousin would catch his scent again. When he did, Dolphus knew he had better be long gone.

Yes, he'd made up his mind. Tonight, after Mariesole was asleep, he would sneak out and make his way to Vienna. It was his only hope.

Elisabetta looked over at Dolphus from her chaise lounge, her voice echoing as though she were talking through a hollow cardboard tube. "Dolphus. Dolphus?"

Realizing his mind had momentarily left their conversation, Dolphus snapped back to attention. "*Ja?*"

"I know I've heard your name before, but I can't remember where."

Flashing a charitable smile, Dolphus said something about life being full of coincidences and then changed the subject by asking Elisabetta about the types of wine her father's vineyard produced. As she began listing them, Marco and Poppy returned from their walk.

Elisabetta, suddenly realizing she had taken someone's chaise, started to get up, but Marco insisted she stay put. He sat down in the sand at the foot of the lounge where Poppy now reclined and introduced himself. "I am Marco," he said. "Marco Bertozzi."

"Ah yes," said Elisabetta. "Mariella told me about you. I am Elisabetta Cavalleri. I met some of your family this morning." After explaining briefly why she had come to Forte dei Marmi, she said, "Your cousins and I are planning to meet again before I leave because Bianca may have more information for me regarding Armida Sigali. By the way, how are you related to Bianca?"

"She is my cousin."

"A rather distant one, I take it."

"In Italy, as you know, no cousin is distant."

Elisabetta laughed. "So very true." She glanced at Dolphus. "Were you supposed to talk to Marco about something, Signor Geller?"

"Ah yes," muttered Dolphus. "Mariella asked if you could drive the signora to her hotel when we are finished here at the beach. As soon as Aarika returns, I think I'll be ready to leave."

"There she is now," said Poppy, pointing to Aarika's approaching figure.

"Who is Aarika?" asked Elisabetta.

"She is my granddaughter." Standing up to gather his things, Dolphus said, "I suppose it's time to go. It was a great pleasure to meet you, Signora Cavalleri. I trust the remainder of your holiday here will be enjoyable."

"As a matter of fact," she replied, rising to face Dolphus, "I will be here for several more days. Bianca mentioned getting together for dinner before I leave. Can I count on you to join us?"

When Dolphus began offering excuses for why that might not be possible, Elisabetta insisted he make every effort to indulge her. "It's not often I meet someone who visited my home during the war," she said. "I am anxious to hear about it. We can't subject fate to convenience now, can we?"

Had Dolphus turned away—had he looked anywhere else but at her—he might have held firm and declined her invitation. But, transfixed by Elisabetta's penetrating brown eyes, he was helpless to reply any other way but with an obeisant, "Yes."

·21·

The Challenge

When Elisabetta Cavalleri contacted me to say she was in Versilia, the first thing I did was call my sisters Rina, Lida, and Bice. After all, we had known Armida Sigali when she was alive, and after Armida's body was brought back to Ripa and buried in the Vallecchia cemetery, we visited her grave many times. A connection between the Cavalleri family in Franciacorta and Armida was a mystery too great for us not to take an interest in.

Then, when Signora Cavalleri mentioned getting together for dinner, I explained the situation to Domenico. I told him I would like to have the others in the family meet the signora, but there were too many people to host the dinner at my villa.

"Would it be possible for you to host a dinner at your casala sometime this week?" I asked him. "I can help with the food."

"I would be happy to, Bianca," said Domenico. "Any dishes you and your sisters want to bring will be welcome, but I can provide most of the food. Are you sure Dolphus is amenable to me hosting a dinner at the casala while he is staying in the fattoria?"

"Oh yes. I asked Marco, and he was certain of it."

What I didn't tell Domenico was that Marco told me he thought Dolphus was smitten with the signora. Smitten! The very idea had me scrambling to arrange the next meeting with Signora Cavalleri soon.

Dolphus, a widower with a newly diagnosed medical condition, I thought, may just have met a new reason to live.

The atmosphere in the car as Marco drove Poppy and the Gellers back from the beach after dropping Signora Cavalleri off at her hotel was as frosty as a glass of cracked ice.

Following an extended period of silence, Aarika blurted, "Opa, I can't believe you took that woman up on an offer to join her for dinner. You don't even know her."

"Actually, Aarika, I met Signora Cavalleri years ago." Dolphus rushed to add that it was during the war. "She was a child. It's a long story and one not worth retelling right now."

"You have a history with her?" gasped Aarika.

"Not so different from the one you and Marco yourselves share," argued Dolphus. "You two met when you were children."

"No, Opa. There's a huge difference. You're old enough to be Signora Cavalleri's father. At least Marco and I are the same age; we were children together."

"It is true there is about a fifteen year age difference between the signora and I," Dolphus conceded. "But what does that have to do with anything? Elisabetta Cavalleri is simply a nice woman who invited me to dinner with the Bertozzi family. You are overreacting, Aarika. Why?"

"Because I'm all you have left, Opa, and it's up to me to

watch out for you since Oma died. Did you bother to see if Signora Cavalleri was wearing a wedding ring?"

Dolphus admitted he hadn't noticed. "Whether Elisabetta is married or not has no bearing on her and I becoming reacquainted."

Weighing in on the conversation, Marco said, "Signora Cavalleri has never been married."

Aarika puffed her lips, making a sound of disbelief. "And how would you know that, Marco?"

"I asked her. While all of you were in the cabana changing your clothes, she told me that when she was in her thirties she was engaged to a man for five years. He was an engineer for a construction company building a new tunnel through the mountains above Lago d'Iseo. Two weeks before their wedding he was killed on the job. He died in a dynamite blast that went wrong. They never found his body."

Dolphus clicked his tongue in sympathy. "Oh, no. How devastating for her."

"She never married," continued Marco. "The signora told me she was convinced she could never find anyone like him again and ultimately resigned herself to being single. She seems to be quite satisfied with her current life." Looking in the rearview mirror, he added, "I hope that clears up any doubts you have, Aarika. Signora Cavalleri is a respectable woman."

"Yes," said Dolphus, nodding his head vigorously. "She is most admirable."

Marco pulled up to the casala, put the car into park, turned off the ignition, and stepped out to help everyone carry their belongings into the house. Entering the kitchen, he proceeded to set out the lunch Domenico had left in the refrigerator for them. Poppy, sweeping through the kitchen on her way to the bedroom, whispered to Marco as she passed.

"Get ready for your alone time with Aarika that I promised," she said. "I'll figure out how you can pay me back later."

After a short interlude, Poppy reappeared. Dolphus and Aarika were seated at the kitchen table while Marco was busy unwrapping an assortment of meats, olives, and cheeses. "How long before lunch is ready, Marco?" she asked, innocently.

Marco glanced at the clock. "Five minutes. Maybe ten."

Poppy turned a beckoning finger to Dolphus. "There's a map of Italy on my wall. Could you come show me where Franciacorta is? I'm interested in seeing where Signora Cavalleri is from."

"My pleasure." Obediently, Dolphus got up and followed Poppy to her room.

Marco stopped what he was doing to address Aarika. "What are you so mad at me about?"

"How dare you make a scene in front of my grandfather?"

"What are you talking about?"

"Ordering me to go on a walk with you on the beach this morning."

"I did no such thing."

"Yes, you did," said Aarika. "You stretched your hand out to me and said, 'Come.'"

"That wasn't an order. It was an invitation."

"An ultimatum is what it was, Marco. You just can't resign yourself to the fact that I've made my decision and that decision doesn't include you."

In the background, Marco could hear Poppy drilling Dolphus for detailed information about the region of

Franciacorta in Lombardy. He knew he didn't have much longer to talk with Aarika, so he took a completely different approach. Sitting down next to her, he said, "You should be happy for your grandfather that there is a woman who has shown interest in him. I'm not saying it's anything more than that, but if a relationship were to develop between him and Signora Cavalleri, where would that leave you?"

"Opa isn't interested in women. He loved my grandmother. No one could ever take her place."

"I'm sure your grandmother would be happy for Dolphus if he found love again. If she were alive, I believe she would tell you that love is the key to living a full life."

Aarika stood up and backed away from Marco. "No. My grandmother would want me to protect Opa from women like Signora Cavalleri. She would expect me to watch out for his best interests."

"Love *is* in your grandfather's best interest," Marco insisted. "And yours."

Aarika raised her voice to a volume that was sure to draw Dolphus back into the kitchen. "Don't put words in my grandmother's mouth. You didn't know her. And stop filling my head with your ideas. It only makes it . . . "

Before Aarika could finish her sentence, Dolphus was back the kitchen, staring at them both and asking Aarika if there was something wrong. In response, Aarika covered her mouth with her hand and rushed out the door into the yard.

"We were talking about your wife," explained Marco, apologetically.

"I see."

The two men looked out the window and watched as Aarika fell into a chair beneath the chestnut tree. Dolphus did the same thing in the kitchen, dropping onto a stool next to the counter. "Sabine," he sighed. "How can I even begin to tell you what she meant to us?"

"Sabine? That was your wife's name?"

"Yes."

Poppy walked into the kitchen, but sensing the men wanted to be left alone, she grabbed an apple and a few slices of cheese and returned to her bedroom.

Marco handed Dolphus a glass of Chianti and pulled a stool up alongside him. "I'm listening," he said. "I want to know about Aarika's grandmother."

"It's a long story, I'm afraid." Dolphus cleared his throat several times before continuing. "Sabine and I met for the second time after I left the Cavalleri estate during the war . . ."

·22·

Sabine

DOLPHUS SNEAKED OFF the Cavalleri estate in the dead of night, leaving an unsuspecting Mariesole snoring so loudly she wouldn't have heard a cannon go off outside her window. Following a seventeen-day journey of brutal proportions, in which he forded streams, rode stolen bicycles, stowed away on a cargo ship, crossed the Italian border into Austria over the mountains by foot, hitched rides on deserted roads at night, and hiked through forests and fields during the day, he found himself standing at last in Café Mozart in Vienna.

By all appearances, Dolphus could easily have been mistaken for a civilian war refugee. His beard was long and scraggly, his dirty hair matted in knots, and his clothes were moldy, stinking rags. The circles beneath his hollow eyes were colored a sickly shade of gray-green and the loose skin on his veiny hands was a dead giveaway that he was malnourished. Worse, his mental state was as unstable as his physical condition.

When the bartender at Café Mozart asked Dolphus what it was he wanted, Dolphus scratched his head in a daze, as though he'd forgotten why he was there. It took a full minute before he finally stuttered, "Are you . . . Kurt?"

The bartender narrowed his eyes. "Who wants to know?"

Seemingly deep in thought, Dolphus stared at the ceiling and then leaned forward, motioning for the bartender to come close. "Jael has Sisera's head," he said, haltingly, his words jumbled.

The bartender's black eyes sparked. He snorted, and with a booming voice shouted, "We don't serve beggars here. Get out, or I'll call the police."

It was bone-chillingly frigid outside, and Dolphus, having barely escaped his months' long ordeal without succumbing to frostbite, wanted to stay inside the café as long as possible. Growls emanated from deep within his bowels. Every joint, every muscle, every fiber in his body ached. He thought of how everything he had endured, he had done so in anticipation of this very moment. Now, to think there might be no victory in his survival, that public humiliation and rejection at the hands of a sneering bartender in a popular café was his reward, that he might meet his end as an emaciated, frozen corpse in a back alley of a world-class city brought to its knees because of its collaboration with the Nazis—all of it was more than he could bear.

Hanging on for dear life to the glimmer of acknowledgement he imagined he had seen in Kurt's eyes, Dolphus resorted to begging. "Please," he implored him, "I need your help."

Kurt exploded. Throwing his towel on the bar, he raced around the counter to confront Dolphus. Seizing him by the collar, he stormed out of the café, yelling obscenities as he heaved Dolphus out the door.

A diner seated near the exit asked if he should summon the police, but Kurt told him it wasn't necessary. "I'll take care of this," he barked.

Outside, in the sub-arctic chill, Dolphus shivered. Kurt looked up and down the street and then made a show of shoving him away from the building. With his feet apart and his arms folded, he positioned himself against the doorframe, waiting for Dolphus to vacate the area. Dolphus lingered, confused and hesitant. Patrons who had been watching from inside the café got bored after a few minutes and turned back to their drinks.

Kurt took a few steps toward Dolphus and pointed south. "Get lost," he growled. Lowering his voice, he added, "Go to the Anker Bakery. At midnight they give away leftovers. Maybe you'll get lucky."

Like a lost, hungry dog, Dolphus made no sign of leaving.

Kurt pointed south again and yelled, "Go on!" but still, Dolphus wouldn't leave.

Lifting Dolphus off the ground, Kurt shoved his lips next to his ear. "Idiot!" he rasped. "Jael is in the city tonight. Get to the bakery before it's too late or it will be your head that has a stake driven through it." With that, he shoved Dolphus into the gutter and stomped back into the café.

It took awhile for Dolphus to struggle back to his feet and stumble in the direction Kurt had indicated he should go. At first everything was a blur. Then he remembered the code phrase "Jael has Sisera's head." It brought back the biblical story of Jael that he had learned as a child, the woman who had lured an enemy commander into her tent only to drive a peg through his temple as he slept. In bits and pieces, the story resurfaced in his memory until the prophecy of the warrior-prophetess Deborah scrolled across the interior of his mind: *"For the Lord will sell Sisera into the hand of a woman. Then Deborah got up and went with Barak . . . "*

Coughing and wheezing, Dolphus forced himself to

retrace the steps he and Sabine had taken together only a few months ago toward the bakery. He recalled it was opposite the Hotel Bristol—the hotel where Ralf had murdered a woman. Knowing he was at the end of his rope and convinced he was lost and without the strength to survive another night in the elements, Dolphus almost considered lying down against one of the ornate Baroque buildings he was passing. It would be so easy to just curl up into a fetal position and relinquish his spirit to the night. But the thought of maybe seeing Sabine again kept him placing one foot methodically in front of the other.

Ten minutes later he emerged onto the the Albertina-platz. Hotel Bristol's skeletal remains towered over a spectral landscape of gutted buildings. The sight stopped him in his tracks. Having only entered Vienna that evening in the back of a grain truck from Berndorf, he hadn't really noticed the extent of the destruction caused by the recent heavy Allied bombing of the city. Now, as he observed his surroundings, he was shocked by what he saw. A major portion of the hotel lay in ruins. Nearby, what had apparently once been an apartment building was now nothing but a pile of rubble. Smoke still rose in acrid curls from the smoldering debris.

He quickened his pace, his heart racing. *One more block, cross the street, turn the corner, on the left—no, on the right.* And suddenly, there it was. Anker Bakery loomed in front of him as warm and inviting as it had been months ago on the evening he and Sabine had stood salivating over the breads and pastries displayed in its window. He burst into the shop, inspecting the dozen or so faces that turned to stare at him.

"May I help you?" asked a stodgy white-aproned woman

standing behind the counter. Her sharp voice, flickering eyes, decisive movements, and graying hair swept into a tight, unforgiving bun, gave him little hope that she might really want to help him.

"I was told to come here," said Dolphus, tenuously.

"We give away our day-old products at midnight," she sniffed. Jabbing her thumb toward an empty table near the window, she added, "Go ahead and take a seat and keep warm until then. It will be about twenty more minutes."

Dolphus scrutinized the customers in the shop one more time before seating himself as told. A harsh overhead light hanging directly above him illuminated his reflection in the bakery window. He flinched, not recognizing the ghost of a man he saw staring back at him. Two German soldiers marched past the front of the shop, one of them doing a double take as he looked in the window at Dolphus.

Locking eyes with the solider, Dolphus panicked. *What if I'm being set up? What if it's Ralf who's going to come walking through the door, his gun aimed at my head?* The soldier, however, apparently looking at his own reflection in the glass, repositioned his hat, smoothed his coat lapels, and continued on.

A moment later, an oxidized copper bell attached to the store's front doorjamb tinkled with the arrival of a new customer. A slender woman wearing a hooded gray wool cape entered. Strolling up to the counter, she placed an order that was quickly filled and handed to her on a small tray. Glancing around the room, she settled on an empty table near Dolphus. Because she didn't lower her hood when she sat down, it was difficult for him to see her face.

"Here, sir."

Startled, Dolphus looked up. The no-nonsense woman behind the counter had materialized with a steaming cup of coffee for him. She set it down next to his elbow. "It's the bottom of the pot, but it's on the house. Enjoy."

Dolphus nodded his appreciation. The woman's looks certainly seemed to have belied her kindess. With a trembling hand, he raised the cup to his lips, but before he could take a drink, he dropped it. The hot liquid spilled onto the tabletop and streamed down the side of the table, just missing Dolphus's lap. The jarring sound of glass shattering on the tile floor caused a stir, and seconds later the rotund waitress was back with a broom, dustpan, and rag to clean up the mess.

Dolphus lowered his eyes in embarrassment, but raising them again he noticed that the caped woman sitting at the nearby table had dropped her hood and was now openly staring at him. Her eyes were the same color as the flowers on the Delft Blue teacup she held in her hands, and her shoulder-length hair, parted on the side, gleamed bright as sunlight falling on marble. Picking up her coffee and pastry, she rose and approached Dolphus.

"May I join you?" she asked.

Dolphus gestured weakly at the empty chair opposite him. Sliding her plate toward the center of the table, she sat down to face him. "I'm not hungry anymore," she said, pointing to what was left of her croissant. "Please. Be my guest."

Snatching the pastry from the plate, Dolphus shoved it into his mouth, keeping his hand against his lips to prevent any crumbs from escaping. While he devoured it, the waitress brought him another cup of coffee.

The caped woman nodded her thanks to the waitress before looking directly at Dolphus and saying, "Odd, isn't it, that in this once beautiful city, one building can be standing proud and untouched while the building next to it is in complete ruins?"

Dolphus stared at her, uncomprehendingly.

"Take this bakery, for example," she continued. "Across the street, the great Hotel Bristol lies wounded, while the humble Anker Bakery thrives unscathed. Such irony, but then, such is war."

Suddenly, a gnarled old baker popped his toque-covered head out of the kitchen and yelled, "Almost midnight. Line up here for a ration."

Chairs scraped away from tables as patrons raced to get in line. A throng of people, not visible in the street just moments before, appeared out of nowhere. They queued from the counter at the front of the bakery, out the partially opened door, and snaked down the sidewalk as far as Dolphus could see. Although the caped woman sitting with Dolphus seemed unfazed by the commotion, he grew alarmed. Not only did he not relish the thought of having to go outside to get a place in line, he was seeing Ralf's face in every person filing by him. He started to bolt, but the woman reached up and pulled him back down to his chair.

"There's no rush," she assured him. "I know the owner. You might as well stay here and keep warm until the crowd is gone. You know, you almost remind me of someone I met once. Right here, in Vienna."

Dolphus caught his breath. The woman was similar to how he remembered Sabine looking, but could he trust his memory?

"Although this particular man I met didn't have any facial hair," she said. "He was heavier than you. Younger too, perhaps. He was an artist and a soldier who had never been to Vienna before. We even stopped here at this very bakery and debated buying something."

Stunned, Dolphus mouthed the words: "Jael has Sisera's head."

"Dolphus?"

"Sabine?"

Throwing the hood back over her head so that her face was again obscured, Sabine shot to her feet. She tossed a coin on the table and as she slid past Dolphus, she pretended to stumble over something. Leaning down momentarily near Dolphus's ear, she whispered, "I'll be standing in front of the ruins of Hotel Bristol. Wait several minutes before following me. Someone may be watching us. Don't let anyone see you speaking to me again." Then, straightening back up, she placed her hand on Dolphus's shoulder. "Poor man," she said loudly. "I pray you find shelter tonight. I'm sorry I can't be of any help to you."

Dolphus watched as Sabine wrapped her cloak tightly around her and made her way toward the front door, squeezing through knots of beggars clogging the entrance to the bakery. He waited another five minutes, as instructed, before getting up to leave. He noticed the waitress behind the counter nodded at him as he vacated his table. *Did she know Sabine? Was she in league with whatever Sabine was involved in?*

Stepping outside, Dolphus was hit with a blast of damp, frigid air. He repositioned his backpack, held his hands up to his mouth, blew on them several times, and then tucked them under his armpits. Across the street, he could just make out Sabine standing beneath a streetlamp at a bus stop in front of Hotel Bristol.

With renewed focus and a burst of energy Dolphus hadn't thought he had left in him, he began walking toward her. But when he was less than twenty feet from her, she turned and took off at a fast pace along the nearly empty Opernring. Traffic was light and very few people were out walking, even though most of the bars and nightclubs were still open. Few of the city's streetlamps were lit, and dense pockets of fog licking through the cobblestone streets and alleys limited his vision even more. As a result, Dolphus eventually resorted to trailing Sabine by listening to the sound of her feet crunching on the snow-packed pavement.

Suddenly, her footsteps stopped. Dolphus paused, his ears straining to hear if they would resume again. When, after at least five minutes, he heard nothing, he continued walking blindly until he found himself at the back of a dead-end alley. Not sure where he had made the wrong turn, Dolphus turned around and retraced his steps. Near the entrance to the alley, a sound—like someone clearing their throat—raised the hair on the back of his neck. All evening, he hadn't been able to shake the feeling that Ralf was somewhere close. Crouching down beside a dumpster, he peered into the dense mist, steeling himself for an ambush.

He heard the same light growl again, but this time he was able to identify it as coming from a stray dog. His relief was short-lived. Seconds later, his ears pricked at the sound of an approaching vehicle. He held his breath and watched as a large boxy contraption, looking as though it were half-tank and half-car, slowed down, turned off its lights, and rolled to a noiseless stop just a few feet from him. Hemmed in on both sides by the alley, and now blocked by the vehicle in front of him, Dolphus reached inside his backpack for his gun. As he did, the back door of the car creaked open and the dome light switched on, illuminating a hooded figure beckoning to him from the back seat. Sabine extended her hand toward Dolphus. Stepping away from the dumpster, Dolphus lunged toward the car, grasped her hand, and slid into the backseat next to her.

It wasn't until they were well out of the Old City, heading west through the outskirts of Vienna, that the car stopped trundling along at a snail's pace and began to pick up speed. Only then, also, did the driver, who had been silent until now, turn to address Dolphus. Grinning widely, and with a thick British accent, he said, "Impressive motorcar, eh? It's a Volkswagen wood-burning Holzbrenner. Being German, you may have seen one before, but I didn't until I got stuck in this hellhole of a war."

"Just drive, Henry," said Sabine. "Let me know when we're close."

"Whatever m'lady says."

Sabine put her hand on Dolphus's knee and apologized. "Sorry about the secrecy, Dolphus. We can't be too careful. Some of us have paid a high price for being careless, but be assured, you were never out of our sight." Lifting her hand, she brushed a long shock of hair away from Dolphus's eyes. "If what you've been through is reflected in how you look, I'm guessing you've had a rough go of it, Dolphus. It took me awhile to recognize you."

Then, pulling a navy silk scarf from her bag, Sabine tied it around Dolphus's head so that his eyes were completely covered. "I hope you don't mind," she said. "Unfortunately, this is standard procedure for everyone we rescue."

From that point on, all that Dolphus could tell was that eventually his ears began to pop, and nearly an hour later the car was parked and he was stumbling—aided by Henry and

Sabine—on gravel and packed snow, with the smell of fir and pine filling his nostrils, for what seemed an eternity.

THE HIDEOUT WHERE Dolphus found himself sequestered, along with several other injured fugitives, was a remote mountain cabin built by Sabine's maternal grandparents at the turn of the century. They had died at the outset of the war, but as her parents were currently prisoners at the Mauthausen-Gusen work camp, the property had been sitting empty and unused for over a year. That is, until Sabine offered it to her partisan conspirators as a safe house for wounded enemy soldiers.

Not including Sabine, there were a total of six fugitives in hiding, all of them male. Henry, the driver of the wood-burning Volkswagen, was—apart from Dolphus—the newest member of the group. A downed RAF pilot, Henry's mother was a German national. He had grown up in a bilingual home, thus equipping him with language skills considered invaluable to British intelligence. Sabine had put him to use as soon as he was rescued from the woods outside Vienna, less than two months ago.

A Jewish boy by the name of Karl, about seventeen, was the youngest among them. He was the lone survivor of a family who had been arrested and sent to the same concentration camp as Sabine's parents nearly two years ago. It was a forgone conclusion that they were dead, although Sabine pretended otherwise whenever Karl was around. The entire right side of the boy's body was palsied—a condition he'd had since birth. Sabine, he said, had saved him after witnessing a gang of Nazi thugs nearly beat him to death outside his home on Kristallnacht, following the Anschluss in

1938. With her help, he had found sanctuary in Vienna, but was eventually forced to flee when the Allied bombing raids destroyed his protector's home. Though he didn't talk about it, he knew, along with everyone else, what happened to the handicapped who fell into Nazi hands. The same thing that happened, and was happening, to each and every Jew in Austria. They disappeared and were never seen or heard from again.

The other three fugitives at the hideout were wounded Resistance fighters whose health, under Sabine's diligent care, was gradually being restored. But of all the men there, it was Karl who stood out the most. Dolphus was amazed at the way the boy carried himself with such confidence, honor, and courage. He never complained, nor did he shirk responsibilities because of his disability. In fact, Karl carried his own weight, whether it was splitting wood one-armed, hauling water, hunting, foraging for food, cooking, cleaning, or whatever it was that needed to be done. And he did it diligently.

Dolphus was able to make such in-depth character judgments about his peers because, since he had arrived three weeks ago, he hadn't stepped foot off the property. He had no desire to leave, and fortunately for him, Sabine didn't think he was ready yet either. She insisted he needed a few more weeks to regain his strength and heal from the minor wounds he'd incurred while on the run from Italy. Dolphus marveled at her fearlessness and deep compassion for others. The level of trust she had shown him when he was still in the army was astonishing. She had taken the initial risk when she gave him the code name by which to reach her if he was ever in trouble. Then, she lived up to her offer by rescuing him in Vienna, no questions asked. Yes, Sabine was incredibly daring.

She was trusting on a personal level too, not just a professional one. Once, when Dolphus tried to give Sabine details of what had happened in Italy, she gently silenced him. "You said you deserted the *Wehrmacht* after nearly killing an officer who was going to rape and kill some innocent women," she said. "That's all I need to know, Dolphus. I just want to see you well again."

Whenever Dolphus imagined Sabine was treating him special, he had to remind himself that she couldn't be playing favorites because she also encouraged his fellow fugitives to stay at the cabin as long as possible. Still, with each day that passed, it grew increasingly more difficult for Dolphus to watch Sabine tend to the others as sensitively as she cared for him. Especially Henry.

Henry had been granted a position of privilege immediately upon his arrival at the cabin. He had supposedly been rescued with nothing more critical than sore knees due to a rough emergency parachute landing. Other than that, he was simply waiting for the Resistance to help get him back to England, or for the war to end, whichever came first. Sabine seemed thrilled to have someone with his expertise accompany her on random secret missions. The two were highly secretive about their capers, plotting them out together privately in the woodshed behind the cabin. Dolphus noted that the only consistent aspect of their subterfuge was that they always left on their assignments under cover of night and returned before dawn.

There was plenty of speculation among the fugitives about where Sabine and Henry went and what they did while they were gone. Dolphus guessed that since there was no more room at the cabin, any Resistance fighters they were rescuing were being escorted to other hideouts dispersed throughout the mountains. Apart from that, the only thing he was confident of—because he remembered it from his own arrival at the safe house—was the route Sabine and Henry took each time they left the cabin. They would have to first cross the meadow on which the cabin was situated and then descend the mountain on a long circuitous footpath to reach the car, which was undoubtedly camouflaged in a thicket off the side of the road.

As Dolphus lay in his bunk bed, in the room he shared with two other fugitives, he continued to ponder the last three weeks of his life. Apart from his companions' sporadic grunts and snores, he treasured the safety and solitude of the mountain hideout. His time there hadn't erased the trauma of his sojourn in Italy—he didn't expect anything would ever completely eradicate those memories—but lying there listening to the soothing hoots of a distant Eagle Owl and the occasional howl of a lone wolf, he believed he was on the road to recovery.

Little did he know that two days later his road to recovery would be hijacked.

DOLPHUS HAD JUST finished his dinner of cabbage soup and rustic bread when he noticed Sabine motioning for him to follow her outside. The air was crisp as a fresh-picked apple, and if the moon would have been fuller it surely would have burst. Dolphus noticed that the deep snowdrifts which had greeted him on his arrival had recently melted down into scattered mounds of dirty slush. Spikes of dead meadow grass poked up in irregular patches between the piles of snow. At the edge of the clearing, Sabine stopped next to an old well. Built in traditional Austrian fashion, it consisted of a low circular stone wall with an overhead wood frame and a blackened oak cover that fit tightly over the opening.

Motioning for Dolphus to sit next to her on top of the well, Sabine explained that her family used to drink water from it when she was a little girl, but it had since gone dry. The cabin now got its water, she said, from a holding tank built below a nearby spring. After a few more minutes of small talk, Sabine cleared her throat. "You can't imagine how comforting it is for me to see your health returning to you, Dolphus."

"Was I that bad?"

"Let's just say when I first saw you in the Anker Bakery, I was convinced it couldn't be you. You looked like an old tramp, not the young soldier I had met on his first visit to Vienna just a few months ago."

Dolphus grinned. "It goes to show what a sharp razor, lots of sleep, home-cooked food, and a good-hearted woman can do for a man."

"You're alive and well today, Dolphus, because you persevered and kept your wits about you. Not everyone is capable of that." Taking note of the satchel slung over his shoulder, she added, "I'm curious, Dolphus. Why do you insist on carrying your backpack with you everywhere you go?"

Dolphus shrugged as though it was obvious. "I like having my gun and ammunition with me at all times."

"I would think by now you would feel perfectly safe here."

"I'm not the only one here who is never without their gun." he argued.

"If you're talking about Harry, he needs to be armed

and ready to go at a moment's notice. Plus, I rely on him to protect me and keep guard over all of us here. He's a good marksman."

Dolphus met Sabine's gaze. "Have you had this discussion with any of the other men?"

Sabine lowered her eyes. "I don't feel for the other men like I feel for you, Dolphus."

Dolphus's euphoria was tempered by a doubt that had been nagging him ever since he had told Sabine about Italy. "Do you think that because I'm a deserter, I'm a failure as a soldier?" he asked. "That I can't be trusted with a gun?"

"I never said that."

"You don't have to, to think it."

"Accidents happen, Dolphus. That's all I'm saying. The truth is, if anything ever happened to you, I'd be . . . devastated."

Setting his backpack on the ground, Dolphus placed his hands around Sabine's waist and drew her close to him. "You really mean it?"

"I've never been more serious in my life."

As Sabine nestled close to him, the hood of her cape slipped off, allowing Dolphus to bury his face in her hair. Then he kissed her eyelids and followed the contour of her face with his lips until, wanting more of her, he began tracing the pink, pliable lobes of her ears with his tongue. Before he knew what he was doing, he had unwound the muffler from her neck so that he could taste the skin on her throat. Discovering the delicate v-notch at the top of her breast bone, he began to feverishly unbutton her cape.

They were so consumed with each other that neither of them saw, nor heard, someone enter the cabin through the back door. And so it was no surprise that they were both startled when, moments later, a light in the rear of the cabin switched on, flooding the clearing with a soft yellow glow.

"Everyone knows the generator is low on fuel," muttered Dolphus, blinking at the unwelcome intrusion. "Why aren't they using the gas lamps?"

Seconds later, several shouts erupted from the house. Shadows jerking behind the curtains suggested there was a scuffle going on inside.

Reluctantly, Sabine pulled away from Dolphus. "The boys are probably just having one of their wrestling matches," she sighed, "but it is a bit strange, isn't it?" Standing up, she wound her muffler around her neck and rebuttoned her cape. "I suppose we should go back and check it out."

Before Sabine took her first step, however, Dolphus tackled her to the ground. Shoving her behind the well, he squatted down next to her and ordered her not to move. Within seconds, he had his gun primed and ready to fire.

"Don't you think you're overreacting?" asked Sabine, her voice a mixture of surprise and irritation.

Before Dolphus could respond, the front door of the cabin opened and six men, walking in a single file—four of them with their hands behind their heads—stepped outside. The last man in the group was several inches taller than the rest, setting him apart from the others. Despite the benefit of a full moon, the distance from the well to the cabin made it impossible for Dolphus to clearly see any of their faces.

"Who's the sixth person?" whispered Sabine, peeking over the top of the well.

Dolphus placed his index finger to his lips for silence and motioned for Sabine to keep her head down.

A harsh, crazed voice pierced the air. "Where are they?"

The response to the question came from Henry, in

German. "They're here somewhere. I just have to find their tracks."

On his haunches, with his back braced against the well, Dolphus inched his way around so that he could look out on the clearing without being seen. He watched as the man he assumed was Henry stepped away from the other men, a flashlight shining in one of his hands. Dolphus could make out the glint of a pistol in Henry's other hand.

Suddenly, Karl cried out, "Sabine! It's not safe!"

Henry spun around, aimed his gun at Karl, and fired. The boy gasped, clutched at his chest with his good hand and crumpled to the ground. With the toe of his boot, Henry kicked Karl's defenseless body several times before raising his gun and firing another shot, this time into his head.

"Well, there's one less burden for the Reich to bear," quipped Henry.

The tall man barked for the rest of the fugitives to line up horizontally in front of him, forming a protective shield. Henry, meanwhile, pointed his flashlight at the well and said, "They're this way."

Dolphus tucked his head back behind the well. Shock and rage had coalesced into resolve. Placing his lips near Sabine's ear, he whispered, "My cousin has caught up with me finally. He's the one I almost killed in Italy. Whatever happens, Sabine, he cannot be trusted."

Sabine nodded in recognition of Dolphus's warning.

Henry was just several yards away from them now. "Come out, lovebirds," he crooned.

Dolphus gripped the handle of his gun. Then, faster than he'd ever moved in his life, he flattened himself on the ground. Thrusting his torso out and away from the well, he aimed and fired twice. The first bullet grazed Henry's hand, flinging his gun into the woods next to the clearing, and the second hit Henry square in the chest. As the traitor keeled backward, slamming to earth with a dull thud, Dolphus ducked back behind the well.

"So you're armed, are you?" screeched the tall man. "Too bad you had to kill Heinrich. Or shall I say, *Henry*. He was one of our best agents. Without him, I would never have found you after I lost your scent in Vienna. Pity. Now it looks like I'll have to kill your friends to get to you."

"It's me you want, Ralf," yelled Dolphus. "Let them go."

"Ah, so you know it's me then. I was hoping for an element of surprise. I tried disguising my voice."

"You can't disguise evil, cousin."

Ralf laughed hysterically. "You, of all people, talk to *me* of evil? I wouldn't call leaving your own flesh and blood for dead 'virtuous,' Dolphus. Treason is a crime, you know. Punishable by death. I couldn't let anyone else have the pleasure of killing you now, could I? Oh, if only you knew how many times I was close to catching you. Why, had I arrived at the Anker Bakery only ten minutes earlier than I did a few weeks ago, we wouldn't be having this pointless, silly little confrontation tonight. I would say, cousin, after all you've put me through, justice rests in my hands tonight."

"Why don't we both drop our weapons and fight it out like men?" shouted Dolphus. "Just you and me. Then we'll see which one of us has justice on his side."

"Ah, Dolphus, Dolphus. You know it doesn't work that way. There's no negotiating with Ralf Geller. If you and the girl don't step away from behind that well with your hands over your heads by the time I count to three, the executions will begin."

Dolphus placed his hands behind his head and dropped

his gun into the fox-lined hood of his parka. Turning to Sabine, he said, "No matter what happens, Sabine, I'll protect you. Do you trust me?"

Sabine nodded.

Ralf began counting. "*Ein, zwei . . .*"

Leaping to his feet, his hands folded behind his head, Dolphus moved away from the well, using the toe of one of his boots to kick his backpack in front of him on the ground. Shadow-like, Sabine followed directly behind him.

"Your gun!" snarled Ralf.

Raising his foot, Dolphus kicked his satchel several yards into the copse of fir trees nearest them, where Henry's gun had landed. "It's in there," he cried out. "Go get it Ralf."

Ralf's field-gray trench coat and shiny, black leather jackboots made him appear larger than life. Moonlight reflected off the visor of his officer's cap and the gold Reich eagle pin near its crown. The overall effect was so sinister, it was no surprise the fugitives jumped when Ralf ordered them to stand aside so that Dolphus could approach him face-to-face.

Dolphus was within spitting distance when Ralf raised his hand for him to stop. "Why would you put your gun back in your satchel and throw it away?" he asked, suspiciously.

"Because I didn't want you to get it," replied Dolphus.

"Idiot." Ralf brandished his gun in the air. "One gun is all I need to finish you off, Dolphus."

"It's your gun, Ralf. The Mauser you gave me."

"Killing me with my own gun? Too bad you'll be denied the pleasure. I'll retrieve it tomorrow morning after I've decided what to do with you . . . or, I should say, your body." Motioning for Dolphus to come closer, Ralf added, "Of course, I'll need to decide what to do with your friends here as well. Ammunition is scarce these days. Rather than wasting bullets on them, perhaps after I've disposed of you I'll torch the cabin with them in it. What do you think?"

Dolphus, now almost nose to nose with Ralf, replied, "I think you're damned."

Thrusting the nose of his gun into Dolphus's belly, Ralf hissed, "Then I'm taking you with me, cousin."

Ralf used his free hand to quickly frisk Dolphus and finding nothing in his pockets he instructed him to take off his boots. As Dolphus bent down to remove them, Ralf got his first look at Sabine.

"Well, well," he trilled. "Who do we have here? Is this the Sabine I've heard so much about?"

Sabine met Ralf's taunt with a defiant glare.

"You know, your old friend at the bakery told me all kinds of fascinating things about you," said Ralf. "It took awhile to extract the information from her, but eventually she gave in."

"What did you do to her?" cried Sabine, lunging toward Ralf.

His boots off, Dolphus leaped to his feet, positioning his body protectively in front of Sabine.

Ralf waved his gun wildly. "Hands back behind your head!"

Obeying, Dolphus growled, "I swear, Ralf. If you touch her, I'll kill you."

Cunning and lithe as a cougar, Ralf began circling around the two of them, his eyes trained solely on Sabine. "Perishing in a fire with her beloved refugees would be a death far too noble for such a traitor to the Führer," he said. "Don't worry, Dolphus, I'll think of an end more suitable for your beautiful little partisan."

Ralf took note of Dolphus's horror and fell into a fit of laughter. Lowering his hands he made a crude gesture below his belt.

In a smooth, split-second maneuver, while Ralf's hands were lowered, Dolphus reached back into the hood of his parka for his gun and rammed it lightning fast into Ralf's temple. Simultaneously, he wrestled Ralf's gun away from him. Handing his cousin's weapon to Sabine, Dolphus then ordered one of his fellow fugitives to get some rope from the shed and secure Ralf's hands behind his back.

Bristling, Ralf hissed, "So, you're going to finish what you started in Italy, are you?"

"What I did in Italy wasn't an attempt to kill you," replied Dolphus. "I was simply trying to stop you from taking the lives of two innocent women." After Ralf's wrists were bound, Dolphus instructed everyone, including Sabine, to go back inside the cabin.

Sabine hesitated. "But he said he would . . ."

"Trust me, Sabine. He'll never kill another soul." Motioning her close, Dolphus added, "Once everyone's in the cabin, keep them away from the windows. I don't want anyone but me ever knowing what happens here tonight. Now go."

Once Sabine had ushered everyone back into the cabin, Dolphus ordered Ralf to march in front of him to the well.

"Your feet must be cold," said Ralf, peering back over his shoulder at Dolphus. "You're still in your stockings. Don't you want to put your boots back on?"

"And give you a chance to pull another one of your tricks, Ralf? I don't think so."

Ralf wavered as they drew closer to the well. "So you think you're going to throw me in alive and let me die of starvation if the fall doesn't kill me?" His voice cracked. "I know you, Dolphus. You can't do it."

Calmly, Dolphus replied, "You don't know me at all."

"You're too much of a coward to go through with it," argued Ralf. "You've always been weak. Besides, you owe me. Remember when I saved you from getting killed by that train?"

Dolphus, struggling with the mention of their shared history, refused to reply. Arriving at the well, he unlatched the lid and lifted it off.

"No!" whimpered Ralf. "Please, Dolphus! I'm your blood relative, for God's sake. I don't deserve to die like a rat!"

"But you are a rat, Ralf," said Dolphus evenly. "And here's where you're wrong about me: I'm not weak, I'm merciful. You've always confused the two. I'm going to give you to the count of three to make your peace with God."

The next few seconds seemed an eternity to Dolphus as he stared into the eyes of his trembling cousin, the man he had once idolized as a child. Boyhood scenes of them fishing together and swimming in the rivers around Passau flooded his mind. Steeling himself, he took a deep breath and counted, "*Ein, zwei, drei . . .*"

The bullet entered just above Ralf's left eye, barely knocking his upper torso over the rim of the well. Dolphus tucked his gun into his belt, and placing his arms around his cousin's legs, he lifted the rest of his body over the ledge and let go. Then, leaning forward, he gazed down into black nothingness and listened. It was the grinding thump of Ralf's body hitting the bottom of the well—the crunch of his bones being broken on impact—that cemented the reality of his death in Dolphus's consciousness forever.

Not allowing himself time to think about what he had just done, Dolphus retraced his steps through the clearing, found his boots, and pulled them back on. Then, grabbing Henry's stiff feet, he dragged his corpse to the well. It took considerable effort to lift the dead weight onto the stone ledge, but once he did, it was a simple matter of using both hands and one of his feet to shove him in. When the dull, fleshy thud of Henry's body breaking over Ralf's reached him, he hurriedly picked up the lid to the well, placed it back over the opening, and secured it tightly. Then he returned to the cabin. Stepping inside, he was greeted by five ashen faces staring at him in gratitude.

Sabine rushed into his arms. "You saved our lives, Dolphus."

But Dolphus, having gone numb, felt nothing. The immensity of what he had done sank into his soul with a vengeance. How could he possibly live with himself knowing he had killed his own cousin? How could he ever face Ralf's parents? Did Henry have a wife, or children?

As he and Sabine embraced, Dolphus realized that Henry's betrayal must have struck her to the core. So he comforted her as best he could and then stepped back to address everyone. "We need to take care of Karl's body," he said. "Tonight. Before the wolves get to him. Who wants to help me?"

·23·

Denial

Sitting in the kitchen of Domenico's *fattoria*, Marco listened as Dolphus finished telling him the story of how he and Sabine had met and survived the war. He told Marco everything but Ralf's real name and the episode on Monte Montignoso preceding his defection.

"He was my cousin," was all Dolphus would say about Ralf. "And he tracked me down in Austria for an incident that happened during the war." With a faraway look in his eyes, he sighed and then added, "Thank you for listening to me, Marco. This is the first time anyone other than my wife has known what happened that night in the Alps at the safe house. What is it about your country that makes a man spill his soul and feel better for doing it? I feel as though I have just been to confession."

"I am no priest," protested Marco, finding it difficult to believe that the mild-mannered man sitting before him had murdered a member of his own family in cold blood. "But I imagine the relief you must feel."

Dolphus massaged his chest, as though he had heartburn. "Relief? Yes, yes."

Marco glanced out the window at Aarika, still sitting dejectedly under the tree. "Your story helps me understand why Aarika is still grieving her grandmother's death. Sabine must have been an extraordinary woman. It took great courage to do the things she did. Just like our partisans here during the war."

"My wife had the courage of a lion," declared Dolphus. "When our son died, it was she who kept our family going. You see, Conrad used my gun—my cousin's gun—to kill himself. Sabine had begged me to get rid of it after the war, but I didn't."

"Why not?

"In hindsight," explained Dolphus, "I realize I had a warped kind of attachment to it. The gun, you see, had belonged to my cousin in the first place. So, sometimes, when I found myself haunted by his death, I would go into the barn where I kept it hidden. I would hold it and weep. It was—how would you say?—a touchstone connecting us. I feared if I got rid of it, it might seem like my cousin never existed. I couldn't allow that. I must never forget what I did to him."

"You killed him in self-defense," said Marco. "And you saved others as well."

Dolphus stopped rubbing his chest. "It doesn't change the fact that I murdered him."

"Where is the gun now?" asked Marco.

"I destroyed it after Conrad killed himself. Sabine did her best to try and convince me that if he hadn't used the gun, he would have found another way to kill himself. But, after we buried my son, I went into the barn, to the exact location where I found his body, wrapped the gun in several layers of burlap, took a sledge hammer, and hit it over and over again until my arms finally gave out. Then I took what was left of the gun down to the River Inn, to a spot where my cousin and I used to fish, and I threw it in."

"As you can imagine," continued Dolphus, "during that time I was too consumed with grief and guilt to be of use to anyone. I spent every waking moment working my farm and doing nothing else. It was Sabine who ultimately became both a mother and a father to Aarika. It wasn't until after she died that I was forced to be fully present for my grand-daughter. I have failed so many people in my life, Marco. Can you see why I have to be here for Aarika now?"

"I do." Marco stood up. "I'm going to go to her."

"Yes," said Dolphus, grudgingly. "You probably should. But before you do, there's one more thing." He struggled to get the words out. "Don't think that Elisabetta Cavalleri changes anything. I was simply shocked to meet her this morning on the beach. That's all."

"I'm not sure I understand."

"Well, Aarika was suggesting, that I . . . that I have feelings for the signora. Elisabetta asked us to dinner and I accepted as any gentleman would. There is nothing wrong with that."

"Of course not."

"I mean, there's nothing more to it."

"If you say so."

"I will never remarry."

"But, that's too bad. I really think . . ."

Dolphus frowned. "What you think is irrelevant, Marco. First of all, I will never find anyone like Sabine, and secondly, as I told you, there are too many differences between our countries. Even if there were feelings between the signora and I—which there aren't—it wouldn't work."

"It is true there are differences between our cultures,"

agreed Marco. "But we are humans first before we are Germans or Italians. The story you just told me illustrates that. Evil doesn't have a nationality and love doesn't discriminate. You are free to do whatever you want with your life, signore. Don't wait until you are forced to make a decision that will determine your destiny. Choose before you run out of choices."

With that, Marco excused himself and stepped outside. When he reached Aarika, he dropped to one knee and took her hands in his. "Aarika, I'm so sorry," he said. "Your grandfather told me about Sabine. What a great, strong woman your grandmother was."

Aarika slumped forward. "I can't believe he told you about her. Opa's always been so tight-lipped about the past."

Marco drew her hands to his lips and kissed them. "Stay here with me, Aarika. Don't go back to Germany."

"Part of me wants to, but . . ."

"Then stay!"

Pulling her hands away from him, Aarika shook her head. "I can't leave my grandfather by himself, Marco. And what about me? I haven't finished college. I can't speak Italian . . ."

"I'll teach you. It won't be a problem, I promise."

"Other than you and your family, I don't know anyone here. The language barrier would make it hard for me to make friends . . ."

"As long as we have each other, we'll be fine."

Smiling sadly, Aarika said, "Most of all, it would be unfair to you, Marco. You deserve someone who is not as crippled by their past as I am. You're full of life. You're happy, positive. I'm, well . . . I'm not."

"I realize we're different in some ways, and maybe it will

be a more difficult road we'll have to travel together than I imagine," Marco admitted. "But everyone has things from their past they need to deal with. We all have our own problems and weaknesses."

"Yes, but I have more than others it seems." Aarika's voice turned hoarse. "That's what I'm trying to tell you. Honestly, Marco, I've felt so unlovable most of my life it's hard to believe anyone could really love me. I keep telling myself you can't possibly care for me the way you claim you do."

"But I *do* love you. Why can't you believe me?"

"Opa doesn't approve. I tell you, Marco, there are too many things at work against us."

"I respect your grandfather," said Marco. "But you realize that he, too, will die one day. What then?"

"You don't think I haven't thought of that?"

"Well?"

"By the time Opa's gone, I'll . . . I'll probably have a husband. And children."

Provoked by the impulsiveness of Aarika's statement, by her tendency to turn on a dime when confronted with decisions that frightened her, Marco asked, almost sarcastically, "You're sure of that?" When she didn't answer, Marco stood to his feet. "And who would that husband be?"

Aarika lowered her eyes. "Whomever I choose."

Taking a step away from her, Marco crossed his arms and scanned Aarika from head to toe. "I know you love me, Aarika, but I will tell you what I told your grandfather: Don't wait until you are forced to make a decision that will determine your destiny. Choose before you run out of choices. It's the only way you'll know you made the right one.

"I'm not saying I can't wait for you," he continued. "But

I'm afraid that when you get back to Germany, you'll talk yourself out of what you're feeling right now. You'll convince yourself our love isn't real."

With a desperate ring in her voice, Aarika asked, "Can't we continue to love each other as friends?"

"I could never just be your friend, Aarika. I'd always want more."

·24·

Armida

MARCO WENT HOME after his conversation with Aarika believing he was no longer needed since the Gellers had indicated they didn't want to go anywhere that evening. About five o'clock, however, he received a call from Domenico.

"Guess what? Have you heard of Signora Elisabetta Cavalleri? She is here to find out about Armida Sigali, Egisto's wife."

"As a matter of fact, I met her on the beach this morning," said Marco.

"She is a beautiful woman, no?"

"For her age, I suppose she is."

"Well, Bianca told her that the Gellers are staying at my fattoria. It turns out a wine merchant the signora was to meet with this evening had to cancel his appointment with her. What with it being Sunday, and everything closed, she asked Bianca if she thought I'd mind if she came up to see the place. Of course, since I've already made dinner, I insisted she come and share a meal with us. Would you mind picking up the signora at her hotel and bringing her to the fattoria, Marco? Of course, I'll need you to stay and interpret for us."

"Does Dolphus know about this?" asked Marco.

"How could he? There is no phone service on the mountain."

"I know, but I thought there were plans for a dinner with the signora another night."

"All I know, Marco, is that Signora Cavalleri would like to visit this evening. Can you bring her or not?"

Marco sighed. "I'll pick her up at her hotel and meet you and Mariella at your house in half an hour."

"*Ciao*, Marco."

"*Ciao*."

Nearly an hour later, the four of them arrived at the fattoria. Domenico hastened the signora to the edge of the property and introduced her to the lay of the land. He showed her the vineyard and olive orchard, telling her its history, his methods of tending the vines, and which years had produced the best vintages. He also pointed out the panorama spread out below them: the dazzling Ligurian Sea, the scattered islands barely visible on the horizon, and the names of all the hamlets and villages dotting the coastline. The signora appeared enthralled.

Meanwhile, Marco and Mariella transported all the food from the car to the kitchen in the casala.

"Where is everyone?" asked Marco.

Mariella waved toward the fattoria. "Dolphus is napping in his room. The girls are out back somewhere drinking tea."

It was Signora Cavalleri's unexpected laughter at one of Domenico's jokes—a full-throated rondo, like the bells pealing hourly throughout the churches in the valley—that made her presence on the property known.

Dolphus, shirtless and rubbing his eyes, his thick silver hair matted to one side of his head, leaned out his upper bedroom window to see what was going on. Apparently catching sight of Elisabetta, he ducked back inside.

Meanwhile, Domenico smiled and waved at Aarika and Poppy who suddenly appeared around the corner of the house. "*Buonasera!*" he cried out to them.

Aarika returned his greeting and skulked into the house. Poppy, however, approached Domenico and Elisabetta, her hand extended toward the signora. "So we meet again," she said cheerily. "Elisabetta, right?"

"*Si*. And you are Poppy." Elisabetta shook Poppy's hand firmly and then kissed both of her cheeks. "Such lovely red hair and beautiful eyes. I could never forget you."

While the two women exchanged pleasantries, Marco returned to the car to retrieve the last of the food. Poppy caught his eye as he was shutting the trunk, and excusing herself from Elisabetta, she approached him.

"Do you need any help, Marco?" she asked.

Marco handed Poppy a flat cardboard box containing dried homemade ravioli and instructed her to take it inside to Mariella, who was setting a pot of water on the stove to boil.

Taking the box from Marco, Poppy whispered, "This ought to be interesting. I'll be back out to help you soon. I've got something to tell you." True to her word, less than five minutes later she was on the patio helping Marco set up chairs and arrange wine bottles, glasses, silverware, plates, napkins, and candles on the table.

Poppy kept her voice hushed. "Aarika was really agitated after you left today," she said. "Remember when Dolphus was thinking of maybe going back to Germany early? I heard her tell him she definitely wants to leave on the tenth when

I leave to go back to the States, rather than staying until the fifteenth like they had originally planned."

"What did Dolphus say?"

"That's what's so funny. Just yesterday, he was still talking about changing their return tickets, even though it would be expensive to do and a huge hassle. But today, when Aarika told him she wanted to leave early, he said they couldn't. He told her they *had* to stay until the fifteenth. When she pressed him to explain why, he just said it was out of the question."

Marco glanced across the yard at Elisabetta, who was still conversing with Domenico.

"Yep," said Poppy, as though reading his thoughts. "That's what I think. Elisabetta threw a big fat wrench in Dolphus's plans and Aarika knows it. She was so mad. I wish you could have seen her."

Pensively, Marco said, "It gives me more time, and time is what Aarika needs to make up her mind."

Poppy, distracted by the sight of an immaculately groomed Dolphus emerging from the house, let out a low whistle. "Wow, what did I tell you?"

Marco followed her gaze. In striking contrast to his deeply tanned skin, the elderly German wore a freshly pressed, white linen shirt and dark dress pants, paired with Italian leather shoes. His hair was perfectly combed, his cheeks smooth from a quick shave. As he passed by Marco and Poppy, he said "good evening," and then hurried toward Domenico and Elisabetta.

"He looks ten years younger, doesn't he," noted Poppy, gaping after Dolphus as he glided across the lawn, his shoulders back, his posture straight and sure. Nudging Marco with her elbow, she added, "If I were a single woman in my fifties, I'd chase him down and reel him in before he had a chance to know what hit him."

"The signora isn't the type to go chasing after men," said Marco.

"Don't bet on it."

Marco reached for Poppy's hand. "I'll bet all the gelato you can eat the next time we go to town."

"I can eat a lot of gelato," said Poppy. "You sure that's what you want to bet?"

They shook hands, laughing, and finished setting the table. Then, at Marco's suggestion, Poppy went to find Aarika. They returned just as Mariella was calling everyone to eat. All of the women selected seats together on one side of the table. Dolphus took a seat opposite Elisabetta, instructing Marco to sit next to him so he could translate, even though the signora spoke English well enough to carry on a conversation. His skills would, no doubt, come into play if someone had to resort to their native language to get a point across.

After Domenico helped Mariella serve the appetizers, he settled down at the head of the table. Lifting his wine glass, he toasted Elisabetta for honoring them with her presence. Everyone but Aarika followed suit.

"*Si! Salute!*"

"*Ja! Prost!*"

"*Hear, hear!*"

The signora waited until they were finished, and then lifting her glass, she thanked Domenico and Mariella for being wonderful hosts. Again, everyone but Aarika clinked their glasses together in agreement. Marco, sitting directly across from Aarika, tried to make eye contact with her several times, but she refused to look at him.

A pastel-scumbled sky signaled the onset of dusk not long

after the second course was served. As it began to cool, Mariella went into the casala and returned carrying several hand-knit sweaters in her arms, passing them around to whoever needed them. Domenico lit a trail of votive candles lining the center of the table and several citronella torches edging the patio.

The darkening sky added an intimate layer of informality to an already unpretentious setting. Some of Domenico's guests crossed their legs, others rested their elbows on the table. All of them leaned close to one another as they talked, their voices lowered out of respect for the neighbors downwind from them, but the volume of their laughter intensified. With their candle-lit faces set against the dark backdrop of the fattoria, the setting could have been a scene from an illustrated fairy tale.

Elisabetta let out a contented sigh. "Oh, what an enjoyable evening this has been! At last I've been able to meet the Bertozzis and see where Armida Sigali was from."

"Bianca has told us only bits and pieces about this Sigali woman," said Poppy. "What was it about her exactly that made you come here?"

The signora bit her lip. Searching for the right words, she turned and asked Marco to help her tell the story, should her English fail her. Then she began. "I don't believe anyone knows the entire story of Armida Sigali. From what I've learned, even if her husband Egisto were still alive, he couldn't say with certainty what made her do the things she did. Her heart was apparently buried beneath an avalanche of unforgiveness."

Aarika slowly raised her eyes to look at the signora.

"It has taken me months to piece together some of her story," continued Elisabetta. "I discovered Armida worked as a nanny and housekeeper for a high-level Fascist officer named Bruno Carditi. He had been reassigned to the town of Siviano on Monte Isola, an island in Lago d'Iseo, after Mussolini set up his republic at Salò. There, they shared lodging with a Nazi officer, Werner Kolbe, and his wife. Kolbe, by all accounts, was extremely powerful and dangerous. He was more evil, some said, than Carditi, who was—in his own right—a notorious thug."

Dolphus stared at Elisabetta, hanging on her every word.

"But I digress," said the signora. "Let me start back at the beginning. Armida and Egisto Bertozzi had barely known each other when they married on the spur of the moment, the night before immigrating to America. They eventually had two children together. Shortly afterward she suffered some sort of mental collapse for which she was institutionalized for several months. Following her release, she divorced Egisto and left him and her children to return to Italy. Her timing couldn't have been worse, since Mussolini had just come into power. There have been different reasons given for why she chose to move back here, but none of the reasons make any sense when looking at the end result of her decision. Once she became involved with the Fascists, her fate was sealed. When Carditi found out she had lied to him about having a husband and children in America, he was convinced she was a spy and used it to blackmail her into doing what he wanted."

Elisabetta's voice had gone dry. She poured some water from a carafe into a glass, took a long drink, and then resumed. Nodding at Dolphus she said, "As some of you may already know, Armida came into our lives one night when she was forced to accompany the Kolbes and Carditis on a trip to Franciacorta, which lies between Salò and Lago d'Iseo. It was the dead of winter. Our family dinner was interrupted by Bruno Carditi bursting into our entry demanding my father open his wine cellar for them. I'll never forget the fear those two men brought into our home. I remember not being able to speak when Commandant Kolbe addressed me, asking what my name was. My father intervened and told him my name was Elisabetta. But the German said, 'Why doesn't she tell me herself? What is she afraid of?'

"My father feared that Kolbe, if he saw that we were terrified of him, would use it to his advantage, and so he said, 'My daughter is a shy girl. She is speechless, no doubt, in your illustrious presence, Herr Kolbe. Rarely does she have the privilege of seeing a highly esteemed officer of the Third Reich at such close range. Once she catches her breath, I am sure her voice, as well as her good manners, will return.'"

Dolphus grunted. "I imagine that did the trick."

"*Si*," said Elisabetta. "From then on, my father was able to play him like a harp. He also knew exactly how to play Carditi—with his overinflated ego, but inferior military position—against Kolbe. Carditi knew what my father was up to and it drove him mad. He couldn't stand the fact that my father, simply by being his charming self, was being held in higher esteem than himself, a Fascist bigwig. It wasn't surprising, therefore, that a few hours later, when they were all drunk in our wine cellar, the situation became volatile. But again, my father was quick to diffuse the tension and turn it to his advantage."

The signora paused for effect while everyone at the table waited expectantly. "He got them involved in a card game," she said, "and he had them bet on the highest stakes possible."

"What were the stakes?" asked Domenico.

"Yes," said Mariella. "What were they?"

Studying their faces, Elisabetta said, "You don't know?"

Mariella shook her head. "My Aunt Bianca knew Armida better than anyone in our family and she has never said anything about a card game. After Armida fled here with the Carditis to Lago d'Iseo, our family had no idea what happened to her, other than what we learned from Egisto."

Elisabetta let this information sink in. Staring into the candlelight, she said, "The jackpot was several of my father's grape seeds."

"Grape seeds?" asked Poppy, perplexed.

"These weren't just any seeds," noted Elisabetta. "They were ancient grape seeds passed down for centuries through my family. You see, my ancestors can be traced all the way back to the Roman Empire."

Marco, seeing how confused Poppy still appeared, tried to explain. "Imagine your family collected art masterpieces, rare wines, or coins," he said, "or any other commodity that has a high market value because of its rarity, its history, or its desirability. Verifiably ancient grape seeds are in the same category. If they can be authenticated, there are people who would pay a fortune for them, although their value today is more in terms of DNA analysis and scientific research."

Poppy tilted her head to one side. "A bit convoluted, but yeah, I get it."

"So, what happened?" asked Domenico. "Who won the jackpot?"

Elisabetta smiled. "My father had waited for the perfect time to suggest the card game—until he knew the Kolbes and Carditis were too drunk to play well—so that he could discreetly help Armida win. When Bruno and Werner realized they had lost the game they got into a fistfight with each other. At that point, it was an easy matter for my father to shut down the evening and escort them out of our house. Mariesole, our housekeeper—she was an Italian-American from Chicago who had moved to Italy with her Italian husband before the war—had struck up a conversation with Armida prior to all this. She had informed my father of the dangerous situation Armida was in. Armida had also told Mariesole about two people in Siviano who had befriended her. 'Angels' is what she called them: a Dr. Leonardo Grassi and his daughter Lara."

"Well," continued the signora, "my father, because of his underground connections throughout our region, knew Dr. Grassi and believed his grape seeds could be trusted with Armida. In fact, aware of the serious danger Armida was in, my father hoped she might be able to use them to buy her freedom. Later, as he related the story to me, he reasoned that they were only seeds. 'Better,' he said, 'for Armida to use them to save her life than for them to sit in my safe doing no one any good.'"

Wrapping her story up, Elisabetta concluded, "Anyway, I believe if Armida had traded the seeds for her freedom, they would have ended up back in my father's possession, as the partisans all knew and respected my father and wouldn't have kept the seeds for themselves."

"I doubt that Armida traded them," said Mariella. "She never made it out of Lago d'Iseo alive."

Domenico spread his hands out. "So the question is . . ."

The signora finished his sentence. "What happened to the seeds?"

"Which is what brought you here," noted Dolphus. "The seeds."

"Exactly," said Elisabetta. "That and more. You see, my

father passed away last year. Cancer." She swept her hand along the top of her chest to indicate the cancer had been in his lungs. "In a way, it was a godsend because it gave my father the opportunity to make peace with everyone before he departed. Had he died suddenly, so much would have been left unsaid, and we would never have learned about Armida."

Her voice wavering, Elisabetta added, "If only you could have met my father. He was a hero in every sense of the word. He saved more lives during the war than anyone else in our region. So many people attended his funeral after he died, hundreds had to stand outside our church in the cold and pouring rain because there was no room inside for them." Elisabetta choked on her last words. "How sad, and how true, that we don't really appreciate our loved ones as much as we should until they're gone."

Dolphus flinched, no doubt thinking of Sabine. Mariella lifted her napkin to her mouth and stifled a sob. Poppy swiped her eyes with the sleeve of her sweater. Aarika remained riveted to her seat, staring at the signora.

Elisabetta composed herself before continuing. "I'm sorry, back to the seeds. Of all the war stories my father told on his deathbed, the one about Armida intrigued me the most, so I decided to find out what I could about her. First, I went to Siviano, where she had lived with the Carditis and Kolbes. I was shocked by how many different accounts of her death I came across, although—given human nature's love of conjecture and exaggeration—I shouldn't have been so surprised. One thing is certain: Armida Sigali was murdered. The official report listed her death as an accidental drowning, but everyone I spoke to said that wasn't true."

Mariella, lifting her finger in the air, mentioned that her

understanding was that a detective hired by Egisto determined an SS officer stationed on the island had tortured and killed her.

Elisabetta agreed that was her assessment as well. "It appears Prince Junio Borghese, admiral of the Decima MAS, the Italian submarine fleet during the war, had heard of Armida's great housekeeping and cooking skills and 'stole' her from the Carditis and Kolbes. The Borgheses lived in a palatial villa on a private island in the lake near Monte d'Isola called San Paolo Island. Although it must have been a relief for Armida to no longer be under the iron fist of Kolbe or Carditi, unfortunately, Borghese—who Hitler suspected of wanting to defect to the Allies—was himself put under house arrest. It meant that SS guards were stationed on San Paolo to prevent anyone from leaving.

"Naturally, the higher one climbed in Mussolini's or Hitler's government, the less freedom one had. Once Armida was trapped with the Borgheses on their island, few people had access to her anymore. The best information I was able to obtain came from partisans who survived the war and knew Dr. Grassi and his daughter."

Elisabetta lifted her hands from her lap and placed them around the stem of her wineglass, a gesture made by someone trying to wrap their mind around an inconceivable reality. "To a person," she said, "the partisans I spoke with agreed that Armida had spent the last several weeks of her life as an informant for Dr. Grassi. By the time she was transferred to the Borgheses' villa, Kolbe and Carditi suspected what she was doing and made it their goal to destroy her. In addition, there were rumors circulating that Armida was in possession of something of great value that she could sell to buy her freedom. I am convinced they were my father's seeds.

One partisan I spoke to told me as much. He said Dr. Grassi's daughter had asked him to find a way to contact Armida at the Borgheses' villa to tell her that *'The seeds are worthless unless they are planted.'*"

Dolphus, who had begun strumming his fingers on the table, asked, "Did the rumor reach Nazi ears?"

"Yes," said Elisabetta. "Although Kolbe and Carditi had been drunk that night in our wine cellar, apparently they could still recall bits and pieces of the card game. They shared their suspicions with fellow officers and soldiers. I'm sure Armida would have denied knowing anything about the seeds—my father had warned her not to let them know— but the black market was so pervasive and so critical during the war, everyone was looking for something to barter. Being an informant aside, even the hint of such a rumor would have been enough to put Armida's life in jeopardy. I am convinced that before she died she was living with one eye over her shoulder at all times."

"So then," asked Marco, "you believe someone killed her for the seeds?"

"Armida was murdered because she was found out as a spy. Of that, I am sure. My guess is she was tortured for the seeds. I could be wrong, however. The SS needed no motive for torturing and murdering innocent people, did they?"

"No they didn't," murmured Domenico, his eyes raised to the tree above their table. "They were without excuse."

Dolphus hung his head. "As a former German solider, I have to agree, Domenico. The SS were an evil arm of the Third Reich. They were without excuse."

Elisabetta gave everyone a moment to reflect before summing up the results of her research. "I began this journey wanting to find out what happened to my father's seeds, but in the process I became so engrossed with Armida's story, I must say I don't care about them anymore. That said, another partisan I spoke to told me that Armida always wore a locket around her neck and guarded it carefully. When anyone asked to look at it, she refused to let them see it. The detective Egisto hired had mentioned in his report that Armida was buried with a locket. All the evidence, I believe, points to the seeds being in that locket."

Mariella went white. "Are you wanting to . . ."

"Oh, no!" exclaimed Elisabetta. "I wouldn't think of exhuming Armida's body. She must rest in peace. If the seeds are buried with her, then so be it. I am content simply knowing she was finally redeemed before her death."

"How do you mean?" asked Domenico.

"Many people I spoke to told me of Armida's transformation while living on the lake. She came to their village a wounded, bitter woman, but through the love of Dr. Grassi and his daughter, she let it all go. They say she became a gentle, trusting soul who touched many lives before her death. It was an absolutely stunning change, I was told."

Marco felt Aarika staring at him. When he turned to meet her gaze, he thought he could see a glow of hope in her eyes.

Dolphus said, "Your father would be pleased with your mission, signora, despite the fact that his seeds were not recovered."

"I do believe he would," agreed Elisabetta, adding, "I sit here tonight, overjoyed, because my journey to find the seeds has also led me to you, Dolphus. Extraordinary, don't you think?"

Even in the dim light of the candles, everyone at the table could see Dolphus blush a deep red. "Extraordinary?" he mumbled. "Well, I must say our meeting today has been . . ."

"Extraordinary," repeated Elisabetta. "It wasn't until this morning on the beach, when you told me your last name, that I realized you were the Dolphus Geller of the wanted posters we were forced to display in our region during the war. You were the deserter with a bounty on his head."

Aarika's jaw dropped. "Opa? What is this?"

Realizing instantly she must have said something she shouldn't have, Elisabetta apologized. "I'm so sorry. I thought you all knew. In our eyes, Dolphus Geller became something of a folk hero because he was a German who dared to go against his own country. Few people defied the Reich and lived to tell about it."

"How exactly did he 'defy the Reich?'" asked Domenico, staring at Dolphus.

Elisabetta begged the question. "Dolphus must share that with you. Not me. I shouldn't have brought it up."

But Dolphus shook his head. "No apology is needed, signora. Keeping secrets helps no one in the end. Just look at the story of Armida Sigali, for example. Better for the secret keepers to let the truth be known than for their families to have to find out after they are gone, with no explanation."

Elisabetta let out a sigh of relief. "I'm glad to hear you say that Dolphus, because I've never forgotten the day that man named Ralf came looking for you in our barn. He told my father that you were his cousin. Of course, we didn't know then that you were the renegade Dolphus Geller. I helped you hide because Ralf was a Nazi and you were—well, I thought you were at the time—a deaf mute. I didn't want him to kill you."

Domenico scratched his chin. "Ralf?" he asked, staring hard at Dolphus. "Your cousin's name was *Ralf?*"

"Yes," said Dolphus. "Ralf Geller."

After dessert was served and eaten, Mariella rose to clear the table, asking Domenico to help her. "What's wrong with you?" she said out of the corner of her mouth as they carried a load of dirty dishes into the casala.

"There's something about the name Ralf that sounds familiar, but for the life of me I just can't place it." Domenico set the dishes down on the counter, muttering, "Ralf. Ralf. Dolphus said his cousin's name was Ralf."

Clicking her tongue, Mariella said, "I don't know anything about Ralf, but that was a shock to hear that Dolphus was a Nazi deserter with a bounty on his head. We'll have to find out what that was all about, eh?"

Domenico and Mariella finished cleaning up, and, saying good night to the Gellers and Poppy, they piled into the car with Marco and Signora Cavalleri. Domenico remained unusually quiet on the ride back down the mountain. That was because one thought—one word—was consuming this thoughts.

Ralf.

Ralf, Ralf, Ralf

It was late when Marco pulled up to the Sacchelli residence, but before Domenico and Mariella opened their car doors to get out, Elisabetta turned to them and said, "I promised Bianca I would get together with her and the other Bertozzis soon. Since you've already hosted a wonderful dinner for me at your casala, please let me arrange a dinner at a local restaurant for all of us before I leave to go back home."

"Absolutely not," said Mariella, in a tone that meant there would be no arguing. "Do you have plans for tomorrow?"

"Not really," said Elisabetta.

Marco asked Domenico what the Gellers had on their agenda for the next day. Domenico told him they mentioned wanting to go to Lucca.

When Elisabetta proclaimed that she had heard wonderful things about Lucca, Domenico said, "Well then, you shall go, signora." He then proceeded to instruct Marco on what he would need to do the next day to facilitate the day trip. "Pick the Gellers up tomorrow morning about nine," he said. "Then go to the signora's hotel and . . ."

Elisabetta objected, saying she hadn't meant to invite herself along to Lucca and that she'd be perfectly fine spending the day by herself, shopping or relaxing on the beach.

Domenico would hear nothing of it. "Every Italian," he insisted, "should see Lucca at least once in their lives."

"My cousin is right, signora," said Marco. "Lucca is so close, you should see it while you are here. I assure you it is *non problema*. I will pick you up at your hotel tomorrow at ten."

"All right, then," laughed Elisabetta. "Since you insist." Thanking Domenico and Mariella once again, she waved good-bye to them as Marco backed out of the driveway.

What followed between Signora Cavalleri and Marco during the ensuing ten-minute drive into Forte dei Marmi was, oddly enough, a rather frank and revealing discussion of love. It started when they passed by a young couple fawning over each other on the sidewalk outside the Arcobaleno gelateria on via Strettoia.

"Isn't that funny," mused Elisabetta. "Each of them is holding a cone dripping with ice cream, yet the mess isn't interfering in the least with their passion for each other."

"But, of course not," replied Marco. "Real lovers don't let anything get between them."

"I detect a note of despair in that comment," said Elisabetta, turning to study Marco's face. "Or is it longing?"

"Both."

"It's the German girl, isn't it. Aarika?"

"How could you tell?"

"When something divides lovers, it shows. What is preventing you two from being together?"

Marco braked for a stop sign. "As I see it, the biggest deterrent is Aarika's past. It keeps her from loving herself and believing that anyone else, other than Dolphus, can love her."

"An all too common affliction, I am afraid," said Elisabetta. "Actually, I wonder if Dolphus struggles with his past as well."

Bluntly, Marco asked, "Do you have feelings for him, signora?"

"Well, given the remarkable way we first met, I must admit to being fascinated by him now." Elisabetta lifted her purse onto her lap and began digging around for her room key.

"Fascinated? That's all?"

"I would certainly be open to developing a strong, deep friendship with Dolphus." Elisabetta grinned. "But for the present, nothing more than that, no."

"Do you believe in destiny, signora?"

"If I didn't before I arrived here this week, I certainly do now. Do you believe in destiny, Marco?"

Marco nodded. "I do. I have also discovered I believe in love at first sight."

"So, you believe Aarika is your soul mate," noted Elisabetta, finally finding her key.

"It depends on what you mean by it."

"I mean, you see someone and it's *literally* love at first sight." Elisabetta used her hands to illustrate her point. "But it's more than that. It's—I don't know—destiny at first sight. You see this person, but you see them through the prism of time, and you discover you're there with them in the future. Your souls are knit together through the best of times and worst of times." Her voice faltered. "I'm not explaining it very well."

"No, you described it perfectly," said Marco. "And yes, I believe Aarika is my soul mate."

Elisabetta sighed. "Here I am in Forte dei Marmi for the first time in my life, and who am I introduced to, but Dolphus Geller. After all these years! Then, I discover he's renting a holiday home from the same family Armida Sigali was married into. And if that isn't strange enough, I find out you're in love with his granddaughter. I don't think it's coincidence, Marco, do you?

"No, coincidences are too random," replied Marco. "They're based solely on odds. For example, what are the odds that there is another planet like earth in the universe? Let alone one that could support complex life forms on it?

"It's inconceivable."

"Exactly," said Marco. "It's like the odds of Dolphus picking your father's vineyard to find refuge in during the war, or Domenico asking me to work for him the very summer Dolphus brings Aarika back to Italy with him again." Coasting up to the curb in front of the Grand Hotel Imperiale, Marco concluded, "That's why I believe in destiny."

Elisabetta unbuckled her seat belt. "Thank you for bringing me back to the hotel, Marco," she said. "I thoroughly enjoyed our discussion of *il vero amore*."

Marco let out a deep sigh. "I only wish Aarika could recognize true love. I've never felt this way about a girl before. If she continues to reject me, I'm not sure what I'll do."

"No doubt, Aarika is allowing many things to dissuade her from committing herself to you. Your different nationalities and cultures, and the fear that you will ultimately reject her because she believes herself to be unlovable are just a few of them. May I speak candidly, Marco?"

"Of course, signora."

"I do not doubt that you are in love with Aarika, or that destiny is in play with your lives. But you must not brush away her doubts. They are serious concerns and you must consider them. I've heard the Americans have a saying: 'Marry in haste; repent at leisure.' The truth of that statement should cause you to think very carefully about what your heart is compelling you to pursue, Marco."

"Thank you for your honesty, signora. But I still believe love overrides everything . . . even reason."

Elisabetta, her hand resting on the door handle, hesitated. "For your sake, Marco, I hope you're right. I guess only time will tell what fabric our destinies are made of, eh?"

"And time is exactly what I have precious little of." Marco got out and walked around the car to open the signora's door for her.

As she stepped up on the curb, Elisabetta kissed Marco on the cheek. "*A domani*, Marco. We will see what tomorrow brings."

Marco escorted the signora into the hotel lobby and returned to his car. Climbing back into the driver's seat, he started the engine and pulled into the flow of traffic heading east. He fumbled with the radio controls until he found a station playing American jazz and blues, hoping it would help lessen his anxiety about what tomorrow really might bring.

WHILE MARCO WAS bidding Elisabetta good evening, Domenico was lying in bed next to his long-suffering wife trolling for answers. "Dolphus's cousin's name was *Ralf*," he said, for what seemed like the hundredth time.

"*Si*, Domenico. That's what Dolphus said."

"There's something about that name . . . " Domenico scrunched up his pillow, elevating himself so his head and shoulders were at a forty-five-degree angle.

"Turn off the light and go to sleep, Domenico. In the morning your mind will be fresh. It will come to you then."

"*Ralf, Ralf, Ralf* . . . " he muttered under his breath. Turning off the lamp on the bedside table next to him, Domenico settled back onto his pillow. "*Ralf, Ralf, Ralf* . . . "

At least ten minutes passed. Mariella, her back to Domenico, began to snore.

"*Ralf!!!*"

Mariella jerked. Rolling over to face Domenico, she lifted herself onto one elbow. "What?" she mumbled.

"I remember now! The two Germans at our fattoria during the war—one of them was named Dolphus and the other one was named Ralf!"

Mariella sat up and rubbed her eyes. Turning on the lamp next to her, she studied her husband. "Oh," she said.

"Dolphus told me there were many German men who shared the same name as his, but the two soldiers who terrorized my mother and Signora Gabrelli behind our house were named Dolphus and Ralf. It cannot be a coincidence." Domenico slid out of bed. "I feel sick," he said, clutching his stomach.

Mariella threw on her bathrobe and followed her husband into the bathroom. Kneeling next to him by the toilet, she placed her hand on his lower back. "I can't believe Dolphus could have terrorized anyone, let alone two helpless women."

"My own mother," croaked Domenico. "And Dolphus has the gall to come here every summer to rent my fattoria?"

Slipping her legs out from under her so that they were splayed out straight, Mariella leaned against the sink. "There must be an explanation. It's too bad your mother isn't still alive, Domenico. She could verify it."

"I'm glad she's not alive. To have to face him again after all these years . . . "

Mariella shook her head. "You don't know if it was both of the soldiers, or only one of them, who hurt your mother. If only one of them was guilty of the act, you can't assume it was Dolphus."

"I recall my mother telling me something about the one who hurt her. I don't assume it was Dolphus," he said. "But then, I can't know for sure unless I ask him."

"When will you confront him about it?"

Domenico struggled to get to his feet. "I must do it as soon as possible. Tomorrow. I'll go with Dolphus to Lucca and find a way to talk to him there."

Mariella stood up along with her husband and watched as he washed his hands and splashed cold water on his face. As they walked together hand in hand back to the bedroom, she suggested he prepare himself well for the upcoming confrontation. "I know it's hard Domenico," she said, "but you must try and recall everything about that day. Did your mother ever tell you what happened to her?"

"I think so." Domenico had blocked details of his mother's death out of his mind, much as he had the war. Bits and pieces occasionally surfaced, such as they had in his dreams lately, but in his waking hours, when he could control his thoughts, remembering was too painful. "I remember Mama died the same year we received our first letter from Dolphus asking if he could rent our fattoria for the summer."

"Good," said Mariella, softly. "It's a start. Keep remembering while I go to the kitchen and make a cup of warm milk to help you sleep."

And so, remembering, and agonizing and gnashing his teeth—and controlling the seething rage that gnawed at the base of his skull, threatening to explode the instant he discovered the truth—was what Domenico set about doing.

$$\cdot 26 \cdot$$

Elvira on Her Deathbed

DOMENICO REMEMBERED THAT once Dolphus had sped away from the fattoria on his motorcycle that fateful summer day in 1945, leaving Ralf unconscious in the shed, he and his father Orazio had shimmied down the tree and raced over to the hillside where Elvira and their neighbor, Signora Gabrelli, lay hidden behind an outcropping of rocks. As they neared the women, they could hear them crying and groaning. Scaling the steep embankment, they finally got a glimpse of the two. Domenico's mother was dirty and bloodied, her dress ripped open. She was bent over the tiny, frail Signora Gabrelli, consoling her as blood poured out of a gunshot wound below her shoulder. Orazio leaned down, placing himself between his wife and their dying neighbor.

Embracing Elvira first, he asked, "Are you hurt?"

"No," she replied, clutching the shredded bodice of her dress close to her.

Orazio gently touched her arm, where her sleeve was soaked in blood. "What is this?"

"It's nothing," said Elvira, trembling. Pointing to Signora Gabrelli, she insisted he look at her.

Domenico, standing mutely near his mother, watched Orazio ease the old woman's head up from the ground and lay it on his lap. Then, with a deftness that comes from a lifetime of caring for animals, his father examined the signora's wound. Horrified, Domenico could see a huge, gaping hole in the old woman's chest. It was filled with raw tissue and bone and gristle, like the innards of a goat he had once seen slaughtered. The signora's eyes fluttered twice in recognition of Orazio and then rolled back in her head. Then, she gave one long, rattling gasp and went limp. Elvira called out the signora's name while Orazio slapped her cheek. There was no response.

"She's gone," said Orazio.

Elvira broke down sobbing.

"Shh!" Orazio covered his wife's mouth with his hand. "It's not safe. We must leave. *Now!*"

"But Signora Gabrelli . . ." Elvira reached toward the old woman as Orazio lifted her to her feet. "We can't leave her here like this."

Pulling her away from the rocks, Orazio said, "We have no choice, Elvira. Come!"

Domenico, frightened and stunned that his mother had yet to even notice him, followed his parents into the woods. After stumbling through forest and dense brush for what seemed like an hour, Elvira asked where they were going. Though no longer nearly hysterical, she was still dazed. "I want to go back home," she cried. "Our animals, my bread . . ."

"We no longer have a home, Elvira," said Orazio. "Your home is with us, with me and Domenico, wherever we can find shelter."

"Domenico?" Elvira turned and finally recognized her son. Collapsing to her knees, she opened one arm to him. Domenico fell into her awkward embrace. He let her smother him with kisses and whimper his name over and over again. It was then he noticed the stiffness of her wounded arm; felt its heat against his own skin. When she released him, he saw that she was holding the arm at an odd angle. Several hours later, around nightfall, they reached an abandoned mill near the entrance of a steep ravine where they would spend their first night in flight. He worried at the concerned look on his father's face as he washed Elvira's arm and gave it a thorough inspection. It was badly infected, his father said.

Elvira didn't lose her arm, though the infection nearly killed her, but she never baked bread again. One can knead bread satisfactorily with one hand perhaps, but Domenico's mother, a perfectionist, couldn't abide mediocrity. And so, after the war, when they were finally able to return to their home, Elvira immediately began teaching her son how to bake. She would stand aside, her limp arm held loosely against her ribs, showing him how to make soups and pastas and breads and desserts, intent on coaching him and praising him through all the culinary basics she thought necessary.

Indeed, thought Domenico, reflecting on those days, his gift of cooking was his mother's legacy to him. Her patience through all of his trials and errors—the burned breads, under-seasoned sauces, overcooked meats, and bland desserts—endowed him with another skill as well. That of teaching. No wonder he eventually chose education as his career. He had studied under the best.

Through the years, Elvira rarely talked about the day the Germans had terrorized her and Signora Gabrelli, the day they had robbed her of the use of her arm. The day they had forever destroyed her ability to sleep through the night in peace. But occasionally, when she was older and suffering the effects of severe arthritis, or when she was waxing particularly nostalgic at the funeral of an old friend or neighbor, details would slip out.

Details like: *The first soldier who had found them had seemed so young, not much older than her own youngest brother who was only fifteen at the time. He had initially appeared shocked at finding them and confused as to what he should do. When the other soldier called out to him, he looked terrified, like a rabbit caught in a trap, ready to be skinned at any moment. The second soldier had steely blue eyes that sucked life in but gave nothing back in return. His lips had a clown-like smile painted on them. Even when he was furious with the first soldier—even when he struck the signora so hard it knocked what few teeth she had left out of her mouth—he kept his hideous smile.*

But it was on her deathbed that Elvira ultimately opened up about all that had happened that day on the mountain. "I have forgiven them both," she whispered at one point to Orazio.

"Who?" he asked. "The German soldiers who hurt you?"

"Yes," she said, her eyes burning intensely. "You need to understand exactly what they did, Orazio. When the first soldier reached us, Signora Gabrelli and I panicked. We begged him for our lives. He lowered his gun, knelt on the ground next to us, and signed for us to be quiet. It was too late. The second soldier had heard us. After he arrived and began pushing Signora Gabrelli and I around, the first soldier seemed to plead for him to leave us alone.

"I couldn't really understand them because they spoke in German, but when the second soldier walked away, the first one started screaming at us. I sensed he was bluffing, because he pointed his gun above our heads into the forest and not directly at us. The signora—you well remember, Orazio—was nearly blind. When the soldier held up his free hand, as though warning us, she must have taken it to mean he was going to hit her because at the exact moment he fired his gun, poor Signora Gabrelli leapt to her feet right in front of him. You saw her wound, Orazio. The bullet hit her in the chest."

"Now, now, Elvira," said Orazio, soothingly. "That's enough for now. We can talk about it more tomorrow when you're rested."

"No, I must tell you now, while I still have my strength!" Elvira rushed to continue her story. "It took several years for me to forgive the first soldier for killing Signora Gabrelli, even though it was an accident. But the second soldier . . ."

Orazio froze. "Elvira, you don't need to—"

"I didn't think I could ever forgive him for what he did to the signora as she lay there dying. For what he did to me afterward."

"Elvira . . ."

"He would have raped me, you know, if the first soldier had not come back." Holding her husband's gaze, Elvira blurted, "Did I ever tell you how much I appreciated you never asking me about what the second soldier did to me? You let me know, just by the way you loved me through everything, that it wouldn't have made any difference to you."

"But he hurt you, Elvira," said Orazio, wiping his eyes with the back of his shirtsleeve.

Elvira tugged at her husband's hand. "You must listen, Orazio. He started ripping my clothes off. When I began to fight back, he pulled out a knife and stabbed me. I screamed, and that's when the first soldier came back."

Choking on his words, Orazio said, "I heard your scream, Elvira. As much as I wanted to climb down the tree and go to you, I knew if I did, it would put Domenico's life in jeopardy."

"You did the right thing, *mio amore*. Domenico was just a child. He needed your protection."

Still choked up, Orazio asked his wife how she could forgive what the soldier had done to her.

"After a few years, I couldn't bear to live with myself, with my lack of forgiveness, any longer. Every time something went wrong—when I'd lose my temper, or failed at something, or was frustrated, or mad at life—I'd blame that second soldier for it. I blamed him for my nightmares, for destroying my ability to sleep, for robbing me of the use of my arm, for—for affecting my relationship with you."

Orazio began to object, but she lifted a finger to his lips. "You can't deny it changed our marriage. We were never as close after that day."

No longer able to keep his emotions in check, Orazio held his wife's hand to his cheek and wept.

"That's why I must tell you that I have forgiven both soldiers," said Elvira. "If I can do it, so can you. Please, Orazio, promise me you'll try to forgive them."

Domenico, who was standing on the other side of his mother's bed during the entire exchange, had been silent. Now, Elvira turned to him. "You too, Domenico. You are a man now. You have a wife and child of your own. Please, son, before I die, promise me you will forgive them."

"The soldiers are probably dead now," argued Domenico. "What point would there be in forgiving them?"

"Whether they are dead or not," said Elvira, shaking her head, "forgiveness works both ways. Forgiving them will heal you, as it did me."

Domenico wanted more facts. Summoning his courage he took a deep breath and asked, "Do you remember what the soldier who stabbed you looked like, Mama?"

"All I remember were his eyes," replied Elvira. "He was the one with the dead blue eyes."

"What color eyes did the other soldier have?" asked Domenico.

Elvira groaned in pain. "It was so long ago. They were blue also, I think. Why does it matter?"

"Papa and I heard them calling out their names to each other that day. Do you remember the name of the soldier who hurt you?"

Elvira looked at the ceiling. "I can't be sure, Domenico. I was too afraid at the time to think clearly."

"Think, Mama."

"His name may have been Ralf," said Elvira, haltingly. "Yes, I think that's what the other soldier called him."

Pressing ahead, Domenico said, "Papa and I watched one of the soldiers carry the other one down after the shooting and put him in the shed. He looked dead. Do you have any idea which soldier was which?"

"Once I was stabbed, I must have gone into shock," she replied. "I vaguely recall seeing them fight each other. One of the soldiers picked up a large rock and hit the other soldier in the head with it. That's all I remember."

When Domenico appeared disappointed that she couldn't be more specific, Elvira chided him for it. "It doesn't matter who was who, Domenico. You will never meet them anyway. As you said, they could both be dead by now."

"Many Germans are coming to Italy these days to holiday, Mama. Some of them were once soldiers here. I just got a request in the mail last week from such a man. He may want to rent our fattoria next summer. His name is Dolphus Geller. He said he had been on our mountain during the war. Perhaps he could give me some information."

Elvira shook her head. "No, Domenico. Do not dig into the past. It will only bring you heartache. You must realize hundreds of German soldiers were here then. They covered the mountain like ants. Anyway, to think any one of them would know about what happened to Signora Gabrelli and I that day is *assurdo*. It is preposterous. Forgiveness comes from your heart, not from a place of knowing everything. It is not necessary that you know anything more than I have already told you."

Elvira glanced at Orazio for support. He nodded his head in agreement. "*Si*, Domenico," he said. "Listen to your mother. She is right. We must leave the past behind us."

"But what if—"

"Please, promise me you will forgive them, Domenico," Elvira pleaded.

Relenting at last, fearing he could no longer stay the hand of death raised against his mother by asking more questions, Domenico said, "I'll try, Mama. I'll do my best to forgive them."

Elvira fell back on her pillow and closed her eyes. Orazio, sitting next to her bed, placed her good hand in his own, stroking it as a father would a child. Domenico bent down low over his mother and reached for her other hand, her injured claw-like one, and tenderly pressed his lips against it. In all the years since the war, he hadn't deliberately touched his mother's contorted hand, nor had she offered it to him. Elvira had always kept it curled securely against her waist. But now, she made no attempt to resist Domenico's final show of affection.

In memory of his mother's Bread of Defiance, Domenico gently traced an outline of three shafts of wheat on her surrendered hand and whispered, "We stay together, Mama. You, I, Papa. We'll be together forever. That, I can promise."

·27·

Comparaggio

MARCO PULLED UP to the fattoria the next morning as instructed, surprised to see Domenico waiting for him.

"They're still getting ready," said Domenico, motioning toward the house as he approached Marco. Catching sight of Elisabetta sitting in the passenger seat of the car, he tipped his cap to her. "Ah, *buongiorno,* signora. You've decided to come with us. It is a beautiful day to see Lucca, no?" Rushing around the hood of the car, Domenico opened the door for her.

"Are you coming with us, Domenico?" she asked.

Glancing at the house, he replied, "I don't know yet."

Elisabetta pointed across the driveway. "Do you mind if I take a short walk while we wait?" she asked. "I'd love to take some pictures of your vineyard and olive orchard."

"Indeed, signora, be my guest," replied Domenico. "I believe the girls will be ready to leave in about ten minutes."

Marco got out of the car and waited until Elisabetta was out of hearing range before saying, "Is something wrong Domenico? You look tired."

Domenico grimaced. "I didn't sleep last night."

"I'm surprised you're here then."

"It's possible I may go to Lucca with you."

Marco stared at Domenico. His cousin rarely behaved so indecisively. "Since Elisabetta is coming, there wouldn't be enough room in the car for all of us if you go."

"Lucca is not that far away," argued Domenico. "The car is designed with bench seating as an option, so if we have to, three of us can fit in the front."

"Did you tell Dolphus the signora would be with us today?"

"How could I? I didn't know for sure until just now that the signora would come. Anyway, Dolphus isn't feeling well. He says he has a headache and may not go to Lucca."

"Dolphus just doesn't like to shop," Marco retorted, rather enviously, since he himself disliked shopping. "But once he knows Elisabetta is going, I guarantee he will want to come with us."

"*Guten Morgen*, Marco." Dolphus emerged from the house, his greeting less vibrant than usual.

"*Buongiorno*, Signor Geller," replied Marco. "I understand you don't feel well. Are you sure you're up for a day of shopping?"

Dolphus tapped his temple with his index finger, thrusting his eyebrows together as he did so. "With this headache, I doubt it. There's nothing to do in Lucca besides shop anyway, is there?"

Marco corrected him. "One could spend days in Lucca touring churches and museums and art galleries."

"No doubt that's true," said Dolphus pulling a face. "I'm just getting a bit—how should I say it—museum-ed out?"

Hurriedly, Domenico said, "It is no problem if you don't go, Dolphus. I'll stay here on the mountain with you while Marco takes the girls to Lucca."

"Well, good morning, Dolphus!" cried Elisabetta,

approaching the three men from the edge of the olive orchard.

"Good morning, signora," stuttered Dolphus, clearly shocked to see her. "What are you doing here?"

"Domenico kindly invited me to come along on the tour of Lucca today. He convinced me that every Italian should see it once in their lives."

Poppy and Aarika emerged from the house just then. Seeing them, Domenico raced to the car and opened the door for Elisabetta, nervously wishing her an enjoyable day in Lucca.

But Elisabetta, appearing to take a quick head count, hesitated. "Wait," she said. "How are we all going to fit in the car?"

Domenico assured her there was no problem. "Dolphus doesn't feel well, so he won't be going. I will stay here with him. There is plenty of room in the car, signora."

"Yes, I woke up with a slight headache," said Dolphus, waving the idea aside. "But it's gone now. I'd like nothing more than to go to Lucca today."

"If that's the case," Domenico blustered, "then by all means, I will go also."

IT WAS, THEREFORE, an overly crowded car crammed with bodies and purses and cameras that pulled out of the fattoria's driveway moments later. Marco drove the scenic route to Lucca, hugging the steep foothills that wound around Pietrasanta and Capezzano and Montramito. Domenico sat in the backseat with Dolphus and the signora, pointing out important landmarks, even though Elisabetta and Dolphus seemed more interested in talking with each other than looking at the scenery.

Poppy, wedged between Marco and Aarika in the front seat, took advantage of her position by talking to Marco almost nonstop, while Aarika spent the entire drive with her nose in a book. The only time she looked up was to shoot visual warnings at Poppy whenever she misconstrued her sister's innocent chatter as being flirtatious.

"Really, Poppy," she said at one point, when Poppy had resorted to whispering to Marco. "I can still hear you. You're embarrassing yourself."

It wasn't until after they parked their car off Lucca's broad Viale Giosue Carducci and began making their way toward the wall encircling the medieval city that everyone awakened to the prospect of an adventure. Entering through the western gate, the girls stopped to study the tourist maps Marco handed them and tried to get their bearings.

"It's ten thirty," said Marco, checking his watch. "What does everyone want to do?"

"I need to get some gifts to take back home for my parents," said Poppy.

"I'd like to shop," said Aarika. "But I'd also like to see some historic parts of Lucca as well."

Marco looked at Elisabetta. "Signora?"

"I'd like to explore and shop too," she replied. "And depending on how long we're here, maybe eat lunch at a good café?"

Marco asked Domenico if he'd made any plans for a meal.

"I have a menu prepared for dinner tonight," said Domenico. "But for lunch perhaps we could agree to meet at, say, the Torre delle Ore—the old clock tower in the historic district. We can decide then where to eat."

Dolphus, his bloodshot eyes betraying the true extent of

his headache, moaned, "Do you really think you'll be shopping for three and a half hours, Aarika?"

"Probably, Opa," she replied.

Elisabetta drew close to Dolphus and examined his face. "You should have stayed back at the fattoria."

"I'm fine," insisted Dolphus.

Domenico turned toward the city wall and pointed to the top of it. "See the trees up there? The wall around Lucca is so thick, there is a park and pedestrian promenade that runs around the entire city. They call it the Passeggiata delle Mura. Dolphus and I could sit up there while Marco takes the girls shopping." He reached into his pocket and pulled out his mobile to make sure it was charged and getting a signal before adding, "Marco can call me when it's time for lunch. If you feel better after we've rested, Dolphus, we can meet them."

Elisabetta told Dolphus she thought it was a great idea. "I'd feel better knowing you and Domenico were enjoying yourselves rather than traipsing around with us while we shop."

"Excellent," said Domenico. "Marco, just call me when you are ready for us to meet up with you."

As Marco and the women disappeared down the bustling via Vittorio Emmanuele II, Domenico and Dolphus located the stone stairway to the left of the Western gate and climbed it in a zigzag fashion to its crest. Once there, they selected a wooden bench beneath one of the beech trees lining the Passeggiata and sat down, stretching out their legs.

Immediately, Dolphus leaned back and closed his eyes. Domenico set his satchel between them and spent a few moments soaking up the view of the city. The morning sun was already intense, reflecting off the hundreds of red-tiled roofs clustered below them. In the distance, he could see the hills near Florence, and behind them, the more rugged Apuan mountains. Dolphus began to snore. Ten minutes later, Lucca's myriad church bells began tolling, a clamoring metal chorus that should have wakened Dolphus, but didn't.

Domenico waited patiently. He watched as lovers strolled hand in hand along the curving tree-lined avenue. He counted scores of bicyclists, young and old, some wearing common street clothes and others adorned in shiny helmets and bold-colored spandex, weaving in and out of the pedestrians. He spent at least ten minutes observing a group of school boys kicking a soccer ball in an impromptu game on the lawn nearby. Their shouts had no effect on Dolphus at all. The German remained slack-jawed, his head slung backward over the park bench like a drunk man sleeping off a hangover.

Studying Dolphus as he slept, Domenico noticed how dark his eyebrows and lashes were compared to his white hair, how thick and muscular his neck was, how broad his shoulders were, and how many sunspots and freckles were broadcast over his hands and arms. He didn't feel in the least guilty scrutinizing Dolphus as he slept. On the contrary, he felt he had a right to know the minutia of this man whose life might be more intimately connected with his than he had ever imagined.

If Dolphus were to wake up and find me staring at him, thought Domenico, *I would tell him what I suspect. I would insist he look me in the eye and tell me what he knows about what happened at our fattoria during the war. I can't stand waiting much longer.*

It occurred to him that he could create a ruckus to wake

Dolphus. Unzipping his satchel, Domenico retrieved a paper sack containing a loaf of bread. He removed the bread, and with great fanfare, scrunched the sack loudly right in front of Dolphus's face.

Nothing.

Another idea came to him. Breaking off a chunk of the bread, Domenico held it directly beneath Dolphus's nose. He watched as the German's nostrils twitched and his eyeballs rolled beneath his eyelids. Just as Dolphus's mouth began working, Domenico barked, "Dolphus!"

"Wha—?"

"Are you hungry?"

Checking the time on his watch, Dolphus declared, "Good heavens, I've been asleep nearly an hour. Have you heard from Marco yet?"

Domenico handed Dolphus the bread he'd been taunting him with. "Not yet. They're probably still shopping. How's your headache?"

"Better." Dolphus stuffed the bread in his mouth and began chewing. "Mmm, you made this, didn't you, Domenico?"

"Early this morning. Before sunrise. I didn't sleep last night."

"I know about sleepless nights," said Dolphus. "They are the bane of old age. But your bread is absolutely the best I have ever eaten. Really, Domenico, I dream of your cooking when I'm back home in Germany. Whoever taught you to bake has my eternal gratitude!"

Domenico felt his stomach flip. His reply was stony, his tone much more harsh, than he intended. "My mother taught me, Dolphus. This is her recipe. My father called it her 'Bread of Defiance.'"

"That's an odd name for bread."

"Not so odd if you consider my mother was handicapped. She didn't have the use of her right arm."

"I'm sorry to hear that." Dolphus glanced at the rest of the bread lying on top of Domenico's backpack. "May I?"

Like a cat offering a mouse a piece of cheese before pouncing on him for the kill, Domenico nodded. He watched Dolphus tear off another piece and eat it before saying, "She was injured in the war . . . my mother."

Dolphus's eyes widened in empathy. "Ach! So tragic, so many people damaged and killed. Too, too many. Thank God your mother survived it, Domenico."

Trying to maintain his civility, but unable to keep his suspicions in check any longer, Domenico blurted, "My mother was stabbed while hiding with our neighbor, an old woman named Signora Gabrelli, on the hill behind our fattoria." As Domenico watched Dolphus's face turn to stone at the news, he fought the urge to throttle the German. Harnessing every ounce of self-control he could muster, he waited for Dolphus to speak.

An eternity of silence passed before Dolphus finally stuttered, "Your mother was . . . at the . . . fattoria?" He pulled on his ear as though perhaps he hadn't heard correctly. "I'm sorry, Domenico. I don't hear well in this ear."

Raising his voice, Domenico repeated himself, adding, "The Germans came so quickly, my father and I were separated from her." Domenico no longer cared if Dolphus could detect his outrage. *Civility be damned*, he thought. "We hid in the chestnut tree in our front lawn. The one with the stone table beneath it."

"So then you saw . . ."

"I saw two soldiers pull up to our house on motorcycles. I remember that one of their names was Dolphus."

"How long have you known?"

Domenico clenched his hands into fists to stop them from shaking. "Last night when I heard Signora Cavalleri mention your cousin's name, it triggered a memory. The name Ralf kept nagging at me until I finally remembered that it was the name of the second soldier. Dolphus might be a common German name, but Dolphus *and* Ralf? It could not be a coincidence."

Before Dolphus could reply, Domenico exploded. Seizing the German by the collar of his shirt he hissed, "Which one of you killed Signora Gabrelli and which one of you stabbed my mother?"

Dolphus didn't resist Domenico's fury. Going limp, he stared directly into Domenico's eyes and said in a small voice, "I killed the old woman. It was an accident. But accident or not, I killed her."

The confession caused Domenico to slowly relinquish his hold on Dolphus. His mother had told him before she died that the soldier who had hurt her was not the one who had killed Signora Gabrelli. And the soldier who had shot the signora, she said, had not done so deliberately. Little by little, Domenico felt his blood pressure return to normal.

Dolphus resumed talking, his tone surrendering, like that of a penitent man on death row. "I had just been conscripted into the Wehrmacht," he explained, "and had never seen military action. When we arrived on the mountain at your fattoria, Ralf ordered me to check the perimeter. That's when I discovered two women—who I know now were your mother and neighbor. As soon as I saw them, I knew what

Ralf would do to them if he realized they were there. I had come to realize by then that my cousin was as an evil man. Fearing for the women, I tried to communicate to them that they should stay low and be quiet until I could find a way to hide them away safely from Ralf, but they were terrified of me and began screaming. As soon as Ralf heard them, he came running . . ."

Domenico knew what Dolphus said was true because his mother's story corroborated it. He nodded for Dolphus to continue.

"Ralf assaulted them," said Dolphus. "He started first with the old woman, hitting her as hard as he could in the face. Then he threw himself on her, straddling her with his legs as she lay crying on the ground."

Grabbing a water bottle from the backpack lying open next to him, Dolphus took a swig and continued. "It was an instantaneous, volatile situation, Domenico. I could have—I *should* have—handled it differently. I should have shot Ralf right then and there. But I didn't. Instead, I pleaded with him to let me handle it. My cousin fancied himself my mentor, in the sickest way, and no doubt thought that I would do to the women what he was planning on doing. I'm sure that's why he agreed to let me take over. When he left, I tried to make your mother and the old woman understand that I didn't want to hurt them. My plan was to fire my gun away from them, into the woods, hoping to somehow stall or trick Ralf into believing they were dead."

Dolphus ran his fingers through his hair. "It all happened so fast. I was young. Inexperienced. I wasn't thinking straight. Just as I turned and pulled the trigger to fire the shot, your neighbor leapt right in front of me." His voice caught as he added, "She reminded me of my own grandmother. Such a frail little woman. So . . . innocent."

Domenico affirmed that his neighbor was just that. "Signora Gabrelli used to call me her *piccolo sognatore*, her little dreamer, because as a child I loved to study the clouds moving across the sky. At least once a week she would make my favorite biscotti, put it in a metal tin, and leave it on our doorstep. 'To keep my dreams alive,' she said. My parents told me she was one of the kindest, sweetest people they'd ever known." Domenico might as well have slapped Dolphus, for the stinging effect his words had on the German.

"I have never been able to forgive myself for what happened," groaned Dolphus. "I have felt more remorse, more sorrow, for shedding your neighbor's blood than you can ever imagine."

Domenico bit his lower lip as he came to grips with the final truth of his past. "And my mother—what do you remember about her?"

Dolphus rubbed his forehead with the palms of his hands as though trying to conjure up the scene in his mind. "I believe she was in shock," he said, "because when I shot your neighbor she became hysterical. Hearing your mother's screams, Ralf was back within seconds. He caught me trying to comfort her. He wrestled my gun from me and tossed it aside. Then he said, 'Watch me, cousin. I'll show you how it's done.'"

When Dolphus gave Domenico a look that asked if he needed to say more, Domenico nodded and said, "My mother told me what she remembered, but I need you to tell me what happened to her from your perspective."

Reluctantly, Dolphus continued. "Ralf starting tearing

at your mother's clothes, groping her, slapping her, calling her names. I was furious, yet paralyzed with indecision as I watched your mother try to defend herself. Ralf was older than me and always intimidated me into submission when we were children, but seeing your mother rabid with fear, I knew the more she fought him, the more certain it was Ralf would probably kill her when he was done with her.

"An unbridled hate and an overriding sense of justice suddenly took control of me," said Dolphus. "I bent down, picked up a rock, and struck Ralf on the back of his head with it. I couldn't believe it only stunned him. Before I knew it, he had whipped his pistol out of his shoulder holster. We fought each other for control of it. When I finally stole it from him, I threw it in the same direction he'd thrown my gun. Then I reached for the rock again. This time I struck him in the temple with every ounce of strength I had. He staggered and went limp, falling forward on top of your mother. I lifted him off of her and even though he was unconscious, I slammed his face into the ground several times until I felt my overriding loathing for him—for what he had become—ebb. I didn't bother checking his pulse because I was sure he was dead, and I was in a panic that I'd be found out any moment by other troops in the area. I retrieved my gun and stuck Ralf's back in his holster so that when his body was found it wouldn't appear as though he had been defending himself from me. Then, because we were both bleeding profusely, I removed my shirt and wrapped it around my head, and did the same with Ralf, so that we wouldn't leave a trail of blood to show where your mother had been."

"Then you dumped him in our shed," said Domenico.

Dolphus nodded. "I forgot. You were watching."

"Yes, but we didn't know who was who."

"Now you know."

The two men sat side-by-side, contemplating their disclosures to each other. Finally, Domenico asked Dolphus what had possessed him to start coming back to Monte Montignoso every summer, given what had happened there during the war.

Dolphus launched into a brief synopsis of how, after the incident with Domenico's mother, Ralf had hunted him down in Austria and how he had ultimately killed him. It was the same story he had told Marco.

"I reasoned if I came back here to where it all started," said Dolphus, "perhaps I could somehow exorcise my demons. Redeem my past. I thought that if I relived what happened in the real location, instead of in my dreams, I would find some kind of deliverance."

"Of course," Dolphus continued, "the first summer I came back was by far the most difficult. You probably don't remember, Domenico, but I came without Sabine and spent most of my time in near total seclusion. I found a measure of closure in confronting my past that summer, but your *fattoria* also became an addiction of sorts. It actually started a vicious cycle. In a perverse way, I found wallowing in my guilt was cleansing . . . like throwing up when you're sick to your stomach. But it didn't last. The nightmares and panic attacks would resume with my return to Passau. So, each summer I was compelled to come back to this location and start the purging pattern all over again. I even told myself that paying to stay on your mountain every summer could be a form of compensation for what your community lost in the war. A paltry reparation, to be sure. Nothing can compensate for the taking of a human life. But such has been my reasoning, rational or not.

"On her deathbed, Sabine said to me, 'Dolphus, you will never find the peace you're looking for in any one geographical place. You will find it when you forgive yourself. Only then will you be free from your past. You must keep seeking it. When I'm gone, you will be all Aarika has left. If not for yourself, promise me you will do it for her.'"

Turning to stare at Domenico full on, Dolphus said, "Perhaps by confessing all of this to you, I can finally find that forgiveness."

Domenico looked away, his continuing internal struggle evident in the setting of his mouth, the grinding of his jaw, the involuntary twitching of a muscle near his eye. Several moments passed before he said, "I believe your version of what happened on the mountain, Dolphus, because my mother, before she died, told me the same thing. As such, I must thank you for saving her life. If my forgiveness means anything, you have it."

"It means everything to me!" Overcome with gratitude, Dolphus rushed to add, "I swear, Domenico, I had no idea that woman was your mother. Our unit had been warned to be on the lookout for partisans hiding in the mountains, but we thought all the homes on Monte Montignoso had already been vacated. When I discovered your mother and your neighbor, I thought they were just that—refugees from the village fleeing into the mountains from our troops. Please believe me."

Domenico involuntarily raised his hand to his heart. "I believe you. And the truth is, Dolphus, life is too short for either of us to live shackled to the past any longer."

"Far too short." Dolphus bowed his head. "I only regret I couldn't ask your mother personally for her forgiveness, and your neighbor's as well."

"My mother's last words were that she had forgiven you. She even forgave your cousin." Domenico's voice caught as he added, "Forgiving you is one thing, Dolphus. You saved my mother's life. She wanted me to forgive both of you, but how can I ever forgive your cousin?"

"I wish I had the answer," muttered Dolphus. "After all these years I still blame Ralf for stealing my peace and my innocence from me, and for making me complicit in his crimes. I have yet to forgive him myself." Peering intently at Domenico, he added, "Yet, the fact that I killed him complicates things terribly, as you can imagine."

Afterward, both men fell silent, the sound of children playing diminishing as families spread blankets out on the lawn in anticipation of eating their picnic lunches.

"Not to change the subject," said Dolphus, after a few moments, "but how did your family escape after I left that day? The mountain was crawling with our troops."

"No doubt, the same way you escaped," said Domenico. "Hiding in caves and abandoned buildings until we found people we could trust who would shelter us. I'm sure you understand what we suffered as a result."

"I do, indeed."

"Occasionally," Domenico added, "I still see some of the families who helped us during the war. There is a special, very unique bond we share with them. In Italy, we call it *comparaggio*. It means kinship by choice. They are part of our family." As his mobile began to buzz, Domenico added, "I believe you and I, Dolphus—by virtue of what has just transpired between us—are now part of the same family also."

Flipping his phone open, Domenico put it to his ear. *"Prego? Sì, Marco, sì.* We'll be right down. *Ciao."* Snapping it closed, he returned it to his pocket and stood up. "That was

Marco," he said. "They're waiting for us at the clock tower. Shall we go?"

Dolphus rose to his feet and extended his hand to Domenico. Grasping it, Domenico said, "Now it is possible to enjoy a kinship with you free of suspicion and fear. I honor and welcome it, Dolphus."

Dolphus smiled. "Yes, my friend. I feel as though a hundred pounds have been lifted from my shoulders. Let's eat!"

· 28 ·

Decision in Chocolat

WHILE DOLPHUS AND Domenico were making amends on top of Lucca's medieval wall, Marco had been guiding the women along via Fillungo, where they stopped at virtually every store to shop. Finding it more than he could bear, Marco opted to wait outside most of the time, stealing glances through the shop windows at Aarika whenever an opportunity presented itself. But it was while they were all in *Chocolat*, a *cioccolateria* on via Cenami, that Marco came to a life-altering decision. Being a chocolate lover, he had followed the women into the shop and was browsing its delectable displays when Poppy sidled up to him to ask his opinion on what kind of confection would be best to take back to America.

"I want to get my mom some chocolates," she told him, "but I'm afraid if it's too hot it will all melt en route."

"What about these?" Marco held up a black box emblazoned in gold, full of assorted biscotti and hard candies.

"Perfect." Poppy took the box from Marco and tossed it in her basket along with some other items. Stealing a glance toward the front of the store where Aarika was absorbed in selecting her own purchases, she added, "Hey Marco, I've got a great idea."

"What?"

"Come back to America with me."

Marco, assuming she was teasing him, continued perusing the chocolates.

"You don't start school for a few more weeks," she said. "Why not come?"

"You're not joking."

"Why would I? Wouldn't you like to see America?"

"Of course, but . . ."

"Look," said Poppy. "You're getting nowhere with Aarika. What's the point of staying here when she might end up just jacking you around until the day she leaves?"

Marco waffled. "Well, I don't think . . ."

"I'm not saying I believe you and Aarika will never happen," Poppy continued. "It's just that nothing's going to happen if something doesn't change."

"That's not necessarily true," argued Marco. "I told Aarika I need a decision from her before she leaves."

"Yeah, like she believes you—like any of us do. You're wearing your heart on your sleeve while she's safe behind all the walls she's built up around herself. With you, what you see is what you get. With Aarika, who knows? I'm telling you, the last thing in the world she would expect you to do is leave with me for America. It would absolutely drive her crazy, and maybe just drive her into your arms. What have you got to lose?"

"Poppy's right."

Poppy and Marco swung around to see Elisabetta standing within inches of them. "Forgive me for eavesdropping," she said. "It was impossible for me not to overhear your conversation."

"Your English is far better than you have led me to believe, signora," said Marco, wryly.

"I understand English better than I speak it," she replied. "Which isn't saying much."

In Italian, Marco asked Elisabetta if she agreed with Poppy.

"If you two are meant to be together, Marco, being separated won't change the fact. Destiny, remember? Go to America and see what happens. Such opportunities don't come around every day." Tossing a sample truffle into her mouth, she added, "I've always wanted to go to America."

Marco faltered. "I'm still working for Domenico," he said, in English. "America is a luxury I can't afford."

"I'm sure Domenico could manage without you for the five days the Gellers will still be here after I'm gone," said Poppy. "And don't worry about the money. My parents have tons of air miles. We can stop at Bianca's, or Domenico's, on the way back so I can call them and work it out. Plus, you'll have free room and board with my family while you're there, so it'll cost you practically nothing."

"Thank you, Poppy, but I can't."

Poppy lowered her voice. "I have an aunt who lives in New York City. I've scheduled my flight so I have a three-day layover there. Three days in the Big Apple? Think of it, Marco! This might be the only opportunity you'll ever have to see it."

"I don't think it will work."

"Look Marco, I realize this is all new territory for you. I mean, I can tell by the way you've fallen for Aarika you've never had a serious girlfriend before."

"For your information," Marco scoffed, "I've had several."

"I said *serious*." Not giving Marco time to reply, Poppy

added, "Take some advice from someone who's been around the block. You won't get anywhere with a girl like Aarika unless she realizes what she's missing. And I don't say that because I'm trying to throw water on your relationship with her. As a matter of fact, as hard as it is for me to admit it, I actually think you two might be meant for each other."

Marco interpreted Poppy's comments for Elisabetta and asked if she agreed.

"It is sad, but true," sighed Elisabetta. "Sometimes girls like Aarika don't realize the extent of their love until it's challenged. Remember our talk in the car last night, Marco? I don't think Aarika will be able to make a decision until her doubts are addressed, and that won't happen as long as you're not willing to let her face the consequences of where her doubts lead her."

"So you're saying I should take Poppy up on this crazy offer to go with her to America?"

"I'm saying do something for yourself. Have you ever wanted to go to America?"

"Of course," said Marco. "I would love to see it someday."

"Then go." Elisabetta flicked her hand at Marco. "At least, that's what I would do if I were you. It's your life, Marco. Do what you think best. Who am I to give advice to anyone?"

Aarika was now queued at the counter near the store entrance. Marco studied her a moment, taking note of her erect stance, her maddening aloofness, the way she acted as though Marco wasn't even there. Although he knew their love needed to be tested, he also understood the time had come to step back and make decisions in his life as if Aarika were not in it.

Turning to Poppy, Marco said, "I'll have to talk to

Domenico first, but if it's okay with him, I will go to America with you."

Fifteen minutes later, Marco and the girls walked out of *Chocolat*, their bags stuffed with an assortment of candy, souvenirs, and gifts. Dolphus and Domenico were waiting for them as they arrived in front of the town's legendary clock tower. After a lengthy deliberation it was decided they would eat lunch at the nearby Trattoria da Giulio. It was there, in the calm of the cool trattoria, that they all took turns sharing highlights from their morning.

Poppy and Elisabetta raved about Lucca's charming streets and shops, displaying their purchases for everyone to see. Dolphus launched into a strange discourse on the healing power of facing one's fears and how his headache had miraculously disappeared, while Domenico spoke cryptically of having just spent one of the most illuminating mornings of his life on the Passeggiata delle Mura talking old times with Dolphus. Neither of them went into details, but clearly something had happened between the two men that had caused their friendship to deepen.

It wasn't until there was a lull in the conversation that Marco calmly made his announcement. "I'm going to America," he said. "I decided this morning to go back with Poppy. She invited me and I accepted."

Aarika nearly spit out the water she had been in the midst of drinking. "What?"

Marco, ignoring her, added, "That is, Domenico, if it's okay with you that I'm gone a few days before the Gellers leave."

"Just be sure to come back, cousin," Domenico teased. "The family needs you here."

As the meal progressed, Poppy began boasting of how much fun Marco would have with her in America. "Wait until all my friends meet him," she trilled. "They're going to love him."

"But of course they will," agreed Signora Cavalleri, raising her glass. "Who wouldn't love Marco?"

Following a round of toasts in honor of Marco's upcoming adventure, Elisabetta settled into a private discussion with Dolphus about his postwar life, while Poppy held Marco in sway with talk of America. Domenico tried to engage Aarika in conversation, but gave up after several tries. Though remaining polite and respectful, she had given herself over to a brooding that had no cure but for her to finally excuse herself from the table.

"I don't feel well," Aarika announced, her hand to her stomach as she stood up. Everyone was so preoccupied in conversation that no one seemed to notice her inching away from them. Raising her voice, she added, "I'll meet you all outside when you're done eating."

Marco and Poppy paid Aarika no heed. Dolphus tore himself away from the signora long enough to nod in recognition of his granddaughter's departure. Domenico alone replied, "Yes, yes, Aarika. Some fresh air may do you good. We won't be much longer."

After her sister left, Poppy said, "Wow, Aarika's already eating her heart out. You won't regret your decision to come to America, Marco. Trust me, you're going to have the time of your life."

PART TWO

Presente

❖ The Present ❖

$$\cdot 29 \cdot$$

America Here and Now

Young people often talk these days about "living in the present," as though it is an option. I understand what they mean, but living any other way is impossible, isn't it? It's Monday, September tenth, and that's all there is to it.

I lived "in the present" when I was a young girl, when I was a married woman, when I had children, when the war engulfed us, and when it was over and we had to rebuild our lives. Each time, a transition from the past to the present was forced upon us. Those who couldn't make the change were left behind in a world haunted by ghosts of their own making, but we survivors planted our feet firmly on the ground and set our faces toward the future.

And what of the future? To live *there*, rather than in the present, is to live untethered to reality. It is a tempting proposition at times, to be sure. But, since no one is promised tomorrow, most of us can only go there in our dreams. I say "most" because there are times the future comes to me when I'm wide awake; unbidden and unwelcome.

My mother called it a gift from God. Sometimes, I wonder.

But tonight, having prepared a huge farewell dinner for Marco and Signora Cavalleri, I am fully present. The past has no effect on me, other than serving as a foundation for my current existence; and the future, as much as I can see it from this moment, looks bright.

It looks especially promising for Marco and Signora Cavalleri, whose imminent departures—Marco to America and the signora to her home near Lago d'Iseo—coincide with each other. As I look out over the forty guests seated on my patio, I am struck by what the future may have in store for some of them as well.

The Gellers are here, of course, as are Signora Cavalleri, Marco and his parents, and Poppy. My sister Rina is here, and my daughter Lucia and her husband Carlo. I even invited several of Armida Sigali's nephews and their wives and children to come and meet Elisabetta. The night is warm and the sky is a riot of stars and planets and sparkling cosmic dust, having finally been swept clean of the sea-haze that had settled over us the last two days.

Being widowed, I live for nights like this: family, wine, food, witty conversation. It rejuvenates me. I forget about my aching muscles and sore hip. But most of all, I delight in the presence of love and all it entails. Tonight, I watch the dance of lovers firsthand in the comfort of my villa. I catch the discreet looks passing between Dolphus Geller and Signora Cavalleri as others engage them separately in conversations. Eventually, the signora extends her hand to Dolphus and draws him to her, a gesture that tells the world there is more to them than meets the eye. This much I know observing Dolphus and the signora: either one will have to learn to speak better Italian, or the other better German. Beyond their body language, English will only get them so far.

Then there's Poppy. I've grown to like that girl. She's friendly, smart, sensitive, strong, and independent. I would never tell Marco this, but if Aarika chooses the path of stubbornness rather than the path of love Marco is offering her, I wouldn't wonder but something could develop between him and Poppy. As soon as I think it, I brush the thought away. It's all too reminiscent of the love triangle that was Egisto, Marietta Tarabella, and Armida.

Marco has returned from my wine cellar armed with several bottles of wine and he's just brushed past Aarika. I watch him deliberately avoid eye contact with her. My, the tension is palpable all the way over here by the patio door, where I'm standing next to my sister. Aarika, I see, is trying not to look crushed. Surely, her grandfather's behavior with the signora tonight must signal a shift in how he feels about German-Italian relationships. After all, Dolphus can't possibly continue to hold Aarika to a standard that he, himself, is not able to maintain. Someone taps me on the shoulder. I turn to see Dolphus and the signora, and Emilio Sigali looking at me.

"Signor Sigali has suggested we visit Armida's grave tomorrow morning," says Elisabetta. "I don't leave until late in the afternoon, so I should have plenty of time. Domenico said he could pick Dolphus and I up and take us to the cemetery after he returns from dropping Marco and Poppy off at the airport. Would you be interested in accompanying us, Bianca?"

"I would love to," I tell them.

"Perfect," smiles the signora. "I believe it is just the closure I have been seeking since starting this journey. You were such a big part of Armida's life; it is fitting you can join us."

Dolphus tells Elisabetta to explain to me her final decision on the matter.

"Oh yes," she says. "After doing some more research with the Sigali family, they concurred that the only sure way to find out what happened to my father's seeds would be to have Armida's body exhumed."

When the signora says this, my chest constricts. The thought is horrific, and the signora, seeing my reaction quickly dispels my assumptions.

"No, no, Bianca," she assures me. "It is not necessary, and I would never do that anyway. From everything I've learned, I am convinced the seeds are with her, in the locket she was buried with, and there they must stay. Perhaps the seeds are meant for the resurrection when Armida and her family are gathered together again. After all, there will be vineyards in heaven, no?"

I breathe a sigh of relief. I know there will be wine in heaven, because my grandfather Luigi is planting and tending vineyards there as we speak. I have seen it in my dreams. "Yes," I reply to the signora's question. "It will be the best wine ever."

As the evening winds down, I find myself unusually tired. Probably my age, I tell myself, but it's also the culmination of summer. I can't help it. Every year, I come alive in the spring. Then summer comes, and with it all the visitors I love to host at my home. I try to make the most of it, for there are only so many summers in one's life. But everyone will be gone tomorrow and I'll have to get used to a smaller circle of activity again. I remind myself that the grape harvest will be on us soon, but then, outside of heaven, there are only so many vintages in a lifetime too.

I say my good-byes and watch the last of my guests leave. Domenico, Mariella, and their daughter, Brunella, stay to cleanup. They insist I go to bed.

"It's late," they say, "and you've already done far too much today, Bianca."

I don't argue with them. I slip into my nightgown, and with some effort crawl into bed, but I can't sleep. Not yet. I'm wishing I knew what will happen to everyone when they leave tomorrow. I'm stuck in the present, but listening for the future.

I'm desperately trying to see what is yet to be.

Aarika Geller

"What have I just done?" I ask myself.

I open my journal to Tuesday, September 11, 2001, and write: "Marco tried to say good-bye to me early this morning. The sun wasn't even up yet. I'm sure he had reservations about waking me, but I'd been awake most of the night anyway, tormented by his leaving for America. I heard his car pull up and then I heard a stone rap against my bedroom window. Two more stones bounced off before I heard him call out, "Aarika! Won't you even say good-bye to me?"

Part of me wanted to cover my head with my pillow so I wouldn't hear his voice lingering in my head after he left, but the other part of me—the one that is recklessly, secretly in love with him—won out. I listened intently for him to say more.

"I know you can hear me," he called out.

So can Opa and Poppy, I thought, wondering if my sister was, indeed, listening from her bedroom where she was busy packing her bags. My excuse for not getting up this morning to see Poppy off was that it was too early, but the truth is I feared drawing out our farewell. And so I said good-bye to her last night just before we went to bed. We hugged, told each other we were glad we finally got to meet and that we must try to arrange another time to get together again. Little did she know I cried myself to sleep thinking about her.

Marco's voice rings out again. "Is this how you want to say good-bye?"

No, it's not how I want to say good-bye. Then what's keeping me from answering him? Is it the same thing that's preventing me from getting out of bed and racing into Poppy's room to tell her I love her?

"If you don't come to the window," Marco calls, "I'll take it to mean your final answer is 'no,' and that you don't want anything more to do with me. Is that what you want?"

I couldn't move. A moment later I heard Poppy trounce down the stairs and say good-bye to Opa. They've grown close during Poppy's stay here, so I'm sure Opa got teary-eyed with her. Then I heard the doors of the car open and close; but it was when I heard Marco start the engine that I finally found my courage. I leapt from my bed and raced to the window, hoping it wasn't too late.

But, of course, it was. I had made sure it was.

I set my pen down, close my journal and wipe my nose, which is running as profusely as the tears down my face.

What is wrong with me?

Domenico Sacchelli

AFTER PICKING POPPY up at the fattoria, Marco pulls up in my driveway. I've never seen anyone look so excited and yet so resigned at the same time, as Marco does this morning. I debate asking him about how it went saying good-bye to Aarika, but change my mind as I get into the driver's seat. It's a forty-five-minute drive to the airport, so if he wants to talk about it, he will.

Halfway to Pisa, Poppy asks me if I have their flight information in case, for some reason, their flight is cancelled, etc. I pull a printed copy out of my shirt pocket and show it to her. I tell her that I also gave a copy to Marco's parents, who will be picking him up when he returns in two weeks.

I feel Poppy's hand on my shoulder. "I know I've already told you Domenico," she says, "but thanks again for everything. It was an unforgettable trip. Momentous in many ways."

"I'm glad I could be a part of it," I tell her.

We pull up to the airport terminal where I find the drop off zone for United Airlines. I help them with their luggage. When Poppy is out of earshot, heading toward the glass revolving doors, I take Marco aside and hug him.

"Come back," I tell him.

He thinks I'm joking and makes light of it.

"I'm serious," I say.

"I'll think about it," he teases. "America is the land of opportunity, you know."

"Your family is here."

He returns my hug. "I'll be back, Domenico."

"And don't worry about Aarika," I add. I'm serious about that too.

Marco turns away from me, toward the barely dawn-lit skies to the east. "I can't very well worry about someone I may have to forget," he says.

I see Poppy waiting for Marco, looking at us through a large plate-glass window. I turn back, give Marco a fatherly pat on the back, and watch as he pulls his suitcase behind him in her direction. As he disappears into the terminal, I feel a keen sense of dread. What if something happens while he's in America and he decides he wants to move there?

Something's just not right.

Dolphus Geller

THIS MORNING, AFTER Domenico dropped Marco and Poppy off at the Pisa airport, he came back and took Elisabetta and I, and Bianca, to the cemetery where Armida Sigali is buried. As we stood over Armida's grave, I saw my life pass before me as though it were nothing but a newsreel of picture frames with a blank ending.

Now, riding in the back of Domenico's car with Elisabetta as we go to the airport this afternoon, I ask myself: *If I had only one year—or even one day—left in my life, could I bear living it without her?* So I turn to face her. I have to speak in English because it's the only language we both understand and I don't care that it will be awkward. Nor do I care if Domenico, in the front seat with his wife, can hear everything I'm about to say.

"Elisabetta, I don't want you to go." I realize immediately what I've just said makes absolutely no sense. I stumble to a halt, frustrated with my verbal inadequacy, before finally adding, "What I mean to say is, can we see each other again . . . soon?"

"Yes," she says, smiling. "If you hadn't asked me, I would have asked you the same question."

I laugh. I don't know whether it's from being nervous, or drunk with happiness, or both. I try not to act like a schoolboy. She allows me to take her hand in mine and caress it. It's a start.

"I'm nearly old enough to be your father," I tell her. It comes out sounding awkward, I know.

"Don't be ridiculous, Dolphus. Thirteen years is not that great of an age difference."

"I have health issues too. I just thought you should know."

"Are they serious?" asks Elisabetta, her eyes sparking with fear.

I assure her they're not. Mostly, I tell her, the doctors are trying to get my high blood pressure under control. "Aarika worries more than I do about it."

"She's your granddaughter," says Elisabetta. "Of course she worries. But, what would she think of us . . . becoming close?"

This is all so new to me, I find myself blurting, "She won't mind. Would you like to visit me in Passau, or shall I come to your vineyard first?"

Elisabetta laughs. "We can take turns, if you like. Why don't you come visit me first?"

I kiss her hand, ecstatic that she is so reasonable. "I always love visiting Italy," I tell her.

"Then that settles it."

"When?" I ask.

"Would you like to come before you go back to Passau?"

Domenico glances over his shoulder at us. Smiling, he teases, "Shall I pull over at the next church?"

Elisabetta and I both blush. Then I think of Aarika and my heart sinks. I remember Sabine and I suddenly go weak.

What am I doing?

Bianca Corrotti

I CAN'T STOP thinking about Aarika.

She was one of the last to leave my villa last night after Marco's farewell dinner. Ever since she had those awful dreams when she stayed at my house, I've worried about her. A beautiful girl like her, so young and with her whole life open before her like an uncharted sea, shouldn't be saddled with guilt and self-condemnation for things that were beyond her control. It will only rob her of present joys and hope for the future.

And so before she left last night, I caught up with her in my foyer as she stood looking at the wall containing my most cherished family pictures. Eerily, she and I looked at each other in the reflection of my wedding photograph.

"That was my husband, Danilo," I told her, in terrible, broken English.

"You both look so in love," she replied, in the best Italian she could muster.

I nodded. "I am still in love with him. Love doesn't die, you know."

Aarika closed her eyes. Probably thinking of her father and grandmother, she sighed, "No, it doesn't."

I reached up then, placing my hands on her shoulders,

and made her look at me. "Aarika," I said. "What do you think God sees when He looks at you?"

It was a question I had once asked myself during the war, when I felt I was a failure for being unable to help several families in our town find refuge. When some of them died as a result, I felt so guilty. Without expecting an answer, I cried out, "God, what do you see in me?"

Do you know what He said? "Bianca, you are my daughter. What do you see when you look at your own daughters?"

Well, I told Aarika this and she began to cry, so I held her in my arms until Dolphus found us. He asked her what was wrong, but Aarika quickly wiped her eyes, regained her composure, and insisted she was only overly tired. But I think Aarika saw who she really is for the first time in her life.

Poppy Doyle

I CAN'T BELIEVE it actually worked out for Marco to come back to the States with me. My parents weren't thrilled at first, but they rose to the occasion and somehow pulled together a free ticket for him with their air miles.

My parents. My mother. I don't want to think about all the stuff we're going to have to hash over when I get back. She's going to want to know all about Aarika and I'm going to want her to come completely clean with me about her past. I mean, what else hasn't she told me? Of course, I shouldn't be too hard on her. It was her idea to have me go to Italy and meet Aarika in the first place. I have to give her credit for that.

We're four hours into our flight to New York. Three

more hours to go. I've been drinking plenty of water, did some leg stretches, and now I'm ready to cover my eyes with a mask to block out the light so I can sleep. I tell Marco to try to do the same, but he's way too excited to do anything but drum his fingers on the seat back tray to the music he's listening to on his headphones, and stare out the window at the flat, deep-blue blanket that is the Atlantic.

I peek over his shoulder at the ocean and it immediately sparks memories of our trip to the Amalfi Coast. Marco had mentioned that he and Aarika had quoted *Ulysses* together one night in Praiano. He said it was one of the pivotal moments in the trip where he realized he loved her. I've never read the poem, but Marco said he often thinks of it, especially when he's looking at the ocean. So, letting my eye mask rest on my forehead, I pull the headphones off Marco's ears and ask him to recite a line from it for me.

"*Come, my friends, tis not too late to seek a newer world . . .* " He shoots me a smile before throwing in the next verse: "*For my purpose holds to sail beyond the sunset, and the baths of all the western stars, until I die . . .* "

"Until you die, huh?" I say, teasingly. "Well, until then we still have three hours to go before we land, so if you don't want to be exhausted when we get to New York, you really should try to get some sleep."

Naturally, he repositions his headphones over his ears and resumes tapping on the tray. Even though he's excited about the trip, I guess he's thinking about Aarika. I know it by the way his eyes glaze over when he's not looking out his window. Well, let him think about her all he wants. I have big plans for him after we land. Two weeks from now, when he flies back home, he may just have a totally different perspective on life.

And on Aarika.

Marco Bertozzi

THOUGH I STILL can't get her face out of my mind, the closer we get to New York, the less I think of Aarika. This *was* a good idea.

I look at Poppy. She's snoring, her mouth wide open. How can she sleep when we're this close to America?

The pilot has just come on the intercom to announce we're landing at La Guardia in thirty minutes. He says the estimated time of arrival is 9:00 a.m. The flight attendant stops to pick up my breakfast tray. She knows it's my first time to the U.S.

"It's a beautiful sunny morning in the Big Apple," she says. "You're going to love it."

I smile and nod. As she moves on to the next row, I check my watch. We've been in the air almost seven hours. I do the math. In Italy, it's six hours later, about three in the afternoon. For a fleeting moment, I allow myself to wonder what everyone is doing.

When the "Fasten Seatbelt" signs flash in our cabin, and an announcement is made that we are beginning our descent into New York, I peer out the window again. But, still, as far as the eye can see there is nothing but water. Gliding as we are, at a lower altitude over the surface of the Atlantic, I entertain the notion that I'm an astronaut on some long space voyage, ready to explode into a new world.

It's that electrifying.

Poppy wakes up and catches me searching the western horizon. "I've been told it comes at you all of a sudden," she says. "It's really clear today, so it shouldn't take long to make out New York's skyline. The Twin Towers are tallest. Look for them."

I keep looking, and just when I'm ready to give my eyes a break, I see something in the distance: a jagged, irregular outline along the otherwise flat contour of what must be the U.S. coastline. After so many hours of seeing nothing but deep blue water, the North American landmass appears emerald: the color of what I'd imagine Ireland to be.

But what is that?

I ask Poppy, who has been staring expectantly at me, trying to gauge my reaction when I catch first sight of America: "Why is there a huge, thick column of smoke over New York?"

The words are barely out of my mouth when several attendants race down the aisle toward the front of the plane. The pilot—or co-pilot, I can't tell which—emerges from the cockpit to meet them. They huddle together. Even from here, in the center of the airplane, I can tell there's something wrong. When the attendants return to our section, their facial expressions are radically changed. Troubled, somber, gritty.

Without warning, our jet banks sharply to the south. The intercom crackles awake as the pilot announces, "We're sorry to inform our passengers that we'll be unable to land at La Guardia as scheduled. Due to an unforeseen and . . . still unfolding situation in New York City, our route has been diverted to Atlanta. Please remain in your seats with your seatbelts fastened until further notice."

Cell phones throughout the cabin start ringing. Others are snapped open as passengers make hurried calls. I hear a woman behind me start crying in the midst of a conversation. Several men get up from their seats and head toward the rear bathroom in an apparent attempt to corner the attendants to find out exactly what's going on. Poppy is talking with the newlyweds across the aisle from us. The bride is clutching her groom, tears welling in her eyes.

I toy with my passport and wait for Poppy to explain to me what all the excitement is about. Finally, she turns to me. She is incredulous, pale and trembling with emotion. Her voice is terse.

"Two passenger jets flew straight into the Twin Towers this morning," she says. "And they say another jet just crashed into the Pentagon. America's under attack."

Suddenly, the world is upside down.

And Italy is a world away.

·30·

Minnesota

It's 7:00 p.m. at Bianca's villa in Ripa and no one is touching the food offered to them. Who could be hungry on a day like this, when the entire world has come to a screeching halt? Marco's parents, the Gellers, and Domenico's family are huddled around Bianca's twenty-inch Zenith television screen in a state of shock. Horrific images broadcast live from New York City dominate every channel. Both of the Twin Towers have collapsed, the Pentagon has been hit, and at least one passenger jet is still unaccounted for.

Aarika paces the floor, chewing her lips so hard they're raw. "Bianca, can I use your telephone again?" she asks, using her hands to communicate her request. It will be the third time in an hour she has phoned to check on Marco's flight. All of her other calls to Marco's and Poppy's mobile phones have been met with a recording saying lines are busy, so her only recourse remains with the airlines.

Marco's parents hover over her as she dials United's international number. When Aarika hangs up after hearing the same announcement—that their information has not been updated—she says nothing. Her slumped shoulders and trembling chin say it all.

Dolphus gets up from his chair to comfort Aarika while

Marco's parents return to their seats in front of the television, no doubt hoping the news anchor will report that no more airplanes have been hijacked.

Mariella, anxiously chewing on her thumbnail as she continues watching the broadcast, suddenly breaks down weeping. "*Dio ci aiuti!*" she sobs. God help us!

Bianca and her sister Rina clutch each other's hands, memories of the war they survived a half-century earlier coming to the surface as they watch a replay of people leaping to their deaths from the World Trade Center and thousands of traumatized New Yorkers running for their lives after the collapse of the first tower. The chaos and fear they are watching on the news seems to suck them into a dimension where they are no longer spectators.

Somberly, Domenico says, "We are all Americans today."

Rina shakes her head, tears rimming her eyelids. "Did you ever dream we'd see a day like today, Bianca? After all we've seen in our lives? An attack against civilians using commercial airplanes? With no warning?"

"Cowards," says Bianca. "To kill so many innocent people; whoever is responsible, they have no soul."

"It is like Hitler all over again," agrees Rina. Tightening her hold on Bianca's hand she whispers, "If it can happen in America, it can happen here too, no?"

Bianca nods, and glances at Aarika, who has collapsed onto a stool near the telephone, her eyes riveted on the television screen.

Another news flash. A jet has just crashed in Pennsylvania. America is in lockdown. No flights are allowed in, or out, of the country. Until further notice, any aircraft violating America's airspace will be shot down. Phone lines are jammed. No one knows if the attack has ended or just begun.

"I'm going there."

Everyone turns to look at Aarika. She sits straight on the stool, her shoulders back, her face resolute, her hands resting calmly on her knees. Then, she says it again.

"I'm going to America."

A WEEK LATER, in Poppy Doyle's modest three-bedroom home in St. Paul's Como district, Poppy's mother Sharon flits about from room to room like a tightly wound band of nervous energy ready to snap. As if the trauma of 9/11 and its aftermath wasn't stressful enough for her, now Aarika and Dolphus Geller are expected to arrive any moment. Aarika, the little girl she'd abandoned, the daughter she hadn't seen since she was a toddler, the grown woman who wanted nothing to do with her. The person Poppy had told her Marco was in love with. She skitters over to the counter where she opens a kitchen drawer, grabs a dust cloth and goes into the living room where Marco and Poppy are sitting, and begins polishing furniture. In a soft falsetto, she attempts singing the first verse of "Amazing Grace."

"Mom!" scolds Poppy. "Dad's going to be here soon. You need to get focused on meeting Aarika, not obsess on how clean the house is."

Dutifully, Sharon stops dusting. "You're right, Poppy," she says. "I'm just so overwhelmed at the thought of Aarika coming here. What if it's only Marco she wants to see and not me? What if I look at her and break down and can't talk, or say something stupid that puts her off? What if she confronts me with all her anger and hurt for what happened and I respond the wrong way? Poppy, you can't imagine what I'm going through right now."

Poppy rises to face her mother. "No, I can't imagine. I had to meet Aarika for the first time when I went to Italy and it wasn't easy either. But if I had run from the challenges it took to reunite with her, I wouldn't be standing here now excited about seeing her again. It took a few weeks to break the ice, but Mom, it was the best thing I ever did."

As Sharon folds the dustcloth and puts it away, Marco asks her if there's anything he can do to help.

"No, but thank you anyway, Marco. You've already done more than enough," she replies. "As a matter of fact, I don't know what we would have done without you this last week."

"We'll get out of your hair so you can relax, Mom," says Poppy. Linking her arm through Marco's, she leads him out to the verandah where she proceeds to pull him down next to her on the porch swing. It's a creaky wooden affair, cloistered behind a trellis of deep purple clematis.

"Way to go making yourself indispensible while you've been here, Marco," moans Poppy. "Now, none of us will be able to handle you leaving."

"You'll do fine," Marco replies.

"Really, you've been the voice of encouragement this last week." Poppy's voice catches. "It's just all still so raw."

Marco gazes down the street at a family taking a late morning stroll and marvels at seeing such a normal scene in such surreal times. "I love your country," he says. "And I'm glad I was here after the attack. It has allowed me to see the best of your people: their unity in crisis, their determination to move forward. I'll never forget seeing your politicians singing 'God Bless America' together in Washington."

"Tragedy does bring out the best and worst in humanity, doesn't it?" asks Poppy.

"It did in my country, during the war."

Poppy sighs. "Anyway, it sounds trite now, but I'm sorry we weren't able to do all the stuff I wanted to do while you were here."

Marco shrugs. "Perhaps the next time I come." He says it as though convinced there will be a next time.

"Sorry about my mom, too. All the talk about Jesus. I hope it didn't turn you off."

"Your mother has been great. Don't apologize."

Poppy breathes a sigh of relief. "She claims ever since she started going to this new church of hers she feels as though she's finally starting to heal from her messed up past. Of course, my memories of mom are pretty normal. It's the stuff that happened in Germany that gets her all bent out of shape."

"My parents taught me that faith can make a difference in how well you can navigate tragedy," says Marco. "I believe it is true."

"Well, since 9/11, I may have to agree." Peeking through the window at her mother, who is downing another cup of coffee, Poppy adds, "You think she's high-strung now? You should have seen her before. She's way more together."

"That's not a surprise," says Marco. "Bianca says the strong have themselves to rely on, but the weak have only one recourse."

"You don't look very nervous, Marco," says Poppy, changing the subject. "I would think you'd be, you know, anxious to see Aarika."

A shadow passes over Marco's face. "I don't want to get my hopes up."

"Tell me again what she said when she called with their flight information."

"She couldn't really talk," explains Marco. "When I asked

her why she was crying she dismissed it as being frustrated with how long it took to get in touch with me over here."

"You don't think she was crying because she was worried about you?"

"I think what happened has everyone rethinking their relationships, but for all I know, her trip here is a peace offering to your mother and has nothing to do with me."

"That's funny. Mom thinks the same thing about you."

"What do you think?" asks Marco.

Poppy leans her head back on the swing and takes a deep breath. "I don't know. Like I said, after 9/11 anything's possible. What about you? Are you rethinking your relationship with Aarika?"

Just as Marco opens his mouth to reply, Patrick Doyle's new black PT Cruiser rolls into the driveway. Taking Poppy's cue, Marco rises slowly to his feet and follows her across the porch and down the front steps to greet them and help with their luggage.

Aarika is the first one out of the car. Her eyes, slightly swollen from either jetlag or crying, or both, hone in on Marco as he approaches. Instead of waiting for him to reach her, she races toward him and hurls herself into his arms, causing him to stumble backward. Her arms are tangled around his neck. One of her legs is anchored around his calf. She's not letting go.

Poppy watches, stunned by Aarika's display of affection. When Marco lifts Aarika completely off her feet and they kiss as though they're alone on a desert island, she mumbles, "I see a brother-in-law in the making. Welcome to the family, Marco."

A moment later, Marco lowers Aarika back to the ground.

When her feet touch the earth it's like she awakens from a stupor. "Poppy!" she cries, flinging herself at her sister.

As they hug, Poppy looks over Aarika's shoulder at Marco, her eyebrows arched in disbelief. "It's okay, Aarika," she says. "We're fine."

Aarika pulls away from Poppy. "I was sick with worry," she blubbers, swiping at her nose and eyes. "You can't imagine what it was like being so far away and not knowing what was happening here."

The screen door slams shut. Everyone turns to see Sharon standing at the top of the porch steps, her face white, clutching the railing to support herself. "Aarika?" She says the name as though it's tarnished from neglect, as though pronouncing it softly might rub away years of omission.

A lifetime passes between the absentee mother and daughter in the silent seconds that follow. Aarika makes the first move. Reaching into her purse, she pulls out a small flat box entwined with scarlet raffia that looks as though it might contain a pair of earrings. Sharon is so transfixed on the daughter she hasn't seen in twenty-two years, she doesn't even look at the peace offering being held out to her. Aarika moves cautiously, approaching her mother as a stranger would approach a wild animal. When she gets close enough that they can touch each other, she raises the box and says, "It's for you . . . Mother."

Sharon accepts the gift, her hands shaking so badly it's a wonder she can unwrap it. Letting the raffia fall to the ground, she clumsily opens the box. Inside is a thin antique gold case, about two-inches square, with the initials $S \sim G$ engraved on the front. She hesitates, looks at Aarika for permission to continue, and unclasps the lock. When the lid springs open, Sharon gasps, her hand over her mouth. Thunderstruck, she sits down on the bottom porch step, pressing the box to her breast, her head resting on her knees.

Aarika lowers herself down next to her mother and for a moment it looks as if she's going to place her arm around her. But she doesn't. Instead, she calls Marco to her side. "Do you know what it is?" she asks Sharon.

When her mother doesn't raise her head, or reply, Aarika says, "It's a lock of Babsi's hair and one of my baby teeth. Oma kept them in that case. Her parents gave it to her when she got married. Those are her initials: Sabine Geller."

Still, Sharon is unresponsive.

Undeterred, Aarika explains, "When Oma died, Opa gave it to me. He said she would have wanted me to have it. I've kept it with me every day since then: at home, school, on the beach, sightseeing, under my pillow or on the table next to me when I sleep at night. Everywhere."

Sharon finally raises her head. Her normally clear complexion is mottled; tears are dripping from her chin. "Why are you giving it to me?" she asks, extending the gold case back to Aarika. "I don't deserve it."

Aarika refuses to take it from her. "The day that Marco and Poppy left Italy to come here," she explains, "and I saw the attack on the Twin Towers, I realized I could fight for my life."

Pausing, Aarika looks up at Marco and reaches for his hand. With his hand in hers, she continues. "We were watching the news at Bianca's house and she said, 'It's the soul of America they're trying to destroy.' Domenico asked Bianca if she thought that was possible, and Bianca replied, 'It's up to the Americans, isn't it? The next move is theirs. They can collapse and implode, or they can fight back. It would be tempting to do the former. No one wants to fight a war. But if you don't stand up for yourself, it's over.' When Bianca said that, it was as though my brain flipped over to face the sun. I realized the power to choose life and death was in my hands."

Aarika, nodding toward Poppy, includes her in her last statement. "I realized I had barricaded myself in a world of my own making, full of fear and rage and guilt and malice and unforgiveness. I thought I had made myself inpenetrable, like one of the Twin Towers, so that no one could ever hurt me again. I had convinced myself that loneliness was preferable to the risk of loving and being loved. But I was wrong. I'd rather risk love and fail—and even be rejected—than go back to a life of running away from the people who love me."

When Aarika finishes, Sharon places her arm over her shoulder. She holds the engraved peace offering between them with her other hand so that it's the only thing separating their beating hearts. Then her body goes limp. "Can you ever forgive me, Aarika?"

"It's all in the past," replies Aarika, her voice breaking. "Buried and gone. Today's a fresh, new day, Mama. There's no going back."

And so, as the calm, sunny Minnesota afternoon fades into a soft, prairie sunset, Marco's presence injects a bit of Italy into the Doyle household. He insists they eat. He brings out a bottle of wine and uncorks it, pouring everyone a glass. With renewed vivacity, he encourages everyone to linger at the dinner table. He fosters laughter and conversation and love, as he keeps Aarika nestled close to his side and showers her with attention.

Meanwhile, back in Italy . . .

PART THREE

Futuro

❖ The Future ❖

·31·

Chiusura

DOMENICO, ALONE AT his *pietra del tavolo*, the stone table beneath the chestnut tree, reads the postcard from America just delivered to him that morning. On the front is a photo of the Twin Cities and on the flip side Marco had written:

> Domenico and Mariella:
>
> We are fine. Dolphus and Aarika arrived yesterday. There is much to tell you. It is good news. I'm happy I came, even though the mood in America is, of course, very sober.
> It is a wonderful country. I wish you could see it. See you soon.
>
> Marco

Marco had actually arrived home from America two days earlier, the postcard taking far longer to get to Domenico's Strettoia mailbox than Marco's transatlantic flight. And though Domenico is anxious to talk with his cousin about his trip, and what exactly the "good news" is, he reasons that Marco will call him when he's over his jetlag. He re-reads the card once more before setting it down next to a plate of fresh, homemade *cornetti*.

It's a fine day, almost October. Summer is over, the vintage has started and the rains have yet to come. He breathes in the fragrant morning air and drinks the last of his espresso before taking another bite of a still-warm chocolate *cornetto*. It brings to mind the time he had made croissants, less than three months ago, shortly after the Gellers had checked in for their summer holiday at the fattoria.

What a difference such a short amount of time had made! In August, he had been captive to his memories. Tormented by them. Today, they are resolved, kneaded thoroughly into his consciousness to such a degree his mind is clearer than it's ever been. He sighs with relief.

A breeze gambols off the sea, rustling the dry leaves above him. He raises his eyes—allowing his imagination to float up through the branches of the tree where he and his father had hidden during the war—and finds his fancy soaring higher yet. Like a lunar rocket, his reverie penetrates the cobalt-blue sky and performs a fanciful figure-eight around the fading ghost of a crescent moon. On its descent back down to earth, his mind's eye screeches to a halt several yards above the crown of the chestnut tree, enabling him to gaze with a bird's-eye view on his little piece of paradise on Monte Montignoso.

He's caught up in the future. It's next summer: 2002. The world is at war, as it always has been and always will be, but at the fattoria time stands still. Dolphus is back, this time with Elisabetta. Domenico sees a ring on her finger. In his dream-like state, he guesses they are engaged. He notes that although her hair is grayer, her skin less elastic, Elisabetta is as lovely as ever. Perhaps more so. Their happiness creates a type of shimmering force field around them made of two hinged halves perfectly molded together—like a priceless Faberge Easter Egg—as though Dolphus's Germanness and her Italianness heave vanished into each other while remaining uniquely distinct.

It's such a beautiful thing to behold, Domenico blushes.

Aarika is there too, he notices. The same long, promise-of-sunshine blond hair, the same penetrating, periwinkle eyes, the same royal yet earthy bearing. But something's strikingly different about her. She's smiling as though she couldn't stop if she tried to. He sees Marco making his way toward the table beneath the tree where Aarika has gathered an assortment of flowers and herbs. She's so preoccupied with arranging them, she doesn't notice him approaching.

Marco sneaks up behind her, gently moving her hair to one side so that he can nuzzle the nape of her neck. Aarika melts at his touch, letting her body relax into his. Encircling her in his arms, Marco places both of his hands on her stomach. It is a gesture that transforms Aarika from a happy, somewhat distracted companion to an ecstatic, carefree lover. She turns around to face Marco, standing on her toes so that her pregnant belly presses firmly into his. Intertwined as they are, Domenico imagines they could breathe from the same set of lungs, they are so full of each other. When Aarika lifts her hands to cup Marco's face, he catches a flash of gold on her ring finger.

Domenico returns to earth, to the present, with a thud. He shakes himself as though he's been sleeping, even though he is wide awake, and wonders if this is what happens to Bianca when she sees into the future. Chuckling, he picks up the postcard and plays with it for a moment before tucking it back into his shirt pocket. A single word resounds within him: *Chiusura*. Closure.

On a whim, he tucks his head down and looks under the table. Peering closely at a particular spot, he rubs his flat hand against the stone. Next summer, he resolves, sitting back up, he will tell Dolphus that the block of stone he used to build his *pietra del tavolo* was cut from the same rock that Signora Gabrelli died on. He assembled it so that her blood stains, mingled with his mother's, face the earth and not the sky, a testament to the power of closure. The next time he and Dolphus sit together at the stone table beneath the chestnut tree and share a bottle of wine, he will let the German see the stains, and touch them.

Chiusura, indeed.

The sound of car tires crunching on gravel diverts Domenico's attention to his driveway. There is Marco, waving at him, smiling as he pulls his car into the parking spot next to the casala. His cousin gets out and bounds toward him, "good news" written all over him. He hasn't seen Marco look so happy since the day he was accepted at the university in Florence. Domenico feels his throat constrict. He rises to his feet and greets his cousin, enveloping him in a bear hug that feels so good he can't let go.

"You're really back," Domenico whispers in his ear. Then he laughs, holding Marco at arm's length to get a good look at him. "I want to hear all about America and what the future has in store for you."

As they sit facing each other over the stone table, with

Marco recounting his experiences, another phrase pops into Domenico's mind. It's one of Bianca's favorite sayings, and as his fingers play along the rim of his *pietra del tavolo*, an idea comes to him. He will carve the saying on the stone, around the edge, where everyone who sits at the table can see it.

"*Chi la dura la vince.*"

He who perseveres wins at last.

Acknowledgments

Sandra Byrd, my incomparable developmental editor and dear friend, I simply don't know what I'd do without you. *Bianca's Vineyard* and *Domenico's Table* are in print largely because of your encouragement and professional expertise.

Copy editor Jennifer Quinlan, thank you, thank you, for your sharp eye and catapulting me into 21st-century editing technology.

Award-winning book designer Jennifer Omner, I can count on you to always deliver a great product in a timely fashion.

Grazie mille to Veronica Arrosti, my beautiful talented *amica,* for her Italian translations, and *danke* to superwoman Karin Meitz for helping with German translations. Any translation errors are mine, not theirs.

Mille baci to my multi-talented son Luke Neumann, and his beautiful wife Marika for designing the book cover for *Domenico's Table.* They are an unbeatable team.

To Jessica Lund Neal for bearing up under an intense sun to pose as Aarika on the book cover. You're a trooper.

Domenico, Mariella, and Brunella Sacchelli of Casali di Montignoso, Toscana: You are an inspiration, not just for this book, but in life. Your pizzas are the BEST!

Carlo and Lucia Stellati: if we could, we'd be on your

doorstep right now wanting to take you to the Arcobaleno for gelato. You are forever in our hearts.

And to Marco Ceccarelli: thanks for giving me the inspiration behind the character Marco Bertozzi.

Without my husband David, I would never have become a member of the "Bertozzi Kingdom" of Tuscany. To him goes my undying love, devotion, and respect.

And to my children, Rachel, Luke, and Hannah, and their spouses: you have made my life more complete than I could ever have imagined. *Ti amo.*

Liam, my heart is insanely, wholly yours. *Ciao bello!*

Author's Note

I met Domenico Sacchelli and his family on our family's first trip to reunite with the Bertozzis in August, 2001. My husband and I were smitten with the Sacchellis and enthralled by Domenico's life story. The book you have just read is the fruit of that visit.

German troops did nearly capture the Sacchelli family in their fattoria as they stormed Mount Montignoso during WWII. Domenico's father had to hide in the chestnut tree near the house to avoid detection. Later, when the talented and enterprising Domenico was a young man, he built, by hand, an enchanting stone casala next to the fattoria. He also built the stone table as depicted in the story.

After the war, one of the German soldiers who had occupied Domenico's home returned to Italy for a holiday. He asked Domenico if he would rent out his fattoria to him. Domenico did. To an American, such a gesture may not seem notable. But to a generation of Italians who lived through the horrors of a war fought on their soil, Domenico's decision was controversial. Today, the descendants of that German soldier continue to rent Domenico's fattoria every summer.

The soldier's name is not Dolphus Geller, and all the events surrounding Dolphus and his family are purely fictitious. Marco Bertozzi, however, was inspired by former

Milanese model Marco Ceccarelli, the remarkably handsome grandson of Bianca's sister, Lida.

For those fortunate enough to travel to Tuscany, do take the time to visit the seaside region of Versilia. Once there, you should be able to see the community of Casali di Montignoso perched atop a verdant foothill overlooking the Ligurian Sea just a few miles northeast of Forte dei Marmi. It's not far from Bianca's home and vineyard and the graveyard where Luigi and Carmela Bertozzi and Armida Sigali are buried.

Indeed, it is the heart of the Bertozzi Kingdom.